A Woman with No Clothes On

A WOMAN WITH NO CLOTHES ON

a novel by VR Main

DELANCEY PRESS
LONDON 2008

Published by Delancey Press Ltd.
23 Berkeley Square
London W1J 6HE

www.delanceypress.com

A CIP catalogue record for this title is available from the British Library.

First published 2008

Jacket painting '*Olympia*' by Edouard Manet
Musée d'Orsay
Photo RMN © Hervé Lewandowski
Jacket by e-Digital Design
Typeset by BookType
Printed and bound by TJ International Ltd.

ISBN 978 0 9539 1197 4

For Rebecca and Hannah Partos

Author's Note

While many of the characters in this novel are based on historical figures, it is important to stress that this story is a work of fiction and that some of the events, as represented in the text, are also the product of the author's imagination.

'Those who live in the next century will see better.'
(Edouard Manet)

'In any exhibition, at a distance of two hundred paces, there is only one painting that stands apart from the others; it is always a painting by Manet.'
(Edmond Duranty)

'Manet, whom people think wild and insane, is simply a very straightforward, unaffected person, as reasonable as he can be but unfortunately touched by romanticism from birth.' (Charles Baudelaire)

'He was greater than we thought.'
(Edgar Degas, following Manet's death)

'We will probably never hear the last word on this strange girl of so many different faces.'
(Adolf Tabarant, Manet's biographer, on Victorine Meurent)

The Prologue

Paris, 1967

Descending a small hidden staircase near the Porte de Lions entrance of the Louvre, just a few steps from the Tuileries gardens, Isabelle thought of the day, more than thirty years ago, when she saw the painting for the first time. They were on a school trip to the Jeu de Paume. She was thirteen, and she had just had her long plaits cut into a fashionable bob. As soon as the class entered the room, she was drawn to the canvas and stood in front of it long after all her fellow pupils had moved on. Many years passed before she could explain what had mesmerised her so much. One thing she was sure of straightaway: she knew who the figures in the picture were and what they were doing. She had known it without even reading the title of the painting or the notes provided.

Absorbed in the painting, she had not noticed one of her teachers standing next to her.

'Oh there you are, Isabelle, we were looking for you, worried that you were lost,' she had said. 'Didn't I say that no one should separate from the group?' Isabelle had nodded.

'We left this room half an hour ago.' Not realizing that she had been alone for that long, Isabelle had apologized. The teacher had responded by smiling at her.

'Well, I understand why you stayed behind. I shouldn't tell you this, but had I been alone, I'd have done the same. The difference is that I know the gallery very well. By staying here, you've missed seeing the other pictures.'

'I don't mind. I was happy to look at this one.' She hadn't planned to justify herself.

'How can you say that since you haven't seen the others?' The teacher's face was serious. Isabelle had had no answer to the question.

A few years later, when she started visiting the gallery on her own, Isabelle learned that she was not the only one whom the painting had intrigued. In a three-year period Picasso produced more than two hundred drawings, paintings, sculptures, ceramic plaques, and lino cuts, all based on the picture. Lesser artists and numerous designers have made it one of the most copied and pastiched paintings of all times.

Generations of critics have written volume after volume on the gaze of the female figure, on the modernism of the perspective, the unfinished canvas, the unusual brushstrokes, and its references to past masters. Everyone in the art world knew the scandal the painting had caused when it was first exhibited in 1863. Critics made numerous suggestions about the identities of the three characters, why they were sitting in the middle of a forest, and what they might be talking about. None were universally accepted.

As Isabelle grew older, she dismissed the story that she had thought of at thirteen for what it was: her own fiction. Questions about what the four figures were doing and who they were no longer mattered to her. Other aspects of the picture became much more intriguing. She wondered why the painter had deliberately flouted verisimilitude and mixed fruit that ripened at different times of the season, while, at the same time, he had rendered the same fruit with so much skill that you could easily imagine birds coming to peck at the cherries? Above all, she wondered who had been the model for the woman in the foreground. Without having any evidence, the painter's best-known biographer assumed that the model was a prostitute who had died young and destitute of alcoholism and syphilis. Isabelle could hardly tell where he had come across that idea.

She rang the staff bell. The night porter let her in. He apologized for having to ask for her identification; he was new and had not had time to learn who was who.

'I'll soon. I'm good at remembering faces, real and painted ones.' He spoke very quickly and blushed slightly. Isabelle smiled as she showed him her pass. Like his two predecessors, he was probably an art student.

Walking quickly through the warren of corridors in the cellar under the main building, all she could hear was the rapping of her high heels on the stone floor. She stopped in front of the door that opened into her department and marvelled at the absolute silence all around her. It would be several hours before anyone else arrived for work. The thought pleased her. Her mind was too preoccupied to be able to accommodate talking to anyone.

Isabelle inserted the key, but could not turn it. The door with its warning yellow triangle was unlocked. She had never left it like that before. It was lucky that the security guard had not been around. The regulations explicitly stated that the lead room had to be locked overnight. She must have been too tired to remember to do that last night when she left.

Slowly, she pushed the door open and peeped in. Claude was hunched over a light box. He was wearing the same stripy shirt from yesterday, both sleeves rolled up. His long black hair was ruffled and only casually tied with an elastic band into a ponytail. There were two empty coffee cups on the desk to his side.

'Morning, Isabelle. So you couldn't sleep, either?' He did not even look up. A stack of handwritten notes lay in front of him.

'Good morning, Claude. Is everything OK?' Isabelle stood next to his chair. He was viewing radiograph number twenty-one and appeared not to hear her question.

She walked into her office, switched on a light box, and placed a film on the screen.

The woman was naked. Isabelle searched for the clothes on the ground but could not see any. Three apples and a bread roll lay scattered next to the woman's feet. Tracing her finger on the screen in front of her, Isabelle identified several faint lines but

3

none resembled the outline of a basket. The two men looked too much alike: their faces and bodies could well have been the same model. It was not obvious whether the figures were sitting on the ground or a floor, outside or indoors. The artist had painted neither trees nor grass. The fourth figure, the woman bather in the background, was missing. Isabelle covered her eyes with her hands. Nothing differed from what she had already observed late the night before. She hadn't expected that it would, but she needed to reassure herself that, in all the excitement that accompanied her first viewing, she had not been mistaken.

Isabelle rearranged the pile of notes on the desk and walked out of the office to the adjoining lead room. Last week, the removal staff had secured the canvas against the long wall. In this position, the picture faced the window, and although not much light came into the basement room, they had covered it as a protection against the sunlight. In two days, the men from the transportation team were coming to take the canvas away. Until then, she will have the privilege of looking at the painting alone and at any time she wished.

Urgently, she lifted the cover and stood back. The features of the painting, such as the spatial relationship between the figures, the shades of colours, and the diversity of brushstrokes were indelibly printed in her memory. She didn't need to look at the picture just now in order to ascertain an idea that had been developing in her mind. However, the canvas was here visiting her in her own space, like an old friend whom she had loved for many years. Isabelle felt greedy for its company. The unease that had tightened the inside of her chest, while she was checking the radiographs, now gave way to pure pleasure at having the picture all to herself. But then a sense of disappointment took over. It was as if she had discovered that a close friend was harbouring a secret, something that she had never suspected.

She stepped back from the picture. The underlying painting, showing only three figures, confirmed what she had already thought of: the fourth, nymph-like figure was an afterthought. Neither the two men nor the woman in the foreground seemed aware of her existence. Her posture and clothes suggested that

4

she belonged to a different world, a mythical one. She might have been a joke on the painter's part. It was as if he were saying, 'You chide me for eschewing nymphs and goddesses, in favour of real people; well, I will give you one. See how out of place she looks in the modern world.'

One of the radiographs had shown a headless dog but the left leg of the man on the side had been superimposed. The dog belonged to yet another layer, the same one that showed a leaping horse and an arm pointing a sword upwards.

Isabelle was sure that this particular canvas contained at least three layers: some kind of heroic military scene, a sketch for the finished painting and the final image. There was nothing unusual about that: from time to time, a painter painted over an already used canvas. But in this case, the story of the layers looked much more complicated.

She raised her arms, took a deep breath, and stretched her body tall. After sitting down for hours, without moving anything but her arms, her back felt stiff, and her movement made her aware of how tired she was; she had hardly slept last night. She paced up and down the small office before plunging into the armchair. After kicking off her high heels, she tucked her feet beneath her.

What next? She needed a second opinion. The expression struck her as funny. Isn't that what they used to say at the hospital whenever they faced a medical problem, usually a patient who was seriously ill but whom the doctor would dare not tell until the diagnosis was confirmed by a colleague?

In this case, the diagnosis was potentially so shocking that she could not proceed without a second opinion.

* * *

'I am Paul Laroque.' A few minutes earlier, the reception told her that the curator from the Jeu de Paume was on his way. The first time he had telephoned her to discuss the idea of x-raying the painting, Isabelle wondered what kind of face went together with such a deep and melodious voice.

A man in his late fifties stood in the doorway. Isabelle thought of El Greco's elongated figures with their serious, religious faces. However, as he stepped towards her, and she noticed a mocking line in the corner of his mouth when he smiled, she changed her mind: his gangly body was more like Picasso's drawing of Don Quixote. The face was gaunt and lined but it was not that of a saint. She stood up. Paul's handshake was firm; he smiled briefly and looked straight into her eyes. Behind the narrow half-moon glasses, perched at the end of his nose, Isabelle detected warmth in the blue of his eyes. Soft, white curls framed his face. He moved and spoke slowly, in calm and measured tone, every inch an elderly academic. Paul Laroque seemed so different from his brisk assistant, who had visited Isabelle at the office a few days after the museum's initial enquiry. There was firmness in her short solid body, in her sharply cut charcoal pin-striped suit and in her manner. Isabelle recalled a little lecture the young woman had delivered to her:

'This painting is one of our most valuable possessions. Indeed, I would say that it is one of the most important paintings in the whole of France, if not in the world. For many people, that canvas marks the beginning of modern painting. Both the treatment of the subject and the technique were revolutionary. We have already commissioned cross-section sampling, so we know the kind of varnish that the painter used. Now, with this damage appearing, we feel we need further diagnosis. We shall not require a report from you. The radiographs will be sufficient. Our experts can interpret them.'

Isabelle hadn't interrupted her. She was used to being treated as an outsider in the art world. Someone, somewhere, must be telling everyone that she was a scientist. Why did they think that her background immediately disqualified her from knowing anything about paintings?

Paul sat down.

'You are well hidden down here. I walked past the Porte de Lion entrance several times before I noticed the staircase to your department. But you are part of the Louvre?'

'Yes, indeed we are.' The Louvre was the first museum she

approached about opening the art radiology department. The lower ground area, part of which was located underground, was the only space they could offer her.

When Claude came in, Isabelle introduced him to Paul: 'My assistant is a professional photographer. His training provides me with a different way of looking at the images.'

'And you are a doctor, a radiologist?' Paul asked before adding: 'How unusual! A medical doctor interested in paintings.' Isabelle disguised her irritation with a smile and nodded. Even a serious man could not hide his prejudice. They always knew who she was and yet they always asked again.

'And an art lover, Isabelle is an art lover,' Claude said smiling, but Paul, already seated by a light box, did not seem to hear him.

While they waited for Claude to bring in the radiographs, Paul said: 'I am looking forward to seeing how science can help art. Perhaps we are not as far apart as it sometimes seems.' Isabelle nodded politely. How many times had she heard the cliché? She was relieved when Claude appeared with the radiographs.

They showed Paul how to insert the film and adjust the brightness.

'Claude is working in the lead room and I'll be in my office, in case you need me.' It was best to leave him to work alone. Perhaps he will not see what she had seen.

Just over an hour later, Paul knocked on her door. That was quicker than she had expected. She invited him in and pointed to a chair next to her desk. He sat down and said: 'I've seen them all. The images are much clearer than I expected. In addition, if I were not afraid of using platitudes, I would say that appearances could be deceptive. The outside doesn't often tell us what's inside. A healthy-looking person may carry a nasty decease inside.' He thought exactly what she thought. Paul paused before adding: 'It cannot be easy for a doctor to break the news to such a patient.'

Isabelle nodded. Paul Laroque was thinking and speaking slowly, stressing every single word and she almost wished for the briskness and self-assurance of his assistant.

'Appearances can be deceptive with paintings as well. Deep down, there is often something else. Something we don't expect.'

Paul paused and looked at Isabelle. She did not react, just waited for him to continue.

'Let me come to the point. I was not surprised to see that the picture had been painted over another one. That often happens. A painter abandons a picture but doesn't wish to waste the canvas, and particularly not such a large one. Alternatively, a painter uses someone else's canvas. Or, a painter paints over a study of his own. Nothing unusual about that.' She knew all of that. Everyone knew that.

Paul looked at Isabelle, waiting for her to agree with him. She nodded and he lowered his eyes. Isabelle was determined not to ask a question. He had to come out with whatever he was going to say without her prompting. The telephone on the desk between them rang and broke the silence. Paul looked up, as if relieved of his responsibility to carry on speaking. Isabelle redirected the call and waited for Paul to continue, fixing her eyes on him.

He stood up, and started pacing up and down the room. She watched him patiently. When he stopped, he took a few deep breaths. Leaning towards her, his hands firmly planted on the desk, he whispered: 'This is in confidence. I am not prepared to put my reputation on line until I have done some further research. I am going to say something for your ears only. For now, at least.'

'You don't have to worry. I'll not speak to anyone.'

Paul looked down, as if to consider her promise.

'From what I can tell, and I cannot be sure, the underlying picture was painted by someone else. Those are not the confident brushstrokes of our master. Not even as a student would he have painted like that. Besides, the postures of the figures are too stiff, even for a simple, quick study of the composition. No trained painter would have done anything like it –'

'I had the same feeling,' Isabelle could not help saying.

Encouraged by her words, Paul continued: 'Do you see, this is not the work of the master. This is someone much less experienced, someone who worked very slowly with a small brush and whose hand was unsure.' Paul readjusted his glasses before continuing. 'This is someone who did not have the master's skill at painting the real landscape, which on the top picture has been identified as that of the family property at Gennevilliers, but who, for the underlying picture, simply copied a mythical scene from another painting. This is someone who probably worked without models.'

Paul sat down in the armchair opposite Isabelle. 'And of course, the sections that we admire so much, such as the exquisitely painted still life of the picnic, have been altered a great deal. The woman's discarded clothes, so important for the way we view the composition, are not there in the hidden picture. And what is that headless dog doing there?'

Paul's words were a relief. Last night she thought of the same idea. However, after she had gone home, she began to wonder whether she really had seen the hidden painting. Unable to sleep, she had to rush back to the lab early this morning and have another look at the radiographs. Now, a respected curator has confirmed her own diagnosis.

Paul leaned forward towards her. 'Does it mean that this other painter, and there is no doubt in my mind that we have two painters here...' Paul paused and waited for Isabelle to nod in agreement.

Isabelle thought of the headless dog, the hand with the sword, and a part of the horse. Possibly three painters, not just two, would have worked on that canvas.

Paul's whisper was barely audible now: 'Does it mean that this other painter, who is clearly far inferior in technique to the master, most likely an amateur, does it mean, dare I say it...?' Paul stopped. His cheeks were flushed. He looked down; he needed Isabelle's support.

She waited; she was going to wait as long as it took him to utter the question that was on her mind.

Eventually, he leaned so close that his mouth was close to her ear: 'Does it mean that this other painter is the originator of the idea for the painting? Does it mean that the master only improved on the original because he was a better craftsman?' Paul stared at Isabelle.

He had done it. She will have to help him not to feel guilty. After a long pause, she spoke: 'It may feel like sacrilege to ask such a question, but we must not be afraid of our research.' What a platitude! She was relieved that the curator did not seem to have heard her. His eyes were looking at something beyond her and the office.

Then, with his right elbow leaning on his knee, and speaking very slowly, as if addressing himself, he said: 'It has always puzzled me that no study drawings have survived. Anyone embarking on such a large canvas would have produced a whole series of preliminary sketches.'

1862

Grandmother knelt in front of me. I thought her eyes were a darker brown than usual. She spoke loudly. I must have done something wrong.

'You are always staring at the world. Now you can make pictures with colour, to show us what you see, Victorine.' My hands gripped the wooden box she had passed on to me and a splinter dug into the tip of my finger. I bit my lip but did not move. My heart was beating as fast as when I stopped running.

In our family, we did not buy presents. Mother brought clothes for me from time to time: a chemise, or a skirt, or a pair of stockings that someone had forgotten or left uncollected at the laundry. Sometimes, grandfather gave me an apple or an egg, still warm.

The walls of the room closed in and held me tight. The air was too warm to breathe. My cheeks burned. Grandmother urged me to open the box.

'Go on, my little one, have a look inside. Grandpa bought them for you. Monsieur Pascal had only two boxes on sale.' Her eyes became lighter. The voice softened. She was not angry with me. I obeyed and lifted the lid. I saw six stubby crayons with sharp points: no one had ever used them before. The smell of resin rose to my nostrils and I inhaled deeply. It was a smell like no other I had known. My mouth was too dry to speak, the lips too tight to smile.

I used the crayons sparingly, only for 'special' pictures that I drew carefully. By my sixth birthday, the box contained only a few waxy crumbs. Sometimes I would open the lid to inhale the powerful smell that still lingered inside the box. It brought back the memory of the day when the grandparents had given me the crayons. The memory made me feel special.

Years later, when mother took me to Paris, the box disappeared in the rush of packing and moving. Dead people didn't take boxes with them and besides my grandparents would not have taken back what they had given me as a present. I asked mother about the box but she ignored my question. All that remained of that day were grandmother's words. I need to show what I see.

Anywhere I go, I observe. I may be alone, I may not speak, or move, but I look. And I see.

1

Here is a world of many pictures.

Whenever I have a spare moment between orders, I snatch a glance in their direction. Standing by the counter behind the pillar, where they cannot see me, I fix my eyes on the couple and imagine that they are in a painting. If I could be invisible for half an hour, I would take out my sketchpad, sit right in front of them and draw.

'Mademoiselle, another glass of red.' I turn towards the voice. An old man is holding up his glass and looking at me. 'Mademoiselle, you're dreaming.'

People are drinking at every table around the man and the woman, talking loudly. Later on, while I am serving at a table near the couple, I hear the man say:

'Is it still no?' He bends his head and looks at the woman. She nods silently, her eyes fixed on her hands in her lap. They were here last week and the week before that. The man holds together the sides of his brown jacket, which has two buttons missing. In doing so, he pulls too hard on the third, tearing the cloth until it hangs by a single thread. He runs his hands up and down his thighs, as if trying to stretch his trousers, which are too short for his long legs. When the woman looks at him, he begins to smooth the cloth of his light blue shirt, drawing attention to its relative newness compared with the rest of his clothes. Perhaps the man is trying to impress his companion.

How much time would I need to paint such details? They say that Monsieur Courbet makes anything he paints look real on the canvas. They say that he takes everything he needs to observe to his studio: men and women, children, horses, dogs, and cats. If they all come to him, he can take his time.

The man's eyes don't wander from the woman. He leans forward as he talks. In contrast, she holds her back straight and moves only when he is too close. She has folded her hands on her lap but, when he attempts to put his hand on hers, she shrinks away and flashes him a warning glance. The hand stops in mid air. The tears in her navy dress have been mended and the white collar is clean and newly ironed. She has pulled back her blond hair with a silver ribbon and, perched on top, she wears a small, black hat.

While I am collecting the glasses from a nearby table, the man whispers: 'But when will you say yes, my dear?' The woman lowers her eyes onto her lap.

The man tries again: 'My dear, I would be good to them. Is that what you're worried about?'

The woman doesn't look up. Her lips tighten. That's an important detail for my picture. He looks at the floor. I stare at his face, at the tension in his brow and the hunched shoulders. Is that the expression and the posture of a man who has not given up?

The sudden rays of the afternoon sun illuminate the woman's face. Before she has time to shade her eyes, the light reveals the softness of her smooth skin and dark lines under her eyes. Why is she so tired, when she is so young? I squint to make myself see better. A pair of vertical lines appears between the woman's eyebrows. When the sunshine fades, the woman lifts her glass, places it close to her lips, but does not drink. As on the two previous occasions, she has eaten the plum but does not touch the brandy.

'Have a sip, my dear. It'll do you good.' The man's back is straight again as he looks at her. She shakes her head and carefully lowers the glass; it doesn't clink when it touches the metal surface of the table. She looks at him and smiles briefly.

'You are a good man,' she waits as if to make sure that he understands the compliment. His face brightens. He moves his hand towards her. 'But,' she says sternly, 'men can change quickly.' All the time she keeps her eyes on his. He sighs and shakes his head.

I move away. Their words disturb me. These two are a picture; I don't want to know their story.

When tobacco smoke from the neighbouring table envelops the couple, the picture becomes more interesting. I think of the paintings in the Louvre where angels sit on clouds hovering above a holy scene. Instead of protecting the saints, the angels should help these two, poor, ordinary Parisians! I'll paint that picture.

'Here she is,' a big hand grabs my arm from behind and pulls me backwards. I try but I cannot free myself. The force of the grip twists me around. The face of my assailant is red and heavily lined, the skin on his nose puckered, with burst veins and purple patches.

'Make her give it back to me,' the man shouts at Monsieur Legrand. Drops of saliva splatter from his mouth. 'She took ten francs from my pocket. I know it was her.'

Monsieur Legrand looks at me and then at the man. 'Let her go,' he thunders. The man releases his grip and I step back.

'I haven't taken anything, monsieur.'

'She is lying,' the man shouts. 'I bought an absinthe and she took the money from my coat as it sat on the chair next to me.'

I want to tell him to search me, but know that Monsieur Legrand would only use the opportunity to run his hands over me.

'You have no proof. I believe my waitress. If you don't leave her alone, I'll call the gendarmes.' The man grabs Monsieur Legrand but the patron, although shorter than his attacker, is sturdy and steady on his feet. He pushes the man away. The man continues shouting while Monsieur Legrand shoos him towards the exit. Once there, he opens the door and throws the man out.

'Don't you dare come back in here,' Monsieur Legrand shouts after him.

The patron disappears into the kitchen, from where comes the clatter of plates and dishes being washed. A couple of minutes later, he is standing in front of me.

'I'm sorry about that, Victorine. A nasty rascal.' I nod.

'Thank you, monsieur. I didn't do it. I swear.' He puts his arm around my shoulders and squeezes me close.

'You look pale.' He takes me by the hand and ushers me to a small room next to the kitchen. 'Have a little rest.'

'I'm fine, monsieur. I can carry on.' I am still standing up, hoping to go back to the bar. 'Please, monsieur. I'm fine.' He steps towards the door, turns the key, takes it out of the lock, and puts it in his pocket.

'Madame Legrand will be looking for me.'

'Don't worry, she is busy with her mother upstairs. It's just you and me. And Henrietta. She can handle the bar for a while.' He gestures towards the bed. I try to move away but he pushes me back. We struggle. He wins. He pins me down; his weight is too much for me.

'Listen to me. There are girls like you asking for jobs all the time…' He doesn't wait for me to comment. 'Just give me five minutes. Then you can go. Had I not helped you, stealing ten francs could have got you into trouble.'

I know that.

His wet mouth stains my face, while his hand lifts my skirt. 'Don't be shy with a man who looks after you.' As he fumbles with the material, I can hear him breathing heavily. 'Shit', he mumbles and lets go of me. I thank heavens that he is old and weak.

I stand up and he throws me the key. When I unlock, he whispers:

'Listen, if you want to stay, let's keep this between you and me.'

I know I've been lucky this time.

Half an hour later, in the bar, Henrietta, the dishwasher, turns towards me: 'Are you better, Victorine? Oh, you have a scratch on your chin. Monsieur Legrand did say that the man was very nasty.'

'I'm all right,' I say. 'It was that customer.'

'Don't cry, Victorine, Monsieur Legrand'll protect you.'

* * *

'Mademoiselle Victorine, come over! I want another drink.' Philippe's voice, husky from smoke, carries above the chatter of the other customers. I set off in his direction, but Robert, who has probably had as much to drink as Philippe, shouts:

'Hey, Victorine. Philippe wants to get you drunk. Mind he doesn't put his hand on your bottom, the old lecher.' With my face burning, I veer off towards the kitchen, dropping the napkin from my shoulder. Robert picks it up and laughs at me. 'Come here, you can exchange this for a kiss.' He holds out the napkin. Stupid bastard! I walk towards him and snatch it from his hand before he can lean towards me.

In the kitchen, I splash water on my face. I wish I could stay here and escape the teasing. However, as soon as I've dried my face, Madame Legrand hands me a tray with four bowls of steaming beef stew.

Passing by Philippe's table, I'm grateful that neither he nor Robert take any notice of me. They are engrossed in conversation: 'Have you seen the paper? Look here, just read about the man who slit his mistress' throat with a razor.'

'Must have deserved it.'

'Of course, he found her with another man. Serves her right.' Robert gesticulates wildly as he speaks, his face stretched into a grimace. I try to memorize what he looks like. I wish I could recall his face later on when I have time to sit down.

Philippe nods, Robert claps his hands and says: 'Women, they cause so much trouble. My friends at work tell me that only the other day a labourer threw his wife down a well.'

'Really? Turned her into a water nymph…' Philippe laughs and Robert joins him.

By lunchtime, Philippe is usually through a bottle of spirits and several glasses of wine. Yesterday, he dropped two one-franc pieces when he stood up to go. I pretended to tie my shoelaces and bent down. He did not see me slip the coins into my pocket.

Philippe started coming to the café about a year ago. He sat quietly and drank the whole day. He would begin with a coffee, pastry, and then move on to absinthe. One lunchtime, he was sobbing loudly. Monsieur Legrand poured him a drink and sat down at his table. It was then that Philippe told us that his wife had run away with another man after twenty years of marriage.

These days, Philippe drinks only alcohol. Around four in the afternoon, Monsieur Legrand takes pity on him, offers him an arm, and walks him home. Leaning on Monsieur Legrand, the old man moves slowly, shuffling his feet and mumbling. A week ago, as soon as they had walked out, he vomited onto one of the two oleanders that stand on each side of the entrance. Henriette and I poured bucket after bucket of water onto the plant to clean up the mess.

I remember the day, nearly a month ago, when Philippe had brought a large bag with him and Monsieur Legrand asked me to help. The apartment wasn't far from the café, but we made slow progress and it took us a good half an hour. Philippe would stop and chat to passers-by or lean against a building and refuse to move.

Inside his apartment, he tripped over a tapestry rug on the floor of the hall. We helped him up but, after one more step, he stumbled once again and hit his head against a walnut glass cabinet. The porcelain dishes, lined on its shelves, clinked and rattled. I peered inside: one of the ballerina figures was toppled over and its skirt was cracked.

We left Philippe stretched out on a *chaise longue* in the salon and Monsieur Legrand opened the doors to the balcony. I stepped out: there was a lovely view of the park below. Snoring loudly, Philippe didn't hear us leave.

On the staircase, Monsieur Legrand put his arm around my waist and tried to pull me towards him. I gave him a sharp look and moved away. 'Oh, you women,' he grumbled, 'you don't know what you need.' For a while, we walked on in silence. When we reached the café, he said that he would gladly swap his lot for Philippe's.

'And them expensive things all around. They all used to be hers, you know; God knows why she didn't take them with her. Old whore, who needs her? If I were Philippe, I would say 'good riddance' and drink to my good fortune. What do you think, Victorine?' He grabbed my arm as if to make sure that I answered.

I thought that Philippe must be very different from Monsieur Legrand. There was no point saying that; it was easier just to listen and nod. After all, he doesn't care what I think.

One morning, while he was still sober, Philippe told me that he used to work as a clerk at the Louvre.

'It's across the road from here, mademoiselle. A very big museum. I could take you there, show you the pictures.' I pretended I didn't know what he was talking about, let alone that I have ever been.

'You don't believe me, do you mademoiselle? I'll prove it to you.' I neither believed nor disbelieved him. He took a piece of paper and drew a floor map of all the galleries. I didn't want to show much interest in the drawing but I could tell that he knew the place well. Philippe went on boasting: 'Mademoiselle, I can tell you where every picture is hung. Big ones I mean. Just try me out.'

I kept quiet. I was dying to ask him how to register as a copyist, but I didn't dare. What would the Legrands have said?

For a couple of years now, I've watched young men and women sitting at their easels making copies of paintings and wondered how they had managed to obtain permission. I wish I had asked him then, instead of hesitating, worried that they might laugh at me in the café. By the time I had plucked up enough courage, Philippe was too far gone to be helpful.

A family, who are also regulars, are walking towards the doors. They could be in another picture, if only I had time to sit in the middle of the café with my paper and pencil. Their table is in the far corner, which attracts very little light from the outside. When they eat, they sit with their heads bowed over the plates: I can't see their faces. They pay weekly and I don't need to take any money today. I like the two boys. No older than five and six, they are meant to be served smaller portions, for which we charge three sous, half the price of the adult ones. Whenever the Legrands are not looking, I put an extra potato or a spoonful of sauce on the children's plates. I pretend that I have overlooked the additional bread slices they ask for and do not charge for them. The boys start eating as soon as I place the food on the table. They eat quickly and finish every single crumb, soaking the last drop of sauce with their bread. The family keep to themselves and, apart from ordering food, they've never said anything to me. The mother must be a washerwoman; the skin on her hands is red and rough and sometimes she brings in a large basket. The man is a labourer of some kind but, surprisingly, he never looks at the workers who regularly meet in the café. Today, one of the workers invited the man to join their meeting.

'We can help you get more money for your work,' he said, but the man just looked away.

When the workers have a meeting, others have to shout their orders if they want me to hear them. The longer they stay, the more they drink and the louder they become. Today, twelve of them share four demijohns of wine. Whenever I look at the table, somebody gestures to me that one of the demijohns needs replacing.

Amidst the glasses, the workers' caps are scattered like blotches of blue paint.

The men are large and muscular. Unlike many others, when they leave the café, they walk straight and upright. Each of them might make a good figure in a drawing, even in their baggy overalls.

In the kitchen, Madame Legrand says that I look tired. 'Are you sure you can manage so many hours, Victorine?'

'Yes, madame. I'm strong enough. I used to do longer hours in my previous job.' This is a lie. A few months ago when I saw the advertisement for a waitress in the window of the Legrand café I went in straight away and told them I had experience. I was lucky that they believed me.

'She works hard,' agrees Monsieur Legrand and slaps me on the back.

'Benôit, leave her alone. Victorine's none of your business.' He looks sheepish and walks away. Once, she caught him touching Henriette's breasts and since then she has watched him closely. If only this morning she had not been busy with her mother in the flat upstairs.

Chastened, he turns towards Jacques, the cook, and they look through the window at the distilling machine in the back garden. They stand side by side in silence, united by their fascination. I used to like to watch it myself, marvelling at the magic of its copper retorts and long tubes that splurt and hiss in unison, as if they were alive. Even this machine, I thought, could serve as a subject for a drawing. I would love to have time to work on the tubes whilst they glistened under the sun.

However, when old Philippe made a mess on the oleander, an image came to my mind of one of those tubes connected straight to his mouth, pumping poison into his body. The thought of the amount of money the old bugger spends here, only to vomit it over the flowers, makes me angry. From now on, I'll keep at least a franc from his change. Pissed as he often is, he'll never notice.

My head hurts and I feel faint, but I don't mention it to anyone. A day's shift brings in four francs and often there are tips as well. I don't want the Legrands to think that I can't cope. Recently, I've been sleeping only a few hours a night. Most evenings, straight after work, I spend a couple of hours drawing.

I stand behind the counter and look at the shining row of glasses, pewter measures and the bowl of fruit. I place my hands on the flat surface and look straight ahead. When it's dark outside, I like to see my reflection in the window opposite and think that one day I'll paint a picture on a large canvas: it'll show me standing here in front of a background of rows and rows of coloured bottles of spirits and shining fruit jars. I imagine the canvas at an exhibition and people coming in and touching the bottles and fruit jars, thinking they were real. I'd love to stand on the side and watch them.

It's a folly to imagine that possibility. The pictures in the Louvre don't involve people like me. They are of nymphs and goddesses, not doing much except lying around.

Later in the afternoon, the bar fills with men. They stand around the counter in small groups. The sound of their fists banging on the metal surface cuts through my head and I want to scream at them to stop.

A man with one arm leans on the counter and asks me to roll him a cigarette. I hold the paper for him to moisten with his tongue, but he insists that I do it. When I place the rolled cigarette in his mouth, he says he can taste me. Several men standing near by laugh loudly and demand that I roll their cigarettes. I blush and the men giggle.

A strong young man, who often sits with the workers, pulls me by the arm.

'Can you lick mine, mademoiselle?' he screams and grabs the crotch of his trousers. More guffawing. The acid in his breath makes me nauseous but I carry on pouring drinks as if I didn't care about their joking and leering. They stop only when Monsieur Legrand stands next to me. He pulls me close to him.

'Leave my waitress, alone,' he says firmly.

'Oh, so she is your waitress,' somebody shouts and the others join in. With Madame Legrand out of the way, his hands move more freely. I flinch at the sight of his fat fingers with thick black hair and dirty nails. If I were to draw a hand like that, I would like the viewer to be able to guess what kind of person it belongs to, perhaps even imagine the face. As I move away, I see that Monsieur Legrand's eyes follow my body across the room.

When Monsieur Legrand goes to the cellar to fetch more bottles, I am serving again, and a small boy, no older than five, lifts himself up on tiptoe so that his hand can reach the top of the counter. He places a sou on the surface in front of him and asks for a glass of spirit. I tell him that it isn't enough for anything, and he starts to cry. He has no more money and, if he doesn't take back a drink, he will receive a beating. Without looking up, an old man, smoking a pipe and drinking alone in the corner at the end of the bar, slides two sous towards the boy. I measure a drink and the boy carries it out, walking slowly and keeping his eyes on the liquid.

The couple stand up to go. The woman picks up her basket and, looking at the mirror by the door, readjusts her hat. An acquaintance stops the man. The woman waits by the door while the two men walk to the counter. The acquaintance is laughing, his head gesturing towards the woman, but the man doesn't look at her. He buys an anisette for his acquaintance and walks out with the woman.

The couple cross the road, walk pass the butcher's and stop at the baker's. The man goes in and comes out with two small parcels, which he places in the woman's basket. She nods and smiles.

Since I can't pay a model, I have to try to store some of the images of the people here in my mind. One image keeps returning. I had my eyes closed most of the time, but even though I saw it for only a few seconds, the face of Monsieur Legrand as he was licking my lips, remains fixed. Earlier on, I rubbed lavender into my skin, but all I can smell is his breath stinking of onions.

Tonight, I'll draw the couple, with him leaning towards her, and her keeping him at a distance with her eyes, rather than with anything she said. If only I could draw their bodies in a way that would show his eagerness and her restraint. I can still see their image in front of me. But will it last until tonight?

I stop to buy fried potatoes and a bunch of radishes from a shop across the road from the café; the owner curses the cold weather.

'Too cold, mademoiselle, much too cold for poor people like me. How can I keep the children warm? The baby, he is only six months and has a chill; he may die, like his sister last year. I keep them here in the shop, it steams up when I cook, and it makes it warmer. I have no money for firewood upstairs.' I watch her as she bends over a pan of frying potatoes, her eyes on the food, while her arms gesticulate wildly, accompanying her words. Wrapped up and surrounded by steam from her pots, she would make a good picture.

The woman's son, a boy of six or seven, plays with sticks on the floor. His sister, a year or two younger than him, sits quietly on a divan in the corner, holding a sleeping baby. The girl stares at me with her big brown eyes. I go over to her and offer her a potato piece from my parcel and she takes it straightaway. The boy runs to me, grabs several pieces, and stuffs them into his mouth. The woman thanks me. I ask the children for their names. The boy answers for both of them: Marcelle and Louis.

Outside, the freezing air penetrates my pelisse and numbs my body. I push my hands into my pockets. I hold the change the woman has just given me. It doesn't seem right. I take the coins out; she has made a mistake and given me back more money than I've originally given her. The extra should be enough for three more meals.

Despite the weather, I leave the omnibus at Place St Michel and walk along the quay. A strong wind is blowing from the Seine and I have to move quickly. The crowd of beggars that usually gathers near Notre Dame has gone: only a very old and sick man, his back forming a proper half circle, totters towards me with his open palm. He would model for me if I gave him a glass of wine but it may be too difficult to get rid of him afterwards.

By the time I reach Maître Albert, my fingers are as hard as bones. I try several times but I can't grip the knob on the large iron door that leads into the hall and the staircase, let alone turn it. The concierge comes out with a shawl wrapped around her shoulders.

'Oh, it's you mademoiselle Victorine. You must be mad to go out on such a cold night. Let me see your hands. Oohhh!' She shivers. 'All blue. No wonder you could not push the door open.' Before she looks for the key, she offers me a cup of tea.

'Too cold to go up straightaway, mademoiselle,' she says, making a sucking noise with her lips. 'Come in here. I have a stove lit.' She makes me go in before I can protest.

Her eyes have shrivelled and her lips tremble as she lifts her tea to take a sip. Strands of grey hair poke through the scarf she has wrapped around her head. I hesitate: shall I stay or not? She would make a good model. However, the memory of the couple from the café flashes through my mind: the prospect of working on them for several hours fills me with pleasure. The concierge shakes her head in disapproval and watches as I turn to walk across the courtyard.

'You will catch your death up there, mademoiselle. And you have hurt your chin. You haven't been in a fight, have you?'

24

'No, I bumped my face against an open window.'

'You young women. Always thinking of something else. Never looking where you're going.' She shakes her head.

Before climbing the staircase, I stop and look up. I like the view from here: those large windows on the top floor belong to my studio. I have a studio, I say to myself.

Taking two stairs at a time, I rush up. No one else calls my two small, adjoining rooms a studio; the concierge refers to it as an apartment. Nor have I mentioned my studio to anyone else. Mother would be shocked and demand I give it up straightaway. The Legrands would laugh at me. Even Marie might. She told me once that I was silly not to see that all the painters were men and all the models were women.

'I don't know about all the painters,' I said, 'but certainly not all the models are women.'

'You are being stubborn, Victorine,' she said. 'Let's not argue.' And we didn't. Not that time, anyway.

When I paid the deposit for the rooms, I had no one to tell.

Studio or no studio, this is the place where I make my art. The windows are large and let in a great deal of light. When I looked around for the first time, last November, I thought that if I had a very large canvas that was too big for the staircase, I could have it hitched up – I have seen that done – through the window. What a fantasy! I have never had a canvas, not even a small one. However, if I am to be a painter, I have to think like one.

On that November day when Madame Conchis showed me around, the weather was mild and some of the residents had their windows open. As we reached the courtyard, I heard someone playing a flute, repeating the same sounds again and again, as if learning. I stopped to listen and Madame Conchis said: 'That's Gabriel, a young man who works at the bank. You never see him, but you can hear him all right. I told him to keep the windows closed but he just wouldn't. I'll tell him, mademoiselle, not to disturb you.'

'It won't disturb me.'

'Ah, he isn't very good.' She waved her hand dismissively.

'He'll get better as he practises.'

Madame Conchis shrugged her shoulders. 'Too sad his tunes, too sad for me.'

However, today all the windows are closed and I can't hear the flute.

Once I open the door, my teeth begin to chatter. The wind rattles the panes of the windows and a draught comes through the roof. I light the iron stove and watch as the flames lick the insides. Although the fire crackles pleasantly, very little heat comes out. The rooms are small but the ceilings are high and it will take a long time before I notice any change in temperature.

I pull a chair close to the stove. Tears well in my eyes, my body aches, my legs tingle from tiredness. I take deep breaths and tell myself that if I am to keep this studio, I'll have to carry on working at the café.

I quickly eat my supper. The potatoes are cold and shrivelled. I take a good swig of brandy, rub my fingers hard, until they turn red, and sit down to work.

I draw slowly, trying to put on paper what my memory holds in front of my eyes. The postures of the figures come out too rigid. There is no life in them. I erase them and start again.

Eventually, I manage to capture the arching of the man's body, but there is too little desire in his movement. I draw the woman with stiff shoulders and a straight back to suggest her detachment. However, when I finish, the lines tell a different story. I start again. I can see the couple right in front of me but, no matter how hard I try, the picture on the paper is wrong. If I could succeed with the shapes of their bodies, I would move onto their faces. I would like to capture the sparkle in his eyes and her level gaze. I fear I can achieve nothing without models. Since the man's face is in profile, the woman's features matter more. If only I could persuade a woman to pose for me. Any woman. The concierge?

On the way down, I knock on her door and hand back the key. Madame Conchis takes it and walks away without looking at me. I dare not ask.

It's eleven o'clock when I reach Pantin. I hear the shouts of the Bottes, who live across the landing from us. He's drunk and she has thrown him out, complaining that he never brings home any money. I've to squeeze past his sprawling body but he doesn't take any notice of me and continues arguing.

Mother lies in bed, asleep. I tiptoe in the darkness, take off my coat, and slip under the covers. A tingling sensation passes through my legs and I move them around to make myself comfortable. I make sure not to wake up mother. I stay awake for a long time.

In my mind I go through a list of all the women I know and think of whom I could ask to model for me. Marie has other things on her mind now. Henriette may not understand what I want to do. Or she, just like Madame Legrand, might ridicule me.

I remember the day when Monsieur Pascal, who ran the stationery shop in the village where I lived with my grandparents, and from whom grandfather had bought a box of paints for me, told me that only men were painters. I was barely six, but I told him that he was wrong because his wife painted. He laughed and said that it was only fans she was doing and a fan was not a canvas, not even a piece of drawing paper.

'Anyway,' he added, turning to my grandfather, 'my wife paints fans only because she can't have children.' I wondered whether some women had children and the others painted fans. Monsieur Pascal looked past my grandfather and me and said:

'Madame Pascal is not a real woman.'

I didn't know what he meant but it didn't matter. Madame Pascal painted fans that opened out into colourful patterns, more beautiful than anything that I'd ever seen. Whenever I visited the shop, I couldn't take my eyes off them. I wanted to be like Madame Pascal.

I kept quiet because Monsieur Pascal's face was serious and I feared he might shout at me. My grandfather nodded and mumbled something into his chin about women.

One day grandmother said that someone from Paris had bought a fan and taken it with her and that it had been seen by a merchant who was coming to order a whole lot.

'They say ladies in Paris adore them. It looks like Madame

Pascal will be making good money. My little one, perhaps you can help her soon.'

When mother came to see us and grandma told her about asking Madame Pascal to let me help her paint with her, mother disagreed.

'Only rich people can be artists,' she said. 'For us, the best we can hope for is to have our own shop and work hard. There is always money doing laundry.'

'There is money in fans,' grandma said but mother just waved it off.

My grandparents died when I was twelve and I came to live with mother in Paris. She had her own plans for me. In the evening of my first day with her, she said: 'Victorine, you are big enough to come to work with me. Delphine is barely a year older than you are, and she has been at the laundry for several months. They will take you on. Mind you, it won't be for long. I've some savings. If we are careful, and do some extra shifts, in a year's time we can open our own laundry.'

Later on, I learned that once before she had been close to having five thousands francs but somebody had cheated her and she had lost more than a half of it.

'Those bastards may have played a trick on me,' she said. 'but none'll stop me from having my shop.'

I asked about going to school. She screamed at me: 'What for? How'll that help us?'

After I had been at the laundry for two days, they said that I was too small and weak and they wouldn't keep me on.

'I'll help her and soon she'll get bigger and stronger,' mother argued.

The owner shook her head. 'Look at her hands. Too small for all the wringing and lifting. There is no strength in them.'

Mother allowed me to go back to school for another year and a half.

Just before my fourteenth birthday, we made another trip to the laundry. This time, they agreed to give me work. Luckily, on the same day, Marie's mother came to see us in the evening. I knew that she wanted to help me out.

'Madame Meurent,' she said, standing very close to my mother, 'a very respectable lady, very rich, a customer of mine, is looking for a young woman to play with her little daughter. The pay is good. They have a lovely apartment with beautiful pictures and tapestries on the walls –'

Mother smirked: 'What good are pictures? I want to teach Victorine to work hard, not to look at pictures.' Marie's mother nodded in agreement but my mother carried on: 'And what will she do when they sack her? Sell her body?'

'Madame Meurent, I go there often for fittings and I thought of Victorine. Madame Duras is a very kind person. If she takes a liking to Victorine, she may help her.'

'No one can help us except us. Laundry taught me the value of hard work.'

'Yes, you work very hard, Madame Meurent.'

'Anyway, what gives you the right to mention Victorine to others, rich or not, respectable or not? I've found work for her. She starts tomorrow.' My mother turned away to go.

Marie's mother put her hand on my mother's shoulder: 'Madame Meurent, I haven't mentioned Victorine by name. I only thought of her. If only my Marie wanted to look after that lovely child. But she doesn't.'

I was glad Marie's mother didn't say that her daughter was modelling for artists. They went on talking and in the end my mother agreed to let me go to work for Madame Duras, provided that I could earn at least as much as I would have done in the laundry.

I loved my days in the house of Madame Duras: little Julie often let me draw her when she played. Madame never laughed at my accent and helped me improve my speech. She had books, and sometimes we read together. My favourite was Stendhal's story *Le Chartreuse de Parme*.

Madame liked Fabrice del Dongo. 'He is so noble with his ideals,' she would say. I wasn't sure I agreed, but I liked him because she liked him. I listened to her and tried to sound like her. I still make an effort to speak like her. People like Madame Duras used many more words than my mother and her friends in the laundry. Sometimes I had to ask her the meaning of the words she used. Madame Duras never shouted.

The family lived very close to the Ecole des Beaux Arts, although at first I did not know what lay in that building on the quay. It was Madame Duras who pointed out the young men going in and coming out of the building.

'Some of them may become great painters one day,' she said. 'Their pictures will be shown at the Salon.'

Madame Duras did not paint or draw herself, but she liked visiting exhibitions. Once when we were looking at a picture in a shop window, I admitted to her that I would like to be an artist. To my surprise, she did not laugh at me.

'You must work very hard, Victorine, if that is what you want.' I nodded.

But when Madame's husband, a soldier stationed on the eastern border, was killed, she took Julie away from Paris and moved to Aix-en-Provence to live with her father. Mother, who had been complaining that I was not giving her enough money from my pay, didn't let me go with them. After two years of looking after Julie, I had become very fond of her and Madame Duras. I was very sad and would have gone with them despite my mother, but I thought I shouldn't leave Paris. Madame Duras agreed with me on that: there are more exhibitions here than anywhere else. And as she said, those who want to learn to paint come here from all over the world. Before leaving, Madame Duras suggested that I should go to the Louvre once a week at least and study the pictures.

I told mother that I would only stay in Paris if she didn't force me to work in the laundry. She relented and let me take the job in the café. Sometimes I help with the washing up, but most of the time I can keep my hands dry. Mother's hands are red and rough, with hard lumps. They ache and twitch. Even if she wanted to, the stiffness of her fingers would prevent her from holding a painter's brush.

2

I wake up to screaming and shouting coming from the staircase. It is still dark outside. Mother's side of the bed is already cold.

'You owe me twenty sous, Claude. If I don't have it today, I'll knock your brains out. And I'm not returning your jacket. The vulture in the pawn shop'll give me a franc for it.'

'You, mean, scrounging bastard. You never pay for drinks, Jean. I don't owe you anything.' The loud voices belong to the young men who have only recently moved to the Hôtel d' Or and occupy the top floor. They work nights and come back early in the morning. When they climb the stairs, they shout at each other and drag their heavy boots as if they were made of lead. Sometimes, in the evening, one of them comes down and bangs on our door asking to borrow a ladle or a saucepan, but mother never lets them have any. On most occasions, she shuts the door in their face.

'They can buy their own; I bet they only knock on the door to look at you, Victorine. Men are cunning. You mustn't let them get close to you. These are such riff raff…not that the well-dressed ones are any better. Once they get what they want, they walk away.'

I sit up and light a lamp. If I leave straightaway, I'll have two hours to sketch at Maître Albert before going to the café.

Mother has fixed a small mirror by the bed. Madame Legrand is right. I'm pale, but that's my natural complexion. In this light, my eyebrows are barely discernible. In a pencil drawing, they would require only the faintest line. The idea of being my own model appeals to me. I could draw my own face on the body of the woman from the café.

When I reach Maître Albert, I remember: damn, I've no mirror

31

in the studio. Nor do I have much else. A previous occupier left an old divan. The concierge let me have two of her own chairs: I was welcome to them; they were only cluttering her office. I use one to sit on and, on the other, I've piled old clothes, collected from market stalls. Whenever I see something unusual or colourful, I think that it might be useful to dress a model, if I ever have one.

On the same day that the concierge gave me the keys to the apartment, I went to a stationery shop and ordered drawing paper, an easel, colours, and brushes. I still had some money left over from Madame Duras. I carried the smaller items myself and the shop delivered the rest. How excited I was! A young boy pulled the easel on a handcart and we carried it upstairs.

A few days later, walking just off the rue de Rennes, I came across a furniture shop and saw a table on the pavement in front. The table was too long and too narrow to be used for dining and the man said I could have it cheaply. He asked for twenty francs. In the end we settled for ten. For two more francs, he brought it here. I use it for my brushes and paints.

I don't know of any useful shops close by, only cafés. If I walk further and look for a mirror, I'll have no time to draw. I must manage without.

When Madame Conchis hands me the key, I catch a reflection of my face behind her. Could she lend me the mirror for the morning? I could bring it back in a couple of hours. The skin between her eyebrows furrows as she stares at me. She turns, walks to the wall, and takes the mirror down.

'Here, mademoiselle. It's a heavy piece, mind how you carry it upstairs. It was in this room when I arrived three years ago,' she says, 'it isn't mine. I never look at myself anyway. You can have it, mademoiselle. A young woman needs a mirror.' She winks.

I walk carefully, one step at a time, making sure that I do not catch my skirt on the edge of the glass. The sun, streaming through the large window, blinds me temporarily as I open the door. A blast of cold air hits my face. I prop up the mirror against a wall and try out different expressions and body postures. I imagine I am the woman from the café, carefully watching the world, but keeping my thoughts to myself. The man sitting opposite me is good and I feel sorry when my rejections disappoint him, but I refuse to trust him.

On that, I agree with the woman and with my mother: I don't trust any man. And, as the woman said yesterday, men change.

I move close to the mirror; my breath mists the shiny surface and I have to keep wiping it to see my changing faces. If only I could draw really fast, I would like to make a series of sketches of all these people staring back at me.

Eventually, I settle for a bland expression that is easy to maintain while drawing. Out of necessity, the woman in my picture will have to look straight out at the viewer. One day, when I can afford a model, I'll be able to choose any position and any expression I want.

I work slowly for almost two hours, erasing the lines that don't work, and improving the face. The eyes are easy to draw, but I cannot get the mouth right. Either the upper or the lower lip has the wrong tension. I shift slightly so that the light on my face changes and I experiment by shading a section of the lower part of my face. By midday, my head and neck hurt and I decide to stop for the day. The sun illuminates the ice patterns on the window and they begin to melt. I wish I could draw them, but it's too late. I need a break before my afternoon and late evening shifts at the café.

I walk along the Boulevard St Germain-des-Prés and, as I turn into Saint Michel, a woman greets me. She is walking arm in arm with a soldier. Her face seems familiar, but it is like so many other faces of young women in Paris. I wonder whether she has mistaken me for someone else. Then the woman says, 'I am Delphine, Delphine Conchis.' I remember that, a few weeks ago, Madame Conchis introduced me to her daughter.

'This is my fiancé,' Delphine says. The man lifts his cap and bows. She smiles: 'We are enjoying this beautiful sunny day.'

I agree with her and wish them a pleasant walk.

I head for Jardin du Luxembourg. When I reach the middle section of the park, my heart leaps at the sight of the bench where Julie and I used to sit. It's empty. A year has passed since

Madame Duras and Julie left Paris and this is the first time since that I have come here. Julie used to run around the fountain. If I close my eyes, I can see her now, chasing small birds, or sitting on the grass and making daisy chains, one for her, one for Madame, and one for me. Sometimes, she would make mine before the one for her *maman*. I can hear the patter of her feet on the gravel, and the joy in her voice as she called me to show me a flower or a bird.

In a letter that arrived only a few days ago, Julie and Madame Duras reminded me that I had promised to visit them. Madame Duras assures me that she would pay for my journey. I would love to go to Aix, but Provence is a long way from Paris and it would mean losing several days' pay.

When my mother said, angrily, that Madame should have compensated me for ending my employment, I kept quiet. The two hundred francs she gave me went towards the rent for the studio. She repeatedly asked if I was to be given anything and when I shrugged my shoulders, she said that I was stupid to be so weak and urged me to demand it. The first time I lied to mother I feared I might blush and that she would press me and find out the truth. As she went on, I became bolder and said that Madame had financial difficulties. I pretended I was sympathetic to her position and could not expect any extra payment.

'Oh, the rich ones, they always moan,' mother said. 'She must have made up the story so that she could avoid paying you. I wouldn't believe them. Ask for money, Victorine. It'd help with our shop. She owes it to you. You tell her that.'

I had no choice but to promise to ask. A day later, I told mother that Madame had cried when I had mentioned the extra payment. I said that she had felt miserable and ashamed that she could not offer me a parting gift.

At first, mother laughed. When she stopped, she shouted: 'Victorine, you are so naïve. You shouldn't believe her. She is putting it on to save herself money.' I didn't like to argue with mother. It was only days after she had agreed that if I managed to find any other work, I wouldn't have to go to the laundry with her. I feared that opposing her might make her reverse her decision. I said I would ask for money again and when, in the evening, I described Madame's tears for the second time, mother waved away my story dismissively.

'Liars,' she shouted. 'Bloody liars, that's what they're, the rich. Never believe them, Victorine.' I was glad she made no further reference to the parting gift. I kept my two hundred francs.

A man sits down on the bench. I feel his eyes boring into my profile. Minutes pass and he neither moves nor averts his gaze. He stares at me and I fear I might blush. I try to forget about him and think about my life in Madame Duras' household.

It was right here on this bench, one sunny afternoon, that Julie said that we should both make a picture. We turned to face each other and I handed her a notebook and a pencil. She was on the side where the man is sitting now and with her paper on the bench between her legs, she drew me sitting in front of her. It took her no more than five minutes and she was pleased with the result.

'You take so long and you still never like it, Victorine.' I said she was right. I've never been happy with any of my drawings.

In almost every letter that comes, she writes that she loves looking at the pictures I made of her. I cried when I read the end of the last letter: '*Maman* and I had a photograph taken last week. I'll send you one when it is ready. Of course, I would prefer if you were here to draw me once again. I would like that better than any photograph. There is no one to make a picture of me here.'

'You have the face of truth, mademoiselle.' His voice is deep and the way he speaks, as if stressing each word, is unusual. I want to look at him – what sort of face goes with that voice? – but I control myself. Men can easily make themselves sound kind and interesting. I stay still. This is what the world is like: men talk to young women who are alone in public. Most of the time, if I ignore them, they go away. Sometimes they insist that they have seen me before; one even claimed that I had promised to call on him.

A few years ago, soon after I started looking after Julie, a man stopped me on the street, saying that I was the same height and build as his sister and that he would be extremely pleased if I could I help him choose a pelisse for her. I hesitated at first, but he insisted. His sister lived outside Paris and it was difficult for her to find well-made clothes. I did go to a shop with him and tried on several different styles but, in the end, he did not order any.

All the time I was aware of his eyes fixed on me as he asked me to turn around while trying on different items, but I excused him by thinking that he was only looking at the pelisse. When we left the shop, he wanted to buy me a drink to thank me. I said that there was no need.

'Mademoiselle, I should be frank with you.' He tried to put his hand on my shoulder and when I moved away, he lowered his eyes. For a moment, I felt sorry for him. 'I have no sister,' he admitted. 'I lied because I wanted to make your acquaintance. I've watched you walk past this way many times. If you allow me to take you for a drink, you will show me that you have forgiven me.' He smiled and touched my hand lightly. I noticed a thick gold ring.

'Rich men are the worst,' my mother always said. But that was not what stopped me going with him. Even then I would have rather used the time for drawing than sit in a café. So I looked him straight in the eye and said that I was married. He apologized and left straight away.

The man's gaze burns my cheeks. I came here first; this bench has memories for me and I shouldn't have to move. The shoes of an old woman creak as she walks on the gravel path in front of me. Each time she moves, she hits the ground with the end of her stick. If she could stand still, I could draw her. With her arched back and the head sticking awkwardly between her narrow angular shoulders, she presents an interesting sight. Even while she moves, I could make a quick sketch if only the man would leave me alone. When she is gone, I can hear the man taking deep breaths. My blouse sticks to my skin. I undo the two top buttons on the pelisse.

'Please, mademoiselle, believe me, yours is the face of truth.' His voice is pleasant but his words do not mean anything. What a silly thing to say! 'The face of truth.' It's more stupid than trying out pelisses for an imaginary sister. When men at the café leer at me and say they want to see me later, I tell them to go away. This time I keep quiet.

'I need to paint your face, mademoiselle.'

Paint?

He stands in front of me, lifts his top hat, and extends his hand with a flourish: 'Manet, Edouard Manet.' He keeps his eyes on me and waits, as if I am supposed to know the name. I don't; I am certain that I've never met him. I'd have remembered the face, if not the name. I look back and he adds, 'I am a painter, mademoiselle.'

A painter? A real painter who shows pictures at the Salon? Anyone could say that.

The skin on his palm is smooth and the grip of his hand firm. His beard and his hair are the colour of a light chestnut. The silk of his top hat glistens in the sun. The dark grey wool coat is perfectly tailored. I think such close fitting cut is fashionable this year. A walking stick and a pair of yellow suede gloves lie on the bench.

His clothes make me feel uncomfortable. Rich men like him don't talk to women like me, unless they think that they can buy them. Now my clothes look shabby: my pelisse is several years' old; I've mended the cuffs and hem more times than I can remember.

His eyes are fixed on mine; he lets go of my hand and steps back, but I still feel trapped by the intensity of his gaze. Heat rises through my body once again and I can't say anything. Aware of my discomfort, he relaxes his stare and, as he smiles, short, teasing lines appear in the corners of his mouth. His lips are delicate and expressive.

'Mademoiselle, you have forgotten to tell me your name.' I haven't forgotten. I am not sure I want to tell him. He carries on looking at me, his face warmed by a wide smile.

'Louise,' I say quickly, 'Louise Meurent.' Victorine is for those who know me.

'Delighted to meet you, Mademoiselle Meurent.' Men like

him always say that. We are both standing up now, facing each other. He is slim and only a bit taller than me. He holds the smile as he stares: his eyes are narrow and deep set. They study me as if I were a still life, a bowl of fruit, or a picture. I have seen copyists in the Louvre maintain the same gaze and concentration. Even if he isn't a painter, he is making a good impression of one.

I try to look back at him, straight into his eyes, but I can't. His scrutinizing look forces me to lower my eyes. I step to the side and it is only when I move out of the focus of his vision that he relaxes his stare and his eyes move to the ground. When he looks at me again, there is kindness in his eyes. They are warm. Once again, the mouth widens into a big smile. I watch his thin lips as he speaks: they are very mobile, with a hint of mockery at the corners.

'I would like to paint your face, the face of truth, Mademoiselle Meurent.' What a silly thing to say! But I don't tell him that. What if he is a painter? I might want to know him.

'Here is the address of my studio. Please come to see me as soon as you can, mademoiselle. Could you come tomorrow? Or the day after? I shall be delighted to welcome you.' He hands me a piece of paper and makes a little twirl with his feet, as if performing a dance. I stand still and watch him.

'May I have your address, mademoiselle?' I don't know what to say. He waits, still smiling. I wouldn't want a rich man like him to turn up at the Hôtel d'Or in the Pantin.

'Maître Albert, Maître Albert 17.' He writes it down in a little notebook that he takes out of his coat pocket. Immediately, I regret telling him. I wouldn't want him to turn up there, either. But it can't be helped now. He doesn't notice my concern.

'Well, mademoiselle, please do come to see me. You will, won't you? I must paint your face.'

I nod. As I turn to go, he says: 'It has been a pleasure meeting you and I very much look forward to painting you soon. Please, come any time, mademoiselle. I shall look forward to seeing you.' A flatterer! He extends his hand and, as he looks at me, I fear a repeat of that prolonged stare. But this time, he lets go of my hand quickly. I dare not look at his mouth; I fear catching a sight of those mocking lines in the corner. I walk away; his eyes lie heavily on me.

By the time I reach the exit on the side of the Palais, I know that he can no longer see me, but his presence remains with me. If he is a painter, he could be helpful to me. But what if he isn't? My steps are light as I make my way down rue de Vaugirard and take the omnibus to St-Germain-des-Prés.

With the sun shining, I walk brusquely to the café. Just before going in, I catch my reflection in the mirror by the door: my cheeks are flushed. I smile at myself. It has been a good morning.

When I enter, the family with the two boys is just leaving. There are several regulars drinking on their own but with no workers' meeting today, it is quieter than yesterday. Philippe is not around, either. He must have left earlier than usual. For a couple of hours, I am not very busy and Madame Legrand asks me to help her in the kitchen. Large, uncovered pots are simmering on the stove and steam covers the windows. The smell of roast meat rises from the oven. The fat sizzles. I roll up my sleeves, undo the top buttons of my blouse, and fan myself with a lid.

Madame Legrand smiles at me: 'You have colour in your cheeks, today, Victorine. The heat in here is doing you good.'

I push my hand into the pocket of my skirt to touch the card with the address of Monsieur Manet. If I finish on time tomorrow, I'll go to rue Guyot and look out for an artist's studio at number eighty-one. I need to be sure that he really is a painter before I visit him. I have no time to waste on nobodies. But if he is a painter, I'll have lots of questions. Perhaps I could watch him work. There is so much I need to learn.

While we chop and stir in the kitchen, Madame Legrand tells me that there had been a fierce argument in the café between the workers. One of them, usually a quiet man, she says, brought in a book by someone he called Saint Simon and started to read sections to the others. The rest of the group kept interrupting him.

'The man,' Madame Legrand points her index finger towards

her head and turns it around, 'must have been off his head. Can you believe it, Victorine? He insisted that a really just society would be one without money. At first, the others laughed but, as he went on saying the same thing, the others shouted angrily at him.

'No money? What justice is that? We want more money, not less.' Several times the man tried to read out passages from his book, but each time they stopped him. The shouting, the way they punched him and threw glasses at him. Their faces were red, spitting violence. He tried to defend himself, but there were too many of them. Soon, his nose was bleeding badly. Monsieur Legrand had to give him a cloth to press on the wound.'

I've seen fights before in the café and wish I could have been present for this one. I would have liked to have watched it from the side and sketched the men as they push each other and fling their arms around.

'How many men were in the crowd? Did they hit him with fists or did they use anything else?'

'Don't think about it. You were lucky not to be here, Victorine.' Madame Legrand passes me a large plate of black pudding to cut. 'The sight of blood all over the floor made me feel faint. I don't want them in here again, but Benoît says we need them. Wine just flows when the workers come in.'

I am arranging portions of black pudding on a platter when Monsieur Legrand rushes in and calls for me to come to the bar straightaway. Madame Legrand gives him a fierce look.

'Leave the girl alone, Benoît.'

'Here, Victorine,' he ignores her. 'It's urgent. Come on!' His face is red and he waves his arms about, gesturing me to move. Madame Legrand sighs and nods towards me.

Philippe is lying on the floor, barely conscious. A young man stumbled across him sleeping in a gutter, not far from the entrance to the café, and brought him in. He couldn't have known that Philippe was a regular at the Coin de Paris; we were the nearest place where he could ask for help. Blood is oozing out of Philippe's forehead and Monsieur Legrand instructs me to clean it. As I approach him, Philippe waves his hands about and knocks down a glass of spirit. The liquid drips onto his forehead and he screams. Monsieur Legrand gives him a glass of water. Philippe takes it eagerly but as soon as he realizes what it is, he spits it out. Now he is coughing and spluttering. We leave him lying on the floor, with the man who brought him in kneeling by his side.

After half an hour, the man manages to help Philippe to his feet, and accompanied by Monsieur Legrand, the two of them take the old man home.

In the evening, the young man returns and orders a drink. He sits alone at the table that the family with the two boys uses at lunchtimes. He smokes and stares blankly in front of him. While I am clearing the empty glasses and wiping the zinc top of his table, he puts his hand on mine and says: 'Mademoiselle, I need to tell you something.' I free my hand but remain standing by the table. His name is Etienne Ducroix and he had met Philippe in the Louvre many years ago.

'It took me a long time to realize that the old wreck in such filthy, stinking clothes was Philippe. He used to be so well turned out… mademoiselle, you can't imagine that once he was so dapper, educated and intelligent. What a transformation, mademoiselle.' He tries to reach out for my hand. I nod in sympathy at his words and move away. Several men are gathering around the bar and calling for me.

At eleven o'clock, I am ready to go. Etienne is still sitting in the corner and drinking. He waves towards me and smiles but when he sees that I ignore him, he stands up. He makes a few steps and then collapses on the floor. Monsieur Legrand tells me that he will get him out. I need to rush. It is a starry night and after all the smoke of the café, I breathe deeply the cool air outside.

By the time I leave the omnibus in the Pantin, a few flakes of snow flutter through the air. I wrap my scarf tightly around my neck and walk quickly to the Hôtel d'Or. In my pocket I feel for the card with that painter's name. When I open the door, I hear mother snoring.

3

What joys, what pleasures for the *flâneur* in Paris! I inhale the crisp air. The sun is shining but its rays have no effect on the frozen ground. The cold, bright weather exhilarates me: I want to paint something in a completely new way, something they have never seen before.

The sky has that luminous quality that I have observed only in Italy when the white facades dazzle in the heat. But on a cold January day in Paris, the blinding brightness is more magical. Perhaps we feel that it does not belong to us in the midst of winter.

Is this the brightness of modernity ushering in a new era? One day our paintings will be full of bright colours. Sometimes I think I should copy all the pictures in the Louvre and bring them alive with chrome orange, Naples yellow, crimson lake, and lead white.

I want to paint the scintillating effect of this light on a canvas.

It would be wrong to die on a day like this; there is too much life in the air. If I ruled France, I would ban funerals on sunny days.

There are crowds on the Boulevard Saint Michel and I cross the road to avoid them. For the briefest of moments, my eyes catch a sight of a face ahead of me. At first, I am not sure that she is more than a vision. The white light shines in my eyes and, as I reach an omnibus stop, the glare from the window blinds me temporarily. When I can see again, she has disappeared. Am I imagining her? A minute later, I am rewarded with another fleeting glimpse of the face, and I have a feeling that I have known her before, sometime ago, perhaps on more than one occasion. Has she emerged from my mind's eye?

When the face turns and its owner walks away in the direction opposite to mine, I know I have to pursue this impression and I change my plans quickly. Eugène, my little brother, is reading in the library at the Sorbonne – an occupation he loves as much as I love rambling around – and it will do no harm if I am late.

She is young and sturdy and moves fast. I perceive an air of determination in her gait: she must know exactly where she is going. When I am with Charles, we roam around without a plan. All of Paris is our destination. But this woman neither looks around, nor slows down. She moves on relentlessly. At one point, the pavement is crowded again and men are digging the road. It becomes almost impossible to keep up with her. Briefly, I lose her – in this light, the colour of her clothes blends easily with the colours of the street – but then a couple emerge from a shop and she stops to greet them. They spend a few minutes talking and this gives me time to catch up. When she proceeds in the direction of the Jardin du Luxembourg, I am certain she will go in for a stroll. This January sunshine must be enjoyed and women like to promenade in parks. But why is she in such a hurry?

With no flowers, the Jardin looks empty: the bright sunlight is imparting an unearthly atmosphere. I have not been here for several months. Next time there is a day like this, I shall bring my large sketchbook. If only I could bring an easel. How can I catch this dazzling whiteness so that the light from my canvas mesmerizes the viewer? I imagine them standing in front of my pictures, fascinated and unable to move on.

I am wrong. Instead of going for a stroll, she makes straight for a bench in front of the fountain. Her body is delicate: a Parisian. She sits perfectly still on the bench. Looking straight ahead, she notices neither me nor anyone else.

I move closer. From the side of the path, I see that her face is hard and melancholy, with beautiful eyes and a fresh mouth. Fully lit, with no shadows, it looks like a mask; it reminds me of a Japanese woodcut.

I need to paint her. The more I look at her, the more certain I am that I have seen her before. Hers is the face that I have carried in my head and have been trying to draw. It never worked. I always need a model to give substance to my imagination.

Quietly, I sit down on the other end of the bench. She does not move and I congratulate myself for being so discreet. Unnoticed, I study her profile. She sits like a marble sculpture, as if she is already modelling for me. I cannot take my eyes off her. As long as she stays here, I have no need to speak.

From such a short distance, her skin is almost translucent. What mixture of colours would create the effect on a canvas? If I were to paint her now, I would want to ensure that her face did not blend with its surroundings. Perhaps I could convey its luminosity – and I make a mental note of the idea – by drawing a black line around it.

After a while, I feel the urge to look at her *en face*. To satisfy my curiosity, I rise and stand in front of her. I move slowly, to avoid startling her. For a while, she remains unaware of my presence. When she looks up and sees me staring at her, her lips part, as if she is about to speak.

I introduce myself. My name means nothing to her.

The bright sun exposes the detail of her face, the tiniest of lines around her eyes. The fluffy strands of hair in front of her ears are like copper, sparkling in the sunshine. She looks straight into my eyes. Her expression is calm, so calm that it appears devoid of emotion. I take a step back, keeping my eyes on her. Velázquez could have painted her like this. There is something very truthful about her look. I tell her that.

In this bright light, she does not appear real. Her light auburn hair, tucked back into a small, black toque, seems to be on fire. A green bush behind her provides a frame that separates her from the rest of the Jardin and the rest of the world. But it is the eyes that I am drawn to. They project an air of indifferent self-sufficiency, almost a touch of arrogance, too much in a woman. She is a modern Parisienne, precisely the woman I need in my paintings.

She is a find; there is no mistake about that. With that face, I can wake up the old, silver heads at the Beaux-Arts.

I give her my address and arrange for her to come to my

studio. She goes away. Finding a good model in Paris is as easy as roaming its streets.

I whistle as I leave the Jardin. What a find! Only when I cross the road, do I remember that I am going in the wrong direction. I have forgotten to collect the aquatint plates that I have had etched. I need to go back. That is what comes from following a woman. Being a *flâneur* in Paris and strolling aimlessly may be the height of pleasure, but there are tasks waiting. Eugène, my dear brother, will have to put up with me being late.

4

'Victorine, are you all right?' Monsieur Legrand stands close to me. His hand touches my waist. I move away.

'Madame Legrand says that you look ill.' He pushes in front of me. 'Are you in some trouble? A pretty young girl like you, it wouldn't surprise me.' His eyes widen while he speaks and then, as he leans his face towards mine, he winks and whispers, 'I can keep your secret.' His breath smells of garlic and black pudding and I move away once again.

'I'm not in any trouble monsieur. I'm feeling very well.'

'You aren't as cheerful as you used to be. You look as if there is something bothering you, as if there is something on your mind. You can tell me, Victorine.'

'Everything is fine, monsieur. If I have a problem, I'll tell you.'

After lunch, there are very few customers and Madame Legrand says I can take a break.

'You work hard, Victorine. Have a rest; a walk by the Seine would do you good. The fresh air should bring some colour to your cheeks.'

I go straight to the Louvre. By the time I reach the Salon Carré, I feel slightly faint and I have to sit on the circular divan in the centre. I had intended to spend some time looking at paintings by seventeenth-century Spanish artists. The view of a picture I am particularly interested in is partially blocked by the easel of a copyist. I stand up and move closer.

The copyist is a woman and, when she sees me looking at the painting, she asks if I like Murillo. How could anyone not like his work? I don't tell her that. She is American, in Paris to learn painting. She knows that the Ecole des Beaux-Arts only accepts male students and has arranged to have lessons with a painter in his studio.

'Monsieur Deschamp tells me what to do. Yesterday, he said I should go to the Louvre and copy Murillo's *Madonna*. When I finish, I will show it to him and he'll pull it to bits, like he always does. He also wants me to do as many drawings of ordinary objects as I can. He expects me to work at home, and sketch even when I'm out and about. "Sketch anything you see and bring it to me", he says each time I leave his studio. Later on, we'll move onto the most important subject, the human figure. I think it's a good arrangement. He has models in the studio, so I can use them.' The woman puts down her brushes, wipes them on a cloth, and stands back from the easel.

'This is more fun, painting, I mean. I like working with colours. I find drawing tedious but he insists on it. He says you can't paint unless you draw. I don't agree.' She waits for me to comment, but when I don't, she says: 'Enough for now, I think.'

While putting away her brushes, she turns towards me: 'Do you paint?' I don't know what to say. No one has ever asked me this question. I want to say that I am in a hurry, but no words come out.

'I am sorry, my accent isn't very good. People have difficulty understanding me.' The woman smiles. She says she needs a break and is going to the café downstairs. 'Come with me.'

Why does she want to talk to me when she has so much work to do?

'I can't, not today.' The woman stares at me and I add, 'I am expected elsewhere. I've to go now.'

'That's fine. I am here most days. I may see you another time. It should take me a week to produce anything worth showing to Monsieur Deschamp.'

On the way out, I wonder how much it costs to join a painting class with an artist. I've heard that women have to pay twice as much as men. If I could earn some extra money, perhaps playing a guitar in cafés on my evening off, I might save for that.

* * *

Late at night, when I open the door of our room, mother is sitting at the table. She looks up at me, but doesn't say anything. Her eyes are red, with black patches underneath. When she is sure that I am looking at her, she lifts her hands and covers her face. All I can see now are her chapped, red fingers with broken skin and her grey hair. She would make a good picture in this position.

I carry on looking at her, but don't know what to say. I wonder if she expects me to do anything.

When I was upset as a child, grandmother always knew how to comfort me. She would hold my hand and press my ear to her heart. 'Listen to the beating, Victorine. It is the beating of love for you. Don't cry, child,' she would say. Amazed with the rhythmical beating, I would soon calm down.

I can't do anything as intimate with mother. We don't embrace or kiss. We sleep in the same bed but we make sure that we never touch. When she visited us in the village on her days off, she would try to stroke my cheeks before she kissed them. I hated the feel of her hand, and I would run away. Grandma would call me back and sometimes, only to please grandma, I allowed mother's fingers on my skin. Even then, I would flinch. Mother's hands have always been so rough, smelling of strong soap that hurt my nostrils.

I stand by the table and edge away towards the door. I want to leave her alone, on pretence of going downstairs to use the toilet. As soon as mother hears me move, her sobs become louder. I watch her shoulders shake as she utters sharp, broken sounds. After a while, a long, piercing cry comes out of her mouth, followed by a sigh. Then she sits up, takes her hands off her face, and looks at me.

I wish I were somewhere else.

'Sit down, Victorine,' she says firmly. I do as I am told. Something cold begins to grow inside me; I am scared.

We have only two chairs around the table. I sit down opposite my mother. I wait for her to say whatever she needs to say but I dare not meet her eyes.

'They've kicked me out of the laundry. Perigôt says I am too old and too slow. When Delphine protested that it wasn't right, the owner gave me a hundred francs on top of my wages and said she didn't wish to see me any more. I've worked there for seventeen years. If only you had had a parting gift from that stingy, rich madame, we could have opened a shop two years ago. Since then, they are asking much more for a place. Now I have nothing.' Her eyes press down heavily on me.

'I am sorry, mother.' What else can I say?

'Victorine, I need your help.' Her voice sounds rough. I keep quiet. She continues: 'I've been thinking…' She pauses and stares at me. I lower my eyes and she continues: 'You could work at the laundry; they pay more than the café.' That's not true. I've lied to mother about how much I earn; I need to keep part of my wages for the rent at Maître Albert. I look down. Mother goes on: 'I've worked it out. In two years' time, with your wages from the laundry, and you know, you can always do overtime, and if we manage carefully, we could open a shop.'

Her hand grabs mine and squeezes it. The roughness of her skin repels me. I say nothing.

'Our own shop. Just the two of us.' I look away. 'Victorine, there is no other way out. I need your help. We have each other. We have no one else.'

She is wrong. I have my drawings and my paintings.

'Are you agreed, then?' mother asks and pulls my arm, forcing me to look up. She makes her voice sound kinder than before, but it doesn't move me.

'I've asked and the owner said that, as a favour to me, they would take you on. They always need strong, young women. You can start tomorrow.'

'I am working in the café the whole day. We expect to be busy. There is a big meeting going on. I can't let them down.' I lie.

She stares at me as if trying to decide whether to believe me or not.

'Just for tomorrow, then. So that you can tell them. I'll go to the laundry and tell them that you'll start a day later.'

I gain one-day's respite.

5

Charles, with his hair newly dyed green, walks around the studio, stops by the wall with the long table, and reads aloud the lines pinned next to the half-finished portrait of the Spanish dancer:

Entre tant de beautés que partout on peut voir,
Je comprends bien, amis, que le désir balance;
Mais on voit scintiller en Lola de Valence
Le charme inattendu d'un bijou rose et noir.

His voice is loud, and he gesticulates with his hands towards an imaginary audience. I don't respond. Today, his histrionics don't amuse me.

'Bravo,' shouts Antoine and claps. I see both of them glance in my direction. They are dear, dear friends, I know, but the din they are making is not helpful. I continue drawing.

I have convinced myself that if I use the red chalk, she will come. What silly superstitions we rely upon. But it is better than doing nothing. I am sick of waiting and feeling helpless. Why did I think of the red chalk? Because her hair is red. I can see it right now: with the evergreen foliage behind her and the sun shining so brightly, her head looked as if it were on fire.

Antoine stands next to me and picks up one of the drawings I have made over the past few days. He peers closely at it, before glancing at the rest that lie scattered on the table. He shuffles through the pile on the side.

'You have dozens of them here.' He stares at me.

Charles laughs: 'Sarrasin and Zambinella.'

I dare not look up. I know Balzac's story.

Charles begins to recite.

'*He became a prey to one of those paroxysms of activity that point to the presence of new principles of existence. He was in love for the first time. His was a love devoted as much to pleasure as to pain. And in order to cope with his impatience and his delirium, he began drawing Zambinella from memory. It was a sort of practical –*'

Why can't he stop mocking?

Antoine walks towards Charles and tells him to stop. Then he turns towards me. 'They are all of the same woman, Edouard.'

Charles resumes his reciting: '*And then Sarrasin made numerous pencil sketches of his lover in different poses. He was, we might say, creating a kind of future for her…Sarrasin, a Pygmalion of our times…*' He pauses before repeating: 'a Pygmalion of our times. Isn't that what every artist wants? To create a woman of his own dreams and to be in charge of her future. A woman just for himself. Creating art is about possession.'

Antoine leans towards me and whispers: 'Ignore him.' I nod. 'But tell me: Who is she? I have not seen her around.'

'She has not been around,' I say without looking up.

Charles opens his mouth to say something but stops. All I can hear is a deep intake of breath. Then, he is standing next to me. His voice is no longer mocking: 'Remember Edouard, that same Zambinella saying, '*the world is no more than a desert to me. Forever, I am a creature doomed to understand happiness, to feel and to desire it. But like with so many others, it will always elude me.*' After that she tells Sarrasine, *I forbid you to love me.*'

'I am not in love.'

'Then, I am relieved.' Charles walks towards the window. 'That's a new one for you: drawing from memory. You always surprise me, Edouard.'

'I have no choice, Antoine. She would not come.'

Charles comes back: 'Antoine, let me tell you: Edouard has found the face of truth. And he needs to possess it.'

I cannot bear the irony in his tone but Charles is not easy to stop: 'As I always say, the streets of our city are full of wondrous subjects. Edouard has found truth on a Parisian pavement.' He moves away.

51

'What do you mean, she would not come to you? Have you asked her? Have you explained that you are a painter?'

'Antoine, of course I have asked her.'

'Which day did you agree on?'

'I said she can come any time. There was no other agreement. I expected her to come the next day. I did say I was going to paint her. I was serious about it.'

'Is it really someone you met on the street?' Antoine asks.

I nod. I think of the woman. I can see her in front of me, right now: she had that typical Parisian way of walking, full of flair. At first, when she didn't turn up, I thought, I would do her from memory, or more or less so. Of course; part of what I saw stayed engraved on my mind. But after trying for days, I realised it was not right. I always find it impossible to do anything without a model. I could paint a landscape perhaps, but I could not do a figure from memory, never.

Antoine leafs through the drawings again.

'How long have you been working on these?' His voice is full of concern. From our days at Couture's, he knows I can sketch very quickly, but there are hundreds of sheets here, all of the same face.

Charles speaks before I can say anything: 'Our dear friend has fallen for the face of truth. He is so much in her grip that all his other muses have deserted him. He cannot draw anything else. And the reality is that Martinet has been sending his boys with messages, but Edouard ignores them.'

'In that case, she has to be found. Louis cannot be made to wait. She has to be brought here. She has to understand the seriousness of the situation.'

Charles agrees: 'She has to be found. She has to be made to understand the seriousness of the situation.' He is mocking again.

Antoine ignores him. He tries to sound practical and helpful as he turns towards me: 'Have you looked in the Pigalle? No? Well, we should go there first. Tomorrow morning, I will pick you up and we shall go there. We can take some of your drawings, to help me recognise her.'

52

'She is not a model,' I say.

'Oh? Who is she, then?'

'I do not know. I have lost her address. I think it was Maître Albert, but I cannot recall the house number.'

'We shall find her, my dear friend. I give you my word, the mademoiselle shall pose for a picture.'

There is a knock at the door. For a minute, no one moves. The knocking starts again.

Antoine looks at me: 'Are you expecting anyone?'

I shake my head. I dare not hope. I have wished for all the visitors in the past two weeks to be her. I have been disappointed each time.

Antoine walks to the door and I can hear his loud voice: 'Oh, come, come in, you are welcome, madame.' I hear the door close and Madame Bijoux, carrying a tray with coffee and croissants, walks towards the middle of the studio.

'I thought the gentlemen would like some coffee,' she says putting the tray down. I nod. Antoine thanks Madame Bijoux.

'What a considerate concierge you have, Edouard,' Antoine says after Madame Bijoux walks out. 'But tell me, Edouard, what kind of clothes did the woman wear? Was she rich or poor?'

I cannot remember.

'What was her speech like?' I can recall only her face, her eyes, and her look.

'She had the face of someone self-possessed.'

Antoine stares at me: 'Yes? Can you be more specific?'

'She seemed strong, indifferent, and defiant.'

'Well, that narrows it down a bit. Your description includes most of the women of Paris.' Antoine looks at Charles, who smiles. 'But, do not worry, Edouard, we shall find her. And you will paint her picture. As many pictures as you want. I give you my word.'

6

I wait until Madame Legrand is alone in the kitchen. But as soon as I say that mother has lost her job and that I'll have to support her, a pot of bubbling stew boils over and she rushes to move it to the side. The spilled sauce splatters onto the stove, leaving large greasy patches. The smell of burnt food fills the kitchen and Madame Legrand complains.

'The smoke'll drift into the café and they'll think we can't cook. Oh, Victorine, help me open the back door. Quick.'

I open the door and fan the air with an old newspaper. All the time I am thinking of how to talk to Madame Legrand. She is too preoccupied with her cooking to pay attention to me. Her husband calls me to help at the bar and when I return to the kitchen an hour later, Madame Legrand is putting on her coat, ready to go out. She holds a basket covered with a napkin. I remember it's her day for visiting her father: she always takes him a bowl of our mutton stew. She gives me instructions on what to do while she is away and then, just as she is about to leave, she turns towards me and says: 'Victorine, you were telling me about your mother. Is there anything I can do to help?' I wonder if she is thinking of offering work to my mother. I couldn't cope with mother knowing where I am every minute of the day.

I tell Madame Legrand that mother has arranged for me to take her place at the laundry, because that way I would earn more.

She waits before saying: 'Victorine, we'd hate to lose you. You have become like a daughter to me. If it's a question of money, we can help you.' I thank her, expecting her to say that she will raise my wages, but instead, she says, 'Henriette is expecting.

She'll be leaving and she already wants to work fewer hours. She has married well; she can manage. If you were to pick up those hours, it'd help both of us.'

I tell her that I'll have to talk to mother first before I accept.

* * *

When I serve the family with the two boys, I forget to include extra bread with the boys' portions and only realize that as I put the plates in front of them. I can't take more hours as Madame Legrand suggests. What would be the point of paying for Maître Albert if I have no time to spend on my art? And if I don't give mother more money, she'll force me to work at the laundry.

The disappointment on the boys' faces when they notice that there is no extra bread on their plates, and less sauce than usual, shames me. I go back to the kitchen and, when no one is looking, make a plate with meat, roast potatoes, and two slices of bread. I take it to the family's table and place it between the boys. They look at me, their mouths open, eyes questioning. I nod and smile and immediately their greedy faces light up. The mother, however, snatches the plate and asks me to take it back. She says that they can't afford it. I assure her that there will be no extra to pay. She looks at me strangely before returning the plate. The boys are already helping themselves. I notice that the younger one pinches the arm of his elder brother, complaining that he has taken more than his share.

As soon as I leave their table, I hear a loud thump. Philippe, who has been drinking since we opened, falls to the floor. With the help of two other regulars, I manage to haul him to his feet. Monsieur Legrand asks Gérard, one of the two, to help me take Philippe back to his apartment. The drunken old man lurches out and totters along the pavement as Gérard and I support him by his elbows. When we reach the building with Philippe's apartment, the concierge gives him the key and he slips it into his pocket. We climb the stairs awkwardly as he is almost a dead weight. Outside his door, he slumps on the floor. He searches his pockets, but can't find the key. While Gérard walks downstairs to check whether Philippe has dropped the key, I look for it in the old man's pockets. When I bend over him, he burps; I can smell alcohol and vomit on his breath. What would Monsieur Manet think of this face of truth?

I find the key, unlock the door, and wait for Gérard. We drag Philippe into the bedroom where he slumps onto the bed. Gérard says that he needs to leave straight away if he is not to be late for work. I protest that I have to rush as well, but Gérard has already gone. On the bed, Philippe snores loudly. He lies on dirty sheets made of fine linen. In this apartment, with its expensive rugs and decorative ornaments on the sideboard, Philippe looks even shabbier than usual.

When I was feeling for the keys, my fingers found a wad of notes in his trouser pocket. Now, I slip my hand in there and, keeping my eyes on his face, I gently pull out the money. Heat rises through my body. Philippe doesn't move. I listen to his regular breathing as I tuck the notes inside my blouse. The edges scrape against my skin and I readjust them. Near the front door, I take out the money, split the wad in half, and tiptoe back into the room. Philippe is still in the same position. I am about to return some of the money into his pocket, when he sneezes loudly and I freeze. Best to get out as quickly as possible. My heart is beating fast as I close the door of the apartment and look up and down the winding staircase. There isn't anyone around. On the way down, I take deep breaths.

Before reaching the café, I enter a porch and for the first time, in semi-darkness, I look at the money. I count one hundred and eighty-five francs. Why does the old fool carry such a fortune around with him? One hundred and eighty-five francs!

No one has seen me and he was too pissed to know how much he had. One hundred and eighty-five francs is mine now. My heart leaps with joy. If I save another fifteen francs, for the next four months I can give mother fifty francs a month. That is twenty francs more than now. And it is more than the extra that mother assumes I would earn at the laundry. Philippe's money will buy me time. I'll have four months to sort something out.

One hundred and eighty-five francs: for Philippe that'd be a lot of alcohol, not to mention, a lot of vomit.

* * *

In the evening, I tell mother that the Legrands have raised my wages and that I'll be earning more than at the laundry. In return, I'll have to work longer hours. She doesn't believe me, but when I produce fifty francs, saying this is the money for the month, she takes it as if it were hers. For the rest of the evening she doesn't mention the laundry.

Soon after we put out the gas lamp, I hear her breathing slowly and regularly. I can't fall asleep for a long time. I wonder if Monsieur Manet has many models in his studio. Does he take students?

7

A month has passed during which I have done nothing but gazed at the sky.

At ten o'clock, Antoine calls to pick me up. Dark clouds gather over the horizon. He has a taxi waiting outside. As soon as we set off, the clouds burst open with such ferocity that the taxi has to stop and we get out. We wait inside a porch, watching rivulets run across the pavements. Once the rain subsides, we resume the ride to Maître Albert.

The street is close to Notre Dame. The area is full of beggars, and the pavements are strewn with rubbish. A young boy walking in front of us, no more than six or seven, trips and falls down, crying with pain. As we stop to help him, the boy tugs on the gold chain of Antoine's watch. I grab hold of his arm before he can run away with his loot. The child starts screaming, pretending that I am hurting him. We are aware of the beggars watching us; one of them walks towards us, threatening us. We give the boy a franc and let him go. He runs away laughing and the beggar turns away.

As we stand at the end of the street, Antoine urges me to think back and remember the address: 'Edouard, my friend,' he says, 'What did the number sound like? You are a painter. Can you visualise the number she gave you? What image did you associate with it?'

I don't know. Was it seven? Seven is yellow; or was it three? Three is green…this is madness. Which colour did I see on that day? I cannot remember anything but her hair, all on fire.

Antoine, my kind and patient friend, says gently: 'Think back, my friend. What do you see? Sun or rain?' I try, but it is not helpful. I can see sunshine, luminously white, but any number I come up with sounds as plausible as the next one.

Maître Albert is not a long street, but we cannot try every door. Once again, it is raining heavily and rubbish floats in the puddles. What a gloomy place this is!

I force myself to recall the mademoiselle's surname, but it does not come to mind. We knock on several doors and speak to each concierge in turn. I try to speak like a *faubourg* and the people are friendly enough, but we have no luck: none of them knows a young woman called Louise. When they hear my description of the woman we are looking for, each concierge shakes her head: 'No, monsieur, she doesn't live here.' Our clothes are soaked and I know that we do not present an attractive sight.

At number seventeen, a large rooming house with boarded windows and a pile of dirty rags on the pavement, there is a large, iron door with a bas relief. Its craftsmanship looks incongruous in the shabby surroundings. We knock, but no one answers. As we are leaving, the door opens and an elderly man comes out. Startled, he winces when he sees us. He is about to go back in and we have to stop him; he immediately says that the concierge is out. When I give him my description of the woman I am looking for, his expression softens, and he nods.

'Yes, I've seen her. The young woman with red hair…she has only recently moved here…or perhaps a year ago…keeps to herself.' He points to the courtyard: 'I think she uses the staircase you approach through the door across the inner yard. If you stand over there, by that bush, you can see her windows, those very tall ones at the top.'

I say: 'Thank you very much, monsieur. You have been very helpful.'

All three of us look up. 'Must be cold up there,' the man says as he turns to leave.

When I ask if her name is Mademoiselle Louise, he shakes his head. 'No, I've heard Madame Conchis call her something else. I can't recall her name, but it's not Louise. I'm certain of that.' His voice becomes soft: 'My wife was called Lousie and I'd have remembered the young woman's name, if it were the same. You must be looking for someone else, monsieur.'

Antoine and I look at each other. I think we will never find her. I am sure the name is Louise.

With the rain still pouring down heavily, we shelter in a porch. Our taxi has left and when the rain turns to drizzle, Antoine looks for another one and asks the driver to take us to Notre-Dame-de-Lorette.

At the rotisserie Pavard, he orders a bottle of fine wine and a roast, but I have little appetite for lunch. Her face is everywhere I look.

I have cancelled sittings with Madame Dumas, and Eugène, my dear brother, is mad with me. Yesterday, he reminded me how many times I had badgered Madame Dumas to pose for me. Eugène said she did not take it well when he told her that we would have to delay her portrait once again.

'Remember,' Eugène said, 'that she has friends in high places. Her husband's cousin is on the jury for the Salon.' Damn that, I think. What's the point of having such connections if I cannot work?

I can neither paint nor do anything else. Today a second letter arrived from Suzanne in Holland. She and Léon are staying with her parents for a couple of months. I have not answered the first one. The poor woman will think that I have forgotten them.

Antoine looks at me and urges me to lift my glass: 'Edouard, be patient. If she is to come, she will come.' He is right. I clink his glass and smile. What else can I do? I know I am not a patient man. We finish the bottle and order another one.

By the time we leave, the rain has stopped and the pavements are glistening in the late March sunshine. For the rest of the afternoon, Antoine indulges me. We stroll to the Ile de la Cité and across the Pont Neuf. I look at the faces we pass by. On several occasions, I have the feeling that I see her, but as soon as I get close, I realize my mistake.

Even the sight of the magnificent building of Hôtel de Ville does not lift my spirits. To show Antoine that I appreciate his efforts, I smile and say:

'If I cannot paint her, I want to decorate the Hôtel de Ville.'

Antoine looks at me with his most serious expression: 'I shall make arrangements for that, my dear Edouard. I promise. Just give me time.'

8

Mother is still in bed when I wake up. I dress quickly. We don't speak; I hope she thinks that I am leaving early on Sunday because I am working an extra day. Dawn is breaking when I take the omnibus to the Boulevard Saint Michel and then walk to Maître Albert.

I've placed the eight drawings of the couple from the café on the long table and I keep looking at them, trying to assess which one I should use as the basis for my first canvas. I pick the one in which only the lower part of the woman's face is visible. She is bowing her head so that her hat covers her eyes. Should they be dressed in the same colours that the man and the woman wore in the café? A blue garment may make the woman look too subdued. Perhaps the angle I have chosen would make the man too prominent, the woman too timid. I'd like the female figure to appear as strong as the woman in the café. For that, I need her face and her eyes. I wouldn't know how to express her strength through her body alone.

I look again at the drawings that show the woman staring out, meeting my eyes. In one of them, she looks strong and confident, as if she is prepared to cope with anything that happens to her. Perhaps the secret lies in the lack of emotion on her face: neither the man, nor anyone else, can tell what she really thinks. Like the real woman in the café, this one knows what she wants. And now that I am her, I am not going to let the man sitting next to me, plying me with drinks and soft words, distract me from my purpose. Perhaps I should draw the woman alone. Or, if not, she should be the centre of my picture. I sketch a series of self-portraits.

When I finish, I stand in front of a mirror and experiment

with different poses for another idea. I hold a basket, change my hat, take a rolled up sheet of paper and imagine that it's a bouquet of flowers. There's a young woman who sells flowers near the Louvre every summer. Sometimes, she comes to our café. Even when her basket is full, she holds her back straight and her head high. I imagine I am her. I try on a wide skirt from the pile of clothes I keep for costumes. I swing my body left and right and the skirt swishes around. If only I could capture the sense of movement. And there I have it! I shall use my first canvas for a full-length painting of this woman. Why bother with a man?

I see her walk the streets, peddling her wares. I see her so clearly. She looks out to catch the eyes of her customers. How could I paint that? If only there were someone I could ask how to capture the movement and her keen eye, looking for trade. If only there were someone who could show me how to prepare the canvas and start.

I'll have to teach myself. I stare at my reflection in the mirror and think: I have the idea; I have the model; now all I need is time and effort. I'll learn.

But there is a quicker way. Perhaps the American woman in the Louvre could help. Would she laugh at my ignorance?

I wonder if Monsieur Manet has students in his atelier.

I rush downstairs. Crossing the courtyard, I hear the sound of a flute coming from the open window just below mine. I listen for a few moments. I recognize an old tune, gentle and emotional: a peddler who sometimes came to our village played it in the square. My grandmother liked to listen to him and she would take me with her. She had no money to give him, but he was happy to receive an apple or a chunk of bread.

Once, when I was seven, he showed me how to play. He was walking through the village and, as he passed by our house, grandmother had given me some bread and cheese and a glass of wine to take to him out in the yard. He told me to put the food on the ground and handed me the flute. I didn't know what to do with it. He placed my fingers on the stops and showed me how to hold my mouth and blow. At first, nothing came out but he persisted, telling me to make an 'o' with my lips, while keeping them relaxed. I remember the excitement I felt when the first proper sound came out. Grandmother watched us from the doorstep and clapped. Later on, grandfather carved a flute for me from a cherry branch. I played it for years. Madame Pascal liked to hear me and when, after her husband's death she had sold the stationery shop and was moving to live with her brother down south, she came to us carrying Monsieur Pascal's guitar. She said she knew no one who could make better use of it. Mother thought it was a waste of time – 'just like your drawing' – but she let me keep the guitar and I taught myself. People always said I was good at music.

But the man who plays the flute now – didn't the concierge call him Gabriel? – is faltering; he is still learning.

When I return the key to Madame Conchis, she claps her hands.

'You look happy today, mademoiselle. Why are you in such a hurry? Who is waiting for you? And so early.'

'No one, madame.' She winks at me. 'It's a lovely morning and I want to walk by the Seine.' Madame Conchis frowns and shakes her head.

I go on foot to Saint Michel and take the omnibus to the Gare St-Lazare. From there it's only a short distance to rue Guyot. At number eighty-one, the top floor has high windows. It may be a studio.

As I pass by the concierge's office on the left, she calls after me. I say that I have come to see Monsieur Manet.

'The third floor, mademoiselle,' she says, without looking at me. As soon as I turn to climb the stairs, I hear her mumble to herself, or to someone in the office: 'Another model, I think.'

I wish I could tell her that I am not a model. I am here because I want to talk about painting with Monsieur Manet.

Before I reach the first landing, she shouts: 'Mademoiselle, mademoiselle, do not go up. I've just remembered, Monsieur Manet is not in today. He does occasionally come in on Sundays, but never in the morning.' I descend.

She says: 'Did he ask you to come today and so early?' I shake my head. She stares at me. 'Shall I tell him that you called?'

'No, thank you.' She continues to stare at me, her eyes travelling from top to toe.

'Young women often visit Monsieur Manet.' I turn my back to her.

I walk on without any particular destination.

Ever since I met Monsieur Manet, I've tried to imagine what it would be like to be in a real painter's studio. Marie told me that the best ones always had large places.

'Lovely rooms with beautiful big windows, sometimes on two sides,' she said 'but always stuffed with so much rubbish. Anything they can find they take in: old furniture, clothes, busts, other artists' work, vases and jugs. So much useless clutter lying all around. Some bring in animals.'

I'd tell her that an artist never knows when a piece of clothing or an object might be useful but she was adamant that it was nothing more than a mess.

'Some of them are very dirty. One of the painters I worked for didn't allow the concierge to sweep the floor, in case the dust settled on his canvases.' I thought that was sensible.

I don't feel like going back to Maître Albert. All the time, while sitting on the omnibus, I was thinking of questions to ask Monsieur Manet. I imagined I was looking at his paintings and telling him about my drawings.

I was ten when Monsieur Lefevre, Madame Pascal's brother, stayed in the village. Like Monsieur Pascal, he ran a stationery shop, except that his was in a large town. All his life he painted with oils. He had never sold any pictures. Madame Pascal used to tease him that he could not part with his canvases. 'They are his children,' she would say. Even when he made a present of a painting to a relative, he claimed that it was only 'on loan' and that he would want it back one day.

When he arrived to stay with his sister for the summer, he'd just sold his shop. Grandpa took me to the Pascals' house. Monsieur Lefevre was old and deaf and so we didn't speak a lot. Besides, I was too much in awe of him to be able to say anything. He sat me next to him and asked me to draw the fruit in the bowl on the table. Sitting at an easel, he was painting the same object.

Later, he gave me his brushes and showed me how to mix the paints and prepare the colours. It was the first time that I'd worked with linseed oil. The smell still brings back the memory of that day. For several weeks, we worked side by side. Often, he would use his paintbrush on my picture, to show me how I could do it better. I spent whole days with him and, one evening, I heard grandfather complaining to grandmother.

'In summer, I've so much work. Now that she isn't at school, I could do with her help. She's old enough to take cows to pasture.'

'Leave her alone, Albert,' grandma said. 'She is working very hard and it's important not to miss this opportunity; she's learning from Monsieur Lefevre. He won't be staying long.'

Grandfather was angry with her, saying that 'pictures had never been of any use to anyone'. To placate him, grandmother said that she would help him. She could clean the chicken coop.

Grandfather threatened: 'Wait until I tell her mother what she is doing.'

It was the only time that I heard grandmother shout at him: 'Albert, you'll do no such thing.'

Grandma looked sternly at him. His face went white and then red. He rushed towards her and I thought that he might strike her. I remembered hearing that Monsieur Pascal hit his wife. But grandma didn't flinch, as I expected; she held her ground and continued to stare at him. He backed off, mumbling something and waving his arms about as he walked away. After that day he never complained about me not helping him, nor did he mention my painting lessons to my mother.

Just before leaving the village, Monsieur Lefevre gave me three of his old brushes and a small box of powder paints. I knew how to mix them then and I still have one of the brushes. Monsieur Manet probably uses paints in tubes. They are very expensive, a franc each. If he has no need for tubes that are almost used up, I would be glad to have them.

I'll have to make another trip to Monsieur Manet very soon. If I tell Madame Legrand that I am not feeling well, she may let me leave my shift early.

The sun is out and, as I have no other plans, I carry on walking. I come across a woman selling winter chrysanthemums. She has a small stall and the flowers are in metal jars. I could buy a bouquet for my flower seller. When the woman sees that I am interested, she asks me whether I'm taking them to a grave.

'I've white ones for young people, yellow ones for anyone older and crimson for women. Men buy them for dead lovers. Which colour do you want, mademoiselle?'

'I don't know, a few of each, I suppose.'

The woman gives me a strange look as she arranges a mixed bouquet of chrysanthemums. Now that I've the flowers, I should go home and work on my flower seller. I could do some more drawings.

I think I will call her Céleste.

Walking on, I find myself on the Boulevard du Temple. I weave my way between the stalls of an open air market. I stop to watch a man selling wooden toys; he picks up an armful of dolls and shows them one by one to a little girl. Her mother, who is standing next to her and holding her hand, seems to like them all, but the girl shakes her head each time the man brings a doll closer to her. The man says he has no others. The girl looks down.

'Let's see them again, Charlotte. There must be one that you like. They have such pretty dresses.'

'I don't want a doll. I have dolls. I want crayons, *maman*.'

The child's mother shakes her head. 'We shall get a doll, Charlotte.'

I smile. If the girl were mine, I would buy her the crayons.

At the meat stall, there are rows of pheasants and rabbits hanging upside down. One day, I'd like to paint them. When I worked with Monsieur Lefevre, he showed me a painting he had done of a bowl of fruit with a rabbit to the side.

'Very hard to do it properly,' he said. 'So many different textures. That's a real challenge for a painter, all those tiny hairs in the fur, their different colours, and direction.'

The crowd is much denser here and I have to push my way through to reach the vegetable part of the market. I buy an apple.

At first the woman can't hear what I want, and I strain my ears to hear her, although we are facing each other across the stall. We both have to shout above everyone else.

I run my hands around the apple, feeling its smooth, shiny surface. I put it in my pocket when I stop in front of a cake seller. Large, round fruit tarts glisten in the sunshine and the smell of fresh yeast rises to my nostrils. Could anyone paint a picture that would make you experience such smells?

At a stall displaying fabrics, someone's hand grips mine. I jump and try to move away but the hand does not let go. Startled, I look up: the face is smiling and black. I've never spoken to anyone who looked like that. I am about to walk away, when she places her hand on my shoulder, to prevent me from moving.

'Hello,' she says. 'Pretty flowers. Who are they for?'

I smile at her. 'The seller told me that they were for dead people, to put on graves.'

'Too pretty, too colourful, too full of life.' She bends down to smell the bouquet. 'I love your hair,' she says smiling. 'With the sun on it, your head looks like fire.'

I nod. For a few moments we stand facing each other and then she says:

'I need you, mademoiselle.' She seems serious now. 'Help me choose a material. I'd like to get something for a head cover. Like this one,' she points towards her elaborately tied headgear in bright blue, yellow and brown.

'Tell me, which one should I have?' Her tone is commanding and for a second I want to walk away but something about her figure and her face makes me stay and obey. I watch her as she moves and think how much I would like to draw her.

I stare at the pile of material. So many patterns, colours and textures that would be good to draw or paint, but I have no idea how to choose one for a headgear. All I can say is: 'The one you are wearing now looks good.'

'But do you like it?'

'Yes.'

'You hesitate. Are you sure?'

'No. No,… I…I do like it.'

The woman smiles and sighs. She doesn't believe me. I don't understand what's wrong. 'They are all nice. Are you looking for something similar?'

'Yes, and no.' She laughs. Her well-shaped teeth stand out against her dark skin.

I run my hands over different samples and look carefully through the display. Eventually, I pick a bale of fabric: 'What about this one? Isn't this special?' I don't think it's much better than others, but I feel I ought to play a role and give the impression of being interested.

She looks at the glossy white material, lifts the bale, unrolls it and examines the cloth against the sky. The golden strands shine, the blue becomes brighter.

The pattern and the colours remind me of the ribbons grandmother used to make. Once a month, a man would come to our house to bring golden threads for her to weave. Sometimes, there was a bit left and she would make a ribbon for me. When it was finished, she would tie my hair.

'No one has hair as lovely as yours,' she would say and run her fingers through my long locks. But when I came to live in Paris, children teased me about the colour. They said I looked like a devil. It became my nickname and they would chant it whenever they saw me. One day, Marie told them to stop. That was the first day of our friendship. After that, whenever I was with her, the other children made faces at me but didn't dare say anything.

'So, this is the one you really like?' The black woman is looking straight into my eyes.

'I think so. No, I am sure, yes, that's the one.'

'Good. If you like it, I will like it, too,' she says and her hand touches me lightly on the shoulder. She asks for three metres. As the stall-holder wraps the parcel, and hands it to her, I begin to move away.

'Don't leave, mademoiselle,' she says and immediately her hand seeks mine. When I face her, my eyes are at the level of her neck. I feel very warm.

'I'm alone here, not just at the market, but in this city. Everyone stares, but no one speaks to me. Walk with me.' I look down, not knowing what to say. 'Just for a while, please.'

Since Marie went to live with Emile, I've had no friends. Women don't talk to me when I am alone outside, although men all too often do.

I raise my eyes towards hers. The tips of her fingers touch a lock of my hair hanging over my ear.

'You have the strangest hair I've ever seen. I spotted you from far away. I thought someone was carrying a torch.' She laughs and her white teeth glisten in the sun.

I wonder whether she would let me draw her, but I dare not ask. She grabs me by the hand, saying, 'Come, I'll show you something.' I let her pull me away. We walk through the market and she buys two apples.

'One for you, one for me,' she says handing me one. I thank her and put it in the pocket, next to the one I bought earlier. She bites into hers: 'Don't you want it?' I say that I'll have mine later. She shrugs her shoulders. I watch her as she chews. A woman eating an apple. It would look interesting in profile. I could do it in half an hour, if she were to stay still.

We walk on and she comments on the goods on display. Whenever she stops talking, she grips my hand and looks at me.

'Please don't go away, I'll show you something else,' she says as she drags me to a cobbler's stall. The man stares at her as she picks up a pair of boots and turns them round, inspecting every stitch. Then she asks me what I think of them.

'They won't fit you,' the cobbler says. 'You are too tall for a woman. No woman has such large feet. My shoes are for Parisian women.' My companion looks at him, drops the boots and walks away.

The cobbler picks up the boots and says: 'You can try them, mademoiselle.' I ignore him and follow the woman. He shouts after me: 'What's a beautiful girl like you doing with her? Where has she come from?'

The woman walks fast and I have to run and push through the crowd to catch up with her.

'I like your height,' I say. 'It's very elegant.' She doesn't respond.

We walk side by side. Once we leave the market behind, the streets are narrow and there is hardly anyone around. She stops in front of a porch, grips my hand and pulls me inside a house. The hall is dark and smells musty. I want to get out.

'Please, don't leave,' she whispers as she bends down, takes my face in her hands, and kisses me. Her lips are soft like velvet and they taste of cinnamon. As her hands move gently across my cheeks and stroke my neck, a tingling sensation rises through my body. I let her push her tongue into my mouth. I want to put my arms on her body but suddenly, she stops and stands back. I breathe fast. She kisses me on the cheeks very quickly.

'I am glad you like it,' she says and giggles. We hear steps on the staircase and move out. A man and a woman brush against us. The woman gives us a long stare. When they are out of sight, my companion starts dancing. I fear someone will come and laugh at us.

'Let's walk on,' I say.

'Let's walk on,' she repeats. She tells me that her name is Lola, that she was born in Martinique and that she works as a maid in the Batignolles area. She asks about me and just as I am about to ask her to let me draw her, she shouts: 'Oh, look ahead.'

We can hear screaming and see people running in panic towards the Hôtel de Ville. Somebody says that a brown omnibus has just run over a man. They think that he is dead but then a woman shouts that he has only broken his legs. A young man runs out of the crowd and calls for a doctor. In the omnibus, the driver is standing holding the reins of the horses. He swears: 'Damn the idiot, he never looked where he was going!'

Women with small children are pushing to get a glimpse of the scene; I notice an old man hobbling on one leg and elbowing his way through the people.

What a scene. If I had a piece of paper now, I could sketch it. I love the constant movement and the sense of excitement of the crowd. What a painting they would make!

'Poor man,' Lola says. 'He must be in terrible pain to be screaming like this. Hope the doctor comes soon. Let's go.'

I want to stay and watch, but she pulls me away. 'He is badly injured; you don't want to see that.'

When we find ourselves close to Notre Dame, I tell her that this time I'll show her something.

I knock on the concierge's window and Madame Conchis hands me the key.

'Who is this?' she says staring at Lola. I don't know what to say. Lola smiles at the concierge. Madame Conchis goes back to her office. We cross the yard and walk upstairs.

'It's freezing in this place,' she says. I light the stove.

'You can sit here.' I pull a chair next to the stove and fetch my sketchpad. Lola ignores my suggestion. She lowers herself on the divan and asks me to join her. I stand in front of her with the sketchpad in my hand but she either doesn't understand what I am trying to do or chooses to ignore it. She pats a place on the divan next to her. I sit down with the sketchpad on my lap. Lola puts an arm around me and squeezes me tight. The sketchpad drops onto the floor. Her lips are cold as she presses them against mine.

'There, that's much better.' She unbuttons my pelisse and puts her hand inside my blouse.

Slowly and gently, she takes off my clothes and urges me to do the same to her. I shiver. In the light coming in from the windows of the apartments opposite, I watch as her hands stroke my breasts and hover above my nipples. Marie used to let me draw her afterwards.

'Hello,' Lola whispers into my ear. 'What are you thinking of, Victorine?'

'Nothing.' After a pause, I add: 'I am thinking of you.'

'Look at me, then.' She has large breasts, much fuller than mine, or Marie's. And the nipples are huge. I run the tips of my fingers around them and they grow harder and swell. She giggles and stands up. Kneeling by the divan, she lays me down, as if I am a doll. Slowly, she climbs on top of me and as her tongue slides inside my mouth, I begin to feel faint. It's more than a year since anyone has kissed me like this.

The weight of her large body pressing down on me feels

good. When she parts my legs and her fingers touch me, slowly pushing inside, I want to scream. Instead, I hold my breath and move her hand away.

9

One very cold January, when I was thirteen, I fell ill. Mother went to work as usual and left me alone.

'Don't get out of bed and don't open the door to anyone,' she said. 'There's cabbage and potato soup that you can warm up for lunch.'

I nodded. The clay stove at the end of the corridor outside our room took an age to light and I had no intention to bother with lunch. Time was too precious.

Just before she closed the door behind her, she added: 'Victorine, you won't need the light. Sleep. Don't use the gas.'

I had to. It was too dark to see.

In the afternoon, there was a knock on the door. I had just eaten some bread and cheese and had placed the rest of the loaf on a plate together with a knife and positioned them on the chair next to the bed. I was lying on my front and drawing. My first thought was that mother had returned early. I jumped up to extinguish the gas lamp and to hide my paper and crayons. In panic I stumbled over the chair. Immediately, the knocking started again, much more insistent. Whoever was there must have realised that I was in. I froze and held my breath. Mother had the key; it wasn't her. Then a voice called me:

'Victorine! You didn't come to school. I know you are in.'

It was Marie. I put away the drawing and the crayons and opened the door.

'What took you so long?'

'I was scared. I didn't know who it was.'

'But even when I called you, what were you doing in here?'

I didn't know what to say. I blushed.

Marie never let go easily. She was younger and smaller than me, but much more confident.

'Tell me, Victorine! What's the secret? Who are you hiding?'

'There's no one here.'

'Can I look?' Marie asked. Of course she could look. It was unlikely to take her long. Apart from the bed that mother and I shared, our furniture consisted of a table, two chairs and a wooden box that had no front side and inside which we kept pots. On top of it we stacked our plates and cups.

Marie remained standing in one place and scanned the room with her eyes, as if she was assessing where a potential fugitive might be hiding. Then she made a bee line for the curtain mother had put up to cover a small recess in the wall where we kept our clothes. With a sudden gesture, she pulled the curtain open and peered in.

'Hello, who's there? Come out, whoever you are?'

I started to laugh. Marie carried on in her exaggeratedly comical voice: 'Come out if you're Victorine's special friend. I want to fight you.'

I was still laughing. She turned towards me.

'They've become invisible. They're afraid of me because they know I'm your special friend.' I smiled. Her face assumed a serious expression: 'I believe you, Victorine. But, tell me, why are you at home? And why in bed?'

'I'm not well. My throat hurts. I was shivering in the morning. Mother said I shouldn't get up but keep warm.'

'Let's get you back to bed, then,' she said. 'Quickly.' I did as she ordered.

'But Victorine, you can't leave me standing here alone.' I didn't know what she expected me to say. She smiled. 'I'll keep you warm.'

She took off her coat, her dress and her stockings. Wearing only a chemise, she climbed into the bed, next to me.

At first, we lay on our backs, side by side. We didn't talk. I thought how exciting it was to be in bed with her. I wondered whether Marie felt the same. After a while, she turned towards me and whispered: 'This is very nice. Don't you think so, Victorine?'

'Yes,' I said softly. I was glad it was too dark for her to see me blushing.

Marie stroked my face before running her fingers through the hair, as if she was brushing it. I closed my eyes. Her touch felt good. She leaned over and kissed me on the lips. I dared not move. She kissed me again and this time I could feel her tongue pushing my lips apart. A wave of heat rose through my body.

She climbed on top of me and placed one of her legs between mine. The weight of her body and the feel of her skin between my thighs, made me tingle inside. I felt the heat from her heavy breathing on my cheeks and put my arms around her back. Her body tensed and I squeezed her tight. By now, the only light came from the moonlight streaming through the window and leaving a line on the floor next to the bed. We held each other and Marie kept pressing her leg against the inside of my thighs. After a while, she said: 'This is what men and women do.' I knew it already but had never thought it could be so lovely. Perhaps it wasn't. Perhaps it was only Marie who was nice. We lay in bed in each other's arms and I wished for time to stop and the after-noon never to end.

But once we heard the church bells ringing, we knew that mother would be home soon. While Marie dressed, I told her my secret. She didn't believe me at first: 'Victorine, you're making this up. What's so secretive about drawing? If I made pictures my mother would be pleased. Why doesn't Madame Meurent like it?'

'She says that only layabouts draw. She doesn't want me to be one of them.'

Marie kissed me again. No longer whispering, she said: 'Victorine, I've an idea. You can draw me. That'll be our little secret.'

'I'd like to. But you must promise never to tell and never to show anyone my pictures.'

'I like sharing secrets with you, Victorine.' She covered my face with kisses.

After that day, we lay in bed together and held each other whenever we were alone. Once, mother almost walked in on us.

When we heard her, we were only half dressed, and Marie pulled on her pelisse quickly, while I said that I had taken off my dress because an insect had crawled on my back.

I loved when we entangled our legs. It always made me feel so light, as if my body had no weight and could float in the air. It was better than kissing. One day, Marie slid her fingers down where I had hair and then pushed them inside me; I screamed. She held me tight and kissed me with her tongue deep into my mouth. Sometimes we removed our chemises and pressed our breasts together. That felt really good.

I loved playing with Marie's breasts. She would lie on her back, and I would cup them in my hands. Then I sucked her nipples and she giggled.

When we got out of bed, Marie always let me draw her. She kept the drawings in a cupboard in her room. Her mother never looked at her things and Marie said that the pictures were safe. I wonder if they are still there.

10

'Monsieur Manet,' Madame Bijoux says as she hands me the key, 'there are several messages for you.'

I look at the scraps of paper. They are all from Martinet. The last one, which arrived this morning, urges me to suggest a line up and confirm a list of etchings for the catalogue. 'Printers always take their time and I would like to stick to the deadline of October for the publication of the catalogue.' Signed: Louis. I may have been ignoring all the commitments, but it does not mean I have forgotten about them.

As I reach the first landing, Madame Bijoux shouts: 'A model came looking for you, monsieur. It was yesterday. I told her you rarely come in on Sundays.'

I turn back. 'What did she look like?'

'Hm. What did she look like?' Madame Bijoux makes a face: her lips take the shape of a letter 'o', her eyebrows arch. She sucks in air. 'The same as all the others. A woman. Young. Pretty, I suppose and you know, monsieur – '

'What colour was her hair?' I hold onto the banister, my heart racing.

'Monsieur Manet, you can't expect me to remember that.' Madame Bijoux lifts her arms and opens them, the palms of her hands turned upwards.

'Was her hair red? Very bright red?'

Now she looks away, screws her eyes and then turns back towards me: 'It might have been. But then, it might not. The truth is, Monsieur Manet, all these girls look the same.' She nods at her own words and when I say nothing, she disappears into her office.

I will never know. It might have been her.

I enter the office. 'Didn't she leave a message?'

'No, monsieur.' Madame Bijoux has her back towards me as she rearranges the keys on their hooks. She knows I am watching her. After a pause, she adds: 'I did ask her, monsieur. She didn't want to talk to me. As soon as she realised that you were not in, she rushed out.'

I sigh.

Madame Bijoux turns towards me: 'She was disappointed as well, monsieur. I could see that.' She stares at me, her face a performance of sympathy and I almost smile.

Upstairs, I place two dozen drawings of the woman from the park – I don't know what to call her; the man said she wasn't Louise; but who was she then? – next to each other in a row. The line covers completely the longer side of the studio and reaches half way along the shorter.

If only the drawings were smaller, I could hold them in the palm of my hand, like a pack of cards, and flick through them very quickly, so that the images merged, as they do when a skilful card player reshuffles a pack and an illusion of movement appears. I wish I could do that with these drawings and bring her to life, Pygmalion-like. Then she could pose for me.

Friends can be a bore but at least I always have models.

Louis Martinet is right: I have to finish Signorina de Valence. There is so little time before the show. For the next couple of hours, I work on the background. Poorly motivated, I work mechanically but that is fine for this part of the picture. I certainly cannot do portraits in this state of mind. My brain would not take in any individual features. I know that all my thoughts are entirely preoccupied by the memory of her face. I work slowly, following the design that I have prepared earlier. Signorina de Valence is on the stage and behind her is the set. I want everyone to know that she is on the stage but that stage is my studio.

I watch the clock as I work. Each time I look, it is earlier than I think. I do not like being alone when I am in this constant state of anxiety. My concentration is too poor for proper work. Nor have I been good company recently. I listen for the sound of steps on the staircase. And yet, each knock makes me jump.

At four o'clock, Charles is coming to take me to visit Jeanne. The beautiful Jeanne Duval moves around with difficulty and rarely leaves the house. She spends most of her time reclining on a *chaise longue* and receiving visitors. 'When they leave,' he says, 'she holds her fan and stares ahead, like a sculpture.' His words remind me of what he had said about my painting of Jeanne: 'You make her look like a doll, a sculpture, an inanimate object.' I don't think he was too pleased with the picture. He walked away from it, repeating 'an inanimate object – perhaps that is the woman.'

And now Jeanne Duval cannot move around much. How prophetic was my painting? Isn't that what makes modernity: life imitating art, rather than the other way around.

Poor Jeanne Duval. What a woman she was!

I fetch Charles's poems and open the volume at random. Here she is:

Je plongerai ma tête amoreuse d'ivresse
Dans ce noir océan où l'autre est enfermé;
Et mon esprit subtil que le roulis caresse
Saura vous retrouver, ô féconde paresse,
Infinis bercements du loisir embaumé!

11

After five days at Maître Albert, she is about to leave. I spent the early mornings and evenings with her.

'We won't have another opportunity for a long time,' she said. 'They don't travel often.'

The family she works for returns tomorrow from Bretagne and Lola needs to prepare the house.

'All the cooking and baking, Victorine. They will expect the rooms to be immaculate, with everything washed, polished and dusted. This has been a holiday for me.'

She looks at me, takes my hands in hers and whispers: 'I'll miss you, Victorine.'

I smile. She is kind.

'But don't worry. I'm free almost every Sunday. I can come early in the morning.'

Last night I rushed back from the café, hoping to have time to do a drawing. Wearing only a chemise and no stockings, Lola waited for me with soup and bread from Madame Martine's across the road. I wasn't hungry, so I suggested that she eat while I draw her.

'But you made a drawing of me yesterday and the day before,' she protested. 'Victorine, all these drawings are the same.'

Of course they aren't. The earlier ones have her standing up holding a basket or moving around. And then there was the close up portrait with only her face. Anyway, the more I draw, the better I get.

I asked her whether she could tell that the more recent pictures were better, but she just shrugged her shoulders. 'They're all good.'

Last night, I wanted to make a picture of her sitting and eating, imagining that she was in the café. I planned to put in the background later, maybe even some other figures in the distance, another table or part of the bar counter. I'd thought about it on the way back from the café and even fantasised that the Legrands might like the drawing and put it up in the bar. People would see my picture.

I couldn't say any of this to Lola. She began to sulk and I had to sit with her and kiss her until she mellowed.

'All right, Victorine. You draw me, but be quick. Afterwards, you'll lie down with me, won't you?' I nodded. As if I didn't know. I don't mind taking off my clothes if she lets me draw her.

Mother used to say that if a woman wanted something from a man, all she needed was to sleep with him. But Lola is a woman.

We walk downstairs and Lola insists on holding my hand. Even after we say goodbye and part, she keeps turning and waving from the other side of the road. I smile and wave back. It goes on for ever and I can't wait to get back. At one point she stops and stares at me. I begin to fear that she might change her mind and return to the flat.

At last, it's time for Céleste. I stand in front of the empty canvas and my heart beats fast. I am scared. What if I can't do it?

I see her walking on the pavement with her basket and a bouquet in her left hand. But how do I move on from all these drawings to a painting? The canvas is large, the drawings small. I stare at the canvas and I dare not go on. It cost thirty-three francs and I don't want to ruin it. Thirty-three francs is a small fortune and I paid that for what the shop owner called a medium size. I don't want to think how much he would charge for a large one.

Over the next hour, I try to sketch an outline of the figure of Céleste but can't do it without a model. I erase part of it and try again but the shape is out of proportion. The next attempt is just as bad and after a while I feel frustrated and give up.

I walk by the Seine as far as the Pont des Arts and then turn left into the little streets behind the Ecole des Beaux-Arts. I look at windows of stationery shops supplying art material. In the first one I enter, the owner is serving a young boy, who is reading from a list of items his employer requires. The owner places them in a pile on the counter, one by one. They are mostly brushes and tubes of paints, also some charcoal and a maulstick. He asks me if I have a list of items and before I can answer, he suggests I leave it with him and come back later or, if the items are too large, he could deliver them. I say that I'll wait for him to finish with the boy.

When we are alone, I ask for everything I need to prime a canvas.

He stares at me for a few moments before saying: 'Not every-one uses the same ingredients or the same technique. What does your painter use, mademoiselle?'

'I don't know. He said you would know.'

The owner stares at me: 'Oh la la, mademoiselle. So, it's up to me. Well, what if he doesn't approve of what I give him?'

'He will,' I say quietly.

The owner looks at his shelves: 'Let's think what we should get him.' After a while, he turns towards me and says: 'On second thoughts, mademoiselle, I think he should come himself. It's no good him relying on me. You see, these days, painters have strong feelings about priming. I can't just decide for him.' I bite my lip and look around.

'He won't mind, mademoiselle. He'll understand that I can't decide for him. Or, just check with him. If he still wants me to choose for him, I'll do so.'

He is an old man with soft blue eyes and a lined face. He's older than my mother.

'Monsieur, I'm…I'm the painter.' I watch him but he doesn't appear shocked, not even surprised. I think I detect a smile on his face. But he isn't mocking.

'I've never painted a canvas, monsieur. Nor have I ever primed one. I'd be grateful if you'd tell me what I need and how to do it, monsieur.' The man looks concerned.

'Don't you have a teacher, mademoiselle?'

'No, monsieur. I'm teaching myself.'

'That's very difficult. You need another pair of eyes to help you judge your work. Would you like me to recommend a teacher? I could give you the address of a good one.'

'No, monsieur. I can't afford the fees.' The man carries on looking at me.

'And you want to paint?' I nod.

'Have you tried modelling? A pretty woman like you, you would easily find work.'

'No, monsieur, I don't want to model. I'm a painter.' The man shakes his head and walks through the door to the store. From there, he shouts: 'Just wait a moment, mademoiselle.' A few minutes later, he comes back, carrying a bottle.

'Here, mademoiselle. This is Haarlem, picture varnish diluted with elemi, some brown fixed oil and turpentine. This is your primer. When it dries, you just paint on it. Or you can draw on it, transfer a cartoon or make a grid. Let me show you.' The man takes a piece of paper, draws a rectangular shape on it and then divides it into squares.

'If you are not experienced, the best is to use a grid on your drawing and then on the canvas. That means you can transfer the drawing square by square. Many experienced artists do, anyway.

'Here you are, mademoiselle.'

'Thank you, monsieur. You've been very kind.'

He smiles. 'Let me know how you get on, mademoiselle.'

I cross the river and walk to the café. I hold the bottle, wrapped in a newspaper, close to my heart. The man refused to charge me for it. 'Come back and pay me when you make some money from your paintings,' he said.

I still have one hour to spare before my shift and I walk to the Louvre. I go directly to the Salon Carré. I want to see the American copyist to tell her that I am just about to prime a new canvas. I won't say it is my first one. I look around. She isn't here. I move from one gallery to another, too restless to pay attention to pictures. Within each frame, I see Céleste. There isn't much point looking at the work of others right now.

As I am leaving the building, I hear someone call my name.

'Mademoiselle Victorine, what are you doing here? Has

someone brought you to see the pictures? I would never have guessed that the Legrands' waitress looks at art in a museum.' Etienne Ducroix laughs at me.

'No, monsieur.' I can't help blushing. 'I was early for my shift so I went for a walk. Someone said it's nice here.'

'For a walk in the Louvre? Not much fresh air among these stuffy old paintings,' Etienne laughs again. I turn to leave.

'Oh, mademoiselle, come back, I can show you around. I don't come to the Louvre often but I bet all the pictures are still hung in the same places.'

'I'm sorry, monsieur, but I am expected at the café.' I lie.

'Oh, of course. I'll see you there later.'

* * *

In the evening, Etienne comes in carrying a folder. When I bring him his order, he tells me that he has something to show me. He says he used to work as a magazine illustrator, mostly drawing pictures to accompany reports of life in Paris. These days, he makes more money from copying works in the Louvre and making small decorative paintings. I only have time to look at two pictures, one of people walking in a park and the other of smartly dressed couples attending the opera. I would like to see the rest, but Monsieur Legrand calls me to the counter. He needs me to help with serving.

When I take the second drink to Etienne, he says that copying commissions are the only paintings worth doing. 'There is no money in anything else.'

He gestures to me to join him at his table but I tell him that I have work to do.

'But no one is calling you now. I need to talk to you; the patron shouldn't mind that.'

'I'm listening, but I mustn't sit down.'

'Well, as I said, there is no money in painting. Remember that, mademoiselle. But it's a different story with illustrations,' he says. 'Magazines pay around thirty francs a piece and I can have as much work as I can manage. It's not a lot, but I'm not starving.

Of course, there is something else I do from time to time, but I wouldn't call it proper painting.' He pauses. 'You see, mademoiselle, I make little oils of flowers in vases. They sell well in England. I know a man who ships them across. Good money and fast work, mademoiselle.'

I nod.

'Victorine, we need you in the kitchen', Monsieur Legrand shouts and I leave Etienne.

* * *

When Philippe falls asleep, Etienne moves to his table and gently wakes him. The two leave together, with Philippe leaning heavily on Etienne. A few minutes later, Etienne rushes in and asks Monsieur Legrand if he could help him with the drunken old man. He says he doesn't think he can manage on his own. Monsieur Legrand hurt his back a few days ago and is finding it difficult to walk. Etienne knows that and I can tell that he wants me to come out with him. He looks at me but I say that we are too busy. Monsieur Legrand interrupts me:

'You be quick, Victorine. I can manage here on my own for a while.'

Philippe is not heavy, but he can barely hold himself up and we progress slowly. He is sick as we take him across the road. People look at us and swear. Somebody assumes that Philippe is our father and shouts at as: 'Poor old man, the two of you should take better care of him.'

When we reach the large front gate of the building where he lives, he slumps on the floor. Etienne lifts him up while I ask the concierge for the key.

Philippe reaches into his trouser pocket and accidentally pulls out a thick wad of bank notes.

'Oh, the old fool; he carries so much money around.' Etienne says, stuffing the money into the old man's pocket. 'This money isn't much use to him.' I nod quickly and look away. 'So much money, what a waste.' Etienne sighs. 'He could enjoy life.'

We take Philippe upstairs and as soon we drag him into his

86

bedroom, I tell Etienne that I need to rush. I don't wish to stay alone with the old man.

'I need an assistant, Victorine,' Etienne says and puts his hand on my arm. 'If I took more work, I could pay you to do the colouring.' He looks at me and waits for an answer. I say that I'll think about it.

At the door, he says: 'Mademoiselle Victorine, I know what we can do: come to my apartment one evening after work and I'll show you the work I have in mind. It's not difficult. If you followed my instructions, you could do it.'

When I enter the café, there is no one serving and I go straight to the counter. The man who usually sits with the young woman in neat clothes is here alone. He orders a large anisette, and then another. When he asks for the sixth one, I wonder whether I would be doing him a favour if I diluted it with some water. By now, he is too drunk to notice, let alone complain.

I hear shouting from the kitchen. A plate is smashed on the floor, followed by another. The Legrands are having a fight. Monsieur Legrand comes out, walks across the café and into the street. Madame Legrand opens the door of the kitchen and shouts after him: 'Good riddance.' Later on, she comes out and stands next to me. It is well after lunch and there are few people around.

'Men. You mind them, Victorine. Don't get involved with one. When they want something from you, they are all sweet words. When they get it, they treat you badly. Pigs. They are pigs. No, worse than pigs.'

I notice that she has a bruise on her face, just below the left eye but I pretend that I haven't seen it. Instead, I nod sympathetically at her words. She is looking at the door. Her eyes are red.

The man who has been drinking anisette is crying quietly at the end of the counter. His half rolled cigarette and an open tobacco pouch lie in front of him.

In the far left corner, an old woman, with a prominent lower jaw, a flat nose and brown eyes, looking like a nice, friendly dog, is sipping spirit from a cup. She sits alone and never looks at anyone else. Yesterday a man joined her but she waved him off without even lifting her eyes of the table.

Here is a world of many pictures!

* * *

In the evening, I give my mother the extra twenty-five francs. Today, as on most evenings, I bring a small amount of left-over food from the café. While I'm out, she doesn't eat anything. With no laundry to go to, she stays in the whole day and never buys any food.

'We must save,' she says if I comment that there is nothing to eat in the cupboard.

Today, when she gestures for me to sit down, I decline, saying that I have already eaten at the café. It's true that throughout the day, every now and then, I can get something. Immediately, she hunches over the paper parcel. She eats quickly, using her fingers to stuff pieces of roast potato, a bit of bread and some cabbage into her mouth. That was all I could manage today. Yesterday, Henriette put aside a whole sausage for me. And the day before, I brought home a large chunk of cheese and some radishes.

12

Unexpectedly, I manage to finish early today. Madame Legrand has her cousin with her and tells me that I can leave whenever I want to.

'This bad weather keeps people at home. Pascale and I can manage.' I know that they like to talk without me listening.

Outside the café, I come across Philippe, who calls and takes me by the arm. I am surprised to see him, as he has not been around for several days. He must have been drinking somewhere else: I smell alcohol on his breath.

'Mademoiselle Victorine, I need your help.' He waves a parcel in front of me: 'Can you take this across to the pawn-shop for me? The man knows me and I'd rather not see him today.'

I hesitate for a second: 'I am afraid, I can't; mother is waiting for me,' I lie. 'She isn't well. That is why the Legrands have let me go early.'

'Tomorrow. Tomorrow, then,' he pleads.

'It is Sunday tomorrow. I do not work on Sundays.'

'Please mademoiselle, there is no one else to help me. I am a bit short of money. I'll give you two francs.' I look at him. Three? Five francs, mademoiselle? How about that?'

'What do you have there?' He unwraps the parcel to reveal a porcelain figure of a young woman.

'It's very pretty.'

'Very expensive as well. German. Please, mademoiselle, I'll give you five francs.'

'Ten.' He opens his mouth and looks up at me. I turn to go.

'All right.'

I go to the shop. The owner offers me ten francs for it. I ask for fifty-five. He says I am mad. Twice I pretend that I am walking out. Eventually, we settle for forty-five francs. I take the pink ticket. Outside, Philippe asks me to walk round the corner with him. We stand in a porch as I give him thirty francs and his pink ticket. Pleased with the money, he doesn't notice that, apart from the ten francs fee, I have kept five francs extra. I watch him as he crosses the road and goes straight into the café.

I take a Batignolaise and then walk a short distance to rue Guyot. As soon as I open the large outer door, the concierge calls me: 'Ah, mademoiselle, it's you. You were here the other day. On Sunday. It was you, wasn't it?' I nod and turn to rush upstairs. She shouts after me but I don't hear what she is saying.

I stand outside the door on the top floor and wait to get my breath back. My heart is racing. I almost wish that he were out. But before I can knock, the door opens. A man with a blank expression and small piercing eyes looks out, waiting for me to speak. His hair is as green as grass.

'I am here to see Monsieur Manet,' I say quickly. I think of the way Madame Duras spoke and try to sound like her. The man's face retains its blank stare, as is he were studying me before making a decision whether to let me in or close the door in my face.

Heat rises through my body. I shouldn't have come.

After a minute or two, the man's brow furrows. I think that I should go away but then he smiles. What should I do? While still keeping his eyes on me, he calls out: 'Edouard, come here. You are wanted.' His voice is very formal, almost mocking. That makes me feel uncomfortable again, and when he bows and gestures with his hand for me to enter, I don't know what to do. His face resumes its blank expression and he stands still. He must be an actor, a comedian.

I step inside a space that would easily house all the residents of the Hotêl d'Or. There are as many pictures here as in one of the larger galleries of the Louvre, some hanging, others leaning against walls. I can see three easels, piles of books, rails with clothes, baskets with hats, busts and lamps. Drawings are pinned to the wall, jars with paint brushes, bottles and palettes stand on tables. There are armchairs scattered around, a *chaise longue* and several tables, large and small, some cluttered with papers. And yet, there is still enough space to move around.

From somewhere else, I hear a voice: 'Charles, I am coming. Why are you always so impatient?'

This Charles stands with his back unusually upright. His heels are pressed together, the tips of his shoes fanning out. With his green hair and immobile expression, he looks like a painted sculpture.

A minute later, a pair of well-polished black shoes appears at the top of the staircase. A man, carrying a top hat in one hand and brushing it with the other, begins to descend. Not looking ahead, he does not notice me until the stairs are behind him and he reaches the middle of the room. Startled by seeing a figure he did not expect, he stops and fixes his eyes on me. They open wider and a slight smile settles on his mouth. Charles stands to the side and watches both of us.

'Monsieur Manet. If you recall, we met in the Jardin du Luxembourg and you asked me to come to see you.' This is my prepared opening sentence. I had hoped I would not have to use it. He keeps staring at me. He doesn't remember me. But when he takes a step towards me, I notice the warmth in his eyes.

'Yes, Mademoiselle... Mademoiselle Louise, isn't it? I remember.' His voice is soft and gentle. He extends his hand.

'Victorine,' I say, determined to maintain my advantage, even if only temporarily. I remember very well that I gave him my second name.

'Oh, yes, yes, Victorine.' He pauses, before saying: 'You look different.'

He may be disappointed and he may no longer wish to paint me. The three of us stand in silence, looking at each other.

After a few moments, Monsieur Manet says: 'Mademoiselle Victorine... ah, Charles, this is my friend Charles, the poet, Charles Baudelaire.' He gestures towards the man who has no expression on his face. 'Charles and I are about to leave. I am sorry about that. Would you be able to wait for me until I return? Half an hour, an hour at the most?' He smiles at me. 'It's my mother I need to attend to. An urgent business.' The thought of being left alone in this place full of treasure fills me with delight.

'Yes, monsieur, I'll wait for you.'

'Oh, you will? That is so very kind of you. I am absolutely delighted that you have found time to visit me.' I blush.

The two of them turn to go.

Just before he closes the door, Monsieur Manet calls out: 'You will wait for me, mademoiselle, won't you? I shall not be long.' A warm smile covers his face.

With the door closed, I can still hear the loud voices of the two men descending the stairs. They disappear quickly and I find myself stranded in the vast space. For a while, I remain standing in the middle of the room, not knowing where to turn. Surrounded by so many objects I feel lost and disoriented. I imagine that many pairs of eyes are watching me from behind the clutter and a fear grips me. This is a different world from my own.

Slowly, my eyes travel around the room and I notice one canvas that looks familiar. I know immediately where and when I have seen it before. It was Madame Duras, in one of her letters from Aix last year, who encouraged me to visit the Salon for the first time. She asked me to write to her about what I had seen, and this was one of the pictures I described. Had I remembered the artist's name, I would have known that it was him who approached me on that day in the Jardin du Luxembourg.

This painting of Monsieur Manet's parents reminds me of a drawing I made of my grandparents, only a few months before grandfather died.

One evening, he was sitting at a table, waiting for his dinner and looking down, when grandma appeared behind him with a plate of potatoes. I asked them not to move, but grandfather was hungry and laughed.

'You are a silly girl to think that I am going to sit here hungry while you draw a picture.' Grandma told him that the potatoes were too hot and made a sign to me to ignore him. I sketched him very quickly in the few minutes that I had. Later, once he had finished eating, and was puffing on his pipe, he didn't mind sitting still. Grandma was much more obliging. For days after-wards, whenever she could spare a few minutes, she would stand on the exact spot behind the empty chair, holding a plate of potatoes. It was the only drawing I ever made of the two of them together. My grandparents never had a photograph taken. My drawing, now in a box in Maître Albert, is the only visual record of their existence. Apart from me, only Marie has seen it.

When I first saw Monsieur Manet's painting at the Salon, it was the similarities in the relationships of each couple, rather than their differences that struck me. In both pictures, the women are standing behind the men. Although Madame Manet is not serving food to her husband, she has a caring look. The men appear focused only on themselves. But the big difference between the two compositions, and I only remember that now, is that, unlike Madame Manet, my grandmother isn't looking down, or sideways, at her husband. My grandmother is actually looking out of the picture. I remember telling her to look at the chair as if grandfather were sitting on it, but she said that she preferred to look at me.

'I've so many things to do, Victorine. If I am standing here for you, let me at least enjoy myself. I love seeing you draw, my little one.'

Thinking about it now, I am pleased that grandma looks out of the picture: it makes her appear strong and confident.

Another canvas attracts my attention: there is a painting of a Spanish-looking woman with a cigarette. I like her. I like her because she is strong. She is not looking out at me, but her eyes are resting on something far away, as if she didn't care for what is around her. She is independent. And she is large; she takes a great deal of space. A cigarette hangs casually from her mouth. She is leaning on a wall and supporting her head with one hand, while the other is resting on her hip, the elbow sticking out. She is standing outdoors: there is a skyline behind her, and the partially visible head of a white horse, but they look more like figures on a painted curtain, than real. The woman's hair is black, her cheeks are rosy and she is smiling in a detached, superior manner. I want to be like her. She is saying to the world:

'I am happy with who I am. I don't need anyone else. I am self-sufficient.'

What a difference between her and the subdued Madame Manet with her downcast eyes looking at her husband.

I walk to a large mirror at the other end of the room and assume the same pose as the woman with the cigarette. The cloth of my grey pelisse hangs down limply and my figure hardly suggests strength and self-possession. I take it off. When I undo the two top buttons of my blouse and roll up the sleeves, my bare arms make me appear more confident.

As a child, I used to dress up in my grandfather's clothes. He didn't have many things, so in winter I would pull his summer trousers and shirts out of the chest by the bed and in summer I would don his heavy woollen trousers and a sheepskin jacket. Standing in front of the old mirror that Madame Pascal had given grandma, I would be either a young man, Albert, or an old man, Victor. I liked Victor, because the name sounded like mine.

In Monsieur Manet's studio there are four baskets and a rail full of clothes. Starting from here, one can impersonate half of Paris. I shift through one of the baskets and pull out three Spanish dancing skirts with layers of frills in bright colours, two black lacy dresses and several scarves. I look at myself in the mirror as I hold each item in front of me.

When I rummage through the baskets again, I find a pair of a torero's knee-length trousers and pull them over my white stockings. I take off my skirt and move around. I start skipping and jumping. What an unusual feeling to wear something so tight that shows off my thighs. The trousers give me a sense of freedom as I turn around. In front of the mirror, I can't take my eyes of my reflection. Later on, I put on an elaborately embroidered short jacket, pile my long hair on top of my head, tucking it under a black hat with a wide brim.

'Off you go, Victorine,' I say to myself. 'Here comes a young Spaniard, a torero.' I bet Marie wouldn't recognise me now. I have to keep the smile off my face as I pose in different positions. Standing sideways, with my arms raised, I pretend I am challenging an imaginary bull. I think of a large audience watching

94

me in trepidation as the angry beast charges towards me. I hear them holding their breath. Their shouts pierce the air once the danger is past and I look up at them, full of pride. I've seen pictures of a scene like that. And I remember a Spanish friend of Monsieur Legrand who once came to the café and talked about the thrill of being in a large crowd when they see a torero facing an enraged bull.

Assuming different positions and speaking to the image of a torero in the mirror, I do not hear Monsieur Manet return. Suddenly, I catch a glimpse of him standing by the front door, quietly observing me. I stop, embarrassed. How can I put my own clothes back on? He notices my discomfort and a faint smile crosses his lips.

'That was good, mademoiselle. Do carry on. Please do not take off the costume. It suits you.'

I look down, unable to move, ashamed. But then another thought crosses my mind: he has exhibited at the Salon, he is a real artist. If he paints me, people would see a picture of me at the Salon. They might recognise me on the street. They might talk about me. Would they also look at the pictures I make?

After a minute or so, he comes to stand close to me. His breath smells of coffee. Slowly and gently, he takes off my hat and looks at me as my hair spills over my shoulders. I try to look back at him. I wish he would not stare like this. I have to speak.

'I have a problem with painting faces that look out.'

The words come out unplanned but he doesn't seem to hear me. His gaze pierces through my face and I have to lower my eyes. I wait.

'Apologies mademoiselle that we have taken so long. I hope you were not bored.'

Charles appears in the doorway. 'It is so difficult to go anywhere with Edouard. He cannot spot a hat without turning it into a fleeting impression. But that's how it is. An artist cannot go out without his sketch book and Paris is full of fleeting impressions.' Charles bows towards me before turning his back and plunging himself into an armchair. There he takes a notebook from his pocket and begins to write.

Monsieur Manet is still staring at me. He takes no notice of his friend. I dare not move. After a minute, Monsieur Manet backs away and says, 'Yes, Mademoiselle Victorine. I have it. I can see it now. An idea.' His voice is relaxed and friendly. I want to ask about his idea, but he doesn't give me a chance: 'But that is for next time. Before that, I need you as you are, as you were when you walked through the door.' I am not sure what he wants.

'Would you take off this costume?'

I've never undressed in front of a man. But it doesn't mean that I'll refuse, or that I'll show that I am self-conscious. Anyway, I had expected him to ask me to pose naked and I was prepared to do as he asked. But, in return, I want something, too.

Marie, who has been working as a model for more than three years, often has to pose in the nude. Sometimes, a painter may want to kiss her or touch her. If the painter was young and she liked him, she didn't turn him down. The first time she worked for Emile, she knew that if he desired her, he would have asked to sleep with her. He never had much money to pay her for modelling, but she liked him and didn't mind earning less. After two months of posing, she was pregnant. She says that she is happy: Emile still wants to paint her and there is somewhere for them to live. Emile's parents keep to themselves. She cooks and cleans for all of them. She says she is lucky, but I don't want that kind of luck, nor babies or in-laws to look after.

I slowly take off the torero's costume. Monsieur Manet turns his back to me, adjusting the height of an easel. After placing a small canvas on it, he drags the easel across the room.

'We'd better get on with this.' I stand still in my undergarments. He turns away and says to himself: 'Whenever possible, I like to work by natural light.'

'Well, mademoiselle, please do hurry up.' He doesn't look at me as he speaks. 'Your clothes are over there. If you could button the pelisse and make yourself look just the same as when you came in this afternoon. We will have light for no longer than another hour. After all, we are only in April. At last the sun is out after all those clouds earlier on.' I dress quickly, pull back my hair and push it into a black woollen toque.

'And the ribbon, please.' Monsieur Manet says, looking at the blue satin in my hands. I tie it in and smooth down the bow. Monsieur Manet gestures to me to sit on a stool that he has placed opposite the large window. He stands by the easel, the window behind him, and looks at me.

'Too much shadow,' he says, pulling the easel to the side of the window and moving my stool so that it is right in front of him.

'That is much better. Please, sit with your back straight.' He begins to work immediately.

I watch him as he studies me. He moves his hand very quickly as he draws straight onto the canvas. I don't see him erase anything. Nor does he speak. When I say that I am looking forward to seeing what he has done, he ignores me. At one point his face tenses and he looks as if he is angry. But all I can hear is a loud sigh. Then he turns his back to me and walks to the window. He opens it and takes a few deep breaths. After a minute or two, he returns to his position by the easel and resumes drawing, again with confident speed.

I sit completely still. Having been on the other side of the easel, I know how important it is not to move. Surprisingly, holding my body in one position is less tiring than I had imagined. Of course, it would be much easier if he talked. If only I could ask questions about painting. I have all those drawings of Céleste and I must start working on the canvas. I understand how to use the grid but it's the colours that are giving me a headache. The brush-strokes shout loudly from my canvas. How can I make them disappear? I've tried using smaller brushes, but it didn't help.

If only he would say something. Should I ask him about pictures in the Louvre? Or about his paintings here in the studio.

I've always held conversations with my models, I mean, with Marie and Lola. That way, the time passed more quickly for them and they were less likely to move or complain. Of course, Monsieur Manet must know that I would not complain to him.

It feels lonely sitting here in front of him. All I can do is watch him and think my own thoughts. I imagine that I am drawing him and that this hour is the time I have to study my subject.

'Mademoiselle, we have to stop. I could light a lamp, but that would destroy the effect I have in mind.' He walks away from the easel and as I am still sitting down, he adds: 'Thank you. You can move now.' Now is the time to tell him about my drawings but he makes me feel as if I have just finished my hours in a bar and want to rush off as quickly as possible. I stand up slowly. I wish I could see what he has done, but he leads me away.

'Next time, I shall start with the colour. You can see the painting when it is finished. Not now, please.' I nod.

'Well, I shall see you tomorrow, mademoiselle. It will be Sunday, so, shall we say, one o'clock?'

I am taken aback by this request, but I don't protest or ask questions.

Monsieur Manet sees me out: 'I would be most obliged, mademoiselle, if tomorrow you would wear the same clothes. Thank you very much.' I nod. He walks away.

13

She arrives ten minutes late. While waiting, I experience a growing sense of anxiety. What if she doesn't turn up? What a fool I was not to have checked her address yesterday. I should have thought of it. It is so much easier to use the people I know well.

Her cheeks are flushed and she is out of breath, but I cannot waste any more time. We start work immediately. She must have been running. At least she understands that she should not be letting me down.

As she sits opposite the window, the light on her face is much brighter than yesterday and she looks as she did on that day in January. The sunshine brings out the paleness of her skin and emphasises the blankness of her expression. For a figure, one needs full light and full shadow; the rest follows. Of course, the idea is even more pertinent when painting a face in close up. And what a face this is!

I congratulate myself on finding her. The blue of the ribbon in her hair shines like silver. I shall use cobalt for that. What a contrast, what a burst of life next to her hair! The more I look at her, the more certain I am of my initial assessment. She is a real find. In this light, her face is like a mask. It will require dense, opaque layers of paint. I feel as if I were looking at the bright sunshine at midday in Italy: I am drawn to it and yet it hurts; it bothers me but I yearn for it.

The emptiness of her powerful eyes as they meet mine, and the expression with no expression, intrigue me more than anything else about her. Her slightly unfocused eyes seem remote and direct, and, at the same time, warm.

I work for five hours and she remains perfectly still. I should be grateful for it, if that were all. On two occasions, I have to rest.

She does not seem to require a break. I walk to the window and inhale deeply, telling myself to keep calm. I am not a patient man, but this stare of hers would test the patience of a saint. Eventually, my irritation causes me to lose control of my hand. I have to speak.

'Would you please stop that, mademoiselle,' I say, looking straight at her. I wish I had not raised my voice. She looks at me but does not say anything. I search her face for the single sign of anger or shock. There is nothing. How can she keep so calm and composed?

'Do not pretend that you do not know what I am talking about. I cannot stand you staring at me like this. It disconcerts me. I am meant to be looking at you, not the other way around. Yes, I do require you to be looking at me, but do not scrutinize me. Your gaze paralyses me.' She continues to stare. 'It drains my energy, my skill, everything. I simply cannot work like this. Do you understand?' I spurt it all out. I want to stop but I cannot. The worst is that she does not move. Nor does she protest. Nor does she raise an eyebrow. But her eyes remain fixed on me. How can she be so insolent?

I pick up a palette and I am about to swing it towards her, when the image of a violent, ugly scene flashes in front of my eyes and I manage to stop myself. Immediately, I feel relieved that the palette is still in my hand. I am shaking.

On the way upstairs, I glance in her direction. She sits as if nothing has happened. Her lack of response angers me further. I grip the banister and lean over it: 'Men are supposed to look at women, not the other way around.' As soon as the words leave my mouth, I know that I do not believe what I am saying. But she probably does. I need to put her in her place. Who does she think she is?

In the room upstairs, I sit on the bed and take deep breaths. I know I must not lose her. After ten minutes, I tell myself that it is the painting that is important, not her, or even me.

Downstairs, she is still sitting in the same place, in the same position, as if nothing has happened. Nothing shatters that bloody composure of hers!

'I am the painter. You are the model.' I mumble, more to myself than to her. Nevertheless, I hope she understands the problem.

'I am not a model.' The softness of her voice shames me, and I feel my anger rising. I stop and turn towards her.

'I don't know who or what you are outside this room.' I snap. 'That's none of my business. But today you are a model. You are sitting for me.' It seems she understands, for she does not argue. 'I am not asking you to adopt an uncomfortable pose. Some painters have a system of rings and pulleys and…' I stop, aware that it is not fair to go on like this.

I return to the easel. It is unfortunate that I have shouted at her, but I am right. She stares at me as if *she* were analysing *my* face, as if *she* were drawing *me*. Her behaviour makes me feel as if it should be me sitting still. The difficulty is that I cannot ignore her gaze. Each time I glance at her, the energy from her eyes seems to suck something from me. It suddenly comes to me. Perhaps that is what I should aim to achieve with this canvas: persuade the viewer that the woman in the picture is draining them.

To keep my temper in check, I remind myself how much I need her. Had Delacroix seen her, he might have changed his mind about the living model never exactly rendering the idea one wants to represent. Until I met her, I used to think how limited human figures are in comparison to what I imagine in my head.

Of course, it is pointless to try to paint a human figure without a model. I need to observe them. I don't know how to invent, nor do I want to rely on memory. Alternatively, if I work according to the lessons I have learnt, I produce nothing worthwhile. If I ever amount to anything, I will have to put it down to precise inter- pretation and faithful analysis of what is in front of me. A good model is bound to play an important part in what I produce. Watching her yesterday, as she tried on different costumes in front of a mirror, I was immediately struck by her powers of transformation. There are so many different figures inside that body, inside that face, inside those eyes. I could paint her for years to come.

Not to mention that she also has a natural way of posing, not like that old model, Dubosc, I think he was called, in my days at Couture's.

'Monsieur Manet,' he said after I complained about the artificiality in his posture, 'Monsieur Delaroche never had anything but praise for me. I find it hard to take criticism from a man as young as you.'

I told him I was not asking him for Monsieur Delaroche's opinion; I was just giving him mine.

'Monsieur Manet,' he said, speaking slowly and choking with emotion, 'many many young men have gone to Rome thanks to me.'

I never cared for the Prix de Rome. I told him so: 'We are not in Rome and I don't want to go there. We're in Paris, so let's stay here.' That shut him up but did not make me popular with Couture.

Often, I wondered what I was doing there. On some days, everything I could see was so ridiculous. The light was wrong and the shadows were wrong. Whenever I arrived, I felt like I was entering a tomb. Why could we not have done studies on life outdoors? Of course, you cannot undress models in the streets, but there is always the country. Which reminds me: I am told that Courbet has horses, oxen and deer in his studio on Notre-Dame-des-Champs.

Does it not cross the old silver head's mind that he could better study these animals in their natural surroundings? That would be realism.

14

It's only a small canvas. He allows me to look at it this morning for the first time. The image puzzles me and I am lost for words. It's not that it's unpleasant. No, not at all. But I didn't expect it to be like this. It doesn't look like any other painting I have ever seen. My face is a mask, or a cut out pasted on the canvas. Didn't Monsieur Manet say that in a conversation with Charles yesterday?

Perhaps what disturbs me most is that I can't tell what it says. The picture seems to say who I am but, at the same time, it's somehow impenetrable. I don't know that face; it could be anyone or no one. The image confuses me.

When I can ignore the fact that this is my portrait, I must admit it's so beautifully drawn and the colour is excellent.

'Do you like it, mademoiselle?' He says, smiling. The corners of his mouth lift as if mocking.

What can I say? The picture intrigues me but I'm not sure of my feelings. He might laugh at me. I look at it for a long time before whispering: 'Yes, I like it.'

We are standing side by side, our eyes on the canvas. Without turning towards me, he says:

'We can put this one aside and start with the next one. The torero. I have already prepared a much larger canvas.'

I nod in consent and, although I try to suppress it, the question comes out: 'What will happen to my portrait?'

He looks at me, puzzled: 'Pictures are to be exhibited, mademoiselle.' He walks towards the easel with the new canvas and then turns towards me: 'What would you like to happen to it?'

I am pleased he is asking me. Perhaps he cares how I feel. The thought gives me confidence: 'I hope you won't show it in public.' I don't know why I say that.

He stares at me and, to my surprise, he consents to the request: 'I understand, mademoiselle. I promise, I will not exhibit it. If that is what you want.'

'Thank you, monsieur.' His kindness on this matter is unexpected. He must know that the portrait shows too much of me. Immediately, I forgive him for all the shouting and all the silences, for the times when he didn't hear or when he ignored my questions. I'm happy to be here with him and that gives me strength to put on the torero costume and stand in any pose that he chooses.

The canvas is large, but not new. Only the other day I saw an unfinished picture of a seated nude on it. He must have abandoned it and reprimed the surface. When I stand close, I can just about see the outline of the woman's arched back. He has turned the canvas upside down. Depending on the composition, my figure could be almost life size.

Once I am dressed, Monsieur Manet stands away from me, asking me to assume different poses. After we try a few, he walks away and comes back with a sword and a large, square red cloth.

'Hold these, Victorine,' he says. I am pleased that he has dropped the 'mademoiselle'. He instructs me how to stand and where to look while he sketches very quickly. Every ten to fifteen minutes or so, he moves me around.

When he has nine drawings, he lines them up on the long table and looks at each one in turn. I stand by his side, hoping that he'll ask me for my preference. He doesn't. When he selects three drawings, he places them next to each other and spends several minutes mumbling to himself. Seemingly unaware of my presence, he picks up each of the drawings in turn and stares at it, unable to decide which one to choose.

I say: 'I like the one in the middle because my figure is leaning forward as if ready for the bull.'

Monsieur Manet lets the drawing fall onto the pile of the discarded ones. 'I see. No, definitely not,' he says without taking the eyes off the drawings. 'It looks too much as if you were in the arena.' Then he focuses on the remaining two drawings. I walk away and stand by the window, looking out. A minute later, he comes to me and says: 'Mademoiselle Victorine, this is the pose I would like you to assume.' He hands me the drawing with my body drawn from the side and my head turned out towards the viewer. Both arms are raised, one holding the sword, the other the red cloth.

I've never attended a corrida, but I've seen bulls. My grandparents had one for a few years. I imagine that an animal of that size, if provoked, is fierce. The torero in Monsieur Manet's drawing would stand like that only if they were posing for a picture, not if they were in action. Monsieur Manet is a Parisian. I don't think he understands animals. But since he doesn't ask for my opinion, I keep my thoughts to myself.

'This time, Mademoiselle Victorine, you will have to stand on a podium. I need to have a good view of your entire figure, head to toe.'

I do as I am told. As with my portrait, Monsieur Manet sketches directly onto the white canvas. His hand moves quickly and I don't see him erase anything.

He works for two hours. It's tiring for me to hold up both arms and, from time to time, he tells me to relax for a few minutes. Apart from that, he never speaks. I've stopped asking questions about painting. His concentration is entirely on my body as a shape that he is placing within a composition upon the canvas.

I wish I could be like that and shut out the world when I draw. It's unlikely that he is ever bothered by the needs of others.

I remember that day, soon after I had met Lola, when I was sketching her and she kept nagging me that we should go out and enjoy ourselves. It was sunny outside and she was suggesting a train trip to a place where we could hire a boat and row on the river. On my days off I preferred to stay in and work.

'You're driven, Victorine,' she shouted, irritated by my lack of response. I kept quiet and she asked: 'But why?'

I didn't know what to say then.

Later on, I heard Monsieur Manet talk to Charles about 'the

illusion to give life meaning'. I didn't understand it at first but the words echoed in my head for a long time and eventually I felt that they described what I'd like to do.

I realized that if I could paint one good picture and someone wanted to exhibit it, I'd feel good. One good picture would make all my difficulties insignificant and worthwhile.

I remember Lola raising her voice: 'Victorine, speak to me!'

'Yes?' Her body was tense, the face looked angry.

'What about loving?' She stood up, facing me.

'Loving, what about it?'

'We could love each other.' I nodded. 'That would help.' She sat down on the floor, next to my feet, her head leaning against my legs. She looked vulnerable and I felt for her. 'When I'm really exhausted with washing and ironing, and my hands are chapped, my back hurts and it's late at night and madame comes to my room and gives me another task, the only thing that helps is thinking of you. That's the only way how I can go on. I need your love, Victorine.'

What could I say in response?

'Don't you get fed up with all the work in the café?' I nodded and smiled in agreement. It was easier than telling her that when I am sick of Monsieur Legrand's advances and the drunks leering at me, I think of the pictures I'll make one day. I don't think of her or anyone else. And even if love helped, it came and went. It was foolish to rely on others. I wanted to have something that was mine and mine only. Unlike men and women, my pictures would stay with me.

But I didn't say any of that. There was no point upsetting her. I needed to finish the sketch.

I don't expect Monsieur Manet to concern himself with my circumstances. For him I'm no more than an object that he's painting. He doesn't think of me having friends or family. When he asked me to return for the second sitting for my portrait on a Sunday, I had to forego my afternoon with Lola.

'This is the only day we have together,' she complained. 'Why did you arrange it for today?' I didn't wish to tell her what I was doing, nor that I had no say in choosing the day. I lied that it was the only day when a painter could help me with my work at a price I could afford.

She sulked; a tear rolled down her cheek. I said I was sorry and that I would miss her. She put her arms around me and said that she would come with me, sit quietly and not bother anyone. Monsieur Manet wouldn't have tolerated it. I could see that he needs full concentration when he works. On several occasions, I had heard him tell the concierge that if anyone except Charles or Antoine came looking for him, she should say that he wasn't in.

Monsieur Manet puts down the chalk. I can see small beads of sweat on his forehead. Looking into my eyes, he speaks slowly and quietly, stressing every word: 'Mademoiselle, do not forget, *I* am painting *you*. You are my model. I am looking at you. You are looking out. You are not studying me.'

But I am studying him. I want to be a painter. I need to train my eyes to see beyond the obvious. It is important for me to learn to see more than most people. If he would let me speak, or if he could at least hear when I speak, he would understand. I want to tell him that my gaze is my own, but I dare not. Instead, I nod.

'I am sorry, monsieur.'

He returns to the easel and resumes drawing. I could have also told him that I wasn't his model. He's never paid me. But as I don't see myself as a model, I don't wish to ask for money.

During the week he worked on my portrait, I was here every day, mornings and afternoons. I told the Legrands that mother was unwell and that I had to stay at home. They didn't complain but, of course, I lost the money. After that, I sent them a message that I wasn't well. That accounted for the second week. Madame Legrand said they could manage without me for a while as her cousin was still around and willing to help.

Now he expects me here every day. I don't know what excuse to make up for the Legrands. I am living off the money I took from Philippe, but if I have another week off, it will run out.

Does it ever occur to him to ask where my money is coming from?

Monsieur Manet's demands mean that I have had very little time to work on my drawings and the canvas with Céleste is unfinished. I can only find the time on Sundays.

Lola let me draw her yesterday. She arrived dressed in a man's suit. When I opened the door, I was startled. She stood in front of me, not saying anything. It was only when she said my name, that I could be sure it was her and not a male relative. She wore a top hat, a grey stripy frock coat, a man's shirt, a burgundy cravat and a pair of black trousers.

As usual, once inside, she took off all her clothes and made me lie next to her. Her breath smelled of tobacco. After we had made love, I said that I'd like to draw her in her new clothes. She told me that she had inherited them from her brother, who died last year.

'I miss him, Victorine.'

I didn't reply. I wondered whether there was a person in my life that I missed. Only my grandmother and perhaps Marie. Most of the time, I am too busy to think of others.

'Wearing his clothes helps me imagine that I am him. The other day, when I spent half the night washing dishes after a large dinner – the family had ten guests and they served six courses – I had time to think. You and he are the only two people I've ever loved. I asked myself whether he'd have liked you. And then I wondered whether you would've liked him. So, I thought, I should try to find out.' She stood up and, lifting her top hat, bowed at me. 'Do you like him?'

I said that she made a very handsome man.

'But you wouldn't lie down with a black man, would you, Victorine?' I said I couldn't be sure. I've never known one.

'I wouldn't lie with any man, black or white,' she said. 'Their bodies can only bruise you. Women I know tell me that sleeping with a man is like having horses gallop all over you.' Lola looked at me, expecting me to comment. How would I know whether she was right?

Later on, she sat on a chair and pulled a small round table over to her. I placed a glass on it and tried to imagine that Lola's brother was sitting in a café. She lit a cigarette and said: 'I was hoping that you would draw me in these clothes. I want to have a picture that reminds me of my brother.'

I spent most of the afternoon on the drawing. We talked very little. Both of us felt content with what we were doing. In the end, I was not happy with the picture. A frightening thought crossed my mind when I looked at the finished piece: perhaps I'll always be a better model than an artist. Lola was delighted to have it. Of course, I let her take it with her.

'Victorine, this'll be my most treasured possession. I'll look at it every night before I go to sleep.'

Since grandma died and Julie left Paris, Lola is the first person made happy by my art.

In the evening, we walked together to St Germain-des-Prés. Although we didn't dare hold hands, people stared at us and some even made loud comments. 'You don't need a black man, mademoiselle,' a café owner standing on the pavement in front of his shop said as he pulled me by the arm.

After I had left Lola, I proceeded on foot to Maître Albert. I like walking around Paris on my own. Monsieur Manet says that it's a good way of getting ideas for pictures. Just as I crossed the Pont St Michel, someone grabbed my arm, causing me to jump. The people staring at Lola and me in the afternoon had made me nervous, and my face must have shown how frightened I was. I struggled to escape, not daring to look, until a man's voice said:

'Mademoiselle Victorine, no need to be so scared. I'm glad you are better. I can see your mind is elsewhere, but at least you are no longer ill.' Etienne smiled.

'I wasn't ill.'

'I've been looking for you in the café. Monsieur Legrand said you're ill.'

Embarrassed, I blushed. Etienne said: 'It's no matter to me. There was something I wanted to talk to you about. Have you thought about what I said before? About helping me?'

We passed by a café and Etienne suggested we go in. It was busy inside and difficult to hear each other but I gathered that recently Etienne had been inundated by requests for small pictures of flower bouquets for the English market.

'They sell for good money and they are easy to make. The English like them in their drawing rooms,' he said.

'Now, mademoiselle, I need your help.'

I let him continue. 'I can produce these flower pictures very quickly. Last week, I was asked to do a big canvas, a copy of a picture in the Louvre, for an American customer. He is prepared to pay handsomely. I don't want to miss this opportunity, mademoiselle.' Etienne placed his hand on mine. I looked at him, making sure that he understood I didn't welcome his attention. He withdrew the hand and continued: 'Mademoiselle, I don't wish to lose the trust of my flower picture dealer. He will expect his delivery. I was thinking that if I were to show you how, you could do these little pictures for me. Of course, I would do the drawing, all the outlines. For you, it would be just a matter of filling in the colour. Many of these pictures are copies of each other, anyway. As long as you are careful and pay attention to detail, it's all very easy.'

'But why me? I cannot draw or paint.' I didn't know why I said it, except that I have grown used to keeping my ambition secret.

'You can. I mean, you can do what I need for these pictures. You were the first person I thought of. Had you been born a man, you would have been a painter.' Etienne looked into my eyes and smiled. 'Oh, mademoiselle, you can do it.'

He leant forward and I smelt cheese on his breath. His yellow teeth had brown stains on. I sat back to move further from him. Etienne insisted: 'Come on, mademoiselle! I know your secret.' My cheeks felt hot. 'I saw you go into a stationery shop near the Beaux-Arts. I went in after you had left. The owner told me that you painted. It didn't come as a surprise. When I met you on the steps of the Louvre, I thought that in a different age you would have been an artist.'

Did he mean this or was he lying to flatter me? Did he know about my studio? I thought back to the occasion, several months ago, when he had first asked me to help with his work.

'Have you been following me, Etienne?' He didn't answer straightaway. 'Have you?' He stared at me. I shouldn't trust him.

'Oh, no, mademoiselle. Don't get so upset.' He laughed. 'I

assure you. I was just passing behind the Beaux-Arts when I spotted you. It was entirely by chance. Anyway, why are you so secretive about painting? I might just as well tell you this: when you served drinks in the café, I noticed the paint stains on your fingers. Besides, I have seen the way you position food on plates, the way you place the cutlery on the table, even the way you wipe the tops of those round tables at the café. You have fine hands and fingers, and good, almost precise control of your movement.'

'I don't understand what you are talking about,' I said. He was a flatterer. I had to be careful.

'You wouldn't. But believe me, mademoiselle, I know what I'm saying. I'm a failure as a painter. I've all of that: fine fingers and precise control of my hands movement. But, that's not enough. I'll never be a good painter as I can only see the world through another person's eyes. I'm a copyist.' His voice faltered and his shoulders dropped. He bit his lip. 'I'll never be anything else but a copyist.'

I felt for him then. When I glanced at him, he must have read a note of sympathy in my eyes. Once again, he put his hand on mine: 'Mademoiselle Victorine,' he said, 'the arrangement would suit both of us. My words shouldn't surprise you. I've told you before that I needed you as an assistant. You could earn as much as in that café, if not more.'

I was thinking whether I could find the time to do the flower pictures. And besides, was he really serious about offering me work? Mother used to say that men were always good and helpful when they wanted something. 'And there is only one thing they want, Victorine. Always remember that.'

'So, what do you say, mademoiselle? It's a good offer.'

'I'm sure there are students who'd be glad to earn money by doing your pictures.'

Etienne looked at me: 'The simple fact is, mademoiselle, I like you. But you need not fear me. I'm a kind man. And besides, the students you mention are so full of themselves that they look down upon this kind of work. They all think they'll be the next Ingres or Delacroix. Many are rich and don't want to waste time on mundane pictures. They are silly. There is good money in it.'

111

'Can I think about it?' I said, withdrawing my hand from under his.

'If you let me know tomorrow, I can wait. I haven't as yet accepted the American customer.'

We agreed to meet the next evening in this same café. Before I left, I asked Etienne whether he thought that painting could be learned. 'Isn't it the case,' I said 'that the more you practise, the better you become and if you also have someone to offer advice and criticism, someone experienced, an artist, then –'

'Mademoiselle, the answer is yes; I would say that painting can be learned. Everyone improves with practice. But practice doesn't earn money. You need to eat while you are learning. Many painters come from rich families. Their parents buy the time so that their sons can develop. My mother is dead, and my father is a drunk. My choice is either to give up hoping to be a painter, or starve. I don't wish to starve. My flower pictures give pleasure, perhaps even more than the expensive paintings. And the American who wants to buy a copy of a big Louvre painting will enjoy what I produce.'

I stood up to go. Etienne wanted to come with me, 'just a little walk', he said, but I insisted that he shouldn't, and in the end I managed to leave without him. I asked him not to mention to the Legrands that he had seen me. He winked at me and nodded.

'Mademoiselle, you are not paying attention; the cloth is falling.' Monsieur Manet's voice sounds concerned. 'Perhaps you are tired. We can stop now. Madame Bijoux has brought the coffee.'

I am glad of the break. This is an opportunity for me to ask how to proceed with my painting. But I'm mistaken. Monsieur Manet pours the coffee, hands me a cup and, carrying his, climbs the stairs to the galleried space. I've a feeling that he smiles briefly, before he turns away, but I'm not sure. He looks tired. I know that he has a bed in the gallery.

I walk to the canvas. He has completed the outline. If he is happy with it, he'll be able to carry on with the paints. I stare at the figure. It's so skilfully drawn that one can sense its movements. Compared with this, Céleste's posture looks rigid.

112

Perhaps the trick is to have the body turned one way and the head the other. Of course, the positioning of the feet helps: the front one firmly on the ground, the other, only slightly behind, raised. I wish I'd done the same in my canvas.

By the time Monsieur Manet descends, I've finished the coffee and I am sitting on the *chaise longue.*

'We can resume when you are ready,' he says.

'I'm ready.'

We work for another three hours, with just one very short break. He looks at me for a long time, before dipping his brush in the palette and, with a movement resembling a click of the fingers, places a light touch of colour on the canvas. Sometimes his brush works up and down, sometimes it follows a contour-like movement. The light, quick touches are followed by strong movements of the wrist, as if he were speeding up or slowing down and lingering over a brush stroke. Sometimes, he seems to apply a good deal of pressure, at other times, he merely dabs at the canvas.

Suddenly, he stops. The maulstick falls on the floor and he lets it roll away. His brow furrows. He stands right in front of me and stares intently into my eyes. I can feel the air coming from his lungs on my skin. For a while, I stare back. When I lower my eyes, he says:

'It is uncomfortable, isn't it? I cannot work like that. Don't you understand?'

'I'm sorry, Monsieur.' I'm not, but I think an apology might help. It does. Unlike on previous occasions, he doesn't shout for long. We work for another hour in complete silence.

When I walk out, I make a decision to accept Etienne's proposal. I'll take the work. But only the work. I'll make sure that we meet in the café. He can bring canvases and paints and, once I have finished the painting, I'll take them back to him in the café. I can do the pictures in my own time. In that way, I can carry on modelling for Monsieur Manet.

15

Charles interrupts me: 'Edouard, may I repeat what you have just said?'

I wait.

'You think that one has to paint what one sees and be accurate in one's drawing?'

I nod. We met at the Tuileries and have been walking and talking for the past hour. In the Avenue de Clichy, we weave our way between the evening strollers enjoying the mild May air. Charles waves his hands as he speaks.

'Well, that is what old Bouguereau said. And damn if I would not swear with my life that you do not want to paint like him.'

'What is the point of painting like Bouguereau? And anyway, he hardly paints what he sees. Those idealized women and children living in some imaginary world...with their dresses hanging down in neat drapes as if they were Greek statues. His shepherdesses in their silly costumes as if they didn't have a care at all. One should be of one's own time –'

'Yes, we must always be modern.'

'Charles, like you, I am also interested in using new techniques. For me, it means new colours. Colour is so much a matter of taste and sensibility.'

'Edouard, you are preaching to the converted. I remember you pointing to the grass and saying that its colour depends on your mood, rather than on the light. You stressed the mood, and said that, therefore you could paint the grass as blue, black, or almost any colour, and not necessarily green.'

I smile at Charles. 'That is right. But that is not all. We also must have something to say – and that has to be of our own time as well – if not, we might as well give up.'

We walk in silence for a few minutes and then I say: 'I love painting. For me, one is not a painter if one doesn't love painting more than anything else in the world. I understand that science is important in our age, but scientific knowledge can only go so far. I think, imagination is much more important.'

Charles nods. 'Your critics could say that Bouguereau and Cabanel use their imagination for their nymphs and goddesses –'

'I am interested in painting people from everyday life, ordinary characters, like street singers, dancers, absinthe drinkers –'

'And whores.'

'And whores, my dear friend.'

'I write about those foul women, those temptresses of the night and you need to paint them, Edouard.'

'And there are so many other people whom we may normally pass by.' Charles looks at me. 'I will tell you. One day, I was coming back from Versailles, and I climbed onto the footplate of a locomotive, alongside the engine driver and fireman. The two men were so calm and patient. I thought it was a wonderful sight. What a marvellous picture they would have made…if only I could have painted them there and then… but theirs is a dog's life, Charles, and it is those men who are the heroes of today. It is people like them that I want to paint.'

'And Victorine. She has changed the way you paint.' Charles looks at me as we cross the road on our way to Guerbois.

'I cannot deny it. But the price I pay. When I work, it feels as if she were holding a long pole that she pokes into my eyes. And yet, I cannot stop painting her. Why does she try to provoke me?'

'Perhaps she expects more from you than she gets.' Charles grimaces.

'She wants me; I would be blind not to see that. But Charles, it is her face that I need, not her body. I have no intention of taking her to bed.'

'What about her? Have you ever asked yourself what she needs?'

'No, I haven't. Sleeping with her would spoil everything for me.'

Charles interrupts me. 'That's women for you. We sleep with

115

the beautiful ones and they drain us dry. We reject the ugly ones and they cast spells on us. *Faire l'amour, c'est faire le mal.'* I can see that Charles is in one of his moods when he speaks such nonsense.

'You are not listening. She is attractive enough; that is not the problem. If I did not wish to paint her again and again, I would be delighted to take her to bed. But as it is, I have plans for many more pictures and that means I need to stay away from her. When you sleep with a woman, you talk and sometimes it brings you close. You discover things about their lives that you would never think from just looking at them. But that is not what I want with Victorine. As long as her life outside my studio remains a mystery, she can take on any role for me. I do not wish to look at her and think of the man she hopes to marry.' Charles laughs. 'The secrets of her heart would only distract me. For her image to remain pure, unsullied by her mundane existence, I must not know anything that I do not see. I have always thought that an artist should paint only what is visible: swathes and dashes of colour. On my canvas, Victorine is a shape, a colour and, above all, she is that gaze.'

Charles responds with a series of exaggerated nods and then says: 'But Edouard, think, what is a woman except a role, forever changing? A woman is her costume. Even her nakedness is her costume.'

'Oh women! When we make love to them, they are never satisfied with the pleasure that we share. They always want something else. And they talk and talk. If only they were capable of discussing art and painting. That is the advantage of prosti-tutes: you tell them to go when you have finished. They do not expect you to listen to their stories.'

Charles sits down on a bench. I watch him as he takes a notebook out of his pocket and writes in it. I sit next to him. The mockery that danced in his eyes has been replaced by a distant, melancholy expression.

'How is Jeanne? You do not bring her along to my studio any more.'

He takes a deep breath before he turns towards me: 'Oh, my

Black Venus! My dancing serpent.' He looks ahead into the distance beyond the paths and strollers, beyond the tops of trees and recites:

Tes yeux, où rien ne se révèle
De doux ni d'amer,
Sont deux bijoux froids où se mêle
L'or avec le fer.

His voice falters. I remember when he used to scream that she was an implacable, cruel beast, a demon without pity, a queen of cruelty. If I reminded him that she was also his angel and his passion, his pleasure and his glory, the words he uttered in my presence so many times before, he would become even more enraged.

Today his tone is gentle: 'I fear Jeanne will never again climb the stairs at rue Guyot. Her legs will not support her. Jeanne, my dear cat. Edouard, she was mad, but madness was part of her beauty.'

The news of Jeanne's illness is not unexpected. I recall the last occasion when she posed for me: she sat on a divan like some giant doll with her legs stiffly propped up, her deeply-set eyes rimmed with black and her dark skin offset by the whiteness of the dress.

We enter Guerbois. It is already crowded but Duranty notices us standing at the door and waves to us to join his group in a corner.

'Come on, Edouard.' His balding head pops up from among the crowd as he stands up. 'Everyone here wants to hear you. You have been denying us the pleasure of your company recently.'

Someone sitting at the bar greets Charles and he stops to talk to him. I walk to the corner. As soon as I sit down, a glass of red wine is placed in front of me.

Duranty says loudly: 'Did you see the article in the *Moniteur* today? I can't imagine that you don't have anything to say about it.'

All the young students sitting around Duranty look at me. I place my elbows on the table and address them: 'First, contemporary life is the only possible subject for art. An artist should walk around with his eyes open and observe what happens on the streets of Paris. He should paint the drunks, the flower sellers, the beggars, the prostitutes.'

Several voices, some approving, some disapproving, try to make themselves heard.

Duranty shouts: 'Edouard, you have forgotten the absinthe drinkers. What was it that Thomas Couture, the revered master, said to you? "If you paint pictures like this, you are the absinthe drinker." Duranty laughs loudly, his blue eyes full of mischief. 'But why paint low life? Why immortalise the immoral and the ordinary?'

'Because we are realists.'

'Bouguereau calls himself one!' someone shouts.

'But there are no nymphs and goddesses in the world. There are wars instead. There is slavery. The poor on our streets. They all belong to our times. Why paint the nymphs and goddesses when there are real Parisian women around?' I am glad Charles is not next to me to say that he has just heard all of this. But these young painters, they need to know.

Duranty winks at me: 'But is it enough to have modern subjects?'

'No, that is not enough. We must have modern techniques. New subjects demand new ways of painting and –'

'Tell us more, Edouard, go on,' Duranty interrupts, 'we have missed these little lectures; '*l' école à la sauce brune*', what do you think of them?'

I realise I am being teased. Why does he always turn a serious discussion into mockery? And why is he making it so obvious that he is not interested in what I have to say?

Recently, I have been spending too much time on my own and now, accused of giving a lecture, I feel out of place. A couple of months ago, my spirits were so low that I avoided café conversations. I could only abide talking to Antoine or Charles, and even then, only one of them at a time. For the past month, I have been painting flat out, morning and afternoon, regularly working after seven in the evening. During the day, I was 'not at home to anyone except Antoine and Charles'. I told Madame Bijoux that under no circumstances was she to let anyone go upstairs. When I am working, I cannot stand all these bloody interruptions.

The Beaux-Arts group look puzzled by Duranty's attitude but dare not protest. I know they want to hear me. Only the other day I saw them passing around a couple of sketches I had done here the evening before. I was flattered by the way they gawped at me in admiration. They sat in silence, open-mouthed, until I addressed them.

I fill up the glasses of the four young men. Then I look at Duranty. He returns my gaze only briefly, stands up and calls a waitress. He needs more wine. In the corner, diagonally opposite us, a man starts to sing.

I wonder whether, in my solitude, I have become too sensitive and have forgotten what Duranty can be like. He is a tease, but he is witty and I know he means well. Most of the time he is gentle and soft-spoken. Perhaps I am taking things too seriously. But, although Duranty is benevolent, he is a parasite. When Degas is here, even when he is in one of his more acerbic moods, we have proper discussions about art. It is different with this man. He doesn't contribute. He feeds on our words, goes off, writes them down and makes money. And yet, he seems to dislike us talking about art, as if he is resentful that we are encroaching on his critical patch. Is this the creation of our times, this parasite, the critic? When art was religious, people did not need anyone to explain it, they experienced it. But now, with our secular pictures, critics have seized control of the meaning: until they say what a picture is about, people do not think it means anything. Most critics are failed artists, anyway.

I smile back at Duranty. This is not the first time that he has irritated me. Have I been more irritable recently? It is true that I have lost my temper more often than before. But only with her.

It is now, sitting here, that a picture gradually forms in my mind. Sections of it have been haunting me for weeks, not allowing me to see it in its entirety. For the first time, one of the three figures has a recognizable face: she is Victorine. She is looking out at me in that irritating way that is hers alone. If only I can capture that gaze with its power and defiance.

'Come on, Edouard, don't go quiet on us. Tell us, we are waiting: is it the linseed oil, the olive oil, or poppy seed oil? Which one do you recommend?' Duranty shouts mockingly.

'Leave him alone, Edmond,' Auguste says. 'Give him a chance to sort himself out. He wants to draw.'

I stand up to go, telling the company that I have just remembered something urgent and that I will be back. Duranty notices that I have taken a sketch pad out of my pocket. A sad smile crosses his face as he says: 'A man who never sells anything needs to do a drawing. Let us wish him well.'

I do not like the jibe but I ignore him. He probably does not realize how much I would like to avoid being so dependent on my family. But when it comes to art, I know Duranty understands. After all, it was he who wrote in *Réalisme* that 'in art one has to reproduce what one has in front of one's eyes'. At the time I had just had an argument with Couture and Duranty's words gave me confidence. There was someone out there who thought the same as me.

Outside the café, I sit on a bench under a street lamp and sketch a composition with three people, one of whom is staring out. Victorine is in every picture that comes to my mind.

Charles joins me on the bench. He takes the drawing from my hand and stares at it. I can see that he recognizes the face.

'Surrounded by spleen, an artist draws the ideal.' For a while, we sit quietly. Then Charles says: 'Edouard, you draw what I write. We see the same world. Let me recite you a poem.'

16

I begin with a lie: 'The Legrands are having problems at the café. They are reducing my wages for a while. They said it would be only for a few weeks or so, until business picked up.'

Mother stops by the table, supporting herself on the chair. I wait for her to say something. When she doesn't, I continue with another lie: 'After all they have done for me, I don't wish to leave them while they are having difficulties. They've been good to me. I am sure they'll appreciate if I help them out now and reward me later.'

Mother stands still, looking at me. Her face is as gaunt as ever. For weeks, I have not brought home any food.

I gave up the café work a month ago. The Legrands didn't seem disappointed when I told them that I was leaving. They had already employed somebody else to cover the weeks I was off.

I've spent most of the money I had put aside. If I am very careful and don't buy cooked meals, I can just about have enough for the rent this week. Of course, that is, assuming that Etienne pays me on time. But while I am modelling for at least half of every day at Monsieur Manet's, and sometimes a whole day, I have little time to earn extra to give to mother.

'Victorine,' mother says at last, 'It's stupid to be sentimental. We've got to look after ourselves. I'll ask at the laundry. I saw Delphine the other day and she said there was work. Of course, they wouldn't have me. But you are young and strong.' I was expecting her to say that.

'Mother, I don't want to work in the laundry,' I say calmly. There is no point embellishing the story about the Legrands' problems. She either doesn't believe me or chooses to disregard my words.

'Victorine,' she says with her eyes on me, and her voice still soft, 'there's no other way. We are almost there with the money for the shop. Another year, or even less than a year, and we'll be working for ourselves.' Two deep, vertical lines appear between her eyebrows as she stares at me. I am prepared for her anger.

'Mother, that's too long. I can't work in the laundry for a year.'

'Why not? You think you're too good?' She is shouting now. Her face is as red as her hands. 'I worked in the laundry for eighteen years. Honest work it is. Who do you think you are? Somebody has been filling your head with nonsense, telling you that you are too pretty for that kind of work. Maybe. But where are the men to marry you? Not a single one has made himself known. You are worse than Marie. At least she has found some-one.'

Mother is screaming now and words come out splattered with her saliva. I am surprised by what she says about Marie. For the past two years, mother has called my friend a fallen woman. She said that as someone who 'dressed above her station and frequented cafés, those places of idle entertainment, Marie was bound to come to a sticky end.' I never opposed her but she would go on: 'Modelling for artists is no job for a decent woman. All that sitting naked in front of strange men will lead to no good. You watch it, Victorine. She'll end up with a baby on her hip and no husband to support her. Both lying in the gutter.'

But now that Marie is married, mother seems to have changed her tune.

Tempted by what mother says, I make a stupid mistake: 'I could do modelling. I've met an artist and –'

Before I can finish, mother grabs her shoe and hits me on the head several times.

'Ah, so that's what it is. A man on the scene. And an artist. You've succumbed to the corruption of Paris. All those lies about the Legrands having problems. You liar, Victorine. Why did I have you brought up in the country? So that you end up loose and immoral like other young women. Oh, no! Tomorrow, I'll take you to the laundry myself. You've had too much freedom to do what you like.'

I raise my arms above my head to protect my face from her blows. As I make a sudden move to avoid her, my mouth hits the edge of the door frame. Mother ignores the blood and shouts: 'I'll ask them tomorrow and you will go to the laundry. That's settled. No more talk.'

Later on, mother sits at the table and eats some cabbage soup. I say I am not hungry. I lie on the bed and watch her hunched figure bent over the bowl. If she is very careful, she can survive on her savings for several years.

Half an hour later, mother descends the stairs to the toilet two floors below us. I make a bundle of the clothes I can grab quickly and walk out of the door. My heart beats fast as I climb to the floor upstairs. I'm relieved that none of the neighbours is here to ask questions. Listening for her steps, I wait on the landing until I hear her go back to our room. When she closes the door, I tiptoe downstairs.

Outside, I look up at the stars and the full moon. There are so many of them, glittering at each other. I hold my head up and make my way to the omnibus stop, all the time looking over my shoulder. A drunken old woman is sleeping on the ground. When I arrive, she wakes, looks at me and stretches out her hand, begging. Like me, she is alone in the world. But compared with her, I'm rich. I have almost ten francs on me and two rooms all to myself. I look in my pocket for something to give her and her eyes light up. I move away. I have to be careful with my money. The woman comes closer and tugs on my skirt. I give her a sou and she lets go. She looks at the coin and says she wants more. I shake my head and she complains but I ignore her. She goes back to sleep.

My broken lip starts to bleed again. In the cold air, the skin pulls back and the cut feels sore. I dab at the blood with a handkerchief, until a clot forms. By the time a yellow vehicle stops in front of me, my feet are numbed. I am the only woman on the omnibus, others are either young workers going for their night shifts or old drunks, sleeping on chairs. The young men stare at me.

I get off at the Boulevard Saint Michel and walk briskly, without looking around. Every now and then, a man calls out, saying he has good money for a pretty one like me. I quicken my pace.

In the apartment, I light a gas lamp and with the door closed, the bundle with my clothes on the floor by my feet, I lean against a wall and survey the scene. In this room, my possessions amount to a small round table, two chairs and a long rectangular table full of drawings, paints, brushes and art material. In the adjoining room there is nothing but a double bed, a wash stand, with a bowl and a jug and a basket full of second-hand clothes. This is my studio and from tonight it is also my home. If I had the money, I would buy a pair of curtains for the bedroom and a bed cover, maybe even some cushions. But for now I mustn't spend any money on such purchases. Rent and some food are my priorities.

I try not to think what mother may be doing.

From now on, every hour that I don't spend in Monsieur Manet's studio will be my own. I can paint for Etienne and work on my flower seller canvas.

It's cold in my bed and the sheet feels damp. I stretch one arm under the pillow and find Lola's shawl. I press it to my swollen lips, imagining that she is lying next to me, her large soft body keeping me warm. I put my hand between my legs and touch myself in the way that Lola does. I fall asleep haunted by her scent.

17

Despite the rain, the day is very warm. I have had an excellent cup of chocolate, courtesy of Madame Bijoux, and there is still an hour left before Victorine arrives. I shall use it to touch up the prints for Cadart.

Yesterday, Charles and I spent half a day strolling around. The plants were all in bud and there was a smell of spring in the air. May is the most beautiful month in Paris. Seeing all those colourful dresses and hats and walking canes pass in front of our eyes in the Tuileries, I was gripped by a sudden desire to work right there. While Charles scribbled in his notebook, I made a few sketches that I could use later for a painting. But then, I thought, why restrict myself to drawings? I could paint in the park. I said that I would bring my easel and set up a studio on the side of one of the avenues. Charles thought it an excellent idea.

'Edouard, an artist of our modern world has to work in the world, among the people, the masses strolling around. That is the only way to create the heroism of our times. Gone are the days when a painter worked in the isolation of his studio.'

We agreed that if the weather were pleasant, we would come back on Sunday.

'I expect you will be quite a sensation, Edouard,' Charles said. 'I shall be on hand to fend off the unwanted, the curious and, most of all, the boring.'

Despite the excitement at the prospect of painting in the open air, the torero canvas played on my mind. I thought that I should ask her, and if she has no objection to it, I would call the painting *Mademoiselle V en costume d' Espada*. Perhaps the name should be obvious enough for the critics to understand what I am doing. Sometimes I feel that unless I tell them what to think, they dismiss my work without any understanding.

Back in the studio, while I looked through the sketches from the Tuileries, Charles nosed around. Suddenly he exclaimed: 'Oh, she is a knowing woman, Edouard. And she is serene. Good. Do not allow sentimentality on your canvas.'

I looked up. He was holding Victorine's portrait in his hand.

'The light, Edouard. It is like what Nadar uses for his photographs.'

I went over and we looked at the picture together. I had not thought of this idea before but I had to admit that he was right. Her face was as fully lit as an object that Nadar requires for his camera.

Charles asked whether I planned to exhibit Victorine's portrait at the Salon or at the Gallery Martinet next year. I told him of her request and my promise. He laughed.

'A portrait is a model complicated by an artist. Without the artist, the model exists only in her daily life. When the artist makes a portrait, he creates a new life for the model. Therefore, only he has a claim to the picture.' His eyes fixed on mine, challenging me to answer.

I did not say it but I had to disagree. A few months ago, I would have thought Charles was right. But since I have met Victorine, although I would not admit it to her, I know that neither the portrait, nor the *Espada*, could exist without her contribution. I could not have used just any model. Only she could give the painting that special quality.

Recently, I have thought of another picture with her that I would like to work on very soon. However, after yesterday, I am also itching to get out and paint the world around me.

Now, standing in front of the *Espada*, it is clear that, apart from a few final touches, her figure and face are almost complete. I have in mind to paint a background based on Goya. There are several copies of his prints lying around that I need to look at: I will place a bull behind the figure.

It will make a pleasant break to work without her. When I am more or less copying, as I intend to do for the background, I can have Charles or Antoine around.

I am used to working with models who are friends or family. They do not exhaust me; we talk while I work. But it is different with her. I do not know her and, often, she scares me. Nor do I know the world she comes from. I want to paint that world, but only what is visible to me, not what I am supposed to know about it.

She arrives as the clock strikes eleven. While she makes herself ready, I sit down and pretend that I am working on an etching. But that does not save me. As she has done on several occasions recently, she stands right in front of me, pretending that she is interested in what I am doing and, when I do not respond, she starts undressing. While still in her undergarments, she walks around, picking up parts of the Spanish costume, one by one. I keep my eyes on the print but cannot fail to notice that she is watching me all the time.

Once she assumes the pose, I start to work on the handker-chief sticking out of her jacket pocket. As I am squeezing the lemon yellow onto the palette, I think that this may be a long session. I'll try to avoid having a break for as long as I can manage. I must not encourage her.

Yesterday, when I took my coffee upstairs and I was sitting on the bed, she appeared at the door. She must have tiptoed, for I did not hear her come up. Looking straight at me, she said: 'Will you need me for anything else, monsieur?' She had a false, coquettish smile. The role does not become her at all. I felt that even her voice had altered; I could hear an affectation in her pronunciation, an unpleasant high pitch.

'No, certainly not,' I said quickly before any misunderstand-ing could take place. She looked puzzled. I lowered my eyes, hoping she would go away.

Instead, she said: 'But we have done only one hour, monsieur. I thought you would make better use of me.' She smiled and fixed her eyes on mine.

She was being purposefully disingenuous. We had worked for a good two hours. The smile widened. I felt challenged and the heat rose to my face: 'I will be with you downstairs in a few minutes and then we can resume, mademoiselle.' She looked even more puzzled. The most annoying thing was that she still did not move. Instead, she stared at me and I had to repeat what I had already told her. At first, I ignored her and pretended that I was looking at a photograph Nadar had recently sent me. When I lifted my eyes, I noticed that the top buttons on her shirt were undone and she was leaning in a way that exposed both of her nipples. Deep pink. Something stirred in me. I cannot deny that. I would have loved to have had her but I managed to exert control over my physical reaction. It would have been stupid to risk my future projects for a moment of pleasure.

She was not giving up.

'I was wondering,' she paused, all smile, 'whether I can help you relax while you are having a break?' She spoke so slowly and I began to wonder whether she was mocking me. I do not understand women like her and their ways.

When she leaned forward, pretending that she was interested in the photograph in my hand, I could see that her nipples were erect. I blushed. What an irritation!

She, on her part, was as white as chalk. Not a fluster. How does she manage it?

I waved her off. I hated her staring at my red face.

'That is fine, monsieur,' she said eventually and turned.

I know she is playing a game but she is after something and I am beginning to think that if I am to have another picture with her, sooner or later I will have to give in and sleep with her.

18

I worked until very late last night. Monsieur Manet needed me for the whole afternoon and by the time I arrived home, it was too dark to work without a gas lamp.

Despite the long hours I spend in Monsieur Manet's company, I don't have a chance to talk to him about painting. Any comments that I make, he ignores. Sometime ago I came to the conclusion that unless he looks at me as a model, which means no more than an object of a certain shape and colour, he is uncomfortable in my presence. He is attracted to me but, at the same time, fears involvement. The way he speaks to me is very different from the way he speaks to Antoine or Charles, or even Madame Bijoux. With them, he is relaxed and friendly; with me, his manner is cold and formal. Or perhaps he has misjudged me and thinks that I wouldn't welcome his attention. I have no desire for him, but from the very first day in his studio, I was prepared to sleep with him if it meant that he would show me how to paint.

Perhaps I should tell him openly that I want to sleep with him.

It was fortunate that all the three pictures that I needed to complete last night were of medium size and the colours were bright. I find it much more tiring to work with dark shades or on small pictures if I don't have natural light. Even so, this morning, my eyes are sore.

I make my way to the Louvre, carrying the pictures parcelled in brown paper and tied with string. I walk slowly through the galleries, stopping from time to time to put down the parcel and look at old favourites.

From a distance, I see Etienne pacing up and down in front of his easel.

'Victorine, you are late,' he says without greeting me, or smiling. Before I have time to reply, he says: 'I've to meet someone downstairs. Will you stay and guard the painting? I'll take the pictures from you when I get back.' I hope he'll pay me for the work from last week and for this new delivery.

Etienne is copying the picture for his American customer. The canvas is much larger than the original; no wonder he is making such slow progress and has had no time to meet me in the café. I'm short of time, too, but my shortage of money is more acute. I couldn't postpone meeting him.

Copyists aren't allowed to use a canvas of exactly the same size but it is not prescribed that the copy has to be so much larger. It amuses me that the gallery fears that a copy could be passed as the real thing. If the copy is good, the pleasure should be the same, and the more are made, the more people can enjoy them.

I can't recall seeing the original before. The picture, by Giorgione, represents four figures: two men and two women placed in a landscape. While the men are making music, the women seem to be lounging about. More interestingly, the men are fully dressed, while the women are naked. But it appears that the men haven't noticed the women; perhaps they are goddesses, invisible to human eyes. That would make sense. But then, does the painting have to make sense as a story?

The picture is more than two hundred years old and its age is obvious from the costumes of the men. I amuse myself by thinking what the painting would look like if the men were to wear contemporary Parisian clothes. If they were dressed, for example, like Etienne or, even better, as elegantly as Monsieur Manet. I've never seen him take off his perfectly tailored jacket, even when he paints. Sometimes, I think that it would not surprise me if I were to go to the studio and see him working in his silk top hat, wearing those finely stitched, yellow leather gloves.

I pick up one of Etienne's brushes and feel the bristles between the tips of my fingers. They are sable. Good for detailed work, that stationery owner told me. Monsieur Manet prefers oven-dried horse-hair and uses brushes with a special grip. I remember how particular he was about his order in a letter to the stationer on rue Lepic.

Etienne's picture is three quarters done. He is working on the tree in the background and on a small figure, most likely a peasant. The four large figures in the foreground are complete. Etienne has copied the colour and the brushstrokes so meticulously that even here, with the two paintings next to each other, it is difficult to distinguish between them. I wonder whether I'd ever be able to paint like this. I have ideas – they come to me all the time – but I have no technique. I hold Etienne's palette and add a touch of brown to the tree.

This morning the galleries are almost deserted. Those who stop by offer a cursory glance at the canvas, and then stare at me. Only a tiny minority of copyists at the Louvre are women, and they attract more attention from the public. A couple of visitors comment on what they assume is my work but I pretend that I don't hear them. I don't want to have to admit that I am not the copyist. Let them believe that I am a painter. I work slowly and carefully with a tiny brush, afraid that Etienne may complain if he notices that I have been meddling with his picture.

Suddenly, a loud voice greets me and a heavy hand lands on my shoulder. I turn; it is the American woman that I met when she was working on the Murillo. She says that she has looked for me on several occasions.

'Today is perhaps the first time that I arrived not expecting to see you. And here you are!' While she is speaking, I try to remember her name. She embraces me and immediately tells me that she hasn't made much progress with her painting. Her loud voice makes people turn their heads towards us. Emma, I think.

'Most of the time, I am left to my own devices,' she says. 'Monsieur Deschamp hasn't been very helpful. He comes to the studio once a week and offers only the briefest of comments. Perhaps he doesn't take me seriously because I'm a woman.' She laughs loudly.

'Well, it is true that I have not been working very hard. I would love to do more, but it isn't easy. There are too many exciting things going on in Paris. I love this city. So different from Boston. Sometimes, I just sit in cafés and talk to friends. I have assembled a whole crowd of my fellow countrymen. Most of them came here to learn to paint.' She turns towards the picture on the easel in front of me.

'Victorine, this is impressive.' She moves closer as if inspecting the brushwork. 'It's fantastic. You are a real painter.' For a second, her words make me feel warm and, if only I knew that Etienne wasn't returning soon, I would keep quiet. When I admit that I am only minding the painting for a friend, she seems a little disappointed because, as she says, she was hoping that I could help her with her work.

'I am only a beginner,' I say.

'Who is your teacher?'

'No one. I teach myself.'

'How can you do that?'

'I observe the world.' Emma looks puzzled. 'Well, I look at people, on the street, in cafés, anywhere. And I draw them.'

'But that cannot be enough.'

'No, I also study other paintings, and I try to listen, whenever I can, to artists talking about their work.'

'That makes sense.' Emma nods. 'But how do you know when your pictures are any good?'

'I don't. At least I don't know straight away. I just assume that they aren't good enough. That's the more likely situation, anyway. After all, there is always something that can be improved. As time passes, and I learn more, I find that I can judge my earlier work more clearly.'

'You are lucky to be able to criticize yourself,' she says. 'I find that I need to be praised. If no one tells me that what I am doing is good, I don't feel like going on. And that's the problem with my teacher. He only comments on the aspects of my pictures that are wrong and that need to be improved.'

She is fortunate to have a teacher.

'If he doesn't make a positive comment on at least one thing in my work, and soon, I think I'll give up. There are too many temptations in Paris. Everything seems to be designed to distract me.'

Once again her voice is too loud for the gallery and people look at us as she asks: 'How do you carry on without praise?' I shrug my shoulders and she continues: 'How do you manage to find the time for painting when there are so many opportunities for socializing?'

She is rich and doesn't have to worry about earning money. 'I don't know. I just do. I live for painting; it's the only thing that matters to me.'

'With that attitude you are bound to become good. But for me, Parisian parties are irresistible. I would not give them up for anything.' That's easy for me: I have no friends and no one invites me. These days, I hardly ever see Marie, either. I nod sympathetically and smile.

The American woman gives me an envious look: 'Perhaps I just haven't the stamina. It is too much hard work for me. I find painting for hours on end too lonely.' She turns to go. 'Right now, I am meeting someone in the café downstairs. But come and see me sometime. There is always someone around in my apartment.'

I promise to visit her.

She writes down her address, together with her name: Emily.

'I live in the Batignolles area. My friends would be delighted if a young French woman painter joined us.'

Before she walks away, she says: 'Perhaps some of your commitment will rub off on me. I envy your discipline.'

Etienne gives me the money for last week's orders and promises to pay me in a few days' time for the pictures I have just completed. He has to do some work at home and he suggests I collect it from his rooms in rue du Four. I tell him that I could come on Sunday, with a friend. When he hears that, he says that Sunday wouldn't be convenient.

I look him in the eyes, not believing what he says.

'My mother, Victorine. I need to do something for her.'

I need the money as soon as possible. We settle for Saturday.

At the corner of Maître Albert, a slight female figure in a brown coat waves and rushes towards me. I quicken my pace. Although she is only seventeen, Marie's face already has two thin vertical lines framing her mouth. We hold each other tightly. Despite her visible pregnancy, her frame feels more angular than I recall.

'Victorine, I'm so glad to have found you. The concierge told me you weren't in and I was about to leave. She said that, these days, she didn't know your comings and goings. A week ago I went to the café but they said you'd left. I've missed you.'

'Dear Marie, I'm sorry. I should have let you know.'

'Your mother doesn't know where you are either.'

'I left Hôtel d'Or without telling her where I was going.'

'She was angry and shouted at me when I wanted to know where you live.'

I dare not ask about her. Since I can't help, I would rather not know. I force myself to smile and Marie doesn't mention her again.

It has been a couple of months since I saw Marie. Her face looks older. When our eyes meet, we stare at each other; for the first time in years, I can't tell what she is thinking about. I wonder if the same thought crosses her mind. She has a new life and I am no longer part of it.

For a while, we walk on in silence. I want to take Marie's hand but decide not to.

'The concierge said that a black woman was looking for you this morning.'

'Oh, Lola.'

'Who's she?' Marie stops and looks at me. I hear the eagerness in her voice and wonder if she is jealous.

'A friend.' Marie smiles briefly. I know she expects me to say more. I don't.

'I miss you, Victorine.'

'I miss you, too.'

'You have new friends now.' No, I haven't. She has. She has a husband and a baby on the way.

I remember the money in my pocket; I invite her to a place down the road where they make lovely stews. We drink a glass of wine each, but Marie leaves most of the food. She sips wine and chews on a bread crust while I finish everything on my plate.

'Don't worry about me, Victorine,' she says when I tell her that she is much thinner than she used to be. 'I'm very happy. Emile has been good to me.' I smile.

'You aren't happy, Victorine.' She puts her hand on mine and our eyes meet. I blush but don't know what to say. She is right. But I am not unhappy either.

'I manage. I draw and paint.' I try to sound cheerful.

We sit quietly and then, without looking up at me, Marie says: 'It's in your blood.'

I smile at her: 'Blood? What about my blood?'

'My mother knew yours when they were young.'

'So?'

'And she knew your father. He was an artist.'

I don't know what to say. Mother said that my father had died before I was born. When I was little, she would hit me if I asked. Grandmother said that mother was still grieving.

'Sorry,' Marie says. 'Mother made me promise not to tell you. But that was when we were children. I thought you knew now.'

I shake my head.

'He used to paint. Mother said no one wanted his pictures, he drank a lot and… he killed himself. You were only a baby.' Marie puts her hand on mine and squeezes it. 'It has been very hard for your mother.'

'Why didn't she ever tell me?'

Marie shrugs her shoulders. 'Why tell you such a sad story?'

'I might have understood why she hates paintings.'

'But it wouldn't have stopped you doing art. My mother says you can't do anything about it.'

Later on, we walk by the river and all I can think of is that doing art is in my blood. I like the thought.

After a while, Marie says: 'We should meet more often and spend more time together, like in the old days.' Her eyes fix on mine, challenging me to agree.

'Yes,' I say, knowing that we won't. 'I'd like to do that.'

'You could show me where you live. You could draw me like you used to.'

'Yes, like I used to.'

Marie smiles and kisses me on the cheek. Is she playing this game for her own benefit? I don't think she is happy.

On the way to the omnibus stop, we walk into a dark porch and I kiss her. I feel her warm tears on my cheek. Before we part, I say: 'Marie, can you ask your mother if she remembers what his pictures were like?'

She nods. 'But there aren't any left. Your mother destroyed them all after his death.'

19

By the time I put my things together, it is late morning. The sun is shining and the air is warm. The weather will bring people out in droves. The prospect of hundreds of models strolling in front of my easel excites me. I carry the sheets of paper and a box of pencils and charcoal downstairs. The driver helps me load my things into his fiacre. As we set out, I think that if the preliminary drawings work well, I might soon, perhaps even today, start drawing straight onto the canvas. I ask the man to turn back. He waits downstairs while I fetch a canvas. At first, I pick up a large one and begin to walk downstairs to ask for help in carrying it. But I realize that there is not much room left in the fiacre, so I change my mind and choose a smaller canvas. Work in the open air requires a degree of organisation and planning. I don't usually have to go through that.

As we ride to the Tuileries, I try to think of the drawings I shall do today, but my mind is still haunted by the *Espada*. I finished it only yesterday, a month after I began. The background took longer than I had expected. I copied the figures from Goya's etchings; I think the borrowing is obvious. If only the scribblers would notice; I suppose Chesneau might. After I had put the final touches to it, I stood back and took a long look at the entire composition. Although I could clearly see the scene with the bulls and matadors in the distance, it was blurred and appeared flat, as if it were a backdrop to her figure, which is painted in sharp focus. I suddenly saw the importance of the contrast, the clear difference between the two. The background looks like one of those painted curtains that photographers deploy to set a scene for a portrait. It emphasises her role-playing. That was not what I originally had in mind. Initially, I did not think of the background at all. It was only her figure, its position and the costume that interested me.

When, on that first day in my studio, I walked in and saw her, posing in front of a mirror, dressed in the outfit of a torero, I knew that I wanted to make a picture that showed her playing the part of a torero. My intention was to make the viewer see her as a contemporary Parisian woman wearing a costume of a torero. I had no idea how to go about it. In fact, it might have been her own objections to the pose I asked her to adopt that helped me develop the idea. I remember that, on the second day of work on the canvas, she said that her position was wrong. She went on to say something about bulls being large, dangerous and fast-moving animals and that in a corrida, a torero would have to be on his guard. I asked her whether she had been to Spain and when she said no, I laughed. How would she know?

'If he held the dagger like this,' and she made an exaggerated upward gesture with her arm, 'he would never be able to use it.'

While I worked, her persistent babble irritated me. I snapped back: 'You are not a real torero. You are only posing as one. Why should you pretend that you are afraid? There are no bulls around. The dagger is a prop.' I had never thought of it like that before. She is playing a role. How can one paint a person unless they take on a role? A painter needs to stage a series of masquerades, dressing up sessions.

She gave me a long look and I thought that she even nodded in acknowledgment. Or perhaps she was just being coy. I felt ashamed at raising my voice. Although the critics do not understand my pictures, I have come to expect her to see what I am doing, simply because she seems to know what to do when posing.

A few days after that conversation, someone at the Guerbois, one of the young people from the Beaux-Arts, passed around a book of Goya's *Tauromaquia*. There was no doubt that the composition of the drawings was powerfully dramatic. Next time Victorine posed, I saw Goya in the background.

Whenever Victorine dressed up, I saw two adjacent images:

that of the role she took on and something beneath. Was that real her? The question bothered me.

When I had finished her portrait, Charles looked at it and said: 'It is a face with no role to play.' It is only now that I can see how astute he was: it is not a face with no identity. That face can play any role. That playfulness is her, rather than something beneath.

And then, there are the eyes, the eyes that shift and do not allow anyone to fix her, even on a canvas. They are the eyes I so much want to paint.

Well, that is it: *Mademoiselle V. en costume d' Espada.* That should convey the play between her role and her shifting identity. But that does not mean that some fool will not come along and interpret my painting as one of those historical reconstructions *à la* Couture.

It was a relief to work quietly, without her overwhelming presence that destroys my concentration. While I was painting the background, only Charles came around, on his daily visits. Nevertheless, as the week went on, I missed working with her. I kept thinking of the next picture that has been on my mind for weeks now and wished for her to be around so that I could ask her to try a few poses that I needed to sketch. I cannot visualise it at all without her standing in front of me.

I pick up Charles on the way to the gardens. We ride along the quai des Tuileries before we enter the park.

People are gathering for the concert and it is very crowded. Looking at the multitude, Charles extends his arm and points ahead.

'For the perfect ambler and passionate observer, a *flâneur*, and that is what our time demands from a painter, this is the perfect domicile: here in the numerous, in the undulating, in movement, in the fugitive and the infinite. To be outside of home and nevertheless to feel oneself everywhere at home, to see the world, be at the centre of the world and remain hidden from the world.'

For a moment, I think that he is reading from his notebook, but his eyes are still on the world passing by. Suddenly, he turns towards me, touches me lightly on the shoulder and says: 'You, Edouard, are an observer. An observer is a prince who partakes incognito of the world around. Think of the world here as your family.' I smile and he continues: 'If you wish to be a painter of modern life, your canvas should be a mirror as large as that crowd.'

The fiacre driver helps us unload. Charles, carrying my large sketch pad, stops suddenly, puts the pad on the grass and says:

'He shall be the true painter who can pull out of everyday life its epic side and make us understand just how great and poetic we are in our neckties and polished boots.' The fiacre driver stares at him and then bursts out laughing.

There is no shortage of onlookers and willing assistants. Immediately, we are surrounded by a group of children begging. But I have anticipated their arrival. My pockets are filled with mandarins. Pierre Lebois, my old school friend, has just sent me a crate of them from Marseilles. The children would probably prefer money, but I would rather give them a share in something I enjoy. The pleasures of this world. Well, they are made of things that mean little to some people but a lot to others.

We set up a studio on the edge of a path and, while I am sketching, Charles sits on a bench writing in his notebook. From time to time, he looks up and makes a comment about the men and women promenading in front of us. 'What a spectacle of elegance. Edouard, this is the heroism of modern life.'

A few people stand around me as I work, the curious, the chatty, the inquisitive, the judgmental and the exhibitionists. The latter gather right in front of my easel, as if compelling me to draw their portraits. Several men try to engage me in conversation; at first, I ignore them, but then, realizing that they won't stop, I offer a word here and there. They want to know why I am working outside. How else is an artist to draw modern life if he does not leave his studio and work in the open air?

The best thing is to paint instantly what you see. A military regiment marches past us. The blare of the brass instruments drowns the comments of the bystanders. After a while, I feel more comfortable working despite all the people talking and giggling.

I shut my ears and open my eyes. The beautiful and the ugly, the old and young, the elegant and shabby, they all pass in front of my easel.

Charles lifts his head and reminds me of the words I have heard from him so many times:

'For a modern painter, Edouard, they are all valuable subjects.'

I think of it as realism: ordinary Parisians, rather than gods and goddesses, are the subject of my painting.

Charles writes in his notebook, looks up and I hear him say: 'Here is the spectacle before the specular eye.'

The music plays, the weather is pleasant and huge crowds stroll through the park. I make several ink drawings of trees, of women sitting down, their heads covered with bonnets with colourful ribbons hanging under their chins, men in top hats and frock coats, little girls in flouncy dresses tied with big bows. As I sketch, the finished painting crystallizes in my head. I shall apply thick colour in rough brush strokes, as if the entire crowd, the entire scene, is just one amorphous shape of different shades. Even the faces will be like masks, unrecognizable, no more than coloured forms. There will be no penetrating eyes in this crowd, no one staring out. The figures in the crowd are blurred and merge together. I imagine that I'll squeeze the paint onto the palette and move my brush very quickly. When I stand back, the picture will be a myriad of touches of colour. If only the colour and the touches could convey the sound of music and the murmur of the crowd.

Charles stands up and looks at my drawing: 'Edouard, here you have drawn the harnesses, scintillations, music, decided glances, heavy, serious moustaches.'

The music has finished and the crowds begin to disperse. It is time for us to go. Charles helps me pack. We carry the canvas, which I have not touched, to the waiting fiacre and arrange to come back in a few days' time.

We stop at Tortoni. Charles does not appear to have much appetite. We eat slowly a dish of jugged hare but, by the time a roast fowl with salad arrives, he refuses to have any more. I look at his subdued face and plead with him to talk to me. I know that on some days he finds it difficult to get out of bed. As the ideal that sustained him in his youth gradually subsides, the spleen takes over. Besides, the pain in his legs is constant. Perhaps the same future awaits me. I remember what it was like with my father. Why are all our lives blighted by the ills of modern living?

20

'Mademoiselle, Victorine,' he says as he opens the door. His eyes are smiling as they meet mine. 'Come in, come in. I need your help.'

This is an unusual welcome. Most of the time, he is polite, but doesn't say much. And when he does speak, it is either about painting or a costume he wants me to try. I notice that today there are no lines on his face and he is smiling in the same easy way as he did on that day in January in the Luxembourg Gardens. My first thought is that I am prepared for whatever he wants to do with me. I have waited a long time for this. And haven't I tried hard enough?

'Can you play the guitar?' I didn't expect this question.

'I used to. I haven't had the time recently.' I want to tell him that I was good at it and that, a couple of years ago, I even earned good money playing in cafés for a few weeks. But he doesn't seem to be interested in hearing more. He hands me a guitar.

'Can you play something for me?' I try a few chords. The instrument is horribly out of tune. He doesn't seem to be able to tell and stares at me questioningly as I stop playing to tune the guitar. Each time I tighten a string, the peg refuses to stay in place.

'The pegs are loose. It won't tune.' He takes no notice of what I say. I fiddle with the strings and pegs but it doesn't work. His eyes are still on me but, by now, his mind is elsewhere. I stand up and move close to him. My proximity seems to unsettle him, or at least break his train of thought, and I can see that he is back with me.

'Mademoiselle Victorine, will you let me satisfy an idea of mine?' At last.

'Of course,' I say, 'anything you want, Monsieur'. I smile coquettishly. Suddenly, the smile disappears from his face. 'What would you like me to do, monsieur?'

'We could play a little game, mademoiselle. I shall position myself over there, just opposite the front door, so that I have a good view of you. Would you mind, mademoiselle, going out and then coming back in, holding the guitar in one arm?' He makes sure not to meet my eyes.

I follow his instructions. As soon as I open the door, I can see him holding a sketchpad and I hear the rapid movements of the pencil. He wants me to stop dead as soon as I step into the room. At least twenty times, I go out, come back, stand frozen and then go out again. He sketches without comment, except to instruct me to vary my entrance slightly. I don't ask questions; I am used to him keeping his ideas to himself. As soon as I think of how different people carrying a guitar would make their entrance, I begin to enjoy the game. At one moment, I imagine I am very young; later on, I become older, and then I take on the age of someone as old as Madame Bijoux. Then I try another approach: I don't think of a particular person; instead, I move very slowly, shuffle my feet and lower my head, keeping my eyes on the ground. Suddenly, the guitar seems very heavy and I have to hold it with both hands. A woman emerges from the movement. I wonder if a painter can create a character only from shapes and sizes, without knowing anything about them first.

Next, I move my body in a jittery fashion. My muscles tense and I grip the guitar. I glance in different directions and shift the guitar from one hand to the other. If only I could change my clothes for each entrance, I could play the people more convincingly. Each time I vary my posture, my movements and my facial expressions. However, I always look straight at him as I enter. I think of people I see on the streets of Paris. I remember people I know and imagine that I am them. Is that what comedians do? Perhaps I should have been an actress. I move around and ideas come quickly. As soon as I close the door behind me, another character leaps into my mind. The game pleases me and I think I could carry on forever. But as I enter in the role of a street

144

woman, seductively unbuttoning my blouse, Monsieur Manet stops me:

'I think I have seen what I need. For now, at least.' He stares over my shoulder and, after a while, I hear him say to himself: 'The outfit is wrong.'

He walks across the studio to the corner where he keeps a clothes stand and a basket. He rummages through the basket, until he finds a yellow skirt and a bright blue jacket. He asks me to put them on. I nod and smile. I start undressing right here in front of him. He watches me. I take off my clothes slowly, so that his eyes can linger on me. Men tend to like it like that. It raises their interest and increases their desire. I move slowly to prolong the undressing to the point where he can't help himself any more and has to touch me.

Since Lola makes love to me as a man, it should not bother me if he does. If we lay down together, we would have to speak differently. I could ask him about art, perhaps even tell him about my ambition. If we were friends, he would show me how to deal with the problems I have with my painting.

I am about the take my stockings off when Monsieur Manet stops me.

'Can you just put these on and quickly, please,' he says, pointing to the clothes he has chosen. His voice is tense. I am not sure what to do. Marie said that once a woman began to undress, no man would stop her from going on unless she was very old and ugly. 'If a man says a woman should not carry on undressing, he doesn't really mean it,' Marie said. I ignore Monsieur Manet's request. My unstockinged foot presses down on the rough surface of the floorboard. Slowly, and gently, I roll down the other stocking, all the time keeping my eyes on him. Monsieur Manet is standing by the table with the prints, reshuffling the pile. While his head is lowered, as if he were looking at the prints, I glimpse his eyes turning aside to stare at my bare calves. He stops reshuffling the prints. It is very quiet in the studio. I carry on stroking my calves, as if I were alone. I wonder whether I should just walk towards him and kiss him. I am not sure how to do it. Slowly or quickly? Do I need to say anything?

I wish I had asked Marie. What if he moves away, or pulls back his head, just as I am close enough to put my lips on his?

Marie said that men always knew what to do. Why doesn't he do it then? Haven't I made it clear, on so many occasions, that I would let him? Either he doesn't like me as a woman, or he has misjudged my reaction. I think of all those outbursts and shouting that I have endured from him. Perhaps I confuse him. It seems to me that he is frustrated and can't control himself any more. Artists often sleep with their models. Why doesn't he sleep with me?

As I walk towards him, with bare feet and uncovered shoulders, I pull down one of the straps of my bodice. If I lean in front of him, he will be able to look at my breasts. Marie told me that most men cannot resist that. I know that he is pretending to be preoccupied with the drawings. As I stand close to him, he turns and his eyes meet mine. I see fear on his face and I stand paralysed. We are locked in a stare. For a while, neither of us moves. I can barely breathe. Very slowly, he places his hand on my breast. I close my eyes. As he moves the hand, the skin of the palm of his hand barely brushes against my nipple. Whispering, he asks whether any man has every touched me like that. 'No,' I say. He sighs.

We hear a single knock on the door. And then another. And again, louder this time. His hand withdraws and he turns away from me. When he looks back, I can't read his face. Then a slight smile crosses from one corner of his mouth to the other and he stares at me, until his eyes force me to back away. He takes the clothes he has chosen for me and throws them behind a screen in a corner. He waits for me to disappear behind it. As I walk across the room, I see that my own clothes are prominently placed on the table in the centre. I decide to leave them there. While I am putting on the skirt and the blouse that Monsieur Manet gave me, he opens the door. His poet friend, Charles, enters.

'I feared you were out, Edouard, it took you so long,' he says. I can hear his steps as he walks around the studio and, when he sees my clothes, including my stockings on a chair by the divan, he adds: 'Oh la la, my dear friend, I am sorry to barge in like this. There is evidence here that you are not alone. But mademoiselle, whoever she is, could not have gone out without her clothes. There is quite a breeze outside. Shall I help you look for her?'

I am still behind the screen and can't see the poet's face, but it would be impossible to miss the teasing note in his voice. Monsieur Manet doesn't answer.

Charles continues: 'I have brought you a present, Edouard. The first of the summer. I am sure an artist, a painter, will appreciate the beauty of the fruit.' I hear the rustling of a paper bag and, as I walk from behind the screen, I see the poet placing a small package on the table, next to the prints. As soon as he notices me, he tears a piece of the paper from the package, places a handful of cherries in it and offers them to me.

'Here you are, mademoiselle. They are as fresh as you.' He bows. I thank him. I am aware of Monsieur Manet watching us closely.

'The skirt is wrong, and so is the blouse, even worse than before.' Monsieur Manet walks towards the clothes stand.

While he is assessing what is available, I look at the sketches. There are at least twenty of them. Anyone could tell that they have been executed with a fast and assured hand, in as few lines as are necessary. The images are clear.

Charles comes to stand next to me and we look at the drawings in silence. In one of the drawings, my face is dominated by two, almost parallel, vertical lines on each side of my nose. With nothing above my eyes, these two lines are like eyebrows that have fallen down, to stand vertically, instead of lying horizontally. They must be the shadows on the sides of my nose. The effect is unusual and makes my eyes appear more prominent. I hear Monsieur Manet's voice: 'Here, mademoiselle. May I ask you to put this on?' He hands me a wide skirt and a matching jacket. I go behind the screen, realizing that the paper with the cherries is still in my hand. I change my clothes quickly and, when I am ready, I pick up the cherries and emerge with them nestling in the palm of my hand.

147

Monsieur Manet comments straightaway: 'That is much better. Only the black toque is missing, mademoiselle, and the guitar, of course.'

I fix the toque on my head and pick up the guitar.

Monsieur Manet says: 'Please, do not eat the cherries, mademoiselle. Not yet.'

I have no time to tell him that I wasn't going to, anyway. I wanted to offer them to him, but I decide not to.

He continues: 'There will be time for that. But do tell me, mademoiselle, what do they smell like?'

Like an obedient child, I pick up two cherries linked by a stalk and place them under my nose.

Monsieur Manet shouts: 'Hold it, hold it, mademoiselle. Do not move.'

I freeze.

He drags over the easel with the canvas so that I am right in front of him and he begins to work. I imagine that, on such a large canvas, my figure will be life-size. We don't have a break for two hours. Finally, it is Charles who reminds Monsieur Manet that if he doesn't stop, 'mademoiselle will turn into stone. She is already like a sculpture.' He pauses. 'Oh, but that could be because she is so attractive.'

At first, Monsieur Manet looks blankly at his friend. Charles decides to speak plainly: 'Edouard, it is time to finish for the day. Mademoiselle must be tired. And if that is not enough, then I have to remind you that I am taking you out.'

Monsieur Manet looks at Charles, smiles and puts down the palette. The maulstick hits the floor and rolls away. While cleaning the brushes, he turns towards me and says: 'Thank you, mademoiselle. We have made a good start. Can we continue at ten tomorrow?'

I nod. I cannot refuse him anything. This is the first time that he seems happy with the picture from the beginning.

* * *

148

At Maître Albert, I peep inside the large iron doors to check if Madame Conchis is in. I know that around six o'clock she leaves to take food from a nearby café to an elderly friend of hers. I wait for her to go out before I sneak in. I am embarrassed about the rent being two weeks overdue. Etienne owes me money but, once again, I need to collect it from his flat. I have not had time to do that. He is still working on the copy of Giorgione. I'll visit him early tomorrow morning.

It is dark outside. I drink a glass of wine and eat some bread and cheese. Every Sunday Lola brings some leftovers from her employers. I still have the two apples that she left a few days ago. I'll have one in the morning, with bread and coffee.

I sit down and look at the sheet with my monthly expenses:

20 francs for the rooms
30 francs for food
8 francs for canvases, brushes and colours
10 francs – laundry and gas
10 francs for small necessities and travel

Total: 78 francs

I receive 10 francs for each small canvas from Etienne; I would need eight of those to cover my basic needs. With all the modelling for Monsieur Manet, I haven't had time to do more than five a month. Last month I pawned a ring that my grandmother had left me. I have fixed the pink ticket from the pawn shop next to the door to remind me of the need to reclaim it. For now, while I am behind with the rent, I have no hope of doing that.

I stare at the expenses. I could spend less on food. Three sous worth of cheese and one sou worth of bread make a substantial meal, particularly if I can accompany it with a glass of red wine. On occasion, I have wasted money on cooked meals, having lunches of soup, beef and bread for eighteen sous and dinners for twenty sous. Of course, I never had both on the same day. But the way things stand now, I should stop all cooked meals.

I light a gas lamp and work on a flower bouquet in a vase, similar to the ones that I have already made for Etienne. He says they are popular with the English. I am tired and paint slowly. I fall asleep. When I wake up, my head is resting on the easel, with one lock of my hair lying across the unfinished and still wet painting.

21

It's dark outside when I wake up but I can't go back to sleep. I watch the dawn break, then dress quickly. I tiptoe towards the main staircase, making sure that I am as quiet as possible. If Madame Conchis is in, she is bound to see me through the little window that overlooks the back courtyard. I am lucky; I pass by her office and no one calls me. Carefully, I close the large iron doors behind me and make my way down Maître Albert. Apart from two men pushing a vegetable cart, and a beggar sleeping on the pavement in front of the baker's, no one else is in sight.

Half the way down the road, after I have long passed the café where Lola sometimes buys our food, I hear Madame Conchis: 'Mademoiselle Victorine, wait, wait, it's important. I need to talk to you.'

I watch as her corpulent body rolls down the street towards me. Despite making an effort to run, she moves slowly and that gives me time to prepare. I wish I could think of something different from what I said last week and the week before. When she finally reaches me, she is out of breath and waves her hand in front of her mouth.

'Madame, I am very sorry to be late once again but I promise, you'll have the money tonight. I am on my way to collect it from someone who owes it to me.'

She looks at me and nods. 'There is something else, as well, mademoiselle. That is why I ran after you.' She looks serious and I am anxious that the landlord might have had enough of me being late with the rent. Madame Conchis searches her pockets. She doesn't seem to find what she is looking for and sighs. She stops for a minute, lowers her eyes and thinks. Then she pushes her hand inside her blouse and extracts a piece of paper from her bosom. 'I was worried I might have lost it. The man pleaded with me to make sure to hand it over to you. He said it was important. There, mademoiselle.'

As Madame Conchis walks away, I look at a small scrap of paper that has been folded several times. Emile left the note last night. Marie is not well. She has been asking for me. Recently, I have been too busy with modelling to see her.

I arrive at Etienne's and, despite my knocking, there is no answer. This means I'll have to return tonight, straight from Monsieur Manet's studio and, if Etienne is not in then, I'll have to wait until he turns up. And if he doesn't, I'll have to get the money another way. I am afraid to break yet another promise.

Over the past few weeks, I have wondered whether there was anything I could pawn. There is still the guitar, but I am reluctant to part with it as it may be the only way I can earn some money quickly. The only other thing I have is the parcel of lace from my grandmother. As a young woman, orphaned at the age of ten, she worked in a kitchen and the garden of a nunnery. The nuns liked her and taught her to read. When she was leaving to get married, the nuns gave her the lace. They had been making lace for centuries, selling it to rich women in the area. Grandma never used it. She said that she had no need for a smart dress. Sometimes, she would lift the lid of the chest by the bed, where she kept blankets and sheets, and take out a small parcel. She would unwrap it carefully and show me the lace. If my hands were clean, I was allowed to touch it.

'I am keeping it for your wedding dress,' she said one day when we were looking at it. I was pleased that such a beautiful thing would be mine one day. But, even at the age of eight, the idea of my wedding did not excite me. It would make me think of Madame Pascal. I always remembered that her husband had said that she painted only because she wasn't a real woman. I had no idea what that meant. But I wanted to paint and be like her. Nevertheless, I am reluctant to part with the lace.

I slowly make my way downstairs and it's only when I reach the ground floor landing, that I hear a voice calling me. I look up.

Etienne is leaning over the banister on the top flight. I climb the stairs.

He owes me one hundred and ten francs but can give me only ninety today. That should cover the rent I owe, a loan from Lola, the credit from the café where I get my lunches and dinner, and leave me with ten francs for food, transport and the paints I need to replace. I have never been able to buy paints in tubes, and this month won't be any different. A tube costs a franc whereas, for a few sous, I can buy powder and mix it myself. I would also like to buy a couple of new brushes and reclaim grandmother's ring from the pawnbroker, but all of that will have to wait until Etienne pays me the remaining money.

I make my way up to the Batignolles and to rue des Arbes. Emile's mother lets me in. She is a dumpy woman with a heavily lined face. As she takes me to the room at the back where the young couple live, she doesn't speak. Marie is lying in bed, propped up with cushions. Her face is pale and she smiles faintly when she sees me. She has lost her baby and has been bleeding for several days. I ask whether a doctor has been around. She shakes her head.

'There is no need,' she whispers. 'They cost a lot of money. Emile has none.' I sit with Marie for twenty minutes and hold her hand. I can barely hear her breathing; it's so low. She dozes off and then wakes up with a start. Her voice is faint and words come out slowly, with long pauses in between.

On the way out, I make Emile's mother promise me that she'll call a doctor. I wish I had time to stay and wait for him. I leave fifty francs with her and rush to rue Guyot.

Monsieur Manet opens the door without a smile or a greeting. Once I am in, he says: 'You do not take our work seriously.'

'I am sorry to be late; I have had some problems.' He walks away and I am not sure he hears me.

'The clothes are over there,' he points towards the screen. 'The cherries have shrivelled. I'll ask Madame Bijoux to buy some fresh ones for tomorrow. Today, we can use just the wrapping. I do not wish to look at the shrivelled fruit. It spoils the effect.'

153

I dress quickly and take my position on the podium, with the guitar in one hand and the paper wrapping in the other. I start by thinking of the particular moment when a street singer emerges from a smoky café. She is carrying a handful of cherries in a paper wrapping that she might have bought herself, or perhaps someone might have just given them to her in the café. As she walks through the door, she presses a couple of cherries to her mouth. The fruit, I imagine, smell fresh and their smooth, red skin feels sensual to the street singer's lips. The touch of the cherries is like a kiss. I try to hold the expression on my face, but my mind wonders back to Marie. I see her pale face and smell the sweat on her brow. I'll go to see her tomorrow.

I watch Monsieur Manet as he works, deep in concentration, both when looking at me and when applying the paint to the canvas. I notice the passion in his eyes and in the movements of his hand. He is completely absorbed, as if nothing else existed. I envy his ability to focus. Without the anger on his face, he is an attractive man.

One hour into our session, he wipes the brushes with a cloth, puts them down and walks away from the easel. The maulstick falls down. I watch as it rolls away, stopping by a leg of a chair.

'I need to fetch something,' he says softly. 'You can relax but, please, stay where you are.'

As Monsieur Manet disappears to the galleried room, I pick up the maulstick and place it next to the brushes on a small table by the easel. A few minutes later, he comes back, carrying three very different hats. He pulls a chair next to me and places them on the seat. Standing right in front of me, he lifts off my black toque very gently, using both hands. I don't move. He is taller than me: his eyes are at the level of the top of my head. I am very conscious of my breath. His breath smells of coffee.

He picks up one of the three hats from the chair and, holding it with both hands, slowly lowers it onto my head. Without taking his eyes off me, he takes two steps back and looks at me for a long time. His gaze penetrates my skin. A wave of heat rises through my body. I have to force myself to stay still and to keep looking at him. He repeats the process with the second and with the third hat. His movements are slow and measured and he does not say a word. I wish I knew what he is thinking. It comforts me to see that there is no trace of the previous tension on his face. I count the golden strands in his beard. The hair on his head is the same colour as mine. Did they call him the devil at school?

Conscious of the rhythm of my breathing, I stand completely still, waiting for him to tell me what he is doing. At one point, just as his hands are lowering the second hat on my head, and the tip of his nose brushes against the tip of my nose, I wonder whether I should put my arms around his neck and kiss him. His cheeks are rosy and I feel their warmth on my skin. But I am afraid to move, lest I interrupt the calm that exists between us now.

Eventually, he speaks: 'I was not happy with the toque, Mademoiselle. The *faluche* suits you much better.' He hands it over to me.

I stand in front of a mirror. The overall effect is very different from before. However, I am not sure that this is the right look. Compared with the women I have seen play music in cafés, I appear too sophisticated. Besides, I've only ever seen *faluches* on male students, never on café singers.

Monsieur Manet returns to the easel and I hear him scrape off bits of paint with a palette knife. When he finishes, he looks at me for a long time and then resumes painting. The movements of his brush are faster than before.

When we finish for the day, he rushes upstairs to the room in the gallery. While I am changing my clothes, I remember that I haven't enough money for the rent. I don't like to ask Monsieur Manet for money. I don't want him to think that I am poor but I feel that I no longer have a choice. A voice inside me says: 'Come out with it. Come out with it, quickly. Get it over and done with.' Once I am dressed, I stand at the bottom of the stairs and call out:

'Monsieur Manet, I have a favour to ask of you.' I remember the first time I heard Charles use the same words, for the same purpose as mine. Unlike me, he didn't seem embarrassed. These days, he borrows money regularly and says simply: 'Edouard, how about a little loan? I am particularly short this week.'

Monsieur Manet stands at the top of the stairs and looks down at me. There is no trace of a smile on his face, although his eyes don't have that penetrating look that I see so often when he paints.

'I am owed some money, monsieur. Until it comes, I am having difficulties with paying the rent. I wonder, monsieur, whether, you could lend me twenty francs?' There, I have said it. The words come out like a spurt. It's all over and now nothing worse can happen.

Monsieur Manet nods and walks downstairs. His face softens. From his trouser pocket, he pulls out a wad of half crumpled notes. I am glad he acts so quickly without asking any questions.

'I'll be happy to help, mademoiselle,' he says, handing me the money.

'Thank you, monsieur,' I say, 'I'll return every sou.'

'Do not worry, mademoiselle. Whatever and whenever. It is not important.' After a pause, he turns towards me and says: 'Now, can you be here at ten o'clock tomorrow?' I nod and see myself out.

At Maître Albert I count the money. Monsieur Manet has given me one hundred and eighty six francs.

22

I open the door and she stands in front of me. Her face is blank and expressionless, as if she has walked out of the portrait I made of her. The eyes, brown and piercing, stare at me. I am reminded of the day I first saw her.

I say I would like her to help me develop an idea and she obliges without asking any questions. The series of quick transformations she can enact with her body, and with her face, fascinates me. She has this incredible gift to change from one role to another almost effortlessly. Sometime I wonder what happens at the core of her, whatever that is. Who is she herself? But, for my purpose now, that is of no importance. Every now and then, I tell myself that her life outside this studio should not interest me.

With this picture, I think I would like to capture the moment, the instant of life on a Parisian street in the same way that Nadar does with his camera. He can freeze the movement and that passing moment of our modern life.

As she goes out and comes back in, I sketch quickly. Just before I stop her, I notice that she has gradually unbuttoned her blouse and that her movements are increasingly flirtatious. She is playing different roles. However, I know I have to be careful, in case she goes too far and creates a situation that turns difficult.

It is clear that the clothes she is wearing are wrong for the role. They are too tight and too dark. I find replacements in my basket. While she undresses, I busy myself with the prints on the table by the long wall. Recently, she has developed the habit of taking off her clothes in my presence. I have mentioned the screen over there a few times but she seems to ignore me. Now

I think it is best not to say anything, instead of drawing attention to what she is doing.

When I glance in her direction, she is removing her clothes very slowly, as if she were in front of an audience. After removing each item, she folds it carefully and places it on the chair. It is a slow moving performance. Surreptitiously, I watch her remove one of her stockings and, as she lifts her skirt, for the first time I see her white thigh. The skin on the inside is almost transparent and I have to suppress a desire to walk over to her to touch it. As a painter, I have an instinctive wish to run my hand on that velvety softness. I have to tell myself not to give in. Another voice tells me that I need to experience it if I am ever to paint it. I lower my head and bend over the table, pretending that I am not aware of her nakedness. I hear her soft footsteps. Her feet must be bare.

When I next look up, she stands in front of me, wearing nothing but a slip. One of the straps has fallen off her shoulder and I can see most of her bosom. Her breasts are small and firm. As she bends, I glimpse her right nipple. It is much bigger than what I would expect to see on a breast of that size. There is no dark aureole. I am a painter; it is not surprising that I am interested in form and shape. It is beauty that excites me.

We look at each other. Her shoulders tremble. I stop breathing. It is just us here and now. Nothing else matters. I want her. Slowly, I reach towards her but before my fingers can touch her skin, just above her left breast, someone knocks on the door. Neither of us moves. My hand remains suspended in the air, lost in the space half way between her and me. The knocking continues. A feeling of irritation rises inside me. The spell is broken.

I hear Charles' voice calling my name. I walk away from the table and away from her, collect the clothes I want her to try on and throw them over the screen. We neither speak nor do our eyes meet. While she disappears behind the screen, I open the door.

Charles wears a rigid smile as he teases me. His voice is strained and the ebullience of his manner forced. He looks tired and older than usual. My friend is a sick and worried man. To hell with my thoughts of pleasure. Here is death.

I am reminded of the occasion, fairly recently, when he first told me about the symptoms of his illness. Until then, he had only spoken of Jeanne's ailments.

'It is no surprise,' he joked. 'Since several of the ladies I am acquainted with have it; it would be a miracle if I had not picked it up.'

I said it could be arthritis, or rheumatism. The symptoms are similar. I could see it with my father. I suppose I was trying to comfort myself as much as him.

Charles laughed as he dismissed my words: 'Edouard you are a young man. You are full of life and hope. I used to be like that. But it is being full of life and desire that brings this perniciousness. Love of women is the death of us.'

When Victorine emerges from behind the screen, the clothes are still wrong. This time it is the colour, not the cut, that I need to change. I let her wear them for a while, just to make sure that my feeling is right.

Victorine tries on another costume and immediately I know that it is the right one. I am lucky to find it in my collection. The piping on the pelisse is particularly suitable for the overall effect. I ask her to turn around: the swirl of the flowing skirt will help convey the movement. I watch her as she swings around again and again. At the last turn, I notice that the movement lifts the hem of the skirt and shows her petticoat. It is visible only for an instant but, during that instant, the lifted hem and its patch of white make it clear to me: the detail looks accidental as if it were frozen in time. I want to create a modern painting that captures the moment, that is, the split second when the street singer emerges from the café into the street, that moment when she is in between the two worlds: one in front of her and the other behind.

Charles stands to the side, watching us for a while. At one point, he walks towards her and while I am sketching, I hear him say: 'Mademoiselle, I would like you to have these. They are the first of the season. As fresh as you.' He kisses her right hand.

Despite the illness, Charles is an old charmer and a flirt. I look up. He bows and hands her a paper bag full of cherries. She takes the bag in her left hand and with the right one picks two cherries, held together by a stalk, and puts them close to her lips. I find myself shouting at her, asking her not to move. She obeys; Charles jumps away, startled. I want both her hands to be occupied, one holding a guitar and a paper bag, the other, lifting cherries up to her mouth. Dear, dear Charles, his gift of cherries is just perfect.

I do not want her to eat them, only to smell them. I shall love to work on their dark red glossiness, a brilliant complement to the brownish red of the polished wood on the side of the guitar.

23

I abandoned the toque. I was not happy with it from the start. It made her seem too formal for a street singer. At night, I would wake up and think about it. It worried me that she looked too much like herself: the face was almost a repeat of *Le portrait*. Charles thinks that picture represents a model who has no role to play. But in this canvas, I wanted her to have a role.

One morning, just before she arrived, I experimented with different hats. I drew her face and then cut out five different hats. I placed the cuts-outs on the picture and more or less decided in favour of a bohemian look. When she arrived, I had to test the correctness of my decision. As always, she was patient. These days, she no longer bothers me with silly questions. She waited for me to tell her what I was doing. The *faluche* is perfect. Now she has style and class without the bourgeois trappings.

We worked solidly for two weeks, every day from ten until four or five. Madame Bijoux would bring in a light lunch, usually some bread, ham and cheese. We had a glass of wine. Often, I would excuse myself and ate upstairs, saying that I had a letter to write or some other business to attend to.

The other day, after she left in the late afternoon, I began to sketch the background. I painted the swinging doors of the café and now all I need is a glimpse of the scene inside, perhaps with a man drinking and peering after the street singer. Now, as I am outlining the small figure of a customer, I have the feeling that it does not seem right. I decide that I do not wish to create a story in the picture. It is simply an instant I have captured. The viewer does not need to know anything else beyond what is visible. Better to go for a shape and colour that will complement the figure. I try out different objects for the background. Then I remember young Jacques at Tortoni's. He always wears a white jacket. It will be the same colour as the petticoat. Yes, I shall have a waiter in the background.

I think back to one afternoon when Antoine and I were walking along the Avenue de Clichy, and a door swung open right in front of us. A woman came out, holding a guitar. We stopped talking, both of us stunned by the sight. I ran after her and asked her to pose for me, but she laughed loudly and walked off. I was not much bothered, anyway. I knew I could ask Victorine.

I stand back to look at the painting. I can already hear the critics and the silver heads at the Beaux-Arts saying that I have not finished it or that everything is too flat, or that there are strange shadows on the sides of her nose.

What is the point of painting anything if it does not make us see the world with new eyes?

If the critics complain, I shall tell them: I paint what I see and not what it pleases others to see. I paint what is there and not what they expect to see. In this case, I painted what I saw, even though it was only there for an instant.

24

Marie is dead. I am sitting on the divan, holding a scrap of paper in my hand. It's a note from Emile. The paper wasn't folded and when I opened the door, I stepped on it. The mark left by the sole of my shoe looks like an official stamp, sealing the end of a life, certifying the poverty and ugliness of a life that could have been different.

She died yesterday, three days after I had visited her. I stare at the note, incredulous that the words have a reality elsewhere. That elsewhere is where Marie lies, her cold body contained in a simple coffin. Will I really never see her again?

In the past year, I haven't had much time for her, but it was good to know that she was in the city and to think that one day, we could be close again. She was part of my past and of who I am. Apart from my grandmother, she was the only other person who knew my secrets and who loved me. Now, there is no one. Her death is also a death of a part of me.

She didn't complain about her new life and family. But I don't think she was happy. Marriage was something she yearned for and I was glad that she achieved it. There was nothing else that she really wanted.

I can't face even the faint light of my gas lamp. I sit in the dark, thinking of the time we spent together. I regret that I never brought her here and showed her my new life. Perhaps it might have made her look at her own circumstances more critically. But I doubt it; Marie was not ambitious. Once I suggested that I should show her where I live, but she said she had to rush back to her family. She was already spending all her time with Emile and besides, she never had much interest in my drawings. After she started sleeping with Emile, she never kissed me again or took me to bed. I missed her then.

I remember the day when I told her that she shouldn't model for Emile if he didn't pay her. She raised her eyes towards me and I could see anger in them. We had just returned from an evening in a café in Montmartre and were standing by her front door.

'He loves me,' she said looking down. When I asked how she could know that, she said: 'I can tell. And as for paying me, money isn't everything.' She stared at me, her face red and her voice raised. 'What do I get from you, anyway? You never pay me for sitting for you.' I looked away. She insisted that I respond: 'Tell me, Victorine. Emile loves me. He says so. Why shouldn't I believe him? What about you? What do I get from you? You have never said that you love me.'

I thought of saying that I had given her pleasure but knew that it would not be enough. She wanted me to say that I loved her. I was sure about my love for painting. I still am. For all I remember, I might have loved her once. But had I said that I loved her, she would have wanted to see me every day. And she would have wanted to do things that she liked, such as going dancing, taking a train to the seaside or hiring a boat in the countryside.

Before she went in, she looked at me and I could see sadness on her face. She lowered her eyes and said softly: 'Victorine, why won't you answer my question? Why haven't you ever said that you love me?'

Would she had married Emile if I had spoken? She might not have become pregnant. She might have been alive today.

After that, I didn't see her for a few weeks. When we eventually met on the staircase at the Hotel d'Or, she seemed happy to see me and said that, in a few days' time, she was moving in with Emile. I meant it when I said that I was pleased for her. She stared at me then, squeezed my hand and said: 'Are you really? You don't mind?'

'How could I mind?'

She looked down. 'I thought you might miss me.' It sounded like a reproach.

'I'm too busy.' Marie put her hand on my arm. 'I need time to

164

paint.' I turned and walked away. I couldn't face her asking me again to tell her that I loved her.

We did meet a few times after she had moved. Sometimes, I went to Emile's or she would wait for me to finish my shift at the café. But since I started going to Monsieur Manet's studio, I had no time to see her.

Had we been seeing each other, I might have prevented her bleeding to death. I might have even been with her when she lost her baby. I know I'd have called for a doctor straight away, rather than wait until it was too late. If need be, I would have stolen the money.

She was a year younger than me and shorter. But she was strong. The first time she stopped other children calling me the devil, I was surprised that they listened to her. I asked her about it. She said she had watched her cat and learned from her: 'Whenever mother has a customer who is afraid of cats, Jujene tries to jump on them. The other day a woman was trying on a dress. Mother pinned it all around and yet the cat wouldn't leave the woman alone. But if a customer isn't afraid of cats, Jujene takes no notice of them. You see, those children are like that. They know you are afraid of them. So am I. But I pretend that I'm not.'

I remembered Marie's words many years later in the café when men were rude to me. I stopped being coy and I answered back. Of course, I can't do that with Monsieur Manet. He makes me so aware that I come from a different place.

I lie down, thinking of the days when Marie and I played outside the Hotel d' Or. The first time I saw her, only a few days after I had arrived in Paris, I was standing outside the door to the building, and waiting for my mother to return from the laundry. Marie walked up to me and said: 'You must be Victorine. I am Marie.'

'How do you know my name?'

'My mother knows your mother. My mother told me your name and said that you had red hair, as red as fire. Not many people do.'

Marie's mother may still be living at the Hotel d' Or. I wonder

165

if mine does. I dare not go to see her. I'll try to save some money and send it to her.

Before I fall asleep, I think of Marie lying dead and cold, small and pale, silent. I wonder if Emile could let me have a picture of her. I'll see him tomorrow at the funeral.

25

I am going to Etienne's apartment to pick up the money I am owed and to collect three new canvases for the pictures he wants me to paint. He has completed the copy of *Le Concert Champêtre*, but we cannot meet at the café, as he is unwell.

On my way out, Madame Conchis hands me a small package, which arrived last night. I take it upstairs. I recognise Emile's handwriting. Inside, there is a note from him, a small red chalk drawing that he made of Marie soon after they were married and the fifty francs that he is returning to me. He writes that the doctor they called would not take any money, as he couldn't help.

I hold the wad of notes in my hand. If Marie had had these few pieces of paper at the time of her miscarriage, her life might have been saved.

I pin the drawing on the wall by my bedside. Later on, I will look for a suitable frame; I know I have some old ones somewhere. Marie looks pretty in the picture. Her long, black hair is tied back and her eyes are bigger than I remember them. She is looking somewhere into the distance. I recognise the dress she is wearing. It had a neat little collar in a lighter shade of blue than the rest of the fabric. When I spoke to Emile after the funeral, he said he would try to find something that I could keep as a memento. He added that Marie had told him that I was her best friend. In the past, I had often wondered whether he was aware that we had held each other naked in bed. At the funeral, I looked at him, hunched in his grief, and thought that it was no longer important if he knows or not.

As I throw away the wrapping paper, a tiny cloth bag falls out. It makes a clinking noise as it hits the floor. Inside, there is a pair of earrings and a note: 'Marie wanted you to have these. She said so on the day that she died.'

I hold the small pieces of gold in the palm of my hand. It feels strange to have them here with me, when Marie is so far away. I remember touching the earrings when we were children and later kissing them when we lay in bed together. They were given to her as a confirmation present when she was ten. I was never confirmed. Grandma felt sorry that I had been left out, but mother said that the whole ceremony was invented to make money for the priests.

Grandma saw me looking at the girls' white dresses and tried to console me: 'It is a silly business, Victorine. Little girls going around as if they were brides. Just you wait: when the day of your wedding comes, I'll make the best wedding dress anyone has ever had in this village.'

I walk downstairs and decide that I'll post the money to my mother.

When I arrive, Etienne is in an exuberant mood. He has received the full payment for the Giorgione copy and miraculously, he tells me, the sight of the money has made him feel better. His throat ache has gone. The American customer has only just left.

'You must have met him on the stairs, Victorine. Had you come just a minute earlier, I could have introduced you. He is rich, a useful man to know. He is off to Boston with my painting but he'll be back.'

Etienne hasn't had a chance to show off in front of anyone else. Proudly, he tells me how much he has received: one thousand, three hundred and fifty francs. He spreads the notes on the table in front of me.

'Look, Victorine, I've never had so much money. If I live frugally, I have enough to last me for a year, even without doing anything else,' he says. I nod and smile. I've never seen so much money.

'Victorine, how silly of me. I've almost forgotten. I need to give you what I owe you.' Etienne counts the money and adds another thirty francs as a special thank you for helping him out. I say it's kind of him but that there is no need for any extras.

'Just a little bonus, that's all. Come on, Victorine, don't turn down good money.' He hugs me. 'Actually, Victorine, I'm taking you out. We need to celebrate. I'll buy you a good lunch, the best you've ever had.'

I am not sure what to say. I am thinking of Marie, cold and small, lying in her grave.

'And over lunch, we can talk about future work. The English market is booming. I can get enough orders for both of us.' I hope so. Monsieur Manet is working on several pictures for which he doesn't need to see me. Now that I have more time, I need to resume my own painting as well as earn some money. Producing pictures for Etienne is lonely, but it pays much better than working in the café. And besides, he gives me paints and brushes that I can use for other paintings.

'Let's go, Victorine.' He puts on a coat and takes me by the hand.

Etienne wants to sit outdoors at a small café on the Champs-Elysées, not far from the Exposition Universale, where the Salon is held. I'd have much rather walked to a more modest place nearby and had something simpler, but I understand when he says: 'Today I am happy and want to do nothing except watch the world go by.'

As soon as we walk out, Etienne looks for a fiacre. Two pass by but he doesn't stop them. After two more, I suggest that we take an omnibus, but he insists that we find a proper fiacre. I don't understand what was wrong with the ones that he ignored.

'Just wait, Victorine,' he says. 'I'll show you what I mean.' Another five minutes pass and we spot two fiacres riding in our direction. Etienne hails the second one.

'The one in front is no good. Can you see what I was after, Victorine?' The only difference is that our fiacre has a white horse. The others were brown. Most of the horses pulling fiacres are brown. 'I wanted to have something special for today.' He laughs.

By the time we reach the café, the sun has disappeared and there is a slight drizzle. We sit inside, by a window, and I let him choose the food. I say I am not very hungry. Etienne frowns.

'Come on, Victorine, make it a day for me.'

I smile. I know I can't mention Marie. After all, he has been good to me and I hope that he will continue to be useful.

We start with oxtail soup. I force myself to eat. The heavy smell rising from the bowl makes me nauseous. When they bring us skate in brown butter sauce, and then fillet of beef with mushrooms, I can eat only a little of each dish and I leave more than half on the plate. Etienne mops all the sauces with chunks of bread. Next, he has ravioli *l'italienne* and then asks for hazel hens from Russia. He has heard that they are a special delicacy. I've never seen anyone eat so much food in one meal.

What would my mother and her neighbours at the Hotel d'Or say if they saw this feast? After a short pause, Etienne orders a truffle salad. I say that I would prefer to draw all this food, rather than eat it. Etienne laughs and calls me silly.

'We've done enough painting, Victorine. It's hard work. Now we must eat and enjoy ourselves' As he leans towards me to kiss me on the cheek, I notice an unshaved hair sticking out from his chin and pull away. Every now and then, he grabs hold of my hand. I keep thinking of Marie and have no energy to resist. By the time a dessert arrives, he is speaking very quickly and I can see that the wine is affecting him. His voice is louder than usual and he gesticulates exuberantly. His mood and behaviour make me feel even more subdued, but I try not to show it.

When they serve us praline ice-cream, fruit and pastries, Etienne wipes his mouth with the back of his hand, smacks his lips and says: 'I was thinking, Victorine, we waste a great deal of time meeting in that café near Notre-Dame and fetching empty canvases or finished pictures. Then you have to come to my flat to collect the money. What a waste! It would be much simpler if you worked in my flat. You would have all the material there.'

I look at him, pretending that I am taking his words seriously and don't interrupt. I can see that this is only a prologue for what he wants to say.

'In fact, I was thinking that it would be much simpler for both of us if you lived with me in my flat.'

His words don't come as a surprise. I have an answer prepared: 'I think it's a good idea, Etienne,' I lie 'but, I like to do my own work. I would like to do a painting that I've thought of for some time, a painting that is neither a copy, nor flowers in a vase and –'

'Victorine, Victorine,' Etienne interrupts me, 'you don't understand, I want you to marry me.'

I lower my eyes. What can I say without spoiling the day for him or losing the orders for the flower pictures?

Even if I had ever wanted to be married, Marie's life with her husband and her death would have made me think differently. But if I knew someone who was a good painter, someone like Monsieur Manet – for I know he'll be a great painter – I'd accept his proposal. Etienne is a better painter than I am, but only because he has had more time to develop his technique and because he has had proper training. He isn't good enough to teach me; there isn't much I can learn from him. There is no point marrying someone like that. Within days, he would expect me to cook and wash for him.

Etienne puts his hand on mine and leans towards me.

'Wouldn't you like to have a man, Victorine?'

What can I say but lie? 'Yes, of course I would, Etienne. But…but…I need some time to get used to the idea of being married.' That's not what I wanted to say.

'So it's yes, Victorine, is it not? Say! Tell me it's yes!' He puts his arms around me and kisses me.

I think of a lie: 'Etienne, I have debts. I owe money. And I am helping my mother. I need to work so that I can repay them. I can't get married until I have cleared my debts.'

'Of course, Victorine. I'll give you some time.'

I nod.

'And I can give you more work to help. Or, even better, look. I have money now. How much do you owe? How much do you need to help your mother?'

'No, I can't do that, Etienne. Just give me a bit of time.' Perhaps I've had too much wine. I keep saying things I don't want to say.

'Three months?'

'A bit longer. Six, at least.'

'It's a long time. But I'll wait. I've lived without love so long; I can last a few more months.' He lowers his eyes. When he looks at me again, he is smiling. He places his hand on mine. 'When I first saw you at that café, something in me turned and I wanted you. You see, I loved a woman once, but she told me that I was ugly. You want me to wait but at least you don't think I am ugly.' He stares at me.

'No.'

Etienne wants to go home with me but I say that I am not feeling well after so much food – which is not far from the truth – and that I need to lie down. We agree to meet in three days' time. Etienne will bring me new canvases for the next order. He says he hopes it'll be the last time that we have to meet at the café. I nod. I know I am in trouble but right now I can't think clearly.

* * *

At home, I look at my face in the mirror. I am wearing Marie's gold earrings. They don't stand out against my red hair; I remember the gold sparkling when surrounded by Marie's long, black locks. The earrings and the drawing, and some of my old sketches, are all that I have left of Marie. Emile must have more drawings and some oils. Other artists she had modelled for before she met Emile may also have pictures of her. But there is nothing left of Marie that she made with her own hands and that others would like to see. That is how it is with most people.

Some women leave children that remember them. Even my grandmother, although a peasant woman, left something to remind the world of her: I still have two ribbons that she wove especially for me, one of them in what Monsieur Manet calls cobalt blue, with golden threads.

Standing in front of the mirror, I catch a sight of the biggest canvas I've ever owned. It's leaning against the wall behind me, and waiting to be made into a picture. For the past two weeks, I've had a clear idea of what I want to paint on it. However, its size frightens me. It'll take me a long time to turn the canvas into the picture that is in my mind.

Here, looking at myself wearing Marie's earrings, with my image as the only witness, I promise myself never to marry anyone, not even if he is a good painter.

I light a gas lamp and begin to prepare the large canvas. I'll start painting tomorrow.

26

Lola notices them as soon as I open the door, but chooses not to comment. Immediately, I see that her large eyes narrow and two fine, vertical lines appear between her eyebrows. Nevertheless, she is still smiling.

I smell rain on her pellise. Today is one of the rare Sundays when she doesn't arrive dressed in her brother's clothes. She stands in front of me and, as she has done many times before, takes my head in her hands, as if I were her child, and kisses me. She is taller than me and has to bend to kiss the top of my head. I understand that this ritual suggests to both of us that she is in charge of what follows. I don't mind at all; I only care to be in charge when she sits for me.

As always, we lie down and make love. She is rougher than usual and doesn't say very much. I can see that she has something on her mind. I know what it is, but I don't want to waste time by talking about it. I want to ask her to pose for one of the figures in the painting on the large canvas. I almost scream when she pushes her fingers inside me and moves them around, without paying attention to how I feel. I am dry but I don't complain. Later on, as she lowers herself on top of me, her large breasts smothering my own, she notices the picture of Marie pinned to the wall next to my bed. I catch the instant when her eyes land on the drawing. Her face tightens, the eyes grow smaller and a wave of heat emanates from her face. She stops moving and sits up. I know she will speak this time. I wait. She turns to look at me. Her voice is loud: 'Who is she?' Fire surges from her eyes and burns me. I can't pretend that I don't understand the question.

'A friend I used to know.' I try to sound casual but I keep my eyes on her. I haven't done anything wrong.

'Used to? You've never mentioned her before.'

'There was no need to talk about her.'

'So what is this picture doing here?' Lola gives me a piercing look. 'Has she come back? What does she want from you?'

I don't feel I want to talk about Marie to someone who didn't know her. I don't answer. Lola has more questions: 'What is she like? When did you draw her? Victorine, it hurts that you have never pinned a picture of me by your bedside and now suddenly this woman comes out of nowhere and you make her drawing and put it where you can see it before you sleep. I bet you have drawn pictures of her naked as well.' I keep quiet. 'You have, haven't you?'

It's true that I have not stuck Lola's picture by my bedside, but there are dozens of drawings of her scattered all around my room. As I expect, my silence makes Lola even angrier.

'She gave you the earrings, didn't she? You couldn't wait to put them on. As soon as I saw you today, I knew there was someone else.'

I keep quiet, which Lola interprets as a confession. She knows I have very little money and that the earrings must be a gift.

'You could have at least been discreet and taken them off when you knew I was coming. Instead, you deliberately placed this drawing by the bedside where I could not fail to see it.'

Lola stretches her arm towards it, as if to grab it, and I fear that she might tear it up. I jump in front of her and shield the picture. I take it off the wall and place it in a drawer of the table where I keep my art materials. Lola's eyes follow me as I move around the room. I didn't dare put it in the walnut chest by the bed.

We sit in silence, at the opposite ends of the divan. Both of us are naked. I decide not to dress, lest I upset her further by giving the impression that our lovemaking is over for today. I am conscious of time passing and of my need to work on the painting. Most importantly, I need Lola to model for me. Eventually, she speaks: 'I can't go on seeing you, Victorine, unless you tell me about the woman in the picture.'

She looks at me. I want to resolve the situation but I can't bring myself to talk about Marie. A few weeks ago, I wouldn't have minded. Now that Marie is dead, I want to keep that part of my life to myself. It's the same with the memories of my grandmother. I never talk to anyone about her.

'How long have you known her, Victorine? You must tell me that.'

'All I'll say is that you have no reason to feel jealous of her.' I know that I could also add that I can promise that I'll never see her again, or bring her here, but I don't think that Lola has the right to expect that from me. There are parts of my life where I don't want to give up my right to make my own decisions. I am fond of Lola, but not enough to lose sight of what matters to me. I don't wish to be tied down to anyone: a man or a woman. My thoughts are my own and that won't be changed. If she is jealous, that's her difficulty. I have to work on improving my painting, rather than spend time worrying about her.

'That's not enough, Victorine. You must tell me more.'

I ignore her.

'I've been so stupid, always waiting for you, never having any fun. You never want to do anything except draw and paint. But now I see that you have time for others. How many times have I suggested that we should go to Asnières, hire a boat and go rowing on the Seine, even swim in the river, have a picnic? I should have known. You don't want me.'

She starts putting on her clothes. I watch her. She dresses slowly, expecting me to stop her, and from time to time, flashes a fierce glance in my direction. Her face is tense and she is breathing fast. I don't want her to storm out in anger. The thought of losing her makes me sad. I know that a few words, a kiss or even a hand on her shoulder could make her change her mind, but something inside me prevents me. At the same time, I am glad that at least we are no longer sitting and waiting for one of us to move. I hate wasting time when I could be painting.

Within minutes, and without saying a word of goodbye, she walks out of my apartment. I rush after her. When she hears my footsteps, she quickens her pace. I stop. I look down from the top of the staircase. She isn't running any more; she listens for my next move. I open my mouth to call her name but my throat is too dry and no words cross my lips. I see her standing motionless three floors down, alert to my moves. As soon as I notice that she is about to look up, I step back. Slowly, I close the door and press my ear to its rough surface. I hear no footsteps. I walk to the window. Lola is standing on the pavement opposite. I hide behind a curtain. My heart beats fast. This is such a silly game to play.

I look at the large canvas. I have just lost a model. She was also a woman who loved me. I rush downstairs and as soon as I walk through the gate, I know I am too late.

I walk upstairs, moving slowly. The painting waits for me. Is there anyone else I could ask to sit for me? Etienne? My chest tightens at the thought of him. I know it would cause more trouble than it's worth. I can only hope that he was too drunk the other day to remember all that talk of marriage.

I spend the rest of the day drawing on the canvas. In the evening, I light the gas lamp and begin to sketch the figure of the woman. I pose for it myself. Outside, it's a warm July evening. I have the windows open. I take off my clothes and sit naked on the floor in front of a mirror. It is very difficult to draw with the shadow from the lamp, and even with a second lamp, I can never make sure that the entire body is fully lit. I hear voices of passers by strolling outside. A group of young people walks past singing loudly. I feel content to be alone and able to work. In the past, I have drawn nude torsos of Marie and of Lola, but this is the first time I have worked on a naked body with a head. As with Céleste, by necessity, my naked figure has to stare out of the canvas.

Before I go to bed, I have half a bottle of wine with bread and cheese. I fall asleep straight away.

27

Yesterday was ladies' day. Madame Lejosne arrived alone, just as I had finished sketching Madame Offenbach. As they have been attending the same soirées for some time, they are well acquainted and have consented to be placed next to each other in the picture. I did not need them to sit together for a long time, and as soon as Madame Offenbach's taxi arrived, I escorted her downstairs. The maid followed. Madame Lejosne was not happy with the colour of her dress. Rightly, she told me that Madame Offenbach's was much darker than her own, and that it would be better if I could show that on the picture. I understand that, as a fashionable woman, she does not like to be seen in the same dress as someone else.

However, as a painter, I need their two figures dressed alike so that the shapes merge. That way, they form a substantial and contrastingly lighter space in the painting. I want the eyes of the viewer to go straight to the light patch on the picture. I have placed the figures of the two women off centre, which makes the entire composition appear less artificial, as if the scene had been taken by an invisible photographer. I want it to be like a picture that Nadar could have taken.

I tried to be diplomatic with Madame Lejosne. I smiled and said: 'Madame, I would like the representatives of the fair sex to be at the centre of my painting. The light colour of your dress, especially when placed close to that of Madame Lejosne, will break the monotony created by the male multitude clothed in dark colours.'

She seemed to consider this point for a while before she said: 'In that case, I shall leave it to you, Monsieur.' I dared not tell her that I intend to use exactly the same colour for their bonnets. I have in mind the magical cobalt blue. There is no other colour like it to attract the eyes of the spectator.

For the rest of the sitting she looked suitably prim and there was little conversation.

I have placed the two women in front of Zachary, slightly to the side of him so that all three are visible. Working with him was most enjoyable. I realized how lucky I am to have such an intelligent and dear friend. He had the ability to keep his face frozen with the same expression throughout, regardless of what he was talking about. Of course, his comments were mostly about art. He said that he could see a direct link between what I have done with Signorina Valence and this picture. I was puzzled at first. I thought they were completely different. I thought of Velázquez and Goya when I was working on the dancer, but they are certainly not on my mind for this picture. Zachary said that he was referring to the brushstrokes. He said that they give the impression of the brush briefly touching the canvas, so that, when one stood close to the picture, one was presented with dabs of colour and it was only when one stood back that the picture emerged.

Later on, Zachary told me a joke about a critic who complained about an unfinished picture. While I laughed, he obliged by not moving a single muscle on his face. He is the first model I have worked with who can talk without distracting me.

Right behind the women, I have already painted the famous trio. Charles, Taylor and Gautier arrived together last Wednesday around ten o'clock. I had intended to place their separate portraits in different parts of the crowd, but each time I asked one of them to pose alone, the others kept distracting him with conversation. At one point I gave up and let them get on with their discussion about what constitutes art in our time. I neither listened to them nor did I make any attempt to contribute and they ignored me, as if I were invisible. I knew that I should be a painter who, rather like Nadar's camera, records what he sees without putting his own personality into the picture.

On reflection, I am not sure that it is possible. Nadar, as any other photographer, must put himself into his pictures as much as we painters do. He has no brushstrokes but, like us, he uses light, the viewpoint and the composition. I sketched my friends as they talked, forming a lively triangle. From time to time, Gautier, in particular, became over excited and began to move around; I had to tell him to keep calm and remain where he was. When I finished, almost two hours later, the three were still in discussion, unable to agree on whether it is the choice of subject, or technique, or both, that define a work of art as modern. They walked out together, intent on continuing in a café. Since then, I have had sessions with each of them separately.

For Fantin, my dear Henri, I painted only a portrait of his head and shoulders. He remains alone, staring out, slightly to the one side of and behind the trio. I would have liked to have given him more prominence – he has such a fine head – but it is difficult to do so in a crowd of people wearing similar clothes and hats. Perhaps I should have placed him in front, so that I could have shown his whole figure. Likewise, Offenbach, is alone but only his head is visible. His wife always seems to be so gloomy and today I felt sorry for him. Perhaps I shall place a young woman next to him. He may appreciate that.

And then, there is Eugène, my dear brother. Have I made him too prominent? When he arrived, he was inspecting a drawing on my table, leaning forward, with his hands crossed behind him under the tails of his jacket. I looked at him and thought that it was just the position I needed. He laughed, saying that I seem to be able to use anything people can offer. By the end of the sitting – and it only took half a morning – he complained that his back ached. Half the way through, I wanted to try sketching him in a different position, but his constant humming – from the moment he arrived, until he left – began to irritate me and I felt I should rather accept what I have than have him in the studio for any longer.

Albert has just arrived for his second sitting. Like Henri, he stares out of the picture, but as he is at the front on one side of the crowd, with his whole figure visible, his stare is more prominent. As a painter himself, he understands my need to concentrate and does not talk. From the days when we shared a studio in the rue Lavoisier, he remembers that I need deep concentration when I work. He stands perfectly still, just like my other ideal model. And, like her, he stares at me. For some reason, with him, I do not find it unsettling. Perhaps I have grown more tolerant or perhaps it is the monocle that acts as a barrier between me and his eyes. No, it is not just the monocle. I understand that Albert needs to stare at me and at the world. After all, he is a painter.

When I finish his face, I stand back and it becomes obvious to me that his position and the air of authority I have given him make him look as if he were the author of the painting. He is meeting the eye of the viewer, as if telling him, 'look at what I have done.' There is something aristocratically detached about his figure. Of course, that is what he is like: a touch arrogant, with a superiority that is justifiable. I cannot leave him alone here. I will have to add someone next to him. But who?

While Albert smokes a cigarette, I catch my reflection in the mirror by the front door and the question finds its answer. I need another pair of eyes next to Albert. Those eyes should also be looking out but in a more relaxed fashion. I shall give Albert a walking stick, while my figure will hold a maulstick or a brush. There is just enough space to squeeze in one third of a self-portrait. It will be my little joke: here is the artist, standing on the side and observing the world. Medieval painters of Biblical scenes used to do something similar: paint a pair of eyes, their own, somewhere in the picture. The eyes are the window between the world of the picture and the world of the spectator.

As I stand here, with Albert's figure almost complete, in my mind's eye I can see how the entire canvas will look when finished. I like the effect created by the partial figures on the edges. They appear as if they have been cut off by the frame of the camera. Or, rather, this picture pretends that it is not posed, and that its composition is an accident, not created to fit the margins of the canvas. It shows life going on while a passer-by has just placed his camera in front of the crowd and taken a picture. He has not planned the arrangement of figures in advance. He has just recorded what is there.

The other day I made Champfleury's portrait. I think I shall place his head in between Albert's and mine.

We finish and Albert looks around the studio. He asks about Victorine. He has not met her but seems to be intrigued by her images. For a long time he looks at her portrait.

'Have you shown this one anywhere?'

When I say that I only finished it a few months ago, he says I ought to take it to Martinet's. Of course, Louis has already tried to persuade me to have it at the show next March. I tell Albert that I am bound by a promise to mademoiselle not to exhibit the portrait. He nods.

Louis laughed when I told him the same thing. 'How would she know? A grisette? She is unlikely to walk into my gallery.' Later on, he added 'After all, the picture belongs to you, Edouard.' Charles, as he has said several times, is of the same opinion.

I do not see it like that. Now that she is not around, I am even more aware what a good model she is. She seems to have an instinct for striking the pose that I need. Not to mention that she is infinitely patient and obliging. Of course, I told Louis that he could have the *Tuileries*. He said he would wait to see it finished first.

Albert goes back to the Tuileries canvas.

'Do you remember, Edouard,' he asks 'when, a few years ago, Duranty wrote that the best draughtsman is the colourist? I recall him arguing at the Guerbois that drawing is not the exterior contour of a form, but that drawing is everywhere, in the middle, above, below, wherever there is light and shadow. Some of us were not sure what he meant. We were taught to do drawing first. The colour was meant to fill the contour. It has only become clear to me now, while looking at your picture, what Duranty meant then. I would say, you cannot use colours if you are not a good draughtsman.'

I admit that I have not thought of Duranty's idea but now I can see that my picture does make drawing with colour, with light and shade, rather than with lines and contours. Albert smiles: 'Even when we were very young, Edouard, you were always a good draughtsman. And, I seem to remember that you were faster than any of us. What was it Delacroix is reputed to have said? Something like, if a man is falling from the fifth floor, a good artist should have a sketch ready by the time the body hits the ground. I have always felt you were one of the few people who could do that.'

I am looking at Albert. What a charming and elegant man he is! I must make sure to convey that in my picture.

28

For a week now, I've been making sketches of *Le Concert champêtre* in the Louvre. Every morning, I arrive as soon as they open and leave at closing time in the evening. The sustained practice has given me a great deal of confidence: not only does my hand move faster than ever before, but there are also fewer lines to correct. With each new day, my concentration improves and I have learned to ignore the frequent comments from visitors to the gallery.

When Etienne lent me a collapsible easel, my first thought was that I should make use of it and produce an oil copy of a picture in the Louvre. I didn't have a particular one in mind, but ever since I've seen his copy of Giorgone's painting, the image of the two women and two men has been stuck in my mind. I see it wherever I go and whatever I do.

For the first time since I've lived alone, I've not thought about money. Nor have I earned anything since last week, when I completed two small flower pictures for Etienne. Perhaps I am becoming more of an artist so that ordinary, everyday things fade into the background. I've noticed that Monsieur Manet ignores everything else in his life when he is in the grip of creating a picture. I've never seen a woman behave like that. My mother always had several things on her mind, even when all she could talk about was her desire to open a laundry. It's the same with all the women I've met. Perhaps only men have that ability to focus on one thing. I want to train myself to be like that: nothing and no one should deflect me from my ambition.

I spend the evenings sketching possible compositions for my large painting. I have a dozen drawings. I need to decide which one to transfer to the canvas. I fear working without a model.

For the sketches, I assumed different positions and used my mirror reflection for both men and women. While I am loosely outlining, that is fine, but I couldn't work like that on a canvas.

I decide that, from now on, I'll refrain from copying in the Louvre. At least for a while. I need to spend more time on my own picture.

But this afternoon I have to visit Emily. A few days ago, I ran into her at the main entrance and she made me promise that I would go to see her. She lives very close to the Batignolles area in a large apartment that is paid for by her father.

'He owns a factory manufacturing hydraulic pumps,' she said. 'There is a great demand for them. I am his only child and he loves spending money on me.'

* * *

We are standing in the hall with its two large mirrors, I catch my reflection and see myself from the front and the back. While I am thinking what an exciting picture that would make, a very tall, robust-looking woman with short blonde hair enters. Her name is Mary and she shares the apartment with Emily. Both of them are from Boston, a large American city on the coast. They are in Paris to study painting. Mary tells me that in America, everyone is interested in contemporary Parisian art. In Boston, they believe that something very exciting is happening in Paris and all the aspiring painters feel that they need to be here.

We sit in the salon, with the windows to the balcony wide open. The curtains dance in the breeze. Emily brings in a tray with a silver and porcelain tea set and a walnut cake. She laughs.

'This is like being back in Boston. My mother forced it on me. "You need a piece of home with you in Paris," she said as she placed the entire set in my trunk.' I smile at her. The stray rays of the afternoon sun bounce off the shiny surface of the silver vessels on the tray. As she starts to pour, holding the heavy tea pot with both hands, a man and a woman arrive. They are John and Anna, a brother and sister. He knows very little French, so I speak mostly to the women. Anna is not studying painting. She is fluent in French and has come to France to interpret for her brother. When Emily says that I paint, John's eyes light up. With the help of Anna, he speaks to me.

'The more French painters I meet, the more I can learn.'

Both John and Mary want to know about my latest picture. At first, I say that it's not much and as I am about to add that I am not a real painter, Emily interrupts me: 'Victorine is too modest. She works very hard. She has produced much good work.'

Everyone looks at me. I realise that, as Americans, these four don't know that women like me become washerwomen, not artists. If they were French, they would not expect me to paint, let alone believe that I could do it well.

Mary turns towards me and says: 'Victorine, we are all here to find out what Parisian painters are working on. Come on, tell us what you have been up to.'

Before I can say anything, Emily adds: 'Please, Victorine. I would be most grateful if you would describe to us what you are painting now. What is ordinary for you here in Paris, will be big news next year in Boston.'

All four of them look at me. I inhale the fragrant steam rising from my teacup and take a sip. The liquid tastes of jasmine; perhaps it's the honey that Emily has added to the pot. I sit back and smile.

'I've just spent a week studying Giorgione's *Concert champêtre* in the Louvre.'

'I know it very well,' John says. 'An intriguing painting.'

'I remember that Emily has seen it,' I say. 'I like that picture and, since I first saw it, I've not been able to get it out of my mind. I thought of doing something similar, but set in modern Paris.' I pause and realise that everyone is waiting for me to continue: 'It is the composition that interests me; the naked women and the fully clothed men –'

'Do you have a model, then? I don't mean a shared one,' John asks.

'Of course, Victorine has a model. You cannot paint figures, human or animal, without a model.'

I am glad that Emily answers on my behalf. I nod: 'The figure

I am working on is looking straight out at whoever is looking at her.'

Emily turns towards me. 'That's very different from anything I can think of and I am sure that –'

John interrupts and his sister translates: 'No, Emily, there are plenty of pictures where a figure meets your eyes. And I don't mean just portraits. What matters is that the eyes of the spectator are met in a particular way. Let me think. Yes, it's as if the eyes in the picture challenge the spectator. Actually, I have seen an etching like that, only I cannot remember now which one it was.' John turns towards me. 'I think there are three figures. They are naked. One of them, on the viewer's left, is looking out…the faces of the other two are seen in profile.'

I know he is right; I have seen a copy of the etching in Monsieur Manet's studio but I can't remember the name of the artist, either. John looks down, his hand on his forehead.

'In my picture, there are two more figures. I remember thinking that while the men in Giorgone are playing music, mine should be idle or, at the most, engaged in a leisurely conversation. At least, that is what I imagined. The woman is listening to them and then, at some point, she becomes bored and turns her eyes away from her companions. Or, perhaps someone stands in front of the group and she is distracted, which is why she looks out.'

There is silence for a while, then Mary asks: 'But why is she sitting naked? People may think she is selling her body.'

'Well, she has removed her clothes because they are in the country and she feels like it.'

Emily looks puzzled. I've never thought of the reason for the woman's nakedness. All that mattered to me was the way the picture looked. I was intrigued by the contrast between the naked women and the dressed men in Giorgone.

'There could be several different reasons,' I say.

'Hmm. It's unusual that as an artist you don't know what is going on in your picture.' Emily looks at me.

'I do know what is going on, except my knowledge doesn't go beyond the visual. What I haven't thought of is the story. Some artists think of stories behind their pictures. I have done it myself. Once, I painted a flower seller and imagined what kind of life she had. This time, it's the shape and colour of a naked female body that fits into the picture. That's all.'

I can see that Emily is thinking hard about my words. Mary looks at me.

'Victorine, what you have said makes sense to me. You aren't a writer, so why should you think of a story? You are a painter. What matters to you are colours and shapes and the way they are put together.'

I nod. She said it better than I ever could.

'Do Parisian women take their clothes off and talk about art when they go to the country?' John asks and everyone laughs.

'One thing I do know is that she is not nude, in the way that Giorgione's women are. Nor is she a nymph or goddess. My woman has taken her clothes off. She is naked. The reason I know that is because I'll paint her discarded clothes, to make it obvious that she is not a goddess, invisible to the humans around her...'

'Yes, John,' Emily says as she turns towards him. 'I am sure you can see what a wonderful idea this is. Who cares why the woman removed her clothes? As you said earlier, Victorine, everyone can make up their own explanation. And since you haven't the answer yourself, you will not argue with us. I also like the idea of a mortal woman being naked, like a goddess.'

John nods and looks at me: 'Interesting. I would love to see your painting, Victorine. Of course, when it is finished and you feel you can show it to the world.'

'Yes, I promise.' I smile at him.

Emily says that it's getting late and that they will be missed at the café where they meet another group of Americans every Friday. She says she hopes that I will be joining them. I say that I would like to, but not tonight. I have something else I need to do. I don't want to say that, for the first time in more than a week, I feel the need, almost a compulsion, to go back to my apartment to paint the large canvas.

We leave together but part at the corner of the Boulevard des Batignolles and rue de Rome. The four of them speak loudly –

passers-by stare at us – and wish me well with my painting. Emily shouts after me that I must visit them again soon.

It's dark when I arrive home. I light a gas lamp. Monsieur Manet often says that a painter works best by natural light but I can't wait until tomorrow.

I arrange a pile of my clothes on the table in front of me: a grey dress, a scarf and a hat. I spend an hour sketching them alongside the woman's figure. There is still a lot of work that I need to do on her. I'll paint her first thing tomorrow morning. And then I'll need to paint the two men. But how can I do it without a model? One option is to pick up some male clothes and wear them myself. That may be very difficult, if not impossible, since at least one of the men has to be painted from the side. I can't think of a man I could ask to sit for me.

I am trying not to see too much of Etienne. Every now and then, he tries to put his arms around me and reminds me of my promise to marry him.

Now, there is John as well. But asking him would mean admitting that I've never painted a male figure from a model. He would be bound to notice my lack of experience. I couldn't bear that. The little bit of confidence that I have would evaporate completely.

Of course, there are male models for hire but, even if I could afford to pay one, I am not sure that I would like to be alone with a man here. I am not good at ordering others around. As a painter, you have to direct a model. I used to talk to Marie and later to Lola about what I wanted from them as models, but neither of them was interested in my explanations. As if they had a secret agreement with each other, they would say exactly the same thing: 'Tell me which position you want, Victorine. Where to stand or sit and what expression to put on. I am not bothered about what it means.'

I've only modelled for Monsieur Manet and he tends not to explain to me what he wants. He chooses the position and the expression and simply tells me to assume them. He likes to be in control. It doesn't seem to cross his mind that I have eyes and can make judgements. When I first went to his studio, I offered my views, but he always ignored them or seemed not to hear. Since then, I haven't bothered making any comments and he has rarely asked me for my opinion.

As a last resort, I know, I'll have to copy the male figures from another painting. I have all these drawings of Giorgione. I may have to use them.

It's after midnight when I put out the light. I feel too excited about the painting and want to carry on, but my eyes ache. For a long time, I can't fall asleep.

29

Gustave, my little brother and my latest model, has just left and I am putting the final touches to the painting. Eugène can be a pain, but Gustave is a darling. And always has been: when we were children, I fought with Eugène, but never with my younger sibling.

I work very slowly, dabbing the brush into the paint and transferring the tiniest amounts to the canvas. These days, my motivation is external and from necessity, from the letters and messages reminding me of the fast-approaching deadlines. Without her around, I seem to have lost any urgency to create something new. Louis Martinet looked at the *Majo* picture yesterday and immediately said that he would like to show it in March. I disagreed. We already have enough for his exhibition. It is clear to me that, if what I am trying to achieve is to have any impact, then the *Majo* has to be on display together with the *Espada*. That should happen at the Salon. Most of those critical scribblers do not see what is in front of them: with two pictures based on a similar idea, they might just catch on.

We are having a wet October; it has been raining incessantly. The lack of bright light is detrimental to the work of a painter like me. I need light and I need Victorine.

I find myself standing by the wall, next to the staircase leading to the room in the gallery, where I have pinned the addresses of various models, although I do not know why I keep them since I have never contacted any of the women. There has been no need; I do not use commercial models. They have neither pose nor perseverance. I prefer family and friends. But with them, too, my main concern is how to arrange regular sittings. When I start something, I worry that sitters will let me down, or that I will not see them as often as I would like, or that the next time will be under conditions I don't like. They come; they pose; and then they go; saying to themselves: "He can finish that by himself." No, no one ever finishes anything "by himself", unless he finishes a picture on the same day as it is begun; otherwise, one has to make several fresh starts and agonize over it. Then, of course, there are some sitters who come back when I don't want them, asking me to retouch this and that. That I won't do.

Why have I never put her address here with the others? Perhaps, from the start, I knew that she was not an ordinary model, not like the ones on hire at Place Pigalle. When I first met her, I wrote her address in a notebook. I remember when I misplaced the notebook, Antoine and I had a great deal of difficulty locating her lodgings. But once we did find her, the address imprinted itself in my mind.

Over the last three weeks, I have sent her two notes. I have not had a response to either, nor has she come looking for me. I have instructed Madame Bijoux that I am expecting Mademoiselle Victorine and that if she arrived while I was out, Madame Bijoux was to take her upstairs and ask her to wait for me. But nothing has happened.

Victorine keeps away from me. Once we had finished *La Chanteuse des rues*, I did say that I had several other works to finish and that I would not be seeing her. But that was two months ago. What I meant was that I would not be seeing her for a week, or two, not longer than that.

When I did not hear from her after the first letter, I assumed that she had not received it. So I wrote again. It was only a week ago; there is still time for her to get in touch.

I have never been a patient man. The waiting frustrates me. Why cannot people take my work seriously?

Yesterday morning, when Madame Bijoux handed me the mail, the first thing I looked for was a note from Victorine. Madame Bijoux said that no one had called for me. I thought, well, there is still Pigalle. So what if I am not in the habit of going there?

I walked to Place Pigalle straightaway. It amazed me how

many women of different shapes and sizes were on offer, ready to model. I imagine they see it as good work, much easier than working in a laundry or being a servant, although the pay must be less.

I talked to quite a few women and, in no time, I engaged two of them, one for the morning and the other for the afternoon.

Mademoiselle Amélie, the first one, had dark red hair and a corpulent physique. Initially, I was interested in her because of the way she looked at people and I suppose I thought that I might find something of Victorine in her. Perhaps it was the colour of her hair and the translucence of her white skin that deceived me. I should have known better. As soon as she arrived, the first question she asked was about the hourly rate. I thought it was a superfluous question: we agreed on the fee when I gave her my address.

'Just to confirm, monsieur,' she said. Clearly, she was in it for the money. That was not a good sign. She claimed to be more experienced than the average model, and therefore charged a little more. But, even with all her experience, she found it difficult to sit still for more than twenty minutes at a time and frequently excused herself to use the bathroom. I wanted to try a sketch based on Marcantonio Raimondi's *Jugement de Pâris*. A copy of the etching has been lying around for months now, ever since I lost my temper with Victorine and told her that the way she stared at me made her look as the figure of Temperance.

Since I had gone to Pigalle on the spur of the moment, I was not prepared when Amélie arrived, only ten minutes after me, and I did not know exactly what I wanted to do with her. I have several ideas that I would like to work on, but, I am saving them for Victorine. Then I spotted *Le jugement* and thought that Amélie could sit for the figure staring out.

She undressed quickly, without any comment or question. Clearly, she was not shy; as an experienced model, she must be used to posing in the nude. But everything about her posture was wrong. Her back was too arched and, when she sat down, her legs splayed in front of her. I explained what I wanted; I did not think that showing her the etching would have been of any use. Worst of all, she did not know where to look. With Victorine, I have become used to a model who understands what I want, even without explanation.

No matter how many times I asked Amélie not to look around, her eyes travelled across the room; I felt exasperated and abandoned the sketch. Oh, what would I not have given at that moment to have Victorine instead of Amélie, even the Victorine with her penetrating stare?

I knew I had not been myself recently and that the debacle of the morning was not entirely the model's fault. I paid her, saying that I had to stop working for the day. I think I added something about having to go somewhere. Mademoiselle looked at me and asked what time she should come tomorrow. I felt embarrassed. I gave her some more money and she misunderstood. As soon as she tucked the money into her pocket, she unbuttoned her blouse and urged me to touch her breasts. For so much money, she was more than willing to sleep with me, she said. I felt angry with myself and sorry for her and, eventually, sorry to have found myself in such an embarrassing situation. I told her that I do not need to pay women to sleep with me. I was relieved when she left.

When I came back after lunch, the second mademoiselle was waiting for me just outside Madame Bijoux's office. Her name was Camille. She was young and shy with a very pretty, innocent looking face. When I asked her what kind of modelling she had done, she lowered her eyes and admitted I was her first engagement. At that point, I thought I should like to draw her just as she was, but then later on, I was not sure of my first impression and I decided to ask her to pose for the figure from Le jugement.

She started undressing and I immediately noticed that she was very embarrassed. I stopped her and said that we might only have enough time for the face. I sketched her but the result was not satisfactory. It was not her fault: my concentration was ebbing. I simply could not develop a visual interest in her face. With Victorine: the most blank expression is so full, so telling, so meaningful. And besides, unlike these Pigalle models, she is patient, understanding and exact. Neither does she complain nor is she given to idle chit chat.

When I finished the sketch and told Camille that she could go, I forgot to pay her. I blamed myself for it. She stopped by door and stared at me. For some reason, the need to pay her completely escaped my mind. She said: 'Would monsieur be able to give me some food to take with me?'

I looked at her and at first did not understand what she was saying.

She spoke again: 'I hope I've been useful. It's been three hours. Could you spare some food, monsieur? Anything you have and you don't want, would do for me. Potatoes. I like potatoes.' I kept looking at her and then it hit me. She was very pale and thin, probably had not eaten. She must have been hungry. I told her to wait and went downstairs to see Madame Bijoux. I asked her to make a little parcel and bring it up, together with a drink.

Back in the studio, I paid Camille and said that the food was coming. It took Madame Bijoux half an hour to come up. For a while, we sat in silence. I did not know what to say. Camille stared uncomfortably at the floor. Eventually, I excused myself and went upstairs, saying that I had to do something while we waited. I only came down when I heard Madame Bijoux calling me. I gave the parcel to Camille and poured us some coffee. She drank it and ate a pastry. She held the parcel on her knees, as if afraid that it might escape or be taken from her.

I watched her and, against my better judgement, went over, put my arms around her and kissed her. She did not resist. She looked so young, much younger than Victorine. I knew that I should not do anything. And yet it was that knowledge that spurred me on. Her thinness excited me. And her pale skin made her face look as if it would break if I kissed it too fiercely. I had to sleep with her. There was some warmth as well. We lay on the divan, next to the *Majo* costume that Gustave had been wearing to model for me. Until her perfume left its traces on me, I thought I could smell my brother. She had small breasts but the nipples were large. I rubbed them against my chest until the vision of her face became blurred. Once I had entered her, it was over in no time and, to my later regret, I could not hold her afterwards; I could not meet her eyes. I walked away. She dressed rapidly and was gone. I was grateful that she never looked me in the eye. I felt less guilty when I reminded myself that it was not the first time for her. Perhaps she lied when she said that I was her first modelling engagement.

I took her address and pinned it next to the others from Pigalle. I am looking at a little flower that I had drawn next to her name; for some reason, I wanted her details to stand out in the sea of the other, identical scraps of paper.

Looking at the *Majo* portrait again, I am suddenly struck by the thought that the *Espada* is not the only one with which it could be paired. I walk to the other side of the studio and, from the canvases leaning against the wall, pull out a portrait of Léon with a sword. I put the three canvases next to each other. They form a triptych. The idea is the same behind each of them. The sitter is playing a role and the painting shows that role as well as the sitter's own character. Léon's sword is a prop and serves the same function as Victorine's and Eugène's costumes. Well, three of the same may be too much for the Salon. I shall give the Léon painting to Martinet. That should satisfy him: he has been demanding one more canvas. I shall submit the *Majo* and the *Espada* to the Salon.

Antoine arrives to take me to the Guerbois. He says he is pleased that I am looking so well.

'I have known you for a long time, Edouard, but I still cannot predict your moods. You swing from depression to elation so quickly. Tell me, dear friend,' he says, 'what has brought this cheerfulness on?'

I smile and tell him what I have just decided: 'I need Victorine. But there is no point waiting for her. I'll look for her in person.' Antoine nods.

'I am ready to accompany you, Edouard, whenever you are ready.'

30

Last night, I lay in bed, thinking about the last two paintings he did with me. For the first time I fully understood the importance of his work: he had captured me, Victorine, as I am and, at the same time and on the same canvas, he depicted the role he had asked me to play. Only a great artist can do that. For a long time I couldn't fall asleep.

I miss working with him; it's been several months and he has probably forgotten me by now. Will he ever ask me to pose for him again? Lying alone in the dark, the question evolved into anxiety. I tried to calm myself and began to fantasise that, not only would he ask me to pose, but also to choose the role. And that would happen very soon. I knew what my choice would be: I would like him to make a picture of me as a painter at work. If his art can turn me into a torero, or a street singer, why not make a painter out of me?

I dreamed that I was in his studio and we were working together, but not as an artist and model, rather, as two painters, sharing the same canvas. He was drawing a figure – we had another model, although I don't remember anything about her from the dream – and I was busy with a bouquet of flowers in a vase that stood on a table to the side of the figure. From time to time, he would ask me to stop painting and to comment on what he had just done. Then he would consider my work and make suggestions. I woke up in seventh heaven. But, within seconds, the disappointment set in. While still sitting in bed, I could see the three figures on my large canvas and I knew that, with the best will in the world, and all the time I can spend on it now, I would never have the skill to turn it into a proper picture. I think the idea is good; unfortunately, I don't have sufficient craft for something so large and so ambitious.

I light the gas lamp and stand in front of the picture. Is there anything I can do to improve it? The female figure is less of a problem than the two men. They look dead and two dimensional, almost as if they were cut out of paper and stuck onto the canvas. Without models, this is the best I can do.

Perhaps asking Etienne is not such a bad idea. Recently, he has been apologetic about his marriage proposal – 'too much drink in the afternoon, Victorine,' he said – and has been paying me regularly for my work. Nevertheless, I must be careful with him: only the other day he told me that he wanted to sleep with me, even if I didn't wish to live in his flat or marry him. I ignored him and he didn't mention the matter again that evening. He knows that I am working on a large oil and, since he is a painter, I wouldn't need to do a great deal of explaining about what I want from him as a model. However, if he helps me out, he may ask for a favour in return.

A few days ago, I spotted Emily and Mary at the Boulevard St Michel and quickly crossed the road before they noticed me. They were laughing and talking loudly. Emily carried a large flat parcel, most likely a canvas. I didn't have the courage to face their questions about my painting. The last time in Emily's apartment, she and her friends expressed so much interest and confidence in me that I feel ashamed to let them down.

I know that I have worked hard but it has been a pure waste. Everything that I've done recently is so horribly bad.

Now that Monsieur Manet no longer requires me to sit for him, I have much more time to spend on improving my own technique. The difficulty is that I have no one to advise me how to do it. I have to be a critic, a teacher and a pupil, all in one. If only I had the money and could afford to pay for lessons. The flower pictures I do for Etienne are routine and after doing so many, I can work on them even when I am tired and under the gas light. But they are not real paintings.

I read in the newspaper that artists have started drawing and painting in fields, forests, and on beaches, delighting in fresh air and natural light. Monsieur Manet, they say, has been spotted in the Jardin des Tuileries. I wondered whether I should try it. Today the sun is shining and it seems a good opportunity to set up a studio in the Bois de Boulogne to sketch the trees and grass. I could use them later for the background. If I place my figures within a landscape, like Giorgione, the group may look less unnatural. On the way home, I could stop at Etienne's apartment and ask him to model for me. If he does insist on anything in return, I'll have to deal with it when it happens.

I begin to pack my paints and brushes and Etienne's collapsible easel. One of the cartoons of an artist working in the open air shows him surrounded by a crowd of onlookers. Apparently, that can present a serious problem. A painter is quoted complaining that a farmer in Normandy tried to frighten him with a bull, and when the animal stopped in front of the canvas and ignored the artist, the farmer set a dog on him. Most of the problems mentioned, fortunately, are not the result of such a hostile reception. One painter is even reported to have been brought meals by villagers. It seems that the main difficulty is the constant barrage of unsolicited comments. In the Louvre, I had gradually become inured to comments from visitors. But at least they were standing next to me because they were interested in art. People in the country often look at artists as strange creatures. I'll try to find a quiet spot to avoid all these problems. I pack an apple, a few dried figs and some bread for lunch.

I am just about to leave, laden with my art materials, canvas and lunch, when I am startled by a knock on the door. It comes as a complete shock to see Lola standing in front of me. It is more than a month since she stormed out of my apartment. She smiles briefly: 'May I come in, Victorine?'

I move aside to let her pass. Once inside, I put down my things by the door and gesture for her to sit down. She takes a chair. I sit on the divan. She looks at me and asks: 'Are you going out?'

I nod.

'Is anyone waiting for you? A man or a woman?' Her large eyes narrow and I can see her fighting jealousy. When I don't answer, she realizes she should not repeat the question: 'I need to talk to you, Victorine. It's important.' She looks serious, but as soon as her eyes meet mine, she forces a smile.

I decide to hear what she wants to say. I have missed her, but right now, I am not overly delighted that she is here. I had set my mind on painting a landscape.

'I am sorry I walked out, Victorine.' She pauses and I can see that she is gauging my reaction. 'I think you were very unfair to me.' I don't say anything, and she continues: 'I have come to apologize.' I nod and smile. She puts her hand on mine and we sit in silence for a few moments.

'But I don't want to see other women here. I fretted that she might be here with you now…the woman who gave you the earrings.' I move my hand from underneath hers. She adds: 'But she isn't, and I'm glad.'

She seems slimmer than I remember and her hair is much shorter. She would do. And why not? If I let her stay, she'll want to make love and then I can ask her to be one of the two men for my picture. That would be a fair exchange. Yes, Lola would do as a male model. All she needs is a different outfit. Her brother's suit is still here and I have several hats that she could try.

'Victorine, please let me stay.' She looks at me. 'I love you. I've brought you a present, something to mark our new beginning.' She takes a paper wrapping out of her pocket and opens it. She walks towards the divan, kneels in front of me and ties a silk necklace with a small teardrop pearl pendant around my neck. Her fingers are warm and moist. I inhale the familiar smell of her breath and of her skin. Her hair brushes against my cheeks. She closes her eyes and kisses me, very slowly and gently, without pushing her tongue inside my mouth.

I put my arms around her and say: 'I am glad you are here.'

We sit on the divan next to each other, holding hands. Lola says that today isn't the first time she has been to see me. She called two, or perhaps three, weeks ago; Madame Conchis had told her that I was in, but when she knocked, there was no answer.

It took her a while, she says, to gather the courage to try again. She looks at the necklace and says: 'I hope you'll wear it,

Victorine and always remember me, whenever we are not together, anywhere you go. The man who sold it to me said that pearls were like tears and I thought of all the tears I've shed missing you.' She can see that I am still wearing Marie's earrings, but she knows better than to refer to them.

We lie down and make love very slowly. Lola runs her hands down my naked body so gently that I can barely feel her touch. She lowers her head in between my legs and caresses me with her fingers. She opens my lips and places a moist kiss on them. I feel her tongue touching gently the soft parts. I've missed her.

Moving very slowly, she parts my legs further and her tongue goes inside me, deeper and deeper. I close my eyes and do nothing. The room disappears and my body seems to take off.

Later, Lola tells me that she was afraid that we would never again be together like this and the thought made her anxious. We hold each other for a long time before she leans over me and, in a very low voice, sings a lullaby. It's not in French. I do not understand a word, but I can tell that the tune is sad. She says that it's a song of a mother singing to her child who is either dead or has been taken away from her.

When we get up, for the first time ever Lola asks about my painting. I tell her that I have been having problems and that I am not happy with what I've been doing. I can see that she is at a loss what to say.

'But you could help me,' I venture.

'Me?' She laughs loudly. 'Victorine, I can sing and dance, but I can't draw or paint.' I explain that I need a male model. She seems relieved and her eyes light up. As soon as I bring her brother's clothes, she puts them on. I notice that her face is serious once again. She comes to stand very close to me and speaks in a low voice: 'Victorine, if we are to have a new beginning, I have to make a confession: I lied to you when I said that these were my brother's. I've never had a brother. Or, at least, I've never known that I had one. I wanted to have brothers and sisters. As a small child, growing up with my grandmother, I begged her to find other children to live with us. But that isn't the only reason why I invented a brother. I wanted to dress as a man. I didn't dare tell you. I thought you might laugh at me. I bought these clothes in the very same market where we met. The woman who sold them to me said that they had belonged to her dead husband. I couldn't tell her that they were for me. I said that I needed them for my brother who was the same height as me. She let me try the jacket. The trousers were too big at the waist, but I took them in.'

I smile.

'That's a lovely story. I like dressing up as other people.'

'Other people? You mean as another woman?'

'Anyone, a man or a woman.'

She kisses me and then takes my hand and holds it in hers: 'Are you not upset that I lied to you, Victorine?'

I can't see the problem. In fact, her story amuses me. I've heard that there are women who like to dress as men, some have even asked for permission from the police. Besides, I remember how special I felt in the torero outfit. I shake my head.

'I've always said you make a handsome man, Lola. The rest doesn't matter.'

'Do you think I make a handsome woman, Victorine?'

'You do.'

She stares at me as if unsure whether to believe my words.

We don't talk much while I paint. I stare at Lola for a long time and realise that the pose I need for the first man is all wrong. I have to do it all over again. We work for two hours without a break. Lola sits patiently and occasionally smiles at me. I manage to sketch the outline of the entire figure and begin to add colour to the clothes.

In the evening, I take out some bread and cheese and Lola brings bowls of soup and a bottle of wine from the café downstairs. She tells me that her employers are away and she can stay until tomorrow night. Of course, if that is what I want. She looks at me and adds, half teasingly: 'And, I mean, if no one else is coming to stay with you.'

I don't like her saying that: 'You can sleep here, Lola. There is no one else tonight. In the morning, we can resume the painting, I hope.'

She nods and smiles but I can see that the word 'tonight' makes her sad. I am aware that I didn't have to use it. I am pleased that she is staying. I hope to make some progress with the male figures tomorrow.

I fall asleep quickly, but in the middle of the night, Lola wakes me up. She is crying. I put my arms around her and she stops. She whispers in my ear that she loves me and wants to be with me forever.

'I could find another job and we could live together, Victorine. It's not enough for me to see you only on Sundays.'

'Yes, we can think about it in the morning,' I say. 'We need to sleep now.' I want to do a lot of work tomorrow.

She holds me tight.

'I love you, Victorine; I love you with all my heart,' she whispers as she squeezes me tight.

I pretend I've fallen asleep.

31

Since my father died two months ago, mother has been in charge of family affairs. I am sure she manages the finances very well but I wish she would not be insistent on what she refers to as 'installing a sense of responsibility'. I suddenly feel a greater pressure to achieve something publicly recognizable and that is not good for an artist. I know that to placate her I need a medal, an honour, some recognition that my work is appreciated. Or, if not that, then at least she would need to see that my paintings are selling for good money. But I cannot pander to the taste of the establishment. I am not Meissonier.

I have a desperate desire to start a new picture with Victorine. I cannot imagine that I will make a real impact without her. And yet she seems to have disappeared from Paris, from France, from the world. Still there is no answer to my messages.

I have a number of ideas that I would like to bring to life. All of them involve her. The last time I saw her would have been at the beginning of July, four months ago.

I have knocked on her door several times recently – Antoine accompanied me on two occasions – but she was out each time. This early on Sunday morning, most people are still in bed or preparing for church. If I am to find her at home, now is the most likely time.

I take a fiacre. The air is freezing; winter is upon us. The driver offers me a blanket. I thank him but say I do not need it. He gives me a strange look and wraps his own blanket around his legs. I am wearing a new coat in fine English wool – it was delivered only yesterday – and a pair of light coloured trousers. The blanket does not look very clean. I turn up my fur collar to keep out the icy wind. There are few vehicles or people about at this hour. The light of the sun is brilliantly white and, from time to time, I have to close my eyes as we ride.

The man stops right in front of Maître Albert, number 17. I tell him not to wait and he expresses surprise.

'Are you sure, monsieur,' he whispers, 'that you want to make your own way back from here? Not many fiacres ride to this area. Do you understand what I mean, monsieur?'

I nod. He can tell that I do not live in this place. The people look poor and there are piles of rubbish on the streets. As I step out of the fiacre, a woman bumps into me. She is drunk and can barely walk. She extends her hand towards me and, as she opens her mouth, I notice that her front teeth are rotten.

'Would monsieur like a kiss? Or love? Only three francs, monsieur. I can give you love, monsieur. You need a woman's love. Only three francs. I have a room, monsieur, just two streets away. Very nice room and warm. Come with me.'

As I give her a franc, she grabs my arm and pulls me towards her. She is weak and wobbly and it is not difficult to extricate myself.

I push open the large double door. I have been here on several occasions and each time I admired the iron decorations. They are too grand for this place. The concierge's office is closed. I walk across the courtyard and climb up to the top floor.

The lodgings must be very cheap. The staircase is dark and narrow and the paint is peeling off most of the woodwork on the way up. I stand in front of her door for a minute or two before I knock. There is some movement inside the apartment. I have a feeling she is in. Indeed, before I knock, I think I hear whispers and then a voice, and the shuffling of feet, but I cannot be sure. I knock louder but now the voice and the whisper have disappeared. Perhaps I was mistaken and she is not at home. The walls and the doors in a house like this are thin and I could have easily heard voices from another apartment.

I knock again, more loudly. I wait; it is completely silent. Perhaps I should slip a note under the door. I take out my notepad, but it is too dark to write anything. I shall have to walk down a flight of steps if I am to find enough light. I remember noticing a small window there. Before I walk away, I call her name. I just feel like shouting it. Again, I think there is some movement and a whisper behind the door. I call her name once again and say, very gently:

'Mademoiselle Victorine, I need to speak with you. It is Edouard, Edouard Manet.'

There is no mistake now: somebody is whispering in there. A man. She has a man in her bed. I turn to leave but then, almost immediately, I hear the sound of feet and the door opens very slowly. With her hair hanging down, unbrushed, she stands in front of me. I have never seen her like this. It is obvious that she has only just slipped on the dress she is wearing. Some of the buttons are undone and she has no stockings. Her cheeks are flushed.

A new Victorine! My first thought is that I would love to paint her like this. I want to scream 'Mademoiselle Victorine! Do not move; wait here until I fetch my easel and my canvas.' I need to fix this look of surprise that, as with her other expressions, is subtly muted. No one has a face like her.

Oh, she is a find. She is a find and I am here with her again. How could I have painted without her?

She keeps her eyes on me and soon I feel embarrassed that I am disturbing her. I should not have come unannounced. She is still looking at me with that blank expression and I cannot tell what she is thinking or feeling. I try to stifle my desire but it keeps coming back: if only she would not move and I could paint her, right here and now. A drawing would do. I can take out my pad and a crayon. She is not moving. As I reach for my pad, I realize that I must say something first: 'Mademoiselle Victorine, I do apologize for disturbing you so early. I need to talk to you.'

She nods but does not move. Her expression does not change.

I smile: 'Well, may I come in? It is important that we talk.'

She carries on looking at me but no words come out of her mouth. In the past, I have often seen her quick and responsive. Now she is confused. Or perhaps not. Perhaps she does not want me inside. I cannot read her face. I ask again if I can come in and it is only now that she appears to understand and moves to the side to let me pass.

I cannot help seeing it straight away. The canvas is huge, bigger than any I have ever worked on, and the room is very small. She has an easel and a long table with paints and brushes and there are other pictures leaning against the walls. Victorine, my model, she paints!

Why has she never told me about it? I can tell immediately from where she has developed the idea for the picture. The composition is based on Raphael's *Jugement de Pâris*. I was the one who showed her a copy of Marcantonio Raimondi's engraving. And it was me who said that she was staring out like the figure of Temperance. She has taken it too literally: she has posed for it herself. The likeness is obvious. But why in the nude? Or rather, why is only her figure in the nude? In Marcantonio Raimondi, all three figures are naked.

The execution is poor, desperately poor. The landscape is a weak imitation of some kind of Arcadia. But the idea intrigues me. If only, if only she could paint properly, this would be a masterful picture. This could be a painting to shake Paris. The way it is now, no one would take it seriously. No idea works without technique, without a skilful execution.

'Monsieur Manet, you said that you needed to talk to me.' She is standing right in front of me, blocking my view of the painting. The tone of her voice tells me that she is not happy that I have seen her work.

'I did. But, it was not anything important. Not as important as what I have just learned. You paint.'

She lowers her eyes. She is holding her hands together, one fist in another. I see her bite her lips. Then she looks up, straight into my eyes and sighs.

'Yes, I paint,' she says in a barely audible voice. I have never seen her so shy before.

I smile: 'I am very pleased to see that you have been working on such a large canvas. This is a very ambitious picture.'

'It's nothing. It's no good. I've tried hard, but I can't do it. I am useless. I am prepared to work long hours but I still can't produce anything of any value.' She blurts out the words fast. There is no false modesty in her voice. She is genuinely disappointed with the result.

'Well, you should not dismiss your work. You could have asked me for advice, mademoiselle. But, now that I am here, let me show you something. There are sections in the picture that we can make better in no time at all. I would be pleased to help.' I am prepared to set to work right now. I look around, not sure which brush to pick up. With just a few strokes, I could improve the male figure in the forefront. I can tell exactly where she has gone wrong. A classic mistake for a beginner, particularly if they do not know how to use a model.

I look around. One entire wall is covered with drawings; they are all of her face. When I move closer, I notice that there are only slight changes of expression on them. There are at least fifty pieces, all arranged next to one another. A self-portrait wall! She shares my fascination with her face.

'Mademoiselle Victorine,' I say removing my coat, 'if you will permit me…could you pass me a brush, a medium size would do.'

Before she moves, a voice interrupts us: 'Victorine, come back to me. What's going on? Who is it? Victorine!'

I look in the direction of the voice and only now I notice a double door leading to an adjoining room. There, a woman lies in bed, sprawled on her back, looking at the ceiling. She is young and black. Her naked body is only partially covered by a blanket. I can see one of her arms stretched above her head and one of her breasts spilling over the cover. A dark brown nipple stands erect. Victorine's eyes follow mine but she does not answer the question posed by the woman.

Something happens inside me very quickly. A kind of force takes over my body and my mind. I do not think what I should be doing. The painting no longer interests me. To hell with it! Who is this woman? What is she doing in Victorine's bed? But as soon as the questions form in my head, I lose interest in them. I do not need anyone to tell me anything. I do not wait for explanations. I can see everything for myself. A wave of heat travels from my feet through my body and reaches my head. I know my face is red. I feel angry. I feel cheated. Situations and images from the past few months fly through my mind. I think of all those occasions when I feared that I would have to sleep with her if she were to agree to pose for me. All those times when I was sure that all she wanted was me.

I hear the black woman calling Victorine's name again. I do not know what Victorine does or says and I do not care. I grab my coat, rush out through her front door and leap downstairs. I do not look left or right; all I want is to be out of there, out of her sight, in the fresh air on the street.

I bump into a couple walking in the opposite direction and they complain about people being drunk early in the morning.

What a fool I have been! Thinking of her as my perfect model. She is a cheat and a liar. She has been dishonest. All along she has been stealing my secrets as a painter. Judging by that canvas, it has not done her much good. How could I have been such an idiot? When she stared at me, she was trying to paint me in her head. I cannot tell what hurts more: the realisation that I have been so blind to her artistic ambitions or her pretending that she wanted me?

I refused to pry into her personal life. That is why I could not have guessed that she painted. But the knowledge that she faked an interest in me…a bitch, a bitch. Women of high society cannot resist me. Why should pathetic little Victorine?

I have to walk quite a distance before I can hail a fiacre. It takes me straight to the studio. I am grateful that at this hour Madame Bijoux is in church. I cannot face talking to anyone. At least no one expects me to be here on Sundays. I need to be alone. I feel such a fool. How could I have been so blind and naïve? Now I understand why she never bothered to answer my messages. All along she has had someone else to think about. My ideal model, indeed!

I do not go out for lunch. As the day goes by, I have no need for either food or company. In the afternoon, I look at the drawings and the three paintings I have of Victorine. As my anger subsides, I am ready to admit to myself that I am jealous. I keep recalling that day – I think we must have been working on *La Chanteuse des rues* by then – when I could no longer ignore her innuendoes without losing her as a model. She had already unbuttoned her blouse and was looking at me, clearly playing a game of provocation. I put my hand inside. As my fingers brushed against her skin, she seemed to shiver.

I said: 'Has any man ever touched your breasts?' She lowered her eyes and shook her head. I assumed that she had never had a lover. Charles would laugh at me now. I can see him saying: 'Edouard, women love women more than they can ever love a man.'

I am angry with her, and yet, for the first time since I have known her, I am attracted to her. This morning, as never before, I saw her as a woman, and not just as my model. If only that other person, that woman, had not been there, I would have taken off her clothes and kissed her. I would have made love to her better than any woman could.

Charles says that lesbians are like artists, the explorers of the unknown, living in the twilight world of transgressive desire. Like artists, they are seekers of the infinite, driven by an overwhelming passion. Damn them!

The painting haunts me as much as she does. As soon as I saw it, I was fascinated and could not take my eyes off it. She has stolen the idea from my mind. I remember that day when I was out in Argenteuil with Antoine. We watched people bathing in brilliant sunshine and I thought of Giorgone and how it was too dark. I knew I wanted to use him and create a brighter place with people like those around us.

I have never told her about it.

Would she have seen the copy I had made of Giorgone?

But what does it matter? She cannot paint.

It is the female figure that I cannot take out of my mind. I have always known that the nude is not just one part of art: it is the essence of all art.

I feel an urgent need to make a drawing of the painting. I must have it on a piece of paper, in case it disappears from my memory. I take a large sheet, although incomparably smaller than her canvas, and work quickly with pen and ink, adding watercolours. I know, and she must know, that she has stolen the idea from Raphael, via my engraving by Marcantonio Raimondi. In that case, there is nothing wrong with me borrowing it from her.

32

'Don't answer. Let's keep quiet and they'll go away,' she says and holds me tighter.

The knocking continues even more loudly. I cannot think who it is. No one would come to see me this early on a Sunday. Etienne has only a vague idea of where I live. Madame Conchis always calls my name when she knocks.

Lola squeezes my body with all her might, as if she were afraid I might escape to whoever is at the door. We lie quietly for a while, her breasts pressed against mine. As the knocking continues, Lola whispers into my ear: 'Do not move, Victorine. Please, don't get up.'

There is a long silence. And then we hear the sound of steps slowly going away. I can tell they are a man's steps. After a minute or so, the person is back outside my door and knocks again. But this time, there is only a single rap before he calls my name. I recognize the voice immediately.

Lola expected a woman; I know that. The male voice confuses her and she eases her grip on me. It is an opportunity for me to free myself. In an instant, I slip on a dress, run my fingers through my hair and open the door. A quick glance at the room makes me regret its shabbiness, but there is nothing I can do about it now. I have no choice but to let him see how poor I am. There is no question of not allowing him to come in. I would never deny him anything.

He stands in front of me in his fashionable coat with its large fur collar. His elegance shows off my poverty even more. Smiling, he strides in, saying that he needs to talk to me. When he notices the large canvas, the smile disappears. His speech trails off in the middle of a sentence. For a long time, he stares at the painting.

I stand next to him, embarrassed. I don't know what to do or say. He must think that I am a fool to paint like this. I see the picture through his eyes. It is worse than it seemed to me before. The male figures are hopeless. Even with Lola as a model, I didn't have the technique to represent their posture. But the figure of the woman is not much better either: a shapeless mass of pasty flesh.

Nevertheless, he can't tear himself away from the canvas. Perhaps I should leave him alone. I remind him that he said he wanted to talk to me. At first, I think he doesn't hear me, but then suddenly, he says, absent-mindedly, with his eyes still on the canvas: 'Oh, no, mademoiselle. It's not important.'

We continue standing in silence in front of the picture, until his face becomes animated and he turns towards me: 'Mademoiselle, you need to do some work on this.' I know that. Is that all he can say after staring at the picture for such a long time?

'Yes, I know what you need to do. Let me show you. We can improve it. If you would pass me a brush, mademoiselle. A medium size would do.' He throws off his coat with such carelessness that for a second I fear it might land on the dirty floor. I catch the coat and place it on a chair.

'A medium size brush is what I need,' he repeats.

I choose a brush from a jar on the table and just as I am about to hand it to him, we hear: 'Victorine, who is it? Are you not coming back to me?' She speaks slowly, emphasizing every single word, teasing me. I had told her about the visitor before I left the bed. I begged her to stay quiet.

At first it seems that Monsieur Manet doesn't hear her. He takes the brush and looks around for my paints. But Lola doesn't give up. She calls again and now he looks in her direction. The lines on his face harden, the skin turns pale and he drops the brush. He won't help me improve the painting.

Lola's timing is perfect. I hate her.

Monsieur Manet turns away from the painting and stares through the double door leading to my bedroom. Lola is lying on the bed, with the covers pushed away and one of her breasts fully exposed. Her nipple is standing erect. It's cold in the room but she doesn't feel the need to cover herself.

His face turns bright red, then purple. He shouts something; I can't tell what. He grabs the coat and rushes out of the apartment without closing the door after him.

I am certain that it's not her colour that upset him. Months ago, I heard him tell Charles about his experiences in Brazil and how shocked he had been at the treatment of black slaves.

I close the door. I imagine him walking away and crossing the road in his characteristic rolling gait but I have no strength to look out of the window.

Lola stands behind me. Naked, she puts her arms around me and tries to kiss me on the neck. I walk away from her. She has just destroyed the single opportunity I have ever had of him helping with my work. The thought that I might never see him again numbs.

We spend the rest of the day in complete silence. I ignore her as I work quietly on a drawing of a jug with a plate of fruit – I have no desire to draw human figures – while she potters around. When I stop working, she leaves me alone and doesn't insist that we go out. Although I don't tell her how I feel, she knows I am angry.

In the evening, she brings up a bottle of wine and a meat stew but I don't feel like eating. She admits that she was selfish and apologizes.

'It's because I love you, Victorine, that I want you all for myself. I was relieved that your visitor was a man but, when he started looking at your painting I became angry. You had something that I could not be part of.'

I don't even bother looking at her. Who will help me with the painting now? I'll never be able to finish it on my own.

'You must admit, Victorine, that your picture was not the only thing he was interested in. He spent quite a bit of time looking at my body.'

She is right. It is my turn to feel a sharp pang of jealousy. In the past, I've undressed in front of Monsieur Manet, but he never stared at me as he stared at her.

Lola smiles at me. He can have her body and look at her for hours, days and months, for ever. I don't mind. If only he would show me what to do with my picture.

I think of his purple face just before he ran out, and of the hard lines around his mouth. I imagine his rolling gait as he rushed away from Maître Albert.

He will never come back.

33

Almost three weeks after that Sunday, Madame Conchis gave me a hand-delivered letter. She said that she had promised a very smartly dressed man that she would hand it to me in person. As I was walking away, she added that she remembered seeing the man before. He had delivered two notes in the past two months. I haven't received anything recently and wondered whether she had confused him with someone else. I turned back to face her.

'Oh, Mademoiselle Victorine, you must have forgotten. You are always rushing around, that's why you can't remember. I'm certain it's the same man. He has a very kind voice. And he wears beautiful clothes. Not many people around here dress like that. One doesn't forget a man of such smart appearance. I remember him very well.'

I rushed across the courtyard and she shouted after me. 'He gave me a franc each time.'

I ripped open the letter upstairs. It read:

Paris, 1 December 1862

Dear Mademoiselle Victorine,

Now that I see you are a painter yourself, I have a proposal to make. If it is convenient for you, I shall call at your apartment on Friday afternoon at four o'clock. I would very much appreciate if you would be alone so that we can talk without being disturbed.

I apologize for rushing out in anger the last time I saw you. It was inappropriate of me to react like that and I trust that you will find it in your heart to forgive me.

Yours truly,
Ed. Manet

I read it again, savouring each word. Then I pressed it to my chest. Tears came to my eyes. He had called me a painter. He was coming to see me a day after with 'a proposal'.

That afternoon my energy soared and I managed to do more work than in the whole of the past week.

If he offers to teach me how to improve the painting, I'll tell Lola that she can't come and spend Saturday nights and Sundays with me. I don't want her interfering. I expect her to be upset and protest but I won't give in.

He arrives precisely at the appointed time. As I open the door, he removes his silk top hat. For several days now, the weather has been milder than it was three weeks ago when he wore the beautiful coat with the large fur collar. Today, he is dressed in dark tails. We sit down at the table.

I have been busy painting a series of pictures for Etienne's English dealer. Five canvases are stacked by the door, ready to be packed and delivered. The last one, which I have still to finish, is on my easel. The large canvas that Monsieur Manet saw is turned towards the wall and covered with a sheet. I haven't been able to look at it for some time. I know it's unfinished and poorly painted but no matter how hard I try I can't improve it. I know I lack the technique. I see his eyes scan the room for the picture.

'I am pleased that you are alone, mademoiselle,' he says.

'I live alone, monsieur.' He looks at me. 'The friend you saw last time is here only on Sundays.' I realise that I didn't need to tell him that.

'I did not mean to pry. It is none of my business how you live and who visits you.' He pauses and looks down. 'Your friend is a beautiful woman.' Now he is saying too much. He checks himself and makes an effort to smile: 'I have come to talk to you about the painting I saw here before.' He pauses, his eyes on me.

I nod. I had expected him to talk about the picture.

'The painting intrigued me. I think you have created something special, mademoiselle. Truly special. I don't know how you came to the idea.'

He is either being too kind or feels that he needs to flatter me. He must know how I got it. We were in his studio, standing by the table with copies of etchings. He picked up *Le jugement de Pâris* and said: 'I like these figures. Sometimes I think of them as Parisians. You see, the one here, staring out, she is Temperance, I see her as a woman, a real Parisian woman of our times, like you.' I remember thinking about it for a long time afterwards.

He pauses for a while, before continuing: 'I have not been able to get it out of my mind. It is a very clever idea. I should also be honest and tell you that the idea on its own is not enough. I am sure you can see, mademoiselle, that the picture is poorly painted. The way it stands, you cannot exhibit it anywhere. People would laugh at you. Ideas work only if they are properly executed.'

'I know all that, monsieur.'

'I am glad you agree with my assessment of the technique.' He never agrees with his critics and their comments on his techniques. How many times have they berated him for not finishing his pictures, slopping on too much paint, and showing brush strokes?

'One day, I'll be a better painter and I'll improve on it.' I think I know what he is about to say. He'll teach me how to become a better painter. He is smiling:

'I am sure, one day, we shall all be much better painters. But we shall not live forever, mademoiselle.' He pauses, and I wait for him to continue. 'Mademoiselle, what I am trying to say is that, until, as you say, you become a better painter, someone else could improve your picture. The idea is too good to waste. I am certain it would make an impact at the next Salon. The sooner it is exhibited, the better.' I keep my eyes on him. My chest tightens. He isn't going to help me.

'To come straight to the point: I suggest I repaint the picture, and make it good enough to be shown in public. We have plenty of time to aim for the Salon. With such a large canvas, anything less than a major exhibition is not worth bothering about.'

I feel a draught blowing through the large window.

Is this the best chance my picture has of being exhibited at the Salon? I can't let it go just like that. It's mine. I know its faults, but it's my picture. With time, I'll get it right. He is wrong; now that I don't pose for him, I have time. I never dream of anyone or anything else. He has a good life; pictures are all I have.

My mother once said that every woman who is unable to bring up a child should give it up to those who can look after it. Is it the same with pictures?

The lines on Monsieur Manet's face soften as he leans towards me: 'Mademoiselle, trust me. I have come to look after your picture; you may put yourself in my hands. I shall tell you what I intend to do. I shall respect your idea.'

His face is close to mine. But things have changed: I am no longer his model. I am an artist with an idea. Monsieur Manet wants that idea. I look at the fine lines fanning from the corners of his eyes and think how much I like the gentleness of his face.

We sit quietly for a while. It's the first time that I see him showing patience. I know that he wants me to consider his words seriously.

I agree to his proposal. What else can I say? His paintings enchant me. If he can improve mine, perhaps I can learn from it. And of course, as he says, there is the Salon in May. Hundreds, if not thousands, of people, would be able to see my picture.

Before he leaves, Monsieur Manet tells me that he has organised for the transport of the painting tomorrow morning. With anyone else, I would consider the haste offensive. The realization that they took me for granted might even make me change my mind. But Monsieur Manet has every right to be confident in his powers of persuasion with me. He is going to be a great painter. I wouldn't deny him anything. Besides, over the past few months, I've noticed that when he takes it into his head that he wants something, he must have it at once.

34

1863

The men were straightforward. With Leenhoff, I had only three sessions, all very productive. He is an amiable fellow, as easy-going and obliging as his dear sister, my beloved Suzanne. For the last session, I was very tired, and I almost cancelled it, but the liveliness of his mind kept me alert. As an artist himself, he understood perfectly what I needed. I said that whenever he wanted a grumpy, bearded model for his sculptures, I would return the favour. He laughed and said that I was too harsh on myself.

'Edouard, when I am asked to do a figure of a handsome and clever painter, you will be my first and my only choice.'

I am pleased I was able to capture his friendly nature in the expression on his face. However, Victorine saw the picture and made it clear that she was not happy with his figure staring out. We had a little argument about it. She said that, if the male figure was looking out of the picture, then the woman's gaze was less striking. As if anyone could ever compete with her.

'On the contrary,' I said, 'his ordinary gaze brings hers out even more. It is only by seeing him next to her that we recognise how extraordinary her figure is.' Victorine is not flattered easily and did not seem convinced. Yet I meant what I said.

I get the impression that she argued because she felt posses-sive about the picture. I think she meant well but the trouble is that she is an intuitive artist, as are all women artists. She cannot rationalise her decisions or understand mine. But in the end, since I have completely repainted the figure, it is up to me to choose the direction of his gaze.

When I look at women artists, sometimes I think it is a pity they are not men. But they could still do something in the cause of painting by each marrying an academician and bringing discord into the camp of those old dodderers, though that would be asking for a considerable self-sacrifice.

I did not dismiss her comment outright. Later I thought about it again and I could see that she had a point. Of course, my idea was perfectly valid, too.

Thinking about it today, I realize that it was clever of her not to insist. Perhaps she has accepted the fact that, after all, the picture is mine now. Since I have known her, I have come to envy her ability to relax and let go of arguments. She knows what she wants, and yet she goes about it in a less offensive way than I could. At first, I used to think that she was unsure of her views, but recently, I have realised that she is as confident as I am. However, unlike me, she knows how to talk to people without imposing her views on them. It helps that she is patient; I am not.

I can talk to Antoine and Charles, but when it comes to loud-mouthed models and waiters, I feel at a loss. I want to cut them short. In the past, I have tried to assume authority but without much success. My other approach is to make them think that I am like them and speak with their vulgar language: slur the words as they do. Again, it rarely works. Usually, they laugh at my feeble imitation.

Victorine is no loud-mouthed model. And yet, she hasn't the language of my friends. Her accent is uneven: when she speaks slowly and makes an effort to explain her views on painting, she can use sophisticated words and pronounces them well. But every now and then, traces of the *faubourg* come out. I find that confusing: who is she?

Yesterday, after Victorine had left without making further reference to the male figure, I looked at it again. I set to work immediately and I altered the direction of his gaze. While the woman is meeting the eyes of the viewer, the man next to her looks out of the picture, but his eyes are set on something undefined in the distance. I think it is important that the woman and the man are not looking towards the same point.

I used Eugène for the second figure, except on the two days when he was engaged elsewhere and my dear Gustave was happy to stand in for him. It is convenient to have two brothers who look so much alike! It was Gustave, always interested in dressing up, who put on the *faluche*, the same one that Victorine wore as *La Chanteuse des rues*.

When I first saw the painting in her room, all I could think of was the figure of Temperance. I envied Victorine for having used the idea before me. Since then, I have thought of other possible influences. I doubt it that she has seen much Watteau. He has that figure of a guitarist looking out and meeting the eye of the viewer. His gaze does not have the same intensity as the woman's here, but then, Watteau was at a disadvantage: he did not have Victorine to model for him.

She comes in and stands briefly in front of the half-finished painting. As she does not comment, I ask her opinion of the two men. She ignores my question.

I ask again: 'I want to know whether you are happy with the composition of the three characters. What do you think of the postures of the men?'

She nods. 'One of my problems,' she says, 'was that the men I painted didn't have real faces. I had a woman posing for them. And she was black. I needed two white men.'

I agree with her: it is important that the men are recognizable as contemporary Parisians.

Victorine takes off her clothes and sits down. What does the black woman think about Victorine being naked alone with me? Does she mind?

I am still preparing for today's session and she does not assume the full pose straight away. Using soft soap, I wash off the woman's face that I painted yesterday. The hard, thick lumps of paint I have to scrape off with a palette knife. Victorine sits with the elbow of her visible arm propped against her knee and the hand holding her chin. She is waiting and thinking. Her head is in profile.

'Please do not move from this position. Just turn your head towards me.' She does as I ask. And there I have it. Here is a thinking woman, rather than just a nude posing in the company of two men engaged in a discussion. A thinking woman. A woman of modernity.

I leave the face for now and go back to the body. I am lucky that the sun is streaming in through the window. I want to show a fully lit body, with no shade, no half tones, very much the same effect as in *La Chanteuse des rues*. I want the viewers to be dazzled by its brightness, just as I was dazzled by Victorine's face when under the white sun on that January day her eyebrows disappeared. I want to make sure that the spectator's perception is arrested instantly by the mass and colour of the woman's body. I want it to feel more like the shock, the immediacy. The abruptness is to work on the eye.

Now that I know what I am doing, I paint quickly and finish the changes to the body in the afternoon. I start on the face and work frantically. Victorine is obliging and sits perfectly still. From time to time, I catch her staring at me in that penetrating way of hers but, these days, it hardly bothers me. On the contrary, today, my mood boosted by the progress with the picture, I find it almost flattering that she is studying me while I am painting her.

I have noticed a certain coldness in her manner towards me and it saddens me. The first time she undressed for this picture, I watched her, making sure that the expression on my face reflected my interest in her. I wanted her to know that I thought she was attractive. I tried to show that I was looking at her as a man looks at a woman; I smiled and spoke softly. As soon as she began to unbutton her blouse, I put down whatever I was holding, a brush or a piece of paper and focused on her, following her movements with my eyes. I even came to stand closer, but as I extended my arm to touch her, she moved away and busied herself undoing a ribbon on her chemise, as if pretending that she did not notice that I was there. Later, probably at the second or third sitting, I made a comment on how well she looked but her face remained impassive. I do not understand

223

why I used to look at her just as a model, flirting with her only because I thought that I had to keep her happy. Why did I not see what a beautiful woman she is?

I have never known a woman like Victorine. Since visiting her lodgings, I know more about her than ever before and yet she is more of an enigma than when I first saw her in the Luxembourg Gardens. She is different from my friends, but she must be different from her friends as well.

Until recently I used to think of her only in terms of shapes and compositions. Her body was an object in my paintings. But now I see more than that and I want her all to myself.

After she leaves, I have an urge to look again at Watteau's engravings. I need to check an idea I have. Would he have seen Giorgione, I wonder? Would he have copied that gaze?

As I leave the studio, I remember a drawing I made of Watteau's *La Villageoise*, based on an engraving. I must have it somewhere. I shall dig it out tomorrow. That may be just what I need for the background. The figure has the right position; I shall not require a model for her. I can copy it straight from the painting.

35

Madame Bijoux brings up a large basket with pastries, apples and dry figs. Monsieur Manet asks me to arrange it. He has finished painting the three figures and is about to start on the landscape. It was his idea that I should paint the still life section. When he came to my apartment to ask if he could repaint the picture, I was working on a series of flowers in vases for Etienne. Monsieur Manet looked at them and complimented me on the craft.

'Your drawings are quite assured. Much better than when you work on figures,' he said. I wasn't surprised. I've had a great deal of practice with flower pictures. In spite of that, I was completely unprepared for his suggestion 'that I should do the picnic food'. My first thought was that he wanted me to buy some fruit from the market for him to paint.

I thank Madame Bijoux and lift the basket onto the table. This morning, on the way to the studio, I stopped at a flower seller to buy fresh foliage, which I use for padding. On top, I place the apples and the pastries arranged on a serviette. In between, I scatter a handful of figs. As I am pulling out some green leaves from below, to make the arrangement look more life-like, the basket overturns and the food spills all over the table. Monsieur Manet looks up. He puts down his brush and the maulstick and walks towards me, his eyes focused on the items on the table.

'This makes a good display. It is much more natural to have an overturned basket than to give the impression that our friends have only just arrived. No, they are in the middle of their little outing. They have eaten some of the food and the rest is scattered on the ground.' Monsieur Manet pushes the fruit and pastries further from the basket.

'What do you think, Mademoiselle Victorine?'

I look at the arrangement on the table, then at the canvas and try to imagine what the picture would look like. I want to say that I like the idea, but Monsieur Manet has already walked away. A minute later, he appears on the stairs leading from the gallery. He is carrying a large straw hat with a blue ribbon, which he places next to the basket.

'We mustn't forget the hat our young mademoiselle has taken off.'

I work on a drawing, starting on a small piece of paper, just to examine the validity of the composition. I move on to a large sheet that allows me to draw life-size objects. I progress very slowly. After more than two hours, I am ready to show Monsieur Manet what I have done. He must find it satisfactory, because he tells me to begin working on the canvas.

By the afternoon, I have finished the outline and I prepare the palette. Again, I work slowly, suddenly unsure how to proceed. Between applications of paint, I pause to study the display, wondering how to convey the differences in textures. I think of my flower pictures and of the techniques I use for them. Everything that I've produced for Etienne is so routine and even the brush strokes are the same in each picture. I don't think I can use that style here. I wish I could make the fruit and the pastries appear real. I work for a while but I don't feel happy with the result and I paint over it again and again. At one point, Monsieur Manet tucks in a folded light blue dress below the basket. I can see what he is doing: he wants the viewer to see that the woman has actually removed her clothes, rather than to assume that her nudity is natural to her. I have thought of it first but he doesn't know it as I never had a chance to paint the dress.

I remember discussing the same idea with Emily and her friends. Since Monsieur Manet has been repainting the canvas, I've forgotten about the woman's clothes. Now I have yet another texture to deal with. I feel completely at a loss but I don't dare admit it to him.

He must notice that I am having difficulties, because he walks towards my easel and stands next to me. Over the past few weeks, I have come to admire his energy and unwavering enthusiasm. He has put long hours into this painting.

'May I,' he says as he holds out his hand for me to pass him my brush. As he works, he explains what he is doing:

'Put the paint down quickly. Don't worry about the background. Just go for the tone of the colour.' With a few brushstrokes, he creates a pastry with a shiny crust and crumbly texture.

'You see? When you look at it, and above all, when you think how to render it as you see it, that is, so that it makes the same impression on the viewer as it does on you..., you don't look for, you don't see the lines on the paper over there, do you...?'

I nod. I have never thought of that. He carries on: 'Let me show you something else.' He fetches a small canvas with a picture of grapes on a plate.

'And the grapes, now, do you need to count each grape? Of course not. What is important is their clear amber colour, and the bloom which models the form and softens it.' He shows me how to paint a grape. I have the apples and figs to work on.

Monsieur Manet leads me to *La Chanteuse des rues* canvas and points to the cherries. I study the brushstrokes. Perhaps I could copy them, scatter them in front of the overturned basket.

'Mademoiselle Victorine, let me show you something else. Have a look at the dress that I have placed here; it is partially covered by the basket. What you have to decide with the cloth is where the highlights come and then which planes are not in direct light.' I nod to let him know that I understand what he is saying. But how can I do it? He makes it appear so obvious and simple. And it is not. It will take me a long time and many attempts. It will involve a great deal of scraping off the paint. And if he sees me doing that, he may lose patience. If that happens, I fear, he may not allow me to paint anything on this canvas.

'Remember, mademoiselle, halftones are for the *Magasin pittoresque* engravers. The folds will come by themselves if you put them in their proper place.' With a few quick brushstrokes, Monsieur Manet demonstrates his technique. I thank him and carry on working.

After a while, he returns and says: 'Painting is all about

creating illusions. There are different ways of doing it. Here I have shown the brushstrokes, the use of light colours. They make the still life realistic. But elsewhere, there are other ways.' He turns away from me and as if looking at some imaginary audience says: 'With the *Espada, La Chanteuse des rues* and, I hope, here, it is your face, your face, Mademoiselle Victorine that tells everyone that the painting is an illusion. If they cannot see that…well, they will not understand what I am doing.' A few moments pass; he looks at me again: 'That's modernism; that's what Charles calls modernism.'

After an hour or two, he asks if he can see what I have done. I am frightened but I nod. He stands next to me and examines the section I've almost completed. He looks at it for a long time. The silence makes me feel uncomfortable; my painting must be all wrong.

'This is good, mademoiselle, very good.' His eyes remain on the painting as he speaks. 'Indeed, I have no suggestions to make at this stage.' With that, he walks away.

I accept his praise as genuine and the words give me courage to carry on. Now, my brushstrokes are more confident and I no longer have to repaint so much.

Around four o'clock, it's too dark for us to work and Monsieur Manet says that we should stop for the day. I wish I could see what he has been working on. I know it's a drawing. Earlier on when I asked, he said, he was 'just copying.' Now, he is covering the large piece of paper and I know better than to mention it again.

Before I leave, I pause by my portrait, the first picture that Monsieur Manet made of me. He is talking to Antoine, who has just arrived, and I feel I can take time to look at the picture closely without being noticed by either of them. It was painted ten months ago. Here, my expression is that of a scared animal who feels frightened and trapped, but is nevertheless prepared to face her persecutors. I compare the portrait to the woman on the large canvas. She is much more confident and self-assured, almost happy to be herself. Compared with Mademoiselle Victorine, the naked woman is almost too proud, conceited even.

Have I changed so much in the past ten months, or have I just become better at playing different roles?

As I reach the door, Monsieur Manet calls me back: 'Mademoiselle, Antoine has just asked me about the title of our large canvas. I did not know how to answer him. What do you say?'

I note that this is the first time that he has called the large canvas 'ours' and that he has said so in the presence of another person. That pleases me. I know that I should say something and show my claim to the painting. At the same time, I am aware that if I make a specific suggestion, he'll go against it. He is a man who needs careful treatment.

'I am not sure, monsieur.' His face is serious and, against my better judgement, I add: 'The three people on the picture seem to be sharing food, perhaps they are having lunch on the grass, in the open air. I'd call it *Le déjeuner sur l'herbe*.'

'Well, we shall see.' He turns towards Antoine: 'My dear friend, I cannot answer your question today. But I think I will have the title shortly.'

I accept that I may not be consulted further. I do mind but, in the context of the whole day, the matter is of no importance. I am no longer the trapped, frightened animal who walked into this studio more than ten months ago. I am working as a painter on the same canvas as Monsieur Manet.

36

Charles and I leave the Martinet show. The Boulevard des Italiens is crowded and we have to weave our way between people strolling in the late afternoon March sunshine. The visit to the gallery, and the reviews I read this morning have lowered my spirits and I need to reflect.

As we turn into side streets, Charles takes my arm: 'Edouard, you often say that for the artist to exhibit is the *sine qua non*. I agree with you on that. And you should be delighted that your one-man show – an honour for an artist as young as you – is so well attended.' His voice is uncharacteristically soft. 'But there is no compulsion to read the critics, let alone to take them seriously.'

'Charles, I need recognition and praise... and –'

'What, for your dear *maman*?'

He is making fun of me. But he would not understand if I were to tell him that I care about what mother thinks of me.

'It is not just the critics. You have just seen that the public do not like my work, either. They come in droves but they complain.'

'Oh, the public.' Charles makes a gesture of dismissal with his hand. 'They are used to standing close to canvases and admiring the delicacy of the brush work. You know that, Edouard. You could see how they were peering at the pictures. With your brushstrokes, they will have to learn to look at paintings in a new way: from a distance. New age, new paintings, new ways of looking at them. And then that fool screaming that there was no point in seeing people wearing the same clothes as his; any nonsense would do for him as long as it was dressed in historical costume. In an age of electricity and steam, artists should not be

230

expected to produce mythological scenes featuring Venus and Bacchus.'

We had barely walked into the gallery when we heard the man screaming that he would take violent action against *La musique aux Tuileries* if the painting remained on show.

'An unfinished canvas like this should not be exhibited,' the man shouted. 'All I can see are brush marks, no real people, no music, no gardens.' The worst was that he wasn't an isolated madman. The crowd around him cheered. The gallery threw him out but, outside on the pavement, he threatened to return.

Martinet was embarrassed by the incident and assured me that there was no question of closing the exhibition.

'Edouard,' Charles says, 'how many times have we agreed that artists need to embrace *la modernité*, the fleeting and seemingly trivial world of contemporary life? We need crowds, street scenes, drunks in cafes, the splendour and the ugliness.'

Charles is right. I can do the dress of the past: *La Pêche* has a couple in seventeenth century costume. But I no longer wish to refer to Rubens. I rather give them my *Le Buveur d'absinthe*, or *Le Vieux musicien*.

And then there are those people who recognise me on the street: some of them shout obscenities, while others laugh at me. I have learned to ignore them.

'At least, no one has attacked you physically. Do I need to remind you of the reception of Delacroix's *La mort de Sardanapale* received in 1828?' Charles smiles at me. It is known that the revulsion of the public at the colours and sensuality was so strong that one visitor even threatened to amputate the painter's hands.

We walk on in silence for a while. I can feel the threat of a headache.

Charles stops, holds my arms and smiles: 'Edouard, the public are vulgar and uneducated. One day they will see better.' We are standing on the pavement outside Gare St Lazare with people pushing around us, porters carrying luggage and a steam engine pulling in. Charles, ignoring the bustle and the noise, says: 'Listen to the words of your favourite poet:

Il te faut, pour gagner ton pain de chaque soir,
Comme un Enfant de choeur, jouer de l'encensoir,
Chanter des Te Deum auxquels tu ne crois guère,

Ou, saltimbanque à jeun, étaler tes appas
Et ton rire trempé des pleurs qu'on ne voit pas,
Pour faire épanouir la rate de vulgaire.

I am grateful for his words but it is difficult to be philosophical when neither the public nor the critics understand what I am doing.

We walk on and Charles says: 'Be an artist and be independent. Who cares what others think?' He is right, but disapproval, even from the vulgar crowd hurts, nevertheless. 'Anyway, you are lucky. You don't need to sell.'

'Just as well. Out of the fourteen canvases at Martinet, none has been sold. There was some interest in *L'Enfant à l'épée*. I told Louis that I would expect 1,000 francs for it, but I would take less.'

The critics are another matter; one cannot ignore them. I could have done without such negative reviews so close to the Salon. My plan, with Louis' encouragement, was to use the show on the Boulevard des Italiens as a preview of the Salon. We hoped that the exhibition, solely dedicated to my work, would have made me the talk of the town and that the jury would be in no position to ignore, let alone reject, my paintings. As it is, I worry that the current reviews may have a negative influence on their decision.

This Salon had been giving me problems even before I had sent them anything. First, there was the publication of Nieuwerkerke's ridiculous rules and all that nonsense about not being able to submit more than three works. At least we all rallied and, the next day, Doré and I were received by Count Walewski and we handed him our petition. He was sympathetic but Nieuwerkerke's just too powerful and can afford to dictate. He behaves like an emperor. And then there was Meissonier publicly announcing that he was boycotting the Salon. I admired him for that but only a man of his reputation can afford to do that. I could not.

We arrive in my studio. Madame Bijoux brings a tray with coffee and cakes. Charles pours me a cup. 'Cheer up, my friend.'

I know he means well but he does not understand my position. Notoriety is enough for him. I have dreams of being shown in the *Salon d'honneur*.

'Edouard, do I have to convince you once again of your own worth?' I sigh.

'It is not easy to remain confident when no one wants to buy my pictures and the critics continue their onslaught.'

Charles sighs: 'What you ask is really too foolish. They make fun of you; you are irritated by the jokes; they are incapable of doing you justice; etc. etc. I agree it is a nuisance and it is annoying. It may be demoralising but do you think you are the first man ever to experience such criticism?' He stares at me as if waiting for a reply. 'Is your genius greater than that of Chateaubriand, or Wagner? And were they not mocked? They survived. And, lest I inspire excessive pride in you, let me say that these men are, each in their own way, exemplary figures in very distinguished fields. You, by contrast, are merely the finest painter in the decrepitude of your art.'

Charles looks me in the eye, worrying how I am taking his words, and then adds in a more mellow voice: 'I hope you do not resent this frank appreciation. You know I am your loyal friend.'

I know that. And I know that I should follow Charles' advice. He knows what he is talking about. He has been through much worse, with the court case and the ban, the accusations of obscenity and all the associated brouhaha. And yet, one day in the future, people will read *Les Fleurs du Mal* and wonder what all the fuss was about.

I say that from now on I promise not to read anything the critics write.

Charles looks away. 'The real criticism should be impartial, but also passionate and political, not to forget that it needs to be amusing and poetic as well.' I am not sure; I have to think about that.

He stands up and walks to the window. The sunshine picks

out the deep lines etched on his face and, with his thinning, dishevelled hair, my friend looks like an old man, well beyond his early forties. Glancing out onto the street, he says: 'The best account of a picture may well be a sonnet or an elegy.' He turns towards me: 'How about that, Edouard?'

I smile and he continues: 'I expect the critic to transform into knowledge my shock of pleasure on seeing a picture.' Charles sighs. His grim, staring eyes settle on my face: 'But you cannot expect that from our little scribblers. Most of them are failed artists. Since they cannot paint or draw, they write, and they write badly. But you cannot avoid them. The trick is not to take them seriously. Snippets of their comments are bound to reach you one way or another. You will hear people talking. The faces of your friends will show you what the critics have written. And public attitudes become influenced by critical views.'

'Not all the reviews are bad. Let me read you what Chesneau writes.' I pick up a newspaper cutting. 'According to him, until now my work has "provided more condemnation than sympathy." And, he adds: "In spite of that I must confess that a certain amount of youthful daring is not distasteful to me and that even if I willingly grant all that, Manet still lacks something to justify his audacity." Well, that's not what I wanted to show you. But listen, he also says, " I do not despair of seeing him triumph over ignorance to become a fine painter. In my eyes, he has one great virtue: he is not commonplace and he does not stick in the rut which leads to easy rewards and cheap success."'

I look at Charles still standing by the window. 'Have you heard that? I am not commonplace and I do not stick in the rut –'

'No, my dear Edouard, you have to learn –'

'Charles, listen, you have to hear a bit more. Chesneau says that I have created "one very fine painting of musical sincerity and feeling for colour"; he is referring to *L'Enfant à l'épée*. Are you listening?'

Charles is shaking his head: 'My dear Edouard, you have to learn not to take the critics' views to heart. If they praise you, you should ignore them. If they condemn you, you should ignore them. Rise above them by not taking any notice of what they say.'

Charles is looking at me, waiting for my reaction. Instead of defending myself, I swallow my words. I simply nod in agreement. He is right. But it is easer said than done. With him looking after me and laughing at 'these critical fools', as he calls them, I can almost join in and laugh at what they say. However, it is different when I am alone. It is true that I have received a few compliments, but the majority of reviews are unfavourable. Whenever I look at the papers, my spirits rise, only to be dashed again and again.

'Edouard, let's start now. We need to immunize you from the critics. They are imbeciles. Listen to this and make sure that you nip in the bud any emotional reaction you might feel. Grow indifferent. Listen. Here we go. Our friend Paul Mantz writes: "Manet, who is a Parisian Spaniard, and who has some mysterious affinity to the tradition of Goya, showed at the 1861 Salon *Le Chanteur espagnol*. That painting greatly impressed us. It was brutal but also truthful. In that rough sketch I could see a promise of a virile talent. Two years have passed since and Manet, still full of his innate bravado, has moved to the realm of the impossible. There is no form in his large portraits of women, and especially in *La Chanteuse des rues*. There the eyebrows have been moved from their horizontal position to a vertical one parallel to the nose, like two dark commas. There is nothing more there than a shattering discord of chalky tones with black ones. The overall effect is pallid, harsh and ominous. At other times, when Manet is in a good humour, he paints *La Musique aux Tuileries*, *Le Ballet espagnol*, and *Lola de Valence*, paintings that disclose his plentiful vigour but which in their strange mixture of red, blue, yellow, and black are colour caricatured, not proper colour itself. In short, this art may be strong and straightforward but it is not healthy, and we feel in no way obliged to plead Manet's cause before the jury of the Salon."'

Charles looks up, gauging my reaction. While reading, he has maintained a neutral tone, clearly not wishing either to applaud, or deride Mantz's criticism. The last sentence causes a tightening in my chest, as if someone is pushing a huge block of ice inside me.

'There are some positive elements here, although it really bothers me what he says about the Salon. I wish he had not made that reference. That could do untold damage to my chances.'

As I speak, Charles shakes his head. 'No, Edouard. No, my little boy. Have we been wasting our time this afternoon? You still do not understand? We, you and I, we do not care what he says. Good or bad, remember? It does not make any difference to us. Who is he anyway? As good an artist as you? No!'

Charles sits next to me. I feel like a helpless child instructed by a sympathetic teacher. Critics make me suffer but I know that their venom also eggs me on.

'Edouard, I need to read you some more. Just to practise.' Charles takes another press cutting sheet from the pile on the side table and reads it out. He looks tired and ill. Suddenly, I feel a surge of affection for him. I know that Jeanne's condition is worsening and that she may not last much longer. He is not well, either. Most certainly, Charles has the same dreaded illness. If that is so, then he has not much time left either. And yet here he is, selfless, helping me deal with what are trivial issues compared with the matters of life and death that regularly visit him now.

I remember him telling me that, when he was a student at the Lycée Louis-le-Grand, his teacher called him 'deceitful and untruthful'. These days, people say that he is 'cavalier and shockingly affected'. And I can see that as he ages, he speaks in paradoxes, he is more cynical, and that he likes to shock. We may disagree when it comes to politics – oh, I could never be a royalist – but as a friend, he is most honest and kind. Suddenly, Chesneau and Mantz appear to be of no significance. It is more important that I have been so lucky with friends. I smile: 'Charles, I honestly do not care for what these parasites write. One day, I shall take revenge for all exclusions. And besides, as someone said the other day at the Guerbois, if one wants to sell, one needs to acquire a certain notoriety.'

Charles nods: 'That's the spirit.' Of course, in his case notoriety goes with impecuniosity. 'Look, my friend, what we have got to

236

do is to go right ahead, without bothering what other people think.'

'Let me take you out for a good dinner,' I say. 'And some very good wine.'

'In that case, I shall come straightaway.' His angular frame springs into life once again. We run downstairs and stop the first fiacre that comes our way. When we sit down, I look at Charles. His face is red and his breathing laboured. I pretend not to notice.

37

I go out to buy newspapers. It's an expense I can't afford, but I don't want to miss any articles about the forthcoming Salon. I'd rather forego my glass of wine tonight.

The last time I saw Monsieur Manet was just before the exhibition on the Boulevard des Italiens, so I can only imagine the effect of those hostile reviews. Two weeks ago, he sent me a note saying that all three of the pictures he had submitted to the Salon had been rejected. He added that, after weeks of agonizing over their fate, he was in real despair. I was saddened that, despite all the work, the picture based on my idea wasn't going to be seen by the public, but I wouldn't say that I was in despair.

I know that Monsieur Manet tends to exaggerate, and in particular when describing his feelings. He is also prone to rapid changes in his mood: he can oscillate between an arrogant self-belief and a conviction that he has nothing to offer. On some days, I thought he banned himself from happiness.

Perhaps he is of 'a nervous and febrile disposition'. I remember Madame Duras using these words to describe her brother after she had received a letter from him that seemed to cause distress. I had never heard the phrase before and it stuck in my mind. When Madame Duras explained to me what it meant, I could not think of anyone I knew who would fit the description. Modelling for Monsieur Manet, I can see that he might be that kind of person. At the time of the first three paintings, we didn't talk much. But working on the last one, with me both modelling and painting, I saw a different side of him. I became more aware of his emotional fragility. Gradually, I realised that he is very susceptible to what others think of him. Quite apart from wanting his work to be admired, he also wants to be popular, to be loved. Any little thing affects him, whether it is a kind word, a smile or an unpleasant remark. I could understand when he told me that sometimes the lack of light depresses him. As a painter, he needs light. But he shouldn't allow people to influence him so much. It is wasteful of time and effort that could be spend on painting.

Once I had the mind to tell him that wasn't the way to go through life. Those of us less fortunate wouldn't survive with such a disposition. I imagined him working in a café or living in the Hôtel d'Or. He would never have managed there. Even Maître Albert would have overwhelmed him with its beggars around Notre-Dame and the rubbish on the pavements.

How is he taking this morning's news? The announcement in the *Moniteur* says:

'Numerous complaints have reached the Emperor in connection with the works of art which have been refused by the jury of the exhibition. His Majesty, wishing to let the public judge the legitimacy of these complaints, has decided that the rejected works of art should be exhibited in another part of the Palace of Industry. This exhibition will be voluntary, meaning that artists who may not wish to participate need only inform the administration, which will return their works to them. This exhibition will open on May 15. Artists have until May 7 to decide. After this date, their pictures will be considered not withdrawn and will be hung in the galleries.'

For a moment, I think of all those artists I saw on 1st April transporting their work to the Palais des Champs-Elysées. The paint on some canvases was still wet to the touch. The sea of wheelbarrows and hand-pulled carts stretched as far as the eye could see. Monsieur Manet wasn't among them. He had hired porters for our painting and for his other two canvases.

Five thousand works were submitted this year and only two thousand, two hundred and seventeen were accepted.

I know that Monsieur Manet was so keen to rally support for his work that he even tried to persuade Monsieur Delacroix to take up his place on the Selection Committee, but Monsieur Delacroix was already too ill.

I can imagine Monsieur Manet pacing up and down in his studio, cursing.

What does he plan to do now? He has often said that if any attempt to do something new in art involves a struggle, it should at least be conducted fairly: the artist should be allowed to show his work.

I don't expect he'll consult me on whether to exhibit or withdraw the large canvas. He regards the painting as entirely his own. The last time I was in his studio, his friend Antonin Proust arrived just as I was about to leave. It was the first time that he had seen the picture. I was standing by the door, when he looked at the canvas and I heard him say: 'Oh, Edouard, here it is.' He paused before adding, 'I remember that day last year at Argenteuil. Was it last August, Edouard? You said something about being expected to do a painting with a nude. Then those bathers came and we both looked at them. I remember you turning towards me and saying that if they wanted the nude, that was what they should have.'

I stopped, intrigued. I noticed that Monsieur Manet glanced in my direction. I couldn't be sure, but I had a feeling that his face told me to keep quiet. I had no intention of interfering and showing him up in front of his friend. Now that he is teaching me how to paint, it would be foolish to make him angry. Learning from him is much more important to me than arguing about who had the idea first.

'And then a few days later, you were still thinking of that scene when you said that you wanted to use the composition from the Giorgone canvas that both of us admired. But you wanted to make it lighter, and with people dressed like us...and here it is...'

As I was closing the door behind me, I could hear Monsieur Proust again: 'But Edouard, I must say that I fear that your prediction that they will slaughter you will prove correct. This picture will make their blood boil.' Monsieur Manet laughed loudly.

Outside, it was a clear starry night, unusually mild for late March. I decided to walk back home. I needed time to think about what I heard. Was it possible that Monsieur Manet had had the same idea as me? And if that were the case, and there was his friend to prove it, why didn't he say anything to me? Why couldn't he have told his friend about my original picture? And moreover, why couldn't he have said that I had actually realised it before him, no matter how poorly? Was it vanity on his part?

As I reached the Boulevard Saint Michel, the pavements were crowded with people out on their early evening stroll, enjoying the weather. Most of them were either couples or families walking together and talking loudly. Alone and silent, weaving my way in between them, I felt isolated. Antonin Proust's words lay heavily on my mind.

Only a few days earlier, I had noticed Monsieur Manet's copy of Giorgone's *Concert champêtre*. When I asked him whether he had only just acquired it, he said: 'Oh, no. I have only just hung it up. Henri, Henri Fantin-Latour made it for me years ago.'

The other painting that might have inspired me is Marc-antonio Raimondi but, even though I had seen it before, I didn't think of it while composing the original picture. If Proust's words are true – and I have no reason to doubt them – then Monsieur Manet's idea, unlike mine, came from life. That would make sense. Doesn't he often say, 'I paint what I see.'

Monsieur Proust's words stayed with me, but there wasn't much point worrying about them. I reminded myself that I've moved a long way from the days when I used to make little drawings, surreptitiously, whenever my mother was out. Now, I have had a studio for more than a year and I have been making money from painting. The most ambitious picture I have ever attempted was finished and, although my visible contribution to it was comparatively small, I was pleased with its execution. Monsieur Manet didn't comment, but the fact that he left my work on the basket and the fruit alone, without adding a single brushstroke, meant that he was satisfied with the result.

By the time I left Boulevard Saint Michel, I was in high spirits. I reminded myself that I had learned a great deal from Monsieur Manet and I was grateful for that.

I cross the street and, as on the day when I heard Monsieur

Proust talk about Argenteuil, I think of how far I have come. It would be silly to allow my spirits to fall. Even if the picture isn't exhibited, if Monsieur Manet decides to withdraw it, I've gained something. I am a better painter and perhaps soon I can attempt something by myself and present it to the Salon. There are other possibilities, too. The brother-in-law of Etienne's dealer, also a dealer, is looking for someone to accompany a number of canvases on a steamboat to America. Etienne recommended me to Monsieur Nouvel.

America must be an exciting place. All the people I have met from there love French paintings. Perhaps, they might like my work.

The sky is cloudy but feelings of warmth and happiness permeate my body. I read the *Moniteur* announcement again. An exhibition of the rejected work is quite a departure from the usual practice.

Suddenly, something sharp prods me in the back. I turn. An old beggar woman shuffles away. Her fist is still clenched. I can't see her face: a loosely tied dark brown kerchief falls over her forehead and her back is so stooped that she looks only at the pavement in front of her.

I watch her, mesmerised by the familiarity of the shape of her body and its movements. She turns towards me and extends her arm. I recognize the mouth with its prominent lower lip. Mother. She is my mother.

For a while, I stand in the middle of the pavement, unable to move. People bump into me while I search my pockets. By now, my mother has given up on me and is almost out of sight. I push through the crowded part of the pavement to reach her. I walk behind her, clutching ten francs. What should I say to her?

I move next to her and try to push the money into her hand. At first, instinctively thinking that I mean to hurt her, she hits back and I feel the strength of her determination to defend herself. She smells of alcohol. My mother never drank and hated anyone who did.

I must speak to her but my throat is tight. When I try to say 'madame', holding the money in front of her, my voice is too

242

quiet and she doesn't hear me. I follow her and once again I try to make her take the money. This time, she realizes what I am doing. She grabs the notes, looks at them, and then quickly pushes them inside her clothes. She stares at me. Sudden fear grips me and I want to move away but the pavement is crowded. She reaches out for my hand and mumbles a thank you before disappearing.

She didn't recognise me.

I walk home slowly. It's been just over a year since I left the Hôtel d'Or. Only once did I send her any money. Whenever I think of her, I experience a terrible tightening of my heart but I try not to feel guilty. I can't; I mustn't go back to that life.

In my apartment, I force myself to focus on my work. A medium size canvas from Etienne, which I need to take back to him in two days' time, is only half finished. And I have barely started on the picture of the fruit bowl, due next week. The real problem there will be the dead rabbit, thrown across the table. Etienne has lent me a small painting of a rabbit in a similar position, which he made some time ago, and suggested that I copy it. I was going to buy a rabbit and work with 'my little model', but today I realize that I am running short of time.

As soon as I set to work, there is knocking on the door. My mother. She has followed me. I decide not to move. The knocking continues. Madame Conchis wouldn't let a beggar past her. Perhaps it is Monsieur Manet coming to consult me on what to do about our picture. As I walk to the door, I tell myself that I'll go along with whatever decision he makes.

It's a surprise to see Lola standing in front of me. She is out of breath and immediately says that she can't stay long as she has been sent on an errand to a vegetable market in the area. As she comes in, I am aware that she is looking around, as if to make sure that I am not hiding a lover. Immediately, she throws her basket on the floor and begins to undress me.

'I want you, Victorine, I want you so much, right now,' she whispers into my ear, and her hot breath tickles me. She unbuttons her blouse and asks me to touch her breasts. Her kisses are more urgent than usual and for the first time in many months, I feel excited. I begin to move, arching my back as Lola glides her fingers inside me. I scream with pleasure. She squeezes me tight.

'I love you, Victorine,' she says. 'I'll come again, but now I really have to go.' She hugs me by the door and rushes down-stairs.

Left alone, I sit on the divan and tears flood into my eyes. I can't remember the last time I cried.

38

I expected *Le Bain* to be attacked, so they can say what they like. Charles is not in Paris to monitor my reactions, but I shall heed his advice. From Brussels, he sent me Thore's review, with a comment scrawled over in red ink: 'Damn the parasites. Do not let them get to you.' Further down, in the margins of one of the press cuttings, Charles has written: 'What can you expect from an age whose etiquette manual advises: "During the bath itself, if necessary, close your eyes until you have finished the procedure."

I read the sections that Charles has encircled.

'Instead of giving us outlines, which the Academy calls drawing, instead of working hard on details, which admirers of classic art call finish, these painters create an effect in its striking unity; they do not bother with correct lines or minute details.

'After Whistler, the artist who attracts most attention is Manet. He, too, is a true painter; several of his etchings, particularly the reproduction of *Les Petits cavaliers* by Velázquez in the Louvre, which is exhibited among the rejected works, are lively, witty, and colourful. His three paintings are a provocation to the public that is dazzled by the too vivid colour. In the centre, there is a bathing scene; to the left a Spanish *Majo*; to the right a Parisian girl in the costume of an *Espada*, waving her purple cape in the bull ring. Manet loves Spain, and his favourite master seems to be Goya, whose vivid and contrasting hues, whose free and fiery touch, he often imitates. There are some amazing materials in these two Spanish figures, the *Majo*'s black costume and the heavy scarlet *burnous*, which he carries over his arm, the pink silk stockings of the young Parisian disguised as an Espada. But underneath these brilliant costumes, personality itself seems to be lacking; he should have painted them differently from the drapery, with more accent and contrast.'

At least the critic recognizes my debt to Velázquez, unlike those critics who talk of the unfinished canvas or of distant blobs. Yes, I have learned so much from Velázquez. He knew how to sacrifice detail to achieve the overall effect.

I want truth rather than likeness. To hell with finishes. Long live the sketches.

I read more of Charles's press cuttings.

'*Le Bain* is very daring. The nude hasn't a good figure, unfortunately, and it is difficult to imagine anything uglier than the man sitting next to her, who hasn't even thought of taking off, out of doors, his awful padded cap. It is the contrast of a creature so inappropriate in a pastoral scene with this undressed bather that is shocking. I cannot see what made an artist of intelligence and refinement select such an absurd composition, which might have been justified only if he had used elegant and charming characters. But, at the same time, there are qualities of colour and light in the landscape, and even very convincing bits of modelling in the woman's body.'

I wish I could shout at them: 'Is there a more sincere work, more free from convention, more true to life?' Had I painted Louis Napoleon, what a success that would have been!

I make a list of the comments, a column of good ones and a column of bad ones. I jot down my response to the bad ones. Perhaps I should write a letter to a newspaper to explain my position. I begin to compose it in my head. I walk around the studio saying the words aloud.

Wait, Edouard, I say to myself. Damn this Thoré! Why should I have to explain my work to him? I am a painter. I paint. I do not write letters to newspapers to educate either the critics or the public. He and the rest are welcome to their opinions. I have my own path to follow.

If only Charles could see me now. I paint what I see. I shall not paint what others expect me to paint. As I go out, a hope, a belief, a conviction, that those who live in the next century will see better begins to grow in my heart. Walking brusquely, I experience a surge of energy and take deep, long breaths. My eyes feast on trees: once again, everything is in full bloom. May is the most beautiful month in Paris. Its pleasures are not to be missed.

After just over half an hour, I reach the Tuileries and sit on a bench under a horse chestnut in full blossom that looks like a bride.

I take out Charles' letter and it is only now that I notice a post scriptum. It is written in tiny letters:

My dear friend, do not worry, but I wish to tell you this: the veritable lady, Madame Verole, has come to claim me. But I shall make her wait. There are other ladies, much nicer than her, who I wish to attend to. And Madame Verole may pester but I know that she will wait. In the past, I cultivated my hysteria with pleasure and terror in equal measure. Now I have constant dizzy spells and today I experienced a singular warning. I felt the wing of imbecility brush over me. Must be her knocking. The impatient woman. Am I so irresistible? But I shall not let her in. I promise you that, dear boy. I shall not let her in. Not as yet.

My dear, dear Charles. I shall no longer be able to comfort him with suggestions that he may be suffering from rheumatism. On a beautiful day like this, thoughts of death depress me more than ever. No one should have to die in May in Paris.

39

The omnibus reaches the Champs Elysées. There are crowds on the pavement, women strolling in the latest fashions, some in flounced skirts, others in silk dresses on the arms of men in black suits. Young and old sit at tables outside cafés. Men are smoking, women laughing. I look down at the pile of newspapers in my lap. Everyone writes about the Salon and I have been through all the reviews several times already. I cannot stop myself from reading every single reference. I try to think of a Lockroy who writes in *Courier artistique* that some of the paintings, and he makes it clear that among them he includes Manet's pictures, 'would have held an honourable place with the work that was accepted'. This Lockroy believes that one day Monsieur Manet will triumph over all the obstacles and says that he will be the first to applaud his success. So will I. But then there are others, like someone called Théophile Thoré who thinks that the composition of the painting is absurd and that the characters lack elegance and charm. Another critic calls the female figure in *Le Bain* 'a commonplace woman of the demimonde'. The words echo in my mind as I fold the paper and walk towards the Annexe of the Palais des Champs-Elysées.

Although some of the critics' views are upsetting, none are as bad as the reaction of the public. I hope the comments won't be as bad as yesterday.

There is a great crush at the entrance and I am caught in the stream. I can't do anything but abandon myself to the current. I go through the door as if I were lifted up.

All the elegance of Paris is here. The women of all ranks, prostitutes, actresses, society matrons, come to show their latest fashion. Their clothes have been chosen with one eye to tomorrow's newspaper reports.

The catalogue sellers, standing by their small tables, shout to the crowd. I've been here every morning since the Salon des Refusés opened nine days ago, but today seems to be busier than ever. Perhaps all those sensational notices are drawing the crowds.

By now, I know the quickest way to the galleries: straight across the courtyard and up the west staircase. I walk quickly between the great velvet curtains and through a porch full of shadows.

I don't stop to look at anything else until I reach exhibit three hundred and sixty-three in the last of the twelve rooms. *Le Bain.* The title irritates me as it draws attention to the second woman. She is an unnecessary addition, put in just to annoy me. But, compared to the other figures, her presence is insignificant.

As on every other day, it's only when I stand right in front of the picture and see it flanked by two others of Monsieur Manet's that I am aware of the size of this canvas. *The Espada*, on the left, is big and so is the *Majo* on the right, but neither is as large as *Le Bain*. I haggled for it for at least half an hour, even walked out of the shop, until the dealer ran after me, dropping the price to a half of what he originally asked. He claimed that he was already selling it for much less than it was worth, but I laughed, and walked away as if I was not serious about acquiring it. I was half the way through the door when he called me back and, buoyed by that, I pointed out that the canvas wasn't a standard size and that it was going to be difficult for him to sell. He didn't argue. Instead, he began to treat me more seriously, realizing that I knew something about art materials. The canvas was partially painted over and I could tell that it was made to order for a specific picture that had been abandoned.

I couldn't discern what the original picture was, except for a figure of a horse, and of a man, presumably a soldier. The colours were very dark. Perhaps that was an example of what Monsieur Manet calls "*l'école de la sauce brune*".

In the end, I was delighted to have it for twenty-five francs, including delivery. It didn't matter to me that it was second-hand.

I walked alongside the young boy from the shop as he pushed the canvas to Maître Albert. I agreed to give him another franc to help me carry it upstairs. We didn't talk on the way upstairs, except to give instructions to each other as we turned corners. It took us almost an hour to negotiate the stairs and my front door. Once the canvas was leaning against the wall in my studio, he asked me: 'Are you a painter, mademoiselle?'

'Yes, I am,' I said proudly.

A look of admiration crossed his face. He was young and shy and the first person to whom I could give an affirmative answer to the question. I was happy to give him a large tip before he left.

Of course, it was much easier for Monsieur Manet to transport the canvas to rue Guyot. Two men came to collect it. They wore soft cloth gloves and were under instructions to make sure that nothing was damaged. When I showed them the painting they were to take, they both laughed loudly, digging their elbows into each other.

'Did you paint this?' The younger of the two asked finally. Embarrassed to admit that it was my picture, I pretended I didn't hear him. The second man said: 'I have seen many strange things but this artist must be off his head.' He winked at his companion: 'Didier, what do you think?'

'Nice fashion this. I hope it catches on: women walking around like that. I wouldn't mind being one of those two men.'

'This is the funniest picture I've ever seen.'

'I know where my hand would be if I was one of those two lucky ones.'

'Me too. But they are stupid. Students probably. Can you see that? What's that one pointing at? Some part of her body?' They both laughed again.

'Just imagine if this becomes the fashion. Naked women on the streets of Paris. That would make life interesting!'

I urged them to hurry up. Even while they were on the stairs, I could still hear them laughing and making lewd jokes. They had thrown a veil over the canvas and I was grateful for that. I dreaded to think what Madame Conchis, or anyone else from the house, would have said had they seen the picture.

Now that the painting is on display, I feel a pang of sadness that it doesn't carry my name. Perhaps it is a punishment for not owning up to its authorship to those lewd porters.

Since then, Monsieur Manet has repainted it completely. There is no question that the finished version is much better than the one I had. I could never have painted so well. I like the way the woman leans her chin on her hand so that she comes over as a thinking person. When I painted her, she was just a naked woman. But why has he reworked my hair?

The trees on the left have wider trunks than on my picture. It looks better to have a stronger background for the figures. The bush, which he added behind the woman and the man in the middle, has the same effect. The two men are much better, too. In my version, Lola posed for both, but we never had enough time. In return for each session, I had to lie down with her. On the occasion of the last sitting, she brought this rubber thing and used it to play with me. I had never seen anything like that before.

'The fashionable ladies have these toys,' she tried to assure me. 'The other day, while serving food at dinner, I heard two female guests talking about them. They were whispering and I could only just hear what they were saying. When I approached them with the soup terrine and ladle, they stopped talking and giggled. I felt like giggling myself. I already had it in my room.'

She smiled and shrugged her shoulders, as if in resignation: 'Victorine, if you expect me to pose as a man, I want to make love as a man.'

I wasn't bothered either way. The sooner we got on with it, the sooner I could work on the painting. Lola tried to convince me:

'Victorine, you'll like it; it's lovely,' she said.

I nodded. 'Let's try it.'

She whispered that I might bleed. 'But I love you and I'll be gentle. We can start slowly.'

I wasn't scared and it didn't hurt. Nor did I lose any blood. She laughed and said she was glad she hadn't hurt me: 'My fingers have been inside you so many times. You must be well stretched by now, Victorine.'

I'll never be happy with the second woman in the background, the bather, as Monsieur Manet calls her. I think she spoils the composition. Besides, her chemise reminds me of the diaphanous wraps on the nymphs and goddesses in old paintings. She is out of place in the company of contemporary people. Monsieur Manet always says that an artist has to be of his own time. Why did he put her in? He thinks I am jealous and would not tell me who she was. Some model, from the place Pigalle, no doubt. He never mentioned that she would be there, let alone asked my permission to add her. Her presence takes some of the attention from the woman at the front.

Monsieur Manet had another surprise for me. I am sure it wasn't there when I last saw the picture in his studio. I only noticed it at the opening and it made me smile. The addition of the little frog, near the naked woman, is a witty touch, typical of him. When his friends are around, he relaxes and they make such jokes. This time, he is sharing the joke with me, as if I were Antoine or Charles.

But the frog also suggests to me that Monsieur Manet, regardless of what he says, had at least partly anticipated the reaction to the painting. Some visitors inevitably see the woman as a harlot, although most of them do not notice the frog. They tend to miss it as they have the habit of peering too closely. But those who spot it, take it as a confirmation that the woman is *la grenouille*, a prostitute. They are so shocked, or sometimes even amused, by the idea that they don't consider the woman's gaze. The beauty of her self-confident eyes that stare directly into the eyes of the spectator passes them by.

I am happy that everyone can see the picture now. But, if I am honest with myself, it bothers me that no one will ever know that I was the one who had painted it first. Monsieur Manet may not think it important. He believes that everything I know I picked up in his studio.

He asked for my permission to have the painting exhibited under his name. He said that it stood a better chance like that.

Well, he was wrong. Even entered under his name, it was still rejected. But what else could I have said? Most of the brush strokes were his. And besides, I am sure he would think it silly to have two names on display: Victorine Meurent next to Edouard Manet. My name would have been in papers and people who have never heard of me would say it as if I were known to them. I might have become famous, the talk of Paris.

I wonder if Lola would feel proud to know me, then. And would someone mention my name to my mother?

After Monsieur Manet had secured my permission to use his name for the painting, he couldn't resist a little sting to my pride: 'You remember, Victorine, I was the first one to show you Marcantonio Raimondi's engraving of *Le jugement de Pâris*. You would not have come across it otherwise.' He almost tried to convince himself that the idea was his. How different he was from that day when he had come to ask to repaint the canvas: he was too polite, or too cautious, to mention it.

When I asked Monsieur Manet for a favour in return, he readily agreed, smiled widely, and added that my request interested him very much indeed.

Although she didn't intend to, Lola also helped me develop the idea for the picture. Once when we were looking at the Giorgione painting, she asked: 'Why can't they look like other people on the street? Why can't they look like you?'

'But that's an old picture.'

'Is it? But it's the same with the others.' She was right.

'Perhaps one day they will look like us,' I said. 'Perhaps one day people will tire of painting gods and goddesses.'

'But why one day? Why not now?'

I shrugged my shoulders. She added: 'No one paints people like me.' I said that one day a picture of her will be in the Louvre. 'I promise.' She squeezed my hand. 'But you'll have to model for me.' She agreed.

While posing for *La Chanteuse des rues*. I tried to think of an idea for a new painting and the conversation with Lola, and my promise, came to mind. At the time, Monsieur Manet did notice that I was not looking at him with the intensity that he found irritating. He had fewer outbursts or, at least, they were not directed at me. Of course, there was always something that annoyed him.

One day, while I was standing on the podium in his studio with a guitar in one hand and the cherries in the other, the staring figure in Marcantonio Raimondi came to my mind and it was followed by the image of Giorgione's women. Eventually, all my thoughts came together in the idea for a picture I wanted to paint. I worked on it for two months, obsessed with it, stopping only to do flowers for Etienne.

But what does it matter which picture inspired me? To be frank, I can't be sure any more. One or the other or both. I just know that the idea has been with me for some time.

There is always a crowd in front of the picture. Their herd-like movement upsets me. I stand back a little and watch the visitors as they file past the other exhibits and stop here. They are devoid of enthusiasm and their harsh voices and drawn faces reek of painted malevolence. Most of them laugh. The other day one man even tried to hit the canvas with a folded newspaper. I can console myself with the fact that no one ignores it. My picture is the talk of the town!

Amidst the laughter, someone says: 'How did he do it, with a floor mop?' The crowd responds with shouts and more laughter.

But they are standing too close to be able to enjoy the overall effect. Monsieur Manet didn't use fine brushes.

Nor can they understand why he doesn't apply undercoat, *la sauce*. Monsieur Manet often uses off-white primers and creates a lighter ground that gives off the luminosity he needs for an outdoor scene. I can see that the technique doesn't allow for the illusion of perspective and the appearance of depth, but perspective isn't what he's after. These people like such tricks.

Two smartly dressed elderly men stand next to me. One of them says: 'It displays poor technique. The woman is too harshly lit. Look at this section here. The folds on the nude's abdomen and the neck are made of too broadly applied lines. No craftsmanship there.'

The other man nods in agreement. 'This Manet cannot paint.

You can see the drawing lines around the baskets. The other two pictures are unfinished, too. And what do they mean? A woman dressed as a matador. Or, say, this one here? What is she doing?'

'Well, you know what she is?' The first man says and winks.

'I do.' The men laugh. 'But why paint her? Has our age fallen so low? Instead of goddesses, we have demi-mondaines.' They move on.

Why is it that when a historical painter takes a nude woman, and makes a portrait of her with a few alterations, or borrows something from older paintings, he can call her a goddess and no one laughs or protests as they do when a nude is represented as an ordinary woman of our time? It's absurd.

Monsieur Manet told me several times: 'You're a model, a modern Parisian woman, not a Venus.' But most of these people want a Venus. As if a goddess in a painting isn't anything but a model.

I watch a family with two young children. When the man sees the picture, he instructs the woman to rush the children past it. He stands in front of the large canvas, staring at it for a long time.

Two couples stop and the women, their arms leaning on the men, laugh loudly. One of the men shouts: But why such a large canvas? Who does he think he is? I can understand if you paint a good heroic scene, but there is nothing heroic here.'

'No.'

'Why is she staring like that? She should be ashamed of herself. It is scandalous how proud she looks.'

The other man says: 'Yes, most unsightly. I wonder who she is. She seems so real. Too real for comfort. This is a real Parisian woman. Somebody's daughter, or wife?'

'She is not a wife,' one of the women says quickly.

'No, I suppose not. No decent man would allow her to do this.'

Such comments don't worry me. The worst fate that a picture can have is not to be noticed. I feared the painting might be skied or cornered, although, I suspect, the size would have made it stand out anyway. Faced with negative comments, I pull out of my pocket a press cutting of an article by Monsieur Manet's friend Zachary Astruc, published only yesterday. The words are reassuring. I know them by heart:

'One must have the strength for two to stand up under the storm of fools who pour in here by the thousand to jeer, with stupid smiles on their lips.'

I look at the woman in the painting in front of me. She has the strength for two. If mine falters, even temporarily, I shall borrow hers. I don't need to remind myself of the other comment by Zachary Astruc: 'Monsieur Manet is one of the greatest personalities of our time, its inspiration and its astonishment.' I have known that myself for some time now.

An elderly man and a younger woman stop in front of the picture. I hear him say: 'I do not know this Manet. But I have heard that while he has some faults, some failings and a lack of balance in his character, he also has irresistible charm. And I think I can see that in this picture: failings and charm.'

'I agree with you, uncle Isidore.'

'My dear Cécile, look at it with your own eyes. But above all, don't let your judgement be clouded by what the newspapers write. Critics often miss the point when something new appears. Manet, I would venture to say, has started a new age in painting.'

The woman nods. The two stand silently in front of the painting for a long time. I remember Monsieur Manet saying that one day people will see better. Here are two of those people of the future.

Cheered by them, I walk on to look at other exhibits. *Le Bain* isn't the only painting provoking sneers. Some of it is reserved for *The White Girl* by an American painter called Whistler. I am intrigued by this large portrait of a very young woman. It is too unusual, too different, too luminous for the crowd to take it seriously.

As I have done every day since the opening, I soon return to painting three hundred and sixty-three. The crowd is larger now than before. They jostle and giggle, nudging each other. I stand at the back of the throng when I notice a woman pulling her male companion towards me. When they are within a couple of metres, she pokes me with a finger. I move away but she pushes even closer and says to the man: 'That's her.'

The man looks at the woman enquiringly.

She says loudly: 'That's the woman.' The man abruptly turns towards me and the woman shouts even more loudly, her face taken over by a sneering smile: 'She is the one in the painting with no clothes on.'

The man gasps. The crowd looks at me. I stand paralysed, not knowing what to do. People come close to me to stare at my face, their backs turned to the painting. Some giggle, others make noises of disgust. I gather all my strength and push my way through the crowd. A man pulls my arm, as if to stop me, but I manage to free myself. Making my way straight to the exit, I run all the way down the Champs Elysées, desperate to reach home, like a wounded animal returning to her lair to lick her wounds.

I sit on the divan in Maître Albert, unable to move, let alone draw or paint. It's dark outside but I don't bother to light a lamp.

Etienne once said to me: 'There comes a time when everyone has to accept that their dream will never be realised.'

None of those people at the Salon thought of me as a painter. Perhaps I will forever be just a model, a woman with no clothes on.

40

Lola is relaxed and takes her time kissing me. Her tongue hovers above my lips, brushing against them, before it begins to explore my mouth. When she slides down, licking my thighs and the inside of my legs, I know that she won't stop until she has proof that I am enjoying her efforts. Slowly, she slips her fingers inside me, pushes my legs wide apart and when her tongue replaces her fingers, a tingling sensation moves through my body.

'There, there, relax, my darling', she lifts her head and whispers gently.

As her hand moves up to touch my nipples, my excitement intensifies and, for a moment, I wish we could stay like this forever. But as I hear the bells of Notre-Dame, I remember that we are expected elsewhere. We shouldn't be late. Monsieur Manet doesn't like to wait. I don't want him to accuse me, as he did once before, of not being serious about painting. What he really meant was that I wasn't serious about modelling. I am about to become a model again. Since the Salon, all my time has been spent painting flower pictures for Etienne. They make money.

Lola looks up at me. 'What's the matter, Victorine? Have I done something wrong?'

I shake my head and smile at her. The bells become more insistent. Lola sits up.

'You're always in a rush, Victorine. You know I like to take things slowly when I'm with you. I have enough of hurrying when I work for the Demains.'

She is being unfair. In the last two months, I've spent a lot of time with her: we met a couple of evenings a week and every weekend we spend together, in bed or out for walks.

Lola lies down on her side. Her head is propped up by her hand as she leans towards me and runs the tips of her fingers down my cheek. At one point, she presses hard on my skin, as if trying to determine out what it's made of. She looks at me for a long time and then asks quietly: 'Why do you no longer enjoy our time in bed?'

She keeps her eyes on me as she waits for my reply. I don't know what to tell her. She has been kind to me but she hasn't made me happy. I know I am useless as a painter; I can't be a lover if I am unhappy.

She continues to stare and I realize that the worst thing is to keep quiet as it means wasting time: until she receives her answer, we won't be able to move on. I say that she is wrong to think like that and that I do get pleasure from her. I can't tell her that my hopes of becoming a painter have been dashed and that my only real chance to be part of the art world is to work as a model. Even if I could overcome my self-doubt, time and money would be so short that I couldn't afford to waste them on a relationship. For her, Sunday is a day off. If I am to do what I want with my life, I can't indulge in such luxuries.

Sometimes I wonder whether it might have been better if the picture hadn't been exhibited. I know that Monsieur Manet considered withdrawing from the Refusés. So did several of his friends. He said that both Henri Fantin-Latour and Whistler had consulted him. In the end they all decided that it was better that the public saw their work and judged for themselves. I am not sure they were right.

Abruptly, Lola turns away from me, lies on her back and stares at the ceiling. I know that she expects me to lean over to kiss her. She needs to feel wanted and waits for me to show her that. But there is no time for kissing. We need to go. Monsieur Manet will be angry if we are late. I want to prevent their first meeting from starting on a bad note.

I sit up and tell her that we have to leave. Without moving, she says: 'A picture can wait. I am alive, I can't. I need to have your kisses. I need to have your arms around me, your fingers on my neck, your lips on mine. ' She pauses, and looks at me. 'When I'm washing dishes and doing the laundry at madame's, all I can think of is you. I see your naked body and feel good, despite the hard work. And then I think that you are doing your painting and thinking of me. We have only each other.'

I don't want to hurt her. There is no time to talk; I realise that all I can do is press my lips against hers and pull her on top of me. I know she likes that best. I think of the time passing but I make sure that Lola thinks I am enjoying our love-making. After a while, as soon as it appears plausible, I throw back my head, and scream with pleasure. Within minutes, she does the same. She holds me tight, kissing me frantically. I am relieved when she says that we can go.

Outside, she hails a fiacre with two horses. I look at her anxiously and she laughs: 'Don't worry, Victorine, I am paying.'

The sun is shining, the morning is warm and the air smells fresh. But instead of enjoying the ride, I think of the cost. It'll be more than I spend on food for the entire week. Lola, on the other hand, doesn't seem to care. She waves to people as we ride past and flashes her broad smile. I keep my head down. They always stare at her, whether she waves or not, but I still wish she would stop drawing attention to us.

While we were dressing, she wanted to put on what she still refers to as her brother's clothes. Recently, she has acquired a walking cane, complete with an ivory handle. There is no doubt that she makes a handsome man, but I wasn't in the mood for all the stares and comments she would attract. Perhaps I was also nervous of what Monsieur Manet might say.

I pleaded with her to wear her dark dress. In the end, she said that as a compromise, she would put on the white one that we had bought together at a market last month. We were running late so I consented. I knew the dress was too ostentatious, pure white with frills around the neck, cuffs and hem. When I first saw it at a stall selling second-hand clothes, I thought it could be used for one of my pictures. I didn't imagine that Lola would want to wear it on the street.

Lola and Monsieur Manet can be explosively temperamental. Both take offence easily, raising their voices at the slightest excuse. At some point, they are bound to clash. Since I suggested the work on this new painting, I shall feel responsible if anything goes wrong.

Monsieur Manet opens the door for us and I introduce Lola. She is taller than him and I have the impression that her height disconcerts him. They shake hands. She doesn't smile and he strikes me as more formal than usual. Madame Bijoux brings coffee and croissants, and as she sets down the tray, I notice her staring at Lola.

Monsieur Manet shows us a sketch for the painting. He says that he has been working on various versions for the last two weeks. On the table where he keeps prints, I can see several drawings with similar composition but with slight variations in the positions of the two figures. He allows us only to see one, drawn in red chalk. I am to be naked, stretched out on a divan, with Lola standing, behind me. Lola says that she would like to pose naked, too. Monsieur Manet shakes his head.

'No, definitely not. No, mademoiselle, that is not what I have in mind.'

She looks serious and her body stiffens. I recognise the first opportunity for conflict. Her request has been ignored and she won't give in. For a moment, I fear that she might stand up and leave. Monsieur Manet is too absorbed to notice her hostility. I don't think that he is used to models opposing him. Nevertheless, he adds, in a more conciliatory tone:

'No, not for this one at least.' I begin to wonder whether he is already thinking of another picture! I wouldn't bet on Lola lasting for more than one; judging by this first meeting, even that's optimistic.

'Who are these two people?' Lola asks him. Her tone is sharp and I know that he won't take to her kindly. 'What's the story of the picture?'

'I do not know who they are. There is no story. At least, I cannot think of one right now.'

Lola's voice sounds aggressive: 'How can you paint them, if you don't know who they are?'

Monsieur Manet stares at her, as if contemplating whether

he should bother to answer. She stares back, defiant. I can see that she knows she has disconcerted him. After a while, he stops, looks her in the eye and says: 'I need their positions, their faces and their bodies. I need to know how the figures relate to each other, in terms of their respective shapes, mademoiselle. I also need to know how they relate to the space around them. That is sufficient for me. It ought to be for you as well. What they did before they came into my picture does not interest me. As far as I am concerned, they do not exist outside the painting.'

As he walks away, he adds in a low voice: 'Anyway, why am I explaining this to you?'

I am relieved that Lola does not hear. Nevertheless, her voice is loud. 'But we do exist outside your painting. Victorine and I have lives that should affect the way you paint us.' Monsieur Manet ignores this comment. Had it come from Charles or Antoine, he would have had a great deal to say. Lola is right. It surprises me that she has noticed that for Monsieur Manet, and for me, pictures and shapes are more important than people and their lives.

I stand to the side, watching them. One thing has become clear: Monsieur Manet developed the idea for the painting from Titian, just as I had my idea from *Le Concert Champêtre*.

Last spring, on one of those rare occasions when Monsieur Manet was prepared to show me his work, he brought out a copy of a painting he had made in Italy, in Florence, I think he said, a few years earlier. I remember the day clearly. I came in immediately after lunch and Monsieur Baudelaire was just leaving. When he saw me, he turned towards Monsieur Manet and said: 'Good luck, Edouard'.

As soon as we were alone, I realized the significance of the remark. They had anticipated my reaction to the introduction of the bather, the second woman in *Le Bain*. After I had made it clear that I thought the figure unnecessary, and Monsieur Manet had tried to argue otherwise, he suddenly stopped and said: 'I have just remembered something that should be of interest to you, Mademoiselle Victorine.' He asked me to follow him to the room in the gallery and there, propped against the wall, along-side the bed, was a colour sketch of Titian's *La Vénus d'Urbin*. I thought it a masterful picture and was extremely glad that he had shown it to me. I knew that he was trying to placate me over the changes in *Le Bain*, which pleased me. I decided not to mention the second woman again. Besides, there was no point. He is too stubborn.

But there is no black woman in the Titian. Where will Lola fit in?

The more I think of the painting, the less I can see myself as the woman lying naked. Does it mean that Monsieur Manet has been thinking of me as a woman, rather than a shape? Or, is he testing my potential to play different roles? I remember him praising my rapid transformations while we were preparing for *La Chanteuse des rues*. But that was a role that I knew.

The idea that Monsieur Manet wishes to paint me in a sensual pose intrigues me. Titian's *Vénus d' Urbin* has a woman on display. I remember that the first thing I noticed about her was the look in her eyes. She is coy, even timid, as if someone had come upon her by accident. In contrast, the woman in *Le Bain* has removed her clothes herself. She is comfortable with her naked body and is defying you when you look at her. I hope that, with Monsieur Manet's permission, the Venus I am to model will look out in a different fashion. If she is on display, she has to be adorned, she has to be proud of her body and feel confident in her beauty. She must not seem shy or ashamed. Even if she is selling her body, she must feel good about it.

'Mademoiselle Victorine,' Monsieur Manet calls, 'we need your help. Tell me, what do you think is the story behind the two figures in my drawing?'

I walk to the table and take a close look at the drawing. 'I don't know, monsieur.'

He smiles: 'And do you want to know?'

'Yes and no. I mean, you don't need to tell me the story. I can make it up. And so can you. And so can everyone.'

Lola looks at me: 'Victorine, these two women on the picture are you and me. What is our story? Monsieur can't tell me that.'

She is very angry now and I can sense that she may turn against me as well. I walk over to her and put my hand on her shoulder.

'It is all right, Lola,' I say gently. 'We'll pretend that we are two other people. It's very amusing to be someone else.'

I squeeze her shoulder and smile at her. Her body freezes under my touch and I slide my fingers down her arm to caress her hand. After a while, she looks at me and I can tell that she has calmed a little.

Monsieur Manet watches us. Knowing that we must not waste more time, I look at him and venture: 'We are ready. Where would you like us to position ourselves?'

He looks straight into my eyes and thanks me. There is still a slight tension in his face.

He has already prepared a divan with several large cushions and he asks me to lie on it. Lola is to stand behind me. She says that she wants to be looking at me. Monsieur Manet allows her, and I sense that she is pleased. At first, he sketches the composition of our two figures and I lie on the divan, fully clothed. Later on, he asks me to undress. I notice the atmosphere change as Lola watches me take off my garments, one by one. When I lie down again, all I am wearing is the string necklace with the glass pendant, the one that Lola had given me to celebrate our reconciliation. When she sees the necklace, she smiles at me.

'That looks lovely on you, Victorine,' she says.

Monsieur Manet agrees. 'Mademoiselle Victorine, that is a good touch, the necklace. Do keep it on.' I am glad he does not know who gave it to me.

Monsieur Manet draws in red ink on a large sheet of paper. Lola never looks at him. As usual, I am amazed at the speed with which his hand moves. At one point, he picks a large, red rosebud from a bouquet of flowers in one of the vases that he has in the studio and pins it in my hair. Later, he asks me to readjust the position of my body and we experiment by moving my hand around my thighs. At one point, Lola runs her hand down my leg, as if to smooth the skin. Monsieur Manet notices what she is doing but, wisely, ignores her.

It's early afternoon, when we stop for the day. He asks us to return together next Sunday. I've already explained to him that Lola works during the week.

When we step out, it's beginning to rain. The sky has clouded over and it's very dark. We walk for a while but, as the rain intensifies, we seek shelter in a porch. While Lola is kissing me, a powerful thunderclap frightens us. Startled, both of us pull back. Lola says: 'The first time I kissed you was under a porch like this. But there was no storm then. It was a sunny, winter day.'

Soon, the rain ceases but the clouds remain. We walk part of the way and then, the rest of the way to Maître Albert, we take an omnibus. Once upstairs, Lola confesses that a couple of months ago, on two occasions when she looked for me and didn't find me at home, she picked up notes from Madame Conchis that were addressed to me. The concierge was out of the office and the door was open. Each time, Lola noticed an envelope with my name. She took them out of curiosity, read them but didn't deliver them to me.

I look at her, shocked. She asks whether I want to know what was in the notes. I don't. She seems surprised and guilty. The messages must have been from Monsieur Manet, most likely the ones Madame Conchis mentioned the other day.

I study her discomfort, hoping that the evening peal from Notre-Dame will soon break the silence. Eventually, Lola says: 'Victorine, I am really sorry. I know I shouldn't have done it. But I couldn't help myself. I feared losing you to someone else.'

I can see that she regrets it. Although it has taken her a few months, I appreciate that she has told me. In the end, what does it matter anyway? Unlike me, Lola is a jealous person and I can't change that.

Before she leaves, she suggests that I draw her. I know she wants to say sorry. Good. I have a full hour with her sitting perfectly still in front of me. I make a life-size charcoal portrait. When I show it to her, she asks: 'What are you going to do with it, Victorine?'

I smile at her as I pin the picture on the wall next to my bed. Lola puts her arms around me and squeezes me tightly. Perhaps she is the woman I can stay with. I can manage her. She doesn't make me feel emotional and lyrical, like Marie did with her kissing and touching and promises of love. I had to leave her. Lola is like a man who wants to possess and penetrate me but doesn't insist on love.

41

As soon as Charles comes in, he says: 'The nude has descended. And, what's more, she has a new companion.'

I smile. I am pleased that Charles understands that what I am doing is inspired by Titian's *Vénus d'Urbin*, a copy of which has been in my room upstairs for several months. My dear friend! Will the public or the critics be able to make the connection?

'Edouard, I am delighted that you are working on a new picture. There have been times, over the past month in particular, when I was concerned that they were getting to you and that you might stop working.' Charles moves closer to the painting.

'If a painter, having to paint a courtesan of the present day, is inspired,' he raises his voice at the last word, 'inspired, Edouard, that is the consecrated word, by a courtesan of Titian or Raphael, it is infinitely probable that he will paint a false, ambiguous and obscure work. It will be insignificant. The study of the masterpiece alone will teach him neither the attitude nor the gaze of the *biche*, the *lorette*, but if a painter uses a modern woman...' He pauses. I wait and he turns towards me. 'Edouard, I need say no more: you paint what I preach. I see, it is Mademoiselle Victorine again. And who is the other woman? Apart from Jeanne, this the first time you have used a black model, I think.' He stares at me. 'She looks, what shall we say, interesting.' His mouth stretches into a teasing smile as he stares at me.

'She is Lola. Mademoiselle Lola Sancho. She is a friend of Victorine's. Once again, Victorine helped me generate a new idea.'

Charles raises his eyebrows.

'Well, she asked me to make a painting with her friend, as a favour to her. I agreed straightaway. However, my initial thought was to have Lola pose in the nude. Just her, with nothing around, no landscape, no objects. Perhaps one day I shall do that.'

'You must introduce me to the mademoiselle.'

'I am not sure she would be interested in you. She prefers women.'

'Oh. So do I. We shall get on famously.' Charles assumes his tragedian pose and recites in a histrionic voice:

Lesbos, terre des nuits chaudes et langoureuses,
Qui font qu'à leurs miroirs, stérile volupté!
Les filles aux yeux creux, de leurs corps amoreuses,
Caressent les fruits mûrs de leur nubilité;
Lesbos, terre des nuits chaudes et langoureuses.'

I sit down and pretend that I am the audience to this impromptu performance. Despite the pain in his limbs, my dear friend recites poetry fit for gods. The sight of his body, ravaged by illness, stops me thinking about the painting.

'Tell me, Edouard. How did the nude make her descend and transform herself?'

'Well, a few days after Victorine had asked me to make a picture with her friend, I was lying on the bed upstairs, with the copy of the Titian alongside. As I turned towards the painting, I imagined that the Venus was Victorine. I kept looking at her and soon I saw Lola standing behind the bed, much closer to it than the woman in the background of the Titian.'

'I like the brightly lit body.'

'I had no option: the light presents itself to me with such unity that one tone is sufficient to render it.'

'Yes, yes, Edouard.'

'I am sure that it is preferable, even if it seems a bit abrupt, to pass straight from light to dark rather than to accumulate things that I cannot see and that weaken the vigour of the lights and the coloration of the shadows. It is important to express them in correct tones.'

Charles nods. 'I understand that. But on a different matter: why can you not do another Venus, like Cabanel?' Cabanel, that merchant of confectionary? Charles must be mocking me. 'This may cause another stir, Edouard, another condemnation from the great and the good. It may become even more provocative than *Le Bain*. Are you aware of that?'

'Does this concern come from a man who was expelled from his lycée for his immoral views?'

'Edouard,' Charles bows, his arms extended in a gesture of supplication: 'I would like to see the entire human race against me. But you? Can you manage?'

'That is not the issue. I paint what I have to, not what is expected of me. Anyway, they have always wanted a nude. I gave them one. They laughed at her. I am giving them another one. Let them laugh again.'

He seems satisfied and smiles at me. For an hour, he sits on the divan and writes in his notebook while I prepare the material for Sunday. Victorine and Lola will be coming early and I plan to start work immediately.

Yesterday, I bought a pair of smart mule slippers for Victorine and a set of stupefyingly expensive silk sheets. They were delivered this morning. I shall partially drape the bed with the spread that I acquired some time ago, precisely for such a purpose. I want to create an atmosphere of luxury and the domestic confidence of a rich household. Although the spread came from a second-hand stall, it cost a great deal of money.

I shall draw straight onto the canvas, with either chalk or charcoal, without the grisaille. With a subject of our own time, the execution should not follow old ways of working.

After I have completed my preparations, we walk to the Guerbois. Charles moves slowly. He makes a joke that his legs are disobeying him. My father used to say the same about his illness, until his whole body disobeyed him. At the corner of Grande rue des Batignolles, we meet a group of students from Couture's studio. They stop talking when they notice us; I can sense that they have been discussing *Le Bain*. I do not know what Couture thinks of it, but it is possible that his response is similar to what he said about *Le Buveur d'absinthe* 'the painter, not the figure represented, is the immoral one.'

The youngsters seem to be in awe of us and they walk in silence, casting sideway glances at us, as if unsure whether to continue their previous debate or to start a new conversation. Inside, I buy drinks for them. As we order another couple of bottles, and then another couple, they relax and admit that they are puzzled by the reaction of the public and the critics to the painting. One of them, Honoré, a thin young man who often comes to the Guerbois but hardly ever speaks, says that, in his view,

'Monsieur Manet is ahead of his time. That is his problem.'

The group starts nodding and, once again, I perceive the loyal adoration in their attitude. That improves my humour. As we drink, I am reminded of what Charles once said to me in the studio, during one of our interminable discussions on art and modernity.

'If the artist is not true to the constellation of his time, he will produce work that is false.'

'But what is the constellation of our time? Is there an agreement on it?' I asked.

Charles shrugged his shoulders. 'A good question. But let me say something else: Our images, Edouard, must have a moral meaning; without that, art would be fashionable but empty.'

I agreed. 'A painter is not a mere translator of images. We have to have something to say, otherwise good night. Knowing one's métier is important, but one also has to be moved.'

Since that conversation, I think I have begun to understand that it is the artist who determines what constitutes 'the constellation of the time'. And why shouldn't he?

I notice that Honoré is looking at me. Encouraged by my smile, he says: 'Monsieur Manet, there is something I have always wanted to ask you.' I nod. 'Why do they say that your paintings are unfinished?'

'Those who say it expect a painter to paint everything. I believe we should leave something for the viewer's imagination. After all, the truth of art is not concerned simply with visual resemblance. I am guided by psychological and moral verity. That is what I call the painting of modern life.'

'I fully agree with you, monsieur. I have heard you say before that the choice of the subject is important.'

I smile at him. At least the young ones understand me. There is hope yet.

Charles nods in agreement: 'It is doubtless an excellent thing to study the old masters in order to learn how to paint, but it can be no more than a waste of labour if your aim is to understand the special nature of present-day beauty. The draperies of Rubens or Veronese will in no way teach you how to depict *moire antique, satin à la reine* or any other fabric of modern manufacture, which we see supported and hung over crinoline or starched muslin petticoat.'

'The beauty in the world around us, that is what we need to paint,' one of the students says.

Charles adds: 'As Stendal teaches us, beauty is nothing but a promise of happiness.' Then he reads his latest poem and the students cheer. We drink late into the night. These young artists make me hopeful. In times to come, people will see better.

42

I walk slowly, carrying three finished canvases, individually wrapped in brown paper and tied with string. Although they are not heavy, their bulk makes it awkward to move quickly. For me, it has always been a matter of pride to arrive on time. But today, I fear I may be late as I've misjudged how difficult it would be to carry the pictures. I hope Etienne won't mind.

Over the past month and a half, I've had enough time to accept all the work that he could give me. I started this as a necessity, but now I welcome the practice as well. I've paid my debts and redeemed grandmother's lace from the pawnbroker. If I can continue like this, I might even be able to save enough for painting lessons or to pay for the occasional model.

It's unusually crowded and noisy at *Les Trois chapeaux*. I walk through the smoke filled café, but I can't see Etienne. I speak to the owner, Monsieur Pons, and he says that Etienne hasn't arrived. It's not like Etienne to be late.

Half an hour later, just as I am about to leave, Etienne walks in and immediately asks to see the paintings. Usually, he orders drinks first and we have a chat before we move onto business. Today, his eyes avoid mine and his voice is strained. He pays me for the work I've brought. For each picture, I receive almost double the standard fee. I think that's fair. The size of the canvases meant that I had to spend much more time on them than usual.

I order a coffee and Etienne has a plum brandy. While I am drinking the coffee, he asks for two more plum brandies and downs them straightaway. Remembering what he was like drunk at the lunch after he had been paid for the Giorgione copy, I make my excuses and stand up to go. Etienne jumps in front of me, grabs my arm and pleads with me to stay. His abrupt manner alarms me and I am determined to leave. He says that his mother died last week and he needs someone to talk to. He hadn't seen her for a long time and is overwhelmed by guilt. She worked as a domestic servant all her life and he knows that he should have been more supportive. It's only in the past few months, he says, that he has been able to send her any money.

Would I know if my mother died? And if I found out, would I feel as he does now? Tears gather in Etienne's eyes and when he leans his head on my shoulder, I am moved enough to put my hand on his head and stroke it. His breath smells horribly but I shouldn't mind. He has been a good friend to me and he needs me now. One of his hands sits in my lap. Gradually it slides down, brushing my thigh. He is upset, it might be accidental and I don't want to draw attention to it.

When his face nuzzles into my shoulder, I am aware of the people at the next table casting dubious glances in our direction, but I don't care. I am used to playing different roles for Monsieur Manet; the idea that they might think I am a prostitute amuses me and, for an instant, I feel like playing the role. But then a vague memory comes to my mind. Didn't Etienne tell me a long time ago that his mother was dead? Or did he mean that she was dead to him because he had no contact with her?

He sobs as he describes the terrible hardship his mother had to endure working through her illness and old age.

'She had nothing but misery in her life. Everyone exploited her. My father was a drunk and beat her regularly when I was a child. Widowed, with no money, she had no choice but to carry on working, and here was me, her only son, painting in Paris. Oh, Victorine, how could I have treated her like that? Good for nothing.'

I want to say something to make him feel better but I am thinking of how to stop his hand sliding up from my thigh. I sit up and ask him to stop touching me and he shouts back that I have no sympathy, after everything he has done for me.

Then his hand drops and all I can hear is his sobbing. He sighs deeply and I wonder how I can leave without upsetting him further.

He wants to order another drink but I persuade him that it would be better for him to go home. He leaves the parcel with Monsieur Pons, promising to collect it tomorrow. As I walk him to the omnibus stop, he leans heavily on my arm. At one point, he puts his arm around my shoulder, pulls me closer and tries to kiss me. I free myself and move away, but he pleads with me to stay. His body is shaking. We wait for his omnibus; I need to make sure that he doesn't follow me home. To my surprise, he climbs up without protest and when the omnibus pulls away, I sigh with relief.

At home, I light the gas lamp and work on a small drawing of a pewter jug on the table. I am teaching myself how to use shading to show the way the light is reflected from the grey surface. I work slowly, taking pleasure in every line. Through the open window, I can hear the sounds of Gabriel's flute. He seems to be able to play only one tune; the rhythm is slow and melancholy. After a while, I find that the movement of my pencil begins to follow the rhythm of the music. Life is good.

When I finish the drawing, I take a break, pour a glass of red wine and eat chunks of bread and cheese. I have an apple on the plate but I don't eat it. It would be a shame to spoil its perfection by biting into it. Looking at its shiny, red surface gives me more pleasure than eating it. I remember the apples grandmother kept in lines on top of the wardrobe; every so often she would take one down and give it to me. I rarely ate it. I preferred to keep it. I would hold it in my cupped hands and run the inside of my palms over its smooth peel.

I work for another hour until around eleven o'clock, I feel too tired to continue. While I am preparing for bed, I am startled by a loud banging on my door; it sounds as if someone is trying to break it down. At first, I hold my breath and don't move. Then I hear Etienne arguing with one of my neighbours. They are both shouting. I learn that Etienne has fallen over and is hurt. How does he know my address?

I consider what to do and, reluctantly, I open the door and he stumbles in, his face dirty and bleeding. There are huge patches of fresh dirt on his jacket and shirt. I lead him to the *chaise longue*, and wash his wounds with a cloth and cold water. He screams with pain but that doesn't stop him from trying to grab my breasts.

Once I have staunched the flow of blood, I can see the size of the gash: it runs from the corner of his left eye, across the eyebrow, and ends just above his nose. I force him to press a damp cloth onto the wound. He says that he tripped and fell onto the edge of the pavement. His face is badly bruised and his left eye is almost completely closed. He can barely speak through his swollen lips and he complains of a throbbing pain in his head. He is drunk.

I offer him a glass of water and tell him to keep still. He asks for wine. Unwilling to oppose him, I pour him a glass. He says that he isn't fit to go home and I can't disagree. I make a bed for him on the divan in the studio. Etienne helps himself to another glass of wine. Perhaps he will pass out.

He wants me to sit down and talk to him. I am tired and want to wake up early tomorrow to work. With a promise that we will talk in the morning, I close the double doors between the two rooms and put out the light. For a while, I listen for any sound, hoping he has fallen asleep.

I wake up with a start. Something heavy is pressing on top of me. It takes me a while to realize what is happening and what it must be. His hand is under my chemise, touching my breasts.

'Etienne, leave me alone, leave me alone,' I say quickly, trying to push him away.

He takes no notice. He forces his lips onto mine and as I turn my face away, he pulls up my chemise. He is laughing. His breath has the stench of vomit. His naked body is in full contact with mine. As he tries to push himself inside me, I beg him to stop. He carries on, murmuring that he loves me. Although he is shorter than me, the weight of his stocky body presses down heavily. I struggle with all my might, but I can't extricate myself. His nakedness thrusts against my body and nauseates me. Just as he tries again to force himself inside me, I gather my strength and hit him with my knuckled fist on the face, close to the wound. I punch again and again.

The pain enrages him and we struggle ferociously. I manage to hold back his hands but one of his knees digs into my left thigh. The sharp pain makes me loosen my grip on him. He tries to push himself inside me once again. In desperation, I dig my nails into the wound and drag them down. Blood gushes onto my face; I taste it. Etienne howls but doesn't give up. I close my eyes and scratch him again as deeply as I can. I feel his skin under my nails. He utters a piercing scream, louder than anything before. Suddenly, he loses his ardour, his body falls limp and with one heave, I push him away from me.

He lands heavily. He lies there, a huge lump of stinking male flesh curled up like a small child. His hands cover his face and I cannot tell whether he is gasping for breath or sobbing.

After a while, his body stops shaking and he is quiet. I dare not approach him. I can see that his eyes are closed; his breath is barely audible and he seems to be asleep. I lift my head: he has passed out. For a moment, I fear that he may be dead. I grab a jug and throw cold water over him. His body jerks and then slowly relaxes, his eyelids half open. Eventually, he comes round. Outside, it's dawn and, in the faint light, I can see the thick trail of congealed blood on the floorboards by the bed.

Filthy bastard. If only I could get him out as quickly as possible. I don't care what happens to him.

After an hour or so – it's daylight now – Etienne stands up, unsteady on his feet, and wipes his face on his shirtsleeve. He pulls up his trousers, throws a jacket over his shoulders and walks to the door.

'You bitch. You whore. I've been waiting for months and months and then you sit naked for him and allow him to paint you for all of Paris to see. I've seen you at the Refusés, like the whore that you are. What do you think it was like for me to stand there and listen to their comments? What hurt most was to hear words like: "No decent man would allow his woman to pose like that!" And there was me, cheated by my woman... And what a terrible picture it is!' Etienne points his finger at me. 'You whore! No decent woman would exhibit herself like that. For a franc, anyone can have you, any day they want. And

I know you slept with him. You can sleep with me, then.'

He pauses by the door, as if waiting for me to change my mind. I don't move. The sooner he goes the better. The door bangs behind him and I hear his footsteps going down the stairs. But within seconds, he turns back and walks up. Standing outside my apartment, he bangs his fist on the door and shouts:

'From now on, you can work for him. That painter who strips you naked. He isn't any good, anyway. Can't even be bothered to finish his pictures. A charlatan! Everyone laughs at him. And don't expect me to provide you with any more work. That's done.'

For a while, there is silence and I think he is gone, but then I hear him shouting again.

'And do you know what they call him? "A painter of ugliness" and "the apostle of decadence". And you are his whore.' He laughs. 'Why not mine, then? Why can't you be mine?' He is sobbing again. 'What's wrong with me? Victorine, please, let me in. I want you. Be mine and I'll give you work again.'

I don't move. After a while I hear him going downstairs.

For a long time I lie curled up on the chaise long. When I look around the room, I can see that the sheets are all twisted up. The cover is torn in places. There is dried blood and vomit on the bed. A large red puddle has congealed on the floor and drops of blood form a path to the door. I can't tell, but I assume that the room smells as badly as I do. I open all the windows.

I stand by the door, listening for sounds. I manage to avoid meeting anyone on the staircase while fetching water from downstairs. Afraid of seeing my bruised face, I cover the mirror and take off my chemise. I pour two pitchers of water into the basin and wash my body with a cloth and the small piece of lavender soap that Lola bought for me. I take the dirty water downstairs and fill two more pitchers. I wash again. I make sure that the cloth scrubs every part of my body. I rub and rub until the skin is red and it smarts. I welcome the pain. My hands are the most difficult to wash. I have to use the tip of a knife to scrape the blood from under my nails. I wash myself again, not sparing the lavender soap. I can still smell Etienne's breath on me, but it is less powerful. Wrapped in a clean sheet I sit on the floor with my back to the wall below the window. I pull my knees up, rest my chin on them and close my eyes. I stay huddled on the floor for a long time. At some point, I fall asleep.

Madame Conchis' voice wakes me. She is sweeping the court-yard below and singing a song in Spanish. Although I don't understand a word, with the windows open, I can hear her clearly and the tune gradually restores me. I unwrap the sheet and run my hands down my body. The touch makes my skin tingle. I feel alive.

For a long time, I managed to keep Etienne at arm's length simply because he considered me respectable. If he, who is an artist, thinks that I am no longer respectable because I have posed naked, what can I expect from everyone else? I am a woman with no clothes on. I am on display for everyone.

Madame Conchis continues her song. I stand up and look out of the window. She has finished sweeping and is sitting in the sunshine on a low wall by the oleander pot. The white flowers have just opened. There is no one else around and she is singing for herself.

I dress and make a bundle of the dirty sheets and my chemise. Before I go out, I scrub the blood off the floor. I hope that when the boards dry, there will be no visible stain. I leave the sheets at the laundry and walk to the Jardin du Luxembourg.

It's a warm, sunny May day and many people are out for an afternoon stroll. The bench, where I used to sit with Julie, and where I met Monsieur Manet, is occupied by two young women and a child of three or four. The little girl is looking at a photograph and the two women are explaining to her what it is. I hear them laughing. I pass by, smiling at them, but they don't notice me.

On the way home, I buy a small potted plant and place it on the window ledge. In the evening, I make supper of fresh bread, radishes and cheese. I drink a glass of wine. Afterwards, I sit at the table and finish another drawing of the pewter jug.

Tomorrow morning, I'll start work on a self-portrait. I feel ready to paint my own image even with its bruises and cuts. One day, I may transfer it onto a canvas.

43

Yesterday, they arrived on time, with Lola already wearing the white dress. On the way to the studio, I had bought a huge bouquet of flowers, so we were set to start work straightaway. Apart from a break for lunch, we worked solidly throughout the day. I wanted to make as much use as I could of Lola's time. It is easier with Victorine; she can come any day.

Madame Bijoux and her daughter Elisa made the bed the day before our first session. She noticed how expensive the sheets were. I watched her run the back of her hand over the pillows. With her usual directness, she said: 'Oh Monsieur Manet, such heavy silk. It drapes so beautifully. So lovely and smooth. It must have cost a great deal of money. And all for a picture. To think that no one will enjoy sleeping in this lovely bed.'

'Madame, I hope that the whole of Paris will have the pleasure of enjoying the luxury of this bed,' I said.

She gave me a stern look. Elisa blushed.

'I mean, madame, I hope that everyone in Paris will see my picture and like it.'

'Oh, I see, monsieur.' Elisa giggled. She is sixteen and such a good girl. She works as a maid not far from here. Whenever I need something, whether it's food or drink, or even art material, she is always ready to oblige. There really are good people, lots more than one thinks. I don't claim to be more democratic than the next man. In fact, I myself am decidedly aristocratic, but nevertheless, when I meet someone like Elisa, I love and admire the whole human race.

We draped the bedspread across the lower part of the bed and propped up the pillows. When Victorine climbed up, I gave her the pair of mules to complete the effect of opulence. She said that they fitted her perfectly and that she was pleased to have such lovely shoes. Was she speaking as Victorine, or as the woman in the picture? I had not thought that Victorine was interested in expensive things. She does not spend much on her clothes or pay attention to what she wears. Most of the time, she wears the same outfit.

Lola, taken aback by Victorine's interest in the slippers, said: 'I've seen such shoes in the market. I could have bought them for you, Victorine. They had them in different colours.'

'They were not from a market. They were made to order by a shoe-maker who brings his wares to my mother's house. He has exquisite goods,' I said. It was not true, but I wanted to say it. Anyway, the mules were expensive. They would have been too expensive for a maid like Lola.

At first, Lola stood behind Victorine while I made an outline of the entire composition. She held the bouquet and kept her eyes on Victorine, just as we agreed last time. Later, as I worked on Victorine's body, Lola asked whether she could sit down, or at least, put down the flowers, since I was no longer looking at her. I explained that, although I was not drawing her figure, I needed to have the entire composition in my vision. She argued with me and said that Sunday was her day off and that, since she worked hard all week, it was very tiring for her to stand still. I put down the brush and stared at her. My concentration was broken and I could not see how I could continue.

Victorine, always calm and composed, intervened, suggesting a compromise: 'Would it be acceptable, Monsieur Manet, if Lola remained where she is supposed to be for a while, and then had a rest? Would you be able to tell her for how long you would need her? I am sure that would help.'

She spoke very slowly, emphasizing every word. Her voice was calm and gentle, persuasive. She was looking straight into my eyes, as if saying that she would do anything for me if only I did not fall out with Lola. I felt for Victorine. I could tell that she was on my side: she saw that Lola was deliberately being difficult. Victorine was trying hard to keep us going. This picture was important to her as well.

I thought for a moment. Blasted woman! Why should I give in? What does she know about painting? Should I allow a model, and an inexperienced one at that, to tell me how to paint? Victorine bit her lip.

I said: 'I shall need Mademoiselle Lola for half an hour and then I could probably manage without her.'

I walked away. I did not wish to see Lola's face. But I could not help hearing her take a deep breath. Or was it a sigh? Or could she have sucked her lips in disapproval?

Victorine whispered something to her and then spoke to me.

'Monsieur Manet, thank you very much. That will be fine. Lola will be happy to stay in this position for another half an hour.'

We continued in silence. Although I tried to keep my eyes away from Lola, I could not help noticing a slight sulk on her lower lip. She may boss Victorine, but I do not tolerate such behaviour in my studio.

Once half an hour had passed, I said, 'I have finished working on the composition for today. Mademoiselle Lola will not be needed for now.'

Lola did not move. I knew she was not tired. She just wanted things to be done her way.

I ignored her and began to work on the detail. I had noticed earlier that Victorine was not wearing the necklace.

'Mademoiselle Victorine,' I said, 'you are not wearing the necklace. Do you have it somewhere with you?'

Victorine looked at me and said nothing. I could tell that she wanted me to drop the subject. But it was too late. Lola moved to stand closer to her.

'Victorine, why aren't you wearing it? Don't you like it any more? Have you lost it?'

Victorine turned towards me: 'I am sorry, monsieur. I was rushing this morning and must have forgotten it. I promise I shall have it for our next session.'

'But why did you need to take it off?' Lola asked. Victorine lowered her eyes.

'It's not a big problem. Don't worry. We can manage for today.'

I said. 'Wait a minute, I have just had an idea.' As I was walking upstairs, Lola shouted 'I see' and rushed off to the window.

I was thinking what else I could give to Victorine to create a sense of opulence. I looked around. No item of clothing would do. It had to be a piece of jewellery, something that looked expensive. There was nothing like that in the studio. All I could find were some strings of beads, cheap looking things. I went upstairs to the room in the gallery. I did not know what I expected to find there, but something just led me. And then, I remembered. As soon as I saw the beige coat hanging on the stand, the one I was wearing last week when Suzanne and I took a ride to the Bois de Boulogne, I knew I had found what I needed. Suzanne had handed it to me for safe-keeping, saying that it was the most precious present I had ever given to her. She had to remove it as it was irritating the inside of her wrist where she had just been stung by nettles as she bent down to readjust the hem of her dress. Later, we both forgot about the bracelet. Worried about the health of her grandmother, and busy arranging an impromptu journey to see her, Suzanne had no time to think of jewellery. Now that she was in Holland, she was unlikely to ask for it until she returned. That would not be for at least another month.

I took the bracelet out of the inside pocket and held it in the palm of my hand. It was sufficiently expensive for my present purpose. I pressed it open. The lock of my hair was still inside. I remember giving the bracelet to Suzanne soon after the death of my father. We snipped a little lock of my hair and placed it inside the pendant. I could picture Suzanne kissing it before she clasped the two sides together. For me, the bracelet was like an engagement ring, but more discreet. Had it been a ring, we could not have been able to keep our engagement secret.

Standing in the upstairs room, with the bracelet still in my hand, I considered whether I should remove the lock of hair. It was the lock of my hair, rather than the bracelet itself, that was a token of my love for Suzanne. In the end, I decided against removing it. Victorine will only wear it for the picture. Besides, I felt a touch superstitious: if I were to separate the lock from the bracelet, would it not doom us to a broken engagement?

'I have found a replacement,' I said, as soon as I came down. I was pleased with myself and immediately handed the bracelet to Victorine. She gasped but did not comment. Perhaps she did not wish to draw Lola's attention to it.

I found Lola standing next to me. She bent over Victorine's naked arm and took the bracelet in her hand. She spoke without examining it properly: 'This is certainly more expensive than the necklace, but it isn't more precious,' she said looking straight into my eyes. She dropped the bracelet on the bed next to Victorine.

I did not know what to say, but I let her remark pass unanswered. I picked up the bracelet and fixed it on Victorine's right arm. As she leaned against the pillow, the gold was clearly offset by the white silk.

We continued. As always, Victorine held her pose perfectly. She is a real professional and can stay for hours, hardly even blinking. Her breathing is always steady, the body relaxed. She held her gaze throughout the morning, without once asking for a break. Lola pottered around, and eventually settled down in the armchair by the window. With her feet tucked under her skirt, she leaned back and closed her eyes. When I looked at her, just before stopping for lunch, the sun was streaming onto her face and, once again, as on that day when I first saw her, her looks intrigued me. I could not take my eyes off her. I recognised something familiar in the shape of her face around the eyes and the mouth. For a moment, I wondered whether I should sneak closer and make a quick sketch of her face, while she was dozing off. I might have done it, regardless of what Victorine thought, had Lola not suddenly moved and opened her eyes. Perhaps one day I will ask her to model for me alone.

When we finished for the day, Victorine handed me the bracelet. I said that I would prefer her to look after it herself, so that she could bring it to the next session. Both women looked at me. I added that the piece was too expensive to be left around in the studio. It could easily be misplaced and lost in the clutter. It was a transparent excuse that I had not planned to make.

Victorine nodded, but Lola said that if someone saw Victorine with the bracelet, they might think that she had a special love token from a man. They might ask questions.

'Or,' and here Lola suddenly turned, raised her voice and looked me straight in the eye as she said: 'they might think that she has stolen it.'

'They may think what they want,' I said. 'Why should that concern us?' Immediately, I felt annoyed with myself to have responded to Lola's remark. Now she could not let go:

'Monsieur Manet, you shouldn't present others with such tokens. It may be misinterpreted. It may not concern you what others think of you, but you shouldn't assume that we feel the same.'

I laughed.

'We need the bracelet for the picture. That is all. There is no other meaning to it.' I wondered whether I should add something about the 'we' that Lola was using. Why did she think she could speak on behalf of both of them? But I could see that Victorine was ready to go. She reminded Lola that they had to collect something on the way home and that they should not delay further. Lola did not seem to understand.

* * *

I hear church bells chiming ten o'clock and Victorine knocks on the door. She has scratches on her face. Some are partially covered by powder.

There is still some coffee left in the pot, but she does not want any. Immediately, she takes off her clothes and positions herself on the divan. She is wearing both the necklace and the bracelet. I do not comment on that, either. But when I notice bruises on her thighs and a deep scratch on her breast, I wonder whether I should ask if someone has attacked her. Months ago, I would have gone out of my way not to have heard what went on in her life outside my studio. Since then, I have learned that she has more integrity than most people I know. And, she cares about painting. Like me, she is prepared to sacrifice everything for art. Perhaps, we are not so different.

'Does it hurt?' I say, and immediately realise that it is not an appropriate question.

She looks at me: 'Someone attacked me, monsieur. But my skin is healing well. I am sorry that it shows and makes it inconvenient for you. I will sit as well as I always do and I'll be as confident and self-possessed as you need me for the composition.'

I nod, ashamed to have asked.

I think back to other images I have made of her. Could I make this one more complex? Charles says that being a woman is to do with costumes, role play and the ability to change constantly. There is the goddess and there is the woman of the Parisian street. I have the two in *Le Bain* – perhaps here I could have both in one woman.

I soften the chin on her image; perhaps I should make this detail in the style of Cabanel. The thought amuses me.

Later, I thank her for the dark pink orchid she has brought and that she pins into her hair. It looks better than either the rosebud or the hibiscus, which we had the other day. As I work, the fingers of her right arm hold the brocade bedspread, as if slightly pulling it from under her body. This is different from the way her hand was positioned last week. In the past, she would never have done something like this without checking with me first. And even then, I might have been annoyed at her initiative. With time, I have learned to appreciate her contribution. The way she sits is perfect.

We stop for lunch and when Madame Bijoux brings up a tray with food, I ask Victorine to share it with me. Since we are not working in the afternoon, she says that she needs to go. On the way out, Madame Bijoux presses an apple into her hand. I wonder whether it is the scratches on Victorine's face that make the concierge feel sorry for her.

44

It was naïve of me to hope that he wouldn't notice. He spends hours staring at me; how could I have expected him to miss the scratches and bruises? I told him very little and I was grateful that he didn't ask further. What could I have said? Because I posed naked for your picture, someone who was almost a friend tried to rape me. Monsieur Manet isn't responsible for what happened. I am the one who opened the door to Etienne and let him stay the night, despite suspecting what he wanted. It serves me right for being so stupid.

I can only hope that, by Sunday, the scratches are less visible, so that I can tell Lola that I fell or that I walked into a bush in the park. I'll have to be more cunning with the bruises. I must make sure that the gas lamp isn't lit, or at least that it is somewhere that doesn't fully illuminate my thighs. If Lola knew what had happened, she would lose her temper. She wouldn't see it from my point of view at all. More likely, she would accuse me of being unfaithful.

But my real problem is that I've lost a source of income. Without contacts, I can't find anyone who would commission me to paint flower pictures. I have the name and address of Etienne's dealer but, after what happened, it's likely that Etienne will have closed that avenue. I better forget about America.

I don't want to return to the Legrands' café. When I left, I felt that a new phase of my life had begun and that I'd never again be a waitress. Besides, I am not sure that they would want me back. Etienne told me that sometimes they complained that I hadn't given them much chance to find a replacement. After what happened, he might have even made up a story about me. During the last six months, I have walked past the café a few times but had no wish to go in, even to say hello.

I still have my guitar. As soon as the scratches on my face heal, I'll try to make some money singing in the cafés in Montmartre. With my face as it is now, I fear I might give the wrong impression and they might think that I am a troublemaker.

For the next two days, Monsieur Manet doesn't need me and I can spend the time on my own work. I pull the easel right in front of the large mirror and sit down to draw my self-portrait. I am not sure how to start, but I have an urge to do it. Immediately, I know that the light is wrong. Monsieur Manet says that a picture for our time shouldn't use half tones. The object must be fully illuminated. I drag the mirror across the room and position it in between the two large windows. As I sit opposite, the sun is full on my face. Now the light blinds me and I may find it difficult to draw at the same time. I have to sit very close to the mirror, as I am drawing only the face. I struggle; I squint. Eventually, I manage to position a large sheet of paper, like a kind of visor, on top of the easel, to shade my eyes, so that I can look straight ahead at the mirror.

I stay in all day and make five drawings. One of them reminds me of the first picture that Monsieur Manet made of me. I thought that I had changed since then, but in my drawing I am the Victorine of a year ago. Maybe, I haven't been attentive enough to what I see. I have drawn the picture that I carry in my head: it is the memory of Monsieur Manet's view of me.

For the second one, I untied my hair and parted my lips in a broad smile. Look at it, I know it's not a Victorine that I have ever come across. She never behaves like that.

In the third drawing, I am wearing a black hat with a veil. I seem to be looking longingly into the distance. It's not clear what the person in the picture wants. She is posing, hoping to be attractive in her melancholy. I don't recognise myself in this image either. In the fourth and fifth sketches, I am laughing: my mouth is wide open and my eyes are sparkling. There is a trace of seduction around my mouth.

With the sun still shining, I place all the drawings on top of each other and stick them onto the window pane. The light penetrates through the sheets of paper and I can see the outlines of all five faces at the same time. I don't like any of the five drawings; together they make much more sense. If only I could have a hundred stacked on top of each other where a viewer could see them all simultaneously. That is what Monsieur Manet calls a palimpsest. I had never heard the word before but there was something in its sound and its meaning that made me remember it. Monsieur Manet said that it was one of his favourite ideas.

It's easy for Monsieur Manet to represent me as a torero or a street singer, or a woman sitting naked somewhere in the country with two fully dressed men. He can choose the different roles for me to play. But what about me? For me, they all exist simultaneously. The roles from my past are the roles that make what I am now. What am I now?

I think of a painting. Perhaps it will be my life's work: a self-portrait as work in progress. It would have to be permanently on exhibition while I worked on it everyday. Visitors could come to the same gallery and always see a different picture.

When the sun sets, I take the drawings from the window pane and place them next to each other on the long table by the wall opposite. In the evening, I make several drawings from memory. I try to recall what I looked like as a small child, as a girl of five and at twelve, when I came to live in Paris with my mother. I wish I had photographs of my childhood, like Monsieur Manet. I can only draw from memory or what I imagine I looked like.

I cut a few chunks of cheese and bread and eat them with radishes. I have two glasses of wine and fall asleep straight-away. I dream that I live with Madame Pascal. In the dream, we are the same age, twenty-five or thirty and we sit together all day painting fans. We have a small house in the suburbs. On Thursdays, a little boy comes to the house and I teach him to play the guitar. His younger sister sits patiently on the sofa and watches us. One Thursday, the parents forget to collect the children. We put them to bed. Days and months pass and no one comes to collect them. The little girl also learns to play the guitar. Her brother has become quite an expert.

When I wake up in the morning, a cold lump settles in my chest. I stay in bed for a long time, curled up, with my knees touching my chin and my arms hugging my legs. I'll never be able to teach the children to play the guitar or to draw. But that also means that I'll have all the time for my own pictures.

I wash in cold water and make myself think how lucky I am to have the whole day to myself.

I stand in front of the mirror and examine my face. In the semi darkness of the cafés and with a bit of powder, no bruises will show. I'll start with *L'Azure*, a small café not far from here. The owner knows me and has often asked me to go back and sing as I used to before I met Monsieur Manet. I'll make my way there in the late afternoon, as soon as the sun has set.

45

I have a clear recollection. We had just finished and Victorine had gone to dress behind the screen at the other end of the room. I glanced towards the window, where Lola was looking out. Her back was stiff and her shoulders raised above their natural level, as if she wanted to separate herself from me and the rest of the studio. As I took a few steps in her direction, I noticed that she had closed her eyes. Why was she standing by the window if she was not looking into the street? When I went closer, I heard her sharp intakes of breath. For an instant, I wondered whether she was sobbing. Certain that Victorine was out of earshot, I told Lola that I would like to do some detailed work on the figure that she was modelling. I whispered, speaking to her in confidence. I asked if she could come alone to the studio one day.

When I glanced at her sideways, I could see that the manner of my approach was effective. The expression on her face gradually mellowed and the rhythm of her breathing slowed. Rather than protest loudly, as she might have done before, she whispered that she could manage Thursday and Friday. That suited me fine. Victorine's figure was almost finished and I needed to focus on the woman standing behind the divan. I had some other ideas, too, but at the same time, I did not allow myself the luxury of thinking that far ahead. Lola has always made me nervous.

On Thursday, she arrived early and I found her waiting for me in the porch. Since Madame Bijoux had gone out, there was no one to let her in. She carried the white dress in a bag and needed to change. I gestured towards the screen, anticipating that otherwise she might try to undress in front of me. I knew I had to be careful, in case she tried something that might destroy our working relationship. The picture was too important to risk it with any indiscretions. But I was wrong. Without Victorine around, Lola said little and certainly kept her eyes away from mine.

I brought in the bouquet, the fresh flowers that I had bought on the way in. I was about to hand it to her when she said that she needed to readjust something on the dress and that I could leave the flowers on the table. I saw that she was trying to avoid being too close to me. Her attitude began to intrigue me, although, at the time, I was determined not to pay too much attention to it.

Surprisingly, whatever I asked from her, she obliged. At one point, I wanted to see whether it might be more interesting if she did not look at Victorine's figure. I feared that she might find that unacceptable and wondered whether I was pushing my luck. But, instead of arguing or complaining, she even asked for further instructions on what to do. I made good progress by the time we stopped, around four o'clock. I offered her coffee but she said that she had to rush.

On Friday, she arrived in the white dress, with a scarf tied around her head. We set to work straightaway. The session until lunch was uneventful and I was grateful to her for that. She stayed perfectly still and had no need to talk. Since we were continuing in the afternoon, I asked Madame Bijoux to bring up some lunch. Although not hungry, I felt that I should keep Lola happy by being friendly. In the end, she hardly ate. But sitting down with bread, some excellent Parma ham, brought to me by a friend recently arrived from Italy, cheese and a glass of full bodied Bordeaux, she seemed to relax and we talked about things other than the painting. At one point, I almost told her about Marcella. I have not mentioned her to anyone, not even to Antoine and Charles. I have thought of her more since I met Lola. They say that women never forget the first man that sleeps with them. I do not know if it is the same for men, but I shall not forget her.

I was barely seventeen and had never loved anyone so much. She spoke no French and I had only a few words of Portuguese.

Every night, when I left her to go back to the ship, I wondered whether I could take her with me to Paris. It was a foolish idea. What would my father have said had I brought back a wife who was black and from the dark recesses of Brazil?

I regret not having made a drawing of her but we always met in the dark and there was little time. When I arrived back in Paris, I sent her a small picture of the port in Sao Paolo, as seen from the ship. I do not know if she ever received it. But I have often thought of her. Even these days, I look for black women in Paris. There are few of them around and I wish I could paint them.

In the end, I did not speak of Marcella to Lola. Instead, I asked Lola whether she would like to model for another painting for me. She said she had very little time as she was not allowed to take days off. Originally, she had agreed to sit for me only because Victorine cared about it. She herself had no interest in pictures.

I persisted: 'I would like to make a picture of you in the nude. Just you. With no one else around.'

To my surprise, she lowered her eyes, thought for a while and then said she would do her best to find the time. We left it at that. Of course, my head was immediately buzzing with ideas for the new painting. Above all, I could not understand why Lola was so pliable. Where had all that temper and anger gone?

On Sunday, after more than twenty sittings, I had almost completed the figure of the black maid. I still had to add a few finishing touches, but I felt I could easily do that without a model. Since it was only two o'clock, I asked Lola to allow me to try out a few ideas for the next picture. I made a few quick sketches. The first three were of her sitting on a chair and looking out. I experimented by moving the easel around and looking at her from different angles. At her suggestion, I drew her lying down on the same bed and in the same position as Victorine. I knew that it was not what I had in mind, but I was happy to humour her. I thought she was either jealous of Victorine, or felt so affectionate towards her that she wanted to imagine that she was Victorine. In the end, I decided that I wanted Lola sitting

292

down, showing only her face and naked bust. I wanted a conventional pose, with her looking sideways.

Yesterday, we spent the entire morning and afternoon on the portrait. I was not very happy with it and after lunch I decided to scrape off all the paint and go back to drawing. I tried out several new ideas, including one with Lola holding her dress, as if she were pulling it over her head, revealing only her naked breasts. She is tall and slim with a large bosom and has a majestic figure. She is too beautiful and looks too seductive for the effect I wish to achieve. In fact, I have had so many ideas that they have become muddled.

In the evening, after she had left, I stayed in and went over what I had done. Charles and Antoine were waiting for me to join them at the Guerbois but, in the end, I spent too long contemplating how to proceed with the painting and it was much too late to go anywhere. I spent the night in the studio. Even as I lay in bed, with the light out, the images appeared before me. They swirled around in my mind as if a strong wind had lifted all the drawings of Lola and made them dance in the air. At some point, as I was falling asleep, a clear vision took hold. It was as if all the drawings had suddenly been blown out of the studio and only one remained. I knew from experience that I might not remember the idea in the morning. I left the bed, lit a lamp and walked downstairs. The canvas had to be fairly small, no bigger than the one I had used for the first portrait of Victorine. I wanted nothing else to show, no background, no chair, perhaps only the dress as it was pushed down, below the line of the breasts. I wanted the figure to look out, not in that challenging way that Victorine has, but in a much less provocative manner. I wanted her strong and beautiful, attractive but not attempting a seduction. Above all, I did not want anyone to think that the figure represented a slave or a maid. She has to be a woman. A black woman. I wanted her to look proud but in a gentler way than Victorine.

As I tried to work out my idea, I could not see why the figure should display her breasts. Who was it for? And it was only then that I thought of a mirror. She was a young woman admiring her own body. The viewer would see her back and the reflection of her face and naked chest in the mirror. I wished I could have drawn the image straight away. If only I had access to my model.

This morning, when she arrived, I noticed that her eyes were red. For a moment, I wondered whether I should ask if she had been crying, but I felt so preoccupied by the idea for the new composition and so desperate to try it out that I thought it would be better not to say anything that might distract me. She seemed a little absent minded: several times, I asked her to move her head, or readjust her hands and she did not hear me, or when she did, even nodding in acknowledgement, she forgot what I was asking. It took a while to set up the mirror and her back at the right angle. But once it was all in place, I knew that I had found what I wanted.

Since it is Sunday, I assumed that she would want to go to spend the afternoon with Victorine. I did not wish to show that I knew their arrangement, so I simply suggested that we continued on Monday. Lola said that she was free to stay on. That surprised me.

The afternoon has been productive. Not once did I feel the need to scrape off what I painted. I have noticed before that if I can work out the overall composition, the actual painting of it proceeds smoothly.

Now that the sun has disappeared and we are sitting in semi-darkness, I have to stop. When I tell her that, she does not move. By now I have moved away from the easel and I cannot see the reflection of her face in the mirror. I walk up to her. She remains perfectly still. I place my hands on her shoulders, at first just one, and then the other. In the mirror, I look at the reflection of my white skin on Lola's dark shoulders. I watch her face. Her expression does not change as I touch her. We are both perfectly still. Several minutes pass. There is absolute silence in the studio. I remove my hands from her shoulders, step to the side, kneel in front of her and bury my head in her naked breasts. When I take a deep breath, I can smell jasmine.

Lola puts her arms around me and rests her chin on my head. I inhale deeply once again, and my head begins to spin. Gradually, she draws me close and places a kiss on the top of my head, like a mother seeing her son off to school. While she holds me, my dizziness subsides and I lift my face. Our eyes meet. I kiss her on the mouth. There is cinnamon on my tongue. We make love on a rug on the floor. Underneath me, she moves very slowly. It takes longer than I have ever known it. When we stop moving, it is completely dark outside and she holds me in her arms. For a moment, I think of Marcella. In those days, I did not have the luxury to be slow.

46

Last week, Lola wrote to me to say that she would have to work on Sunday and wouldn't be able to see me. Her employers were going away soon and she would have time off during the week. This was the first time since I've known her that she wasn't free on a Sunday. Lola had told me that the family she worked for were very religious and always made sure their servants were free on Sundays to attend church.

I felt some relief that we wouldn't be meeting: the bruises on my thighs were still visible and the scratch on my stomach was oozing pus. Lola would have seen through any lies and we would surely have had an argument. But when the second note arrived, saying that she couldn't see me on this coming Sunday, I was puzzled: What was happening?

Finding work in cafés hasn't been easy. *L'Azure*, the place I tried first, has a regular singer and she was in no mood to negotiate with me. Although her guitar playing isn't very good, she is well liked by the customers and the owner was keen to keep her. I suggested that we could sing a duet, with me accompanying us on the guitar, but she wouldn't hear of it.

I walked to three other cafés on the first night and they either already had someone or weren't interested. In one of them, I had to leave after singing two songs as there was too much shouting and no one paid attention to me. When I went around to collect the money, all I got was a few sous. I realised that if I was going to get work, I'd have to make friends with an owner.

On the second night, I walked further towards St-Germain-des-Prés and I was lucky that the regular singer in the café at the corner of rue de Rennes was ill. They allowed me to stay the entire evening. Towards the end, I had to repeat several songs, as

I didn't have anything else to sing. The tips were much better than on the first night. I received three francs and thirty, two francs and forty more than the first night. Before I left, the owner, Monsieur Tombé, thanked me.

'You've been good for business, mademoiselle,' he said and pressed two more francs into my palm. His wife, standing next to him, with a boy and a girl behind her and a baby in her arms, smiled and nodded. The boy came forward and asked if I could play the guitar for him and he would sing. I did and when we finished, the whole family clapped. On the second night with them, I was treated as a regular by the customers and they kept making requests for particular songs. I earned better money than I expected.

As they closed for the night, Monsieur Tombé said that they hoped I would be able to stay with them for some time. That pleased me. Madame Tombé brought me a plate of potatoes and a lamb stew. The children sat with me at the table and talked to me while I ate.

But a few days later, she was not well and Monsieur Tombé said that she was staying in bed. As he walked past me, his hand brushed against my breasts. I assumed that the movement was accidental and ignored it. But later on, when everyone had gone, he leaned towards me, his face so close to mine that I could feel the heat of his skin, and squeezed my hand. That made me uncomfortable but I couldn't fail to notice his azure eyes and perfectly shaped nose. He is a handsome man, with a gentle voice and I used to think that his wife was a lucky woman. When he placed one of his hands on my bottom, my palm closed tightly around the five francs that he has just given me on top of the tips from the customers. I forced myself to smile.

He opened a small door off the corridor, close to where we were standing. It was a pantry and there, among the sacks of potatoes and with hams hanging above us, I let him put his hand inside my blouse. He undid the buttons and sucked on my breasts, mumbling: 'Ah, mademoiselle. You are lovely. Yes, yes, oh, mademoiselle.' I let him lift my skirt and place his hand between my legs.

His wife called: 'Albert, where are you? I need you here. Albert, I have been looking for you. Simone is crying and I cannot pick her up.'

With his voice shaking, he shouted that he had been inspecting the hams. I managed to free myself.

The next day, I had to walk much further than St-Germain-de-Prés before I could find a café without a singer.

In the morning, I pawned grandmother's lace again. On the way to the shop, I changed my mind several times. Once inside, I bargained until I was offered twenty francs. That was more than I'd expected and yet a voice inside me kept telling me not to bargain and to walk out. I knew that if I managed to get a good price I wouldn't be able to resist the temptation to take the money. I was reluctant to part with the lace and had he offered me just a few francs I could have told myself that it wasn't worth it. As once before, I pinned the pink ticket on the wall by the door. As soon as I manage to earn some money, I'll redeem the lace.

In the late afternoon, I went into four cafés, but none of them made me welcome. In the first two, the clientele were very noisy and I had to sing louder than usual if I wanted to be heard. In the third, a drunken man announced at the top of his voice that my lips were kissable and that he wanted to have a better look at my breasts. 'Could you undo a few buttons?' he shouted. Several men laughed and cheered him; one of them sneaked behind my back and attempted to pinch my bottom. Since no one intervened, I left after two songs. Altogether, I had barely one franc and ten sous. On the way back, I stopped at Monsieur Tombé's café. Although another singer was there, he allowed me to perform. When she complained, he gave her some money and asked her to leave. She shouted abuse at me.

I played the guitar and sang for two hours, with just one short break. Monsieur Tombé brought me a bottle of wine.

'All that singing, you need to drink, mademoiselle,' he winked at me.

Despite sparing on food and paints, I am two weeks behind with the rent. I appreciated Madame Tombé offering me some bread and cheese.

'You eat, mademoiselle. Our customers liked your music and you've worked hard. But it's late. I am going to bed. My husband'll talk to you about tomorrow.'

I was going to ask whether I could make arrangements with her, but she had already gone.

Monsieur Tombé ushered me into the pantry. There was no light, except for a candle he placed on the floor. I needed the money and said so. He gave me ten francs: I submitted to him. He pointed to the barrel, turned me around and asked me to bend over. As he lowered his trousers, I could hear him smacking his lips. Then he pulled up my skirt, and immediately pushed himself inside me. It hurt; I held my breath and waited for him to finish. As soon as I had counted twelve hams hanging above me, he pulled out.

Since then, I've spent two weeks singing in that café, and every night before I leave, Monsieur Tombé gestures for me to go to the pantry. He always has ten francs ready in his pocket. Most of the time he is quick, but sometimes he can't make himself hard, and fumbles with my breasts instead. Yesterday, while he was kneeling in front of me and sucking my nipples, I managed to take out several bank notes from his back pocket. I made noises as if I was enjoying his attention and he never noticed that his money had gone.

This morning the sun is streaming through the large window. I go downstairs where Madame Conchis is singing, in French this time, and I pay the rent, everything that I owe. I am relieved that she doesn't comment on all the money that I give her or ask how many pictures I've sold. Tomorrow morning, I'll redeem the lace.

Back upstairs, I set to work on my self-portrait. I draw myself wearing nothing but an enormous hat, with a large feather. I pull down the brim of the hat until all I can see in the mirror is my mouth, my neck and my breasts. I experiment by changing the shape of my lips to suggest a different mood or character. This is the kind of work I like, but it doesn't bring in any money.

In the afternoon, Madame Conchis knocks on my door and hands me a note. I recognize Monsieur Manet's handwriting.

The last time I went to his studio, he was very agitated. That was hardly anything new and I would never have asked what had upset him. But he seemed to want me to know. He carried on shouting, although the person who had caused his agitation had already left.

While climbing the stairs, I had noticed a smartly dressed, middle-aged man with a monocle walking down, mumbling to himself. A fiacre with a coat of arms was parked by the entrance. Apparently, as I soon learned, this man had come to ask Monsieur Manet to make a portrait of his wife. Monsieur Manet had told him that he was not a society painter. The man said that he would pay him very well as long as Monsieur Manet followed his instructions on how to represent his wife. As I can easily imagine, that threw Monsieur Manet into a rage. The man then named the sum he would pay for the finished portrait. At that point, Monsieur Manet, as he assured me, grew even angrier and insisted that the man left. But the man was so shocked that for a while he just stood in the middle of the studio, not knowing what to do. Monsieur Manet continued to shout at him and, in the end, he had to push him out with his hands. I remember hearing him bang the door, just as I passed the concierge's lodge.

'What does he think? Does he see me as a society portrait painter? As someone who paints wives to order? I would have thought that the scandal following the Salon would have cured anyone of that misapprehension. And to imagine that this nobody would tell me how to paint his wife. Has the world gone mad? Some stupid bureaucrat imagines he knows about art. What does he know about painting? And I spit on his money. Mademoiselle Victorine, you understand what I mean?'

I did and I nodded but it wasn't enough to calm Monsieur Manet. He told me the entire episode all over again, shouting as if I were the one to blame for what had just happened.

Eventually, we settled to work. I sat for two hours while Monsieur Manet put the finishing touches to the figure of the naked woman. He allowed me to look at the painting. I was surprised to see that the maid had been completed, as well as the background. He never worked on a human figure without a model. Lola must had been posing for him without me. I couldn't understand it: whenever we came together, she couldn't hide her dislike of him. It was strange that she would have gone to the studio alone. Was that why she had no time to come to Maître Albert?

When Monsieur Manet came to stand next to me, I commented only on the drapes that he had painted in the background. Made from heavy brocade and expensive looking, they reminded me of theatre curtains: framed by them, the figure I modelled appeared as if she were on the stage. That background suggested that the woman was on display. Monsieur Manet just stared at the painting, lost in thought. I wondered if he expected me to ask about Lola.

Although the matter bothered me, I decided to let it rest. I had another idea to pursue. In my new circumstances, with no work coming from Etienne, that idea was much more important. I explained to Monsieur Manet that I had recently lost my main source of income. I told him that I no longer received orders for flower pictures for the English market. As I didn't wish him to think that there was a problem with the quality of my work, I added that it wasn't through any fault of mine. Before I could finish, he pulled a pile of notes from his pocket and said that he was glad to be of use. For a second, I wondered what to do, as I was in no position to refuse the offer. I thanked him. I said I didn't need a loan but that perhaps, the next time someone asked him to do a portrait, I would be very pleased if he would pass the request on to me.

Monsieur Manet looked at me blankly. I thought he didn't understand what I was asking. Or perhaps I had gone too far to ask for such a favour. He said: 'Mademoiselle Victorine, tell me honestly, is it true that you would not mind doing portraits for the *nouveaux riches*, for people who expect you to do exactly what they tell you to do?'

'Not at all, monsieur. I assure you, I wouldn't mind. And even if I did…' I didn't want to tell him that I was destitute, but I wanted to say something about the pleasure one can create for ordinary people with simple, uncomplicated paintings. I had in mind something that Etienne had said about the flower pictures, but Monsieur Manet was already looking at a canvas. I could see that he was disappointed by my attitude.

I left without mentioning the matter again. I didn't think anything would come out of it. But I was wrong. Here is the note from Monsieur Manet. He has enclosed the address of a woman – rue du Mont Thabor – who wanted her portrait painted. I decide to go there straightaway. I pack some drawing material, just in case the woman wants me to start today, although I'll have to be back by late afternoon. Someone told me of a café where the regular singer hasn't turned up for the past two weeks and they allow anyone else who turns up first to sing for the evening.

As I pass the concierge's office, I almost bump into a tall, thin young man, with a pale face and a shock of black hair. I nod at him, and move on to hand the key to Madame Conchis. I realize that he has stopped and is watching me. Just as I am about to leave the hall, he says: 'Mademoiselle, my name is Gabriel. I live on the second floor,' he extends his hand. His palm is warm and moist, the handshake light. I know he is the flute player. I am too much in a hurry for conversation. If I don't arrive at the café before six, they may have someone else. And who knows how long it will take at rue du Mont Thabor.

'Mademoiselle, I've noticed that you carry a guitar. I never hear you play. I was wondering if you –'

'I am sorry, monsieur. I have to go.' Madame Conchis turns to Gabriel and asks about his flute.

Rue du Mont Thabor has an expensive look with its smart facades and shops. The woman lives on the second floor. The concierge accompanies me upstairs. A young maid, dressed in black, opens the door, ushers me in to the salon and disappears. I look around. I expected the people to be rich and, indeed, they are. The household is opulent, but the décor is stiflingly ugly. The walls are covered with antique tapestries showing hunting scenes. A collection of old weapons sits alongside some busts of strange looking men on a table in a corner. On another table, various oriental objects, fans, lacquered boxes and small Chinese statues, are fighting for space. There are more things here than in a painter's studio.

I sit down. The seat and backrest of the chair are covered with embroidered pictures of a deer chased by two dogs. Other chairs have similar animal scenes. Ten minutes pass before the double doors open and an elderly lady enters. Her clothes are as magnificent and as bizarre as the room. She wears a skirt of black lace with embroidered butterflies stitched all around the hem. Her deep-green jacket has a pattern of large flowers in red and yellow. A pair of white lace gloves covers her hands and, on her head, she has a small hat with a black lace veil.

I stand up but she gestures to me not to move. She says she expected a proper artist. I don't know what to say. I want to appear confident but I don't want to upset her. I need the job.

'I did not know that women can paint. All artists are men. My brother made enquiries and looked for a male painter. Obviously.'

'Madame, you are right: most artists are men. But there are a few women. I can assure you, I am as good as most men,' I lie. I know I can do what she wants me to do.

'You do come with a recommendation, mademoiselle. But it came by word of mouth and no one told me that you were a woman.'

I smile: 'I understand, madame.'

The woman comes to sit next to me: 'Oh, you are very young,' she says. She peers closely at me and adds: 'And pretty, you are pretty.'

'Thank you, madame. I understand you are looking for a portrait painter. Would the painting be of you?'

She looks surprised. 'Oh, yes. Were you not told that?' As I shake my head, she continues: 'Yes, me and my little Angélique. A double portrait, mademoiselle.' She brings a photo of a little girl, her granddaughter. She says that the girl lives far away, which is why she wants a picture of the two of them together. She would like me to start as soon as possible.

'I miss her terribly.'

When I ask when the girl would be able to sit for me, since she doesn't live in Paris, Madame Chevens says that she wants me to use the photograph. Only she will sit for me. We agree on a fee of seventy-five francs. I would like to start as soon as possible.

I ride the omnibus back and then take a short stroll along the quay by Notre-Dame. There is drizzle in the air but I don't mind. As soon as I enter the hall next to the concierge's lodge, I see Lola. She jumps in front of me, very excited: 'Victorine, I've been here for two hours. Where have you been?'

'I've been out.' She frowns.

'But it's Sunday.'

'I go out on Sundays. I didn't expect you to come today. I had your note.'

'Well, in the end, I managed to find the time. But where have you been?'

I don't feel that I want to tell her. I could ask her why she has been seeing Monsieur Manet without telling me. But I never ask such things.

'I went to see someone,' I say.

As we walk upstairs, I can sense that she is trying hard to be pleasant. By the time we are inside, we are both less tense. Lola fetches some food from the café downstairs: sorrel soup and a potato stew. We eat quietly. I have a feeling that there are things that she wants to talk about but doesn't dare mention. For my part, I don't like to waste time on talk about anything that isn't to do with painting.

When we finish, as I expect, Lola undresses me and takes me to bed. Immediately, she notices the bruises and the scratch on my stomach. Convinced that I have a lover, she becomes angry and shouts: 'It's a man, isn't it? No woman would have done this to you. How could you, Victorine? You have just been with him, haven't you?'

I don't answer. I need to prepare for the singing tonight. I was told that I would be able to earn as much as five francs if I am good. I really don't wish to miss the opportunity.

'You have spoilt what we had. And I loved you so much. You have no heart, Victorine. You will die alone. How could you do this to me?'

I lower my head, hoping that she might calm down if I look

penitent. But she doesn't. Still shouting, she grabs her clothes and dresses very quickly.

'I hate you,' she shouts as she rushes out.

I don't bother to look through the window. I sit still for a few minutes, then tidy my hair and put on a clean blouse.

One hour later, I enter the café and make enquiries. To my surprise, the owner doesn't ask many questions. I tell him that I am experienced and that anywhere I play, people stay longer and drink more.

'You are a blessing, a god-send, mademoiselle. I always like to have music on Sundays. You can stay the whole evening.' He offers me wine and I take it. It helps me sing.

47

Warm sunshine penetrates the thick branches of the trees lining the main avenue of Père Lachaise. As we walk, I watch the shifting pattern of shadows on the ground. Birds are singing. Is that a song thrush? When a butterfly flutters past, I think that there is too much life around for a man to go on his last journey. The funeral procession turns off the main avenue and winds down one of the pathways. We must be getting closer.

I walk between Charles and Henri. Alfred and Zachary are in front of us. We move quietly, occupied by our own thoughts.

Charles is unusually pale. During the funeral service in Saint-Germain-des-Prés, I was shocked by his stooped figure, looking much older than his forty-two years. The rouge on his cheeks appears silly in the sunshine and does not hide the ravages of his illness. But what does a coat of paint matter? My friend is a genius underneath all his make-up.

Some people whisper behind us. Today will be remembered: 17th August 1863 is the day we bury the famous, the magnificent Delacroix. He will be celebrated for showing us that colour is not an accessory, but that it has an expressive role.

In years to come no one will remember the fatuous celebrations of two days ago: silly street parties, clowns and fireworks, just to commemorate Napoleon's birthday.

Almost the entire art world is here. Théophile Gautier's elegant figure is a few rows in front of me. The silk of his top hat glistens in the sunshine. And among the pallbearers I can see the bulk of Nieuwerkerke and the familiar figure of Hippolyte Flandrin.

I think of what Charles said the other day: 'Eugène Delacroix was the last of the great artists of the Renaissance and the first modern.' I agreed and Charles added that Delacroix was the

306

only artist who, in our faithless generation, had conceived truly spiritual pictures. I concur with that, too.

I think back to when I saw *La Barque de Dante* for the first time and how I was immediately struck by its power. When I realized that Delacroix was only twenty-four when he had painted it, I felt jealous: at that age, I had nothing to show. Even before I left the Luxembourg gallery, I knew I had to copy the picture. What impressed me most was the drama of the composition. It was the only time I felt the need to copy a painting by an artist who was still alive.

In 1855, I went to see him in his studio in rue Notre-Dame de Lorette. Antonin accompanied me. Monsieur Delacroix was as old as my father and looked very respectable, well-bred, a man of quality. He was small and thin, all nerves. A solitary man. But contrary to what we were told to expect, he was not cold. He received us with great courtesy and as soon as I had explained the purpose of our visit, he gave me permission to copy his painting. Then he questioned us about our preferences in art and told us what mattered to him, all the time speaking with perfect grace.

'The colour,' he said turning towards me, 'the colour, messieurs, do not mix it to give us half tones. They have no power.'

Before we left, he told us to look at Rubens, because 'Rubens was a god'.

He died before I could tell him how I had taken his advice to heart. Most of what I know about the relation between light and colour comes from *La Barque*. And I do not blend my colours. I do not use half tones. The critics hate that, as much as they dislike my visible brushstrokes. I think of Delacroix's murals in Ste Sulpice. The large, separate brushstrokes blend naturally at a distance and give energy and freshness to the colour.

He came to see my show at the Martinet last March, although he was already ill. Louis said that on hearing the rude comments from the public, Delacroix said he regretted not being strong enough to defend me.

Henri looks across at me, as if he has guessed my thoughts. I nod silently. I wonder what he is thinking.

My mind turns to my own paintings. I shall need only another two or three half-day sittings to finish Lola's portrait. Although she has followed my instructions on how to pose, she seems to have adopted an enigmatic expression. I fear she may be imitating Victorine. The problem is that her gaze makes her look as if she is on show. It makes me think of those poor souls in the São Paolo slave market, the most wretched people I have ever seen. I do not want to produce a black woman on display. Nor do I want to produce a painting where black people represent no more than a colourful addition to the overall composition. My black woman has a canvas to herself. I intend to use Lola's name for the title of the portrait. I could call her Mademoiselle L. Sancho. I do not want the picture to be known as "the black woman" as if she were all the black women in the world. In the painting, she is a person, an individual.

The procession turns onto a narrow pathway and slows down. The whispers cease. The only sound we can hear is the rhythm of shoes crunching the gravel. The birds have stopped singing.

I think about the background to the portrait. Since I do not want anything to distract the viewer's attention from the figure, I shall paint no curtain, no set, no landscape behind her. Even the chair will not show. But what colour shall I use for the background? How much should I offset her black skin? The white dress already emphasises her colour.

Suddenly, I am gripped by panic: I am not sure what I am doing with that picture. She is too beautiful for my purpose. The naked breasts are the most difficult. I am still puzzled why I asked her to pull down the dress. Charles mischievously suggested that I could always claim that I had painted an allegorical figure, perhaps symbolizing the idea of plenty, of abundance.

'That is how you painters explain, justify even, all these naked female bodies. That is the easiest way of getting away with it. It is the only explanation the public can accept.' He knew I would not be able to go along with any allegorical nonsense. Not only do I want the image to represent an individual, but I also want her to look as if she had just walked off the streets of Paris, just like Victorine.

Now I can see that the naked breasts make the figure too erotic. They thought the same of Victorine because they did not know how to read her gaze in *Le Bain*. But with Lola, there is nothing to counteract the idea of a woman offering herself. There is no challenge in her gaze, only provocation. Perhaps, I might look at her differently if I did not want her myself. For me, she is Eros, and yet, I do not want to paint her for others to consume.

What shall I do with her head? At first, I painted her with the turban that she usually wears. Once, when we were making love, she let me unwrap it and I stroked her hair. I used to do that with Marcella. Without the head cover, Lola looked vulnerable, so I gave her various hats to try. She giggled a lot, looking at herself in the mirror. I liked her with a fashionable, wide brimmed fedora. When I stuck a feather in it, I though she looked exquisite. Perhaps that is what I should do next: paint her in a ball gown and an elegant hat and call it *A l' Opéra*. Later, I scraped off the paint from the canvas and painted the hat. I am still not sure that it is the right thing to do.

Perhaps a maid might have been best after all. Couture always told us that servants and laundresses, ordinary workers, they were all legitimate subjects. But not if they are black. Oh, yes, Lola at the opera, that is what I should do next.

I cannot leave her alone, neither her, nor her image. She is the best lover I have ever known, the only one who senses what pleases me before I say it. And she is the most affectionate. She never tires of me and I never tire of her. She takes pleasure in being with me and is never timid to show what she wants from me. What I like best is when I can bury my head between her breasts and wait for her to plant a kiss on the top of my head. Sometimes, she holds me quietly for five or ten minutes. I try not to think of anything, but the moment. Her smell. To be buried there, in between her breasts.

The procession stops. We stand around the freshly dug grave, surrounded by monuments and gravestones. François Jouffroy, president of the Académie des Beaux-Arts, speaks. Another butterfly flutters in front of me. The sun shines on the magnificent graves around us. The words 'great Delacroix' echo in my head. Paul Huet delivers another oration and says that 'Delacroix is one of the few artists who characterize an epoch'. Then there is the priest. They lower the coffin and we throw earth into the grave.

I think of him sitting in rue Notre-Dame de Lorette, an older, respectable painter, with a reputation for hostility, and Antoine and me, our voices trembling with fear and excitement, asking for a permission to copy *La Barque*. I think of his voice and the expression on his face when he asked us about our artistic preferences. He did not humour us. We were young and he wanted to know what we thought.

Although Couture and his cronies threw out my *Le Buveur d'absinthe* from the 1859 Salon, it pleased me that Delacroix was one of the few jurors who voted for it. He was a horse of a different colour.

I see Lola, sitting on a chaise longue and me kneeling in front of her and burying my head in her breasts. I like the smell of her skin after we had made love. I like to lick the droplets of perspiration from her forehead. Who will throw the earth onto my coffin?

48

On the way back from the second sitting with Madame Chesnes, I stop at *L'Azure*. Fed up with the advances from the foul Tombé, I went back there; luckily, their singer had left. It's an hour before they expect me to start playing, but I prefer to rest rather than rush home. The patron offers me a bowl of potato and beef soup. I eat it with chunks of bread and sip red wine. I chew slowly, preferring to sit in the corner to study the scene, just as I used to in my days as a waitress. I am pleased that I don't have to pay for the food and can keep all the money that I collect. The best is that the patron, Pierre Lebois, is a young man and very much in love with his wife, who is pregnant, so that I don't have to fear his advances. If I didn't have to sing, I could draw what I see. There are few people around at this hour but the place fills up in the evenings. Pierre Lebois says that having music makes a huge difference to his trade.

When I finish eating, I start tuning my guitar. As soon as they hear me strumming, two little children, a boy and a girl, run to my table. The boy is older than the girl; they are both younger than the children in my dream.

'Can I try to play?' the boy asks. I show him how to produce a sound with his fingers on a string. He smiles each time he touches a string and it makes a sound. I offer to show the girl what to do but she is too shy and stands away from us. I let the boy hold the guitar and he tells me that his father has a piano in the house and that soon a teacher will come to give him lessons. After a while, a woman comes to collect the children. Her short coat has a tapered waist, much too fashionable for this café.

Today, I had a very long session with Madame Chesnes; her portrait is coming along. But the thought that she may not approve of the painting makes me nervous. I encouraged her to look at the work in progress but she said that she only wants to see the picture when it's finished. Since I'll be painting Angélique from a photograph, I suggested to Madame Chesnes that I could complete it in my studio. She said she would prefer me to continue working at her place, as she liked to keep an eye on little Angélique. I understood then.

'She can be so naughty,' she added. 'Always running around. Such a lovely child.' I nodded and said that it was a pity I wouldn't be able to see her. I felt ashamed thinking that at least having to paint a dead child I'd have no problems with keeping her still.

'You would love her, mademoiselle; if only she could be here,' Madame Chesnes said wistfully. Then she looked down and I noticed a tear roll down her cheek.

Madame Chesnes sat primly and, apart from an occasional remark about the weather, she let me work in peace. I've already sketched her reclining on a divan and, since the photo of the little girl shows her sitting on a chair, it should not be too difficult for me to copy her image and position her next to her grandmother. The divan is green and Madame Chesnes insisted on wearing a white skirt and a white blouse. I am allowed to choose a colour for Angélique's dress, although Madame Chesnes said that she hoped I would go for red. I have to please her: red it shall be. On the instructions of Madame Chesnes, the maid has placed two busts, one on each side of the divan. Altogether, it is a strange composition, too symmetrical for my taste. I would much rather paint a family doing something, with people in different parts of the room. But Madame Chesnes has a strong idea of what she wants the painting to look like. I am here only to paint that idea. I can see why a man like Monsieur Manet could never work with people like this.

Even before I started the picture, Madame Chesnes had already given it a title: *La Famille*. One of the busts represents her deceased husband, and the other is her dead father.

'Can you paint busts, mademoiselle?' she asked me on the first day.

'Most certainly, madame,' I said. I've never done them, but I have to pretend that I am confident and that I know what I am doing.

She also wanted to know how long it would take me to finish the painting. I thought I would need seven or eight days, if we work both mornings and afternoons. She was pleased with the time scale. So was I. The sooner I complete the picture, the sooner I shall be paid.

Today, she looked at the two busts and said: 'They are good likenesses. Monsieur Chesnes looks just the same as I remember him. I shall expect you to make him look alive, mademoiselle.'

I nodded and we carried on working until a maid interrupted us by bringing in coffee and a cake. Madame Chesnes cut a piece and handed it to me, before pouring the coffee and serving a piece of cake for herself.

While we ate, she talked about Angélique. I listened attentively. On my way out, the maid whispered to me that Angélique didn't exist. I looked at her, and before I could ask what she meant, she said: 'Every now and then I am asked to prepare a room for Angélique, supposedly coming to stay, and to cook her favourite food. Sometimes I even have to set her place at the table. But she is dead.'

The maid made me even more aware of my responsibility as a painter: I have to make Angélique look alive. If I can, my painting will give a great deal of pleasure to a lonely, old woman. Would Monsieur Manet consider this worthwhile?

Now the café is filling up with people. Pierre Lebois brings me another glass of wine and says I should start in fifteen minutes.

Half the way through the evening, just as I stop for a break, a well-dressed man calls me. He says that he needs to talk to me: 'You are Mademoiselle Victorine, aren't you?'

I look at him, trying to determine how he knows my name. I can't place him. There are many men like him on the streets of Paris. He extends his hand: 'We have met before, Mademoiselle Victorine. Very briefly, though. We may not have even been introduced properly at the time. I am Emile Nouvel. My brother-in-law, Monsieur Rosiers, deals in flower pictures for the English market.'

At that point, the little boy who showed interest in my guitar earlier on, runs to me and says to the man: 'Papa, why are you talking to her? She is my friend.'

Monsieur Nouvel says that he noticed me when I allowed Claude to strum the guitar. They were passing by and would not have come in, had it not been for the boy, who saw me carrying the guitar and insisted.

'You should blame Claude that I have found you, mademoiselle.'

'I am pleased to have met you, monsieur.'

'Well, I am pleased to see that you are well. Etienne said that you had fallen ill and that you were no longer painting.'

'I am painting, monsieur. I'll always paint.'

'Etienne claimed you were no longer interested in the assignment. For the past month, it has been impossible to get anything out of him. Words or pictures. I began to wonder whether I should believe what he said about you. He is a fallen man, mademoiselle. What a tragedy. He used to be so reliable, never missing a deadline. And now? Drinks all the time. My brother-in-law no longer gives orders to him.'

I nod. 'I am sorry to hear that, monsieur.'

'Well, so am I. Etienne was a good and prolific painter. But, these things happen. More often than not. I am so glad to see you, mademoiselle. Do you remember the American trip? It is hard to find anyone. Ideally the person should know about painting. I have asked at the Ecole des Beaux-Arts. Several students are a possibility but none can set off soon.'

'I am interested, Monsieur Nouvel.'

'Are you? Well, would you be able to go in six weeks' time? The gallery where my contact works needs the paintings by January. You should be in America before Christmas. And despite the Civil War, I can assure you that Boston is quite safe.'

'That would suit me, monsieur.'

He gives me his card. His office is on the Champs-Elysées. We arrange for me to see him to work out the details of our arrangement. The patron gestures to me: it's time to continue. As I am about to go, Monsieur Nouvel says:

'I like your singing, mademoiselle. You have lots of feeling. That's essential for a café singer.'

I smile. Suddenly, I feel full of energy. I sing late into the night. I collect eight francs and fifty sous. Pierre Lebois and Juliette, his wife, thank me.

'Will you come tomorrow, mademoiselle?'

'Certainly, monsieur.'

The streets are almost deserted as I make my way home. To my surprise, the light is on in the concierge's office. As soon as she hears me, she jumps out. I wonder whether I should tell her that I may be going to America. I smile but she doesn't smile back.

'Mademoiselle Victorine, a terrible thing has happened.' She stares at me, willing me to ask.

'Yes, what is it?' Has there been a fire?

'It's Gabriel.' She lowers her eyes and takes a deep breath. 'He has hanged himself. In his apartment. The gendarmes came and took down the body.'

'No. No, it can't be true.' I've become used to his music. The thought that I won't hear it again saddens me.

'Mademoiselle, come in, take a seat.' She ushers me into her office and hands me a glass of water.

'His sister came this afternoon to collect his things. She didn't say much but I think he was unhappy in love. Why else would someone so young kill himself?'

It was only ten days ago that he tried to talk to me but I was in a hurry.

49

The shreds of the torn canvas hang down, lifeless. I lift them one by one. It is useless. There is no point trying to repair the damage. Before slashing the picture, she smeared paint over it. Even as I hold the strips of the canvas together, the figure of the black woman, whom we had agreed to call Mademoiselle Agnès, is barely discernible.

I feel a terrible sadness: the picture I worked on with so much enthusiasm for three weeks lies in front of me like a corpse. It died before it was given the chance of life at an exhibition. There is nothing I can do to revive it now. I am left to mourn the loss.

At least I arrived before she managed to do any more damage. She was about to attack *Olympia*. It was not easy restraining her: although slim, she is taller than me and surprisingly strong. My priority was to pull her as far back as I could from the picture before trying to take away the knife. I dragged her across the studio, her writhing body knocking over chairs and tables in its wake. Who knows what Madame Bijoux thought when she heard all the noise and the commotion.

Once I secured the knife, I pinned Lola down, but she went on struggling. She bit my hand, calling me a monster. She screamed something about an attack on Victorine, the bruises on her thighs but, under the circumstances, I had no time to consider what she meant. Somehow I managed to keep her away from the pictures; she carried on shouting, and spitting venom. It is only now that I think I understand what she was saying: did she think that I had hit Victorine and given her those bruises and scratches?

I cannot come to terms with what she has done. Nor can I understand her hatred. I think back to the evening I was leaving the studio for Guerbois and as soon as I stepped onto the street, Lola called me. It was dark and raining heavily: at first, I could not see her. She said that she was in trouble. I asked what kind of trouble, but she pleaded with me to take her upstairs. As soon as we were indoors, she explained that she had been thrown out of the house where she had worked for five years. That meant that not only had she lost her job, but also that she had nowhere to live. Her employers had lost their patience with her frequent absences.

'I told them that I was ill and that a friend was looking after me.'

I wondered whether she wanted me to feel responsible. I did not. She had never protested when I asked her to sit for me, never told me that her job was in jeopardy. She made the decision to lie to the family without saying anything to me. As she spoke, I thought it strange that she had not gone to Victorine's apartment.

'I have nowhere to go, monsieur. I was stupid to lose this job. They were good to me. They were better than anyone else I have known.' She paused and caught my eye. Then she lowered her voice and added: 'I have not told this to anyone. Monsieur, I was born a slave in Martinique. Before I was taken away, everyone on the farm said I was lucky to be bought by Monsieur Lapage. He was French and was taking me to Paris. On the farm, everyone knew that once you reached France, you would no longer be a slave. The Lapages made me work hard but they also paid me. As a slave, I worked for nothing.'

My mind filled with images of the slave market in São Paolo. I saw handsome young men, as strong as horses, being forced to kneel and open their mouths so that prospective buyers could examine their teeth. And there were young women, with fat merchants fondling their breasts and bottoms in the guise of inspecting how healthy they were. Then there were small children, old women, old men, all of them on display like cattle at a market. They must have been the most downtrodden people on earth. Here in front of me was one of them, a beautiful young woman who was destitute in Paris, a woman I had been sleeping with. Without thinking further, I said:

'Lola, you must stay here tonight. You can sleep in the bed-room upstairs.' I immediately added: 'I must tell you that I need peace and quiet, no disturbance of any kind, so that I can work. Therefore, this offer is only for a few days, until you can sort your affairs.'

She nodded: 'Of course, monsieur, just for a few days. Thank you. I'll start looking for another post tomorrow.'

We left it at that.

I did not go to the Guerbois that evening. I took Lola to the upstairs bedroom and we made love. Afterwards, I buried my head in her breasts and cried. I carried the smell of her skin back with me to my apartment.

When I returned in the morning, she was ready to go out to seek another position as a maid, but I was keen to continue with the portrait and told her so. She did not argue. I thought she seemed relieved that she could stay. The same thing happened the next day and for a few days after that. I did not ask questions about her situation, nor did I think about it. I was too preoccupied with the painting. Two weeks passed. Only once did she make a reference to her search for a job. She said that she was experiencing difficulties because of her colour. That surprised me because I know rich families who prefer to have a black servant. But I did not wish to doubt her. In many ways, she was little trouble. If I did not need her for modelling, she either went out or stayed out of sight.

Charles noticed that she was living here; he teased me. But that did not bother me.

This afternoon, as soon as she stopped fighting me, I said that I was prepared to allow her to explain why she wanted to destroy my pictures. But I made her realize that, regardless of what she said, I could no longer allow her to stay in the studio. I reminded her that the arrangement was to be temporary.

She calmed down and accepted my invitation to talk. I wanted to know why she had destroyed the portrait. She raised her voice once again:

'Because I don't like the way you want to display me to the world. I don't like being a servant, and I don't like exposing my breasts for everyone to see. When I looked at the painting this morning, I remembered my white master who, whenever his wife wasn't around, insisted that I pull down my dress and work with my breasts uncovered so that he could touch me anytime he wanted. If I objected, he whipped me and forced himself on me.'

'Why did you not tell me that before?' I said.

'You wouldn't have been interested. All you talk about is colours and shapes and how they fit together. And then something about the texture of the skin and that of the white dress material. You never said you liked my breasts. You liked the contrast with the white cloth.'

She was partially right. In a picture, a person is always primarily a shape, an object of colour, an element in the composition. She could never understand that. But, I did not wish to argue now.

'You treated us as if we were marionettes on the Champs Elysées.' I sighed but she carried on with her accusations: 'And you lusted after Victorine. She was mine and you wanted to take her away from me. She was everything I had. I loved her. You came between us. I decided that the only way I could prevent you taking her from me was by giving myself to you. I hated when you touched me. The only way I could put up with your hands on my body was by thinking about Victorine. I told myself that it was for her that I endured your embraces. I hated you.'

I did not believe her. She may have felt like that then, but I did not think it was true when we had started sleeping together. She was trying to hurt me. Clearly, she would have to go. I gave her some money, a good deal of money, I think, and asked her to leave straightaway. She went up, gathered her possessions, and when she came down, she asked if we could talk more. I said no. There was nothing else to say. I was angry and wanted her out of my sight. She lingered, perhaps thinking that I would change my mind. I stuffed more money into her hands and pushed her out. She did not struggle this time. Once I closed the door behind her, she started screaming that I was a bastard and that I would pay for ruining her life. A few minutes later, I heard Madame

319

Bijoux asking her to leave before she called a gendarme. Lola shouted some obscenity at her.

Now it is quiet. My canvas is ruined. I am looking at it and yet I cannot believe it. I almost expect to find the portrait somewhere else in the studio. I realise, with regret, that I shall never be able to make that picture of her visiting the opera.

50

This morning, two men have erected a white board outside the entrance to Maître Albert 17: *A Louer. Un atelier, et une chambre à coucher.*

I feel no emotion as I walk past. I gave my notice three days ago. It's a strange feeling that in two weeks' time, I'll no longer live here, or anywhere else in Paris. I'll be on board a ship bound for Boston. In ten days, I leave for Le Havre. Most of my possessions, few enough, but many more than there had been when I first moved in, are packed for storage. Monsieur Nouvel has made the necessary arrangements. He has even given me money to buy new clothes.

'An interesting Parisian mademoiselle like you will be a sensation in Boston. All the ladies will want to know about the latest French fashion and you'll have to be very careful what you wear.'

It took me two full days to find out what is fashionable. I went to the Bon Marché, the Bazar de l' Hôtel de Ville and to the Louvre and each time gave a list of items to a couture assistant. When I told them what I needed and for what reason, they said that they would have to take proper measurements.

I had never visited any of these *grands magasins*. Inside, they are huge, like cathedrals. The assistants are constantly busy, measuring, cutting materials, discarding. They looked tired but were very kind to me.

The head of the women's fashion section and her deputy helped me choose the styles of dresses and jackets from the ones they had on display. Despite their advice, I shied away from the voluminous crinolines and I needed a great deal of persuading before agreeing to purchase one.

I watched the women shopping as they searched through

piles of handkerchiefs, scarves, and silk blouses trimmed with lace. I saw one woman try on a velvet coat priced at 1,800 francs. I could live on that money for two years. She bought it after hardly a moment's consideration. Most women carried several parcels. Some even had carts piled up with parcels attended by one of the numerous page boys in green uniforms with shining brass buttons. The excitement in the eyes of the women and the urgency with which they handled the goods, made me think that this spectacle of female desire would present a good subject for a modern painting. If I wasn't going to America, I would set up my easel here. The shops were like dream landscapes where women were instantly transformed into alert, feline hunters skilfully weaving in and out of displays, and snatching their prey in front of each other. It occurred to me how different my dreams have been from the dreams of these women.

Outside the store, the crowds were just as excited as those inside and new customers were arriving in rows of carriages. It is a women's world and while I could see how seductive it could be, it didn't hold much attraction for me. A page boy found me a taxi and I gave him a tip. I realized I was expected to.

Today, I am wearing one of my new dresses, which has a very pronounced waist. The bodice is skin tight, moulded over a *cuirasse* corset. I wonder if Monsieur Manet will notice. We have arranged that I should see him before I leave. Yesterday, when I visited Emily, she and her friends said that I would turn heads in Boston. I laughed. I said that I hoped they would take me seriously as a painter.

'They will,' Mary said. 'They are mad about French painters. You will be swamped by orders for portraits.'

'And marriage offers,' Mary added. I was not sure whether to look forward to either possibility. I was not proud of the portrait I made of Madame Chesnes, but I needed the money and I had to do what she wanted. However, I can console myself with the fact that I gave pleasure to a grieving grandmother. I never revealed to Madame Chesnes that I knew Angélique was dead. What mattered was that my painting helped someone: Madame Chesnes was pleased with the finished result and recommended me to a friend. Unfortunately, I had to disappoint her. I've been too busy with the arrangements for the journey.

Emily has given me the address of her family and, since they speak only a few words of French, she said they were likely to find an interpreter for me. I can say a few things in English now. Mary has been teaching me for the past two weeks.

Monsieur Manet opens the door himself and as I enter, he turns towards a tall man standing in the middle of the studio and says: 'Alfred, this is Mademoiselle Victorine, a promising young artist.'

Alfred steps towards me with his hand extended, while Monsieur Manet says that Alfred is Alfred Stevens, a painter. This is the first time Monsieur Manet has referred to me as an artist.

Alfred Stevens asks whether I have been taught by Monsieur Manet. I say that I have learned a great deal from Monsieur Manet, but Monsieur Manet interrupts me: 'Oh, Alfred, you know I could never take any pupils. Anyway, what would I teach them? Nothing that cannot be summed up in just a few words: black does not exist, that's the first rule; don't do anything that is seen through someone else's work, that's the second. I would just tell them to go back home and paint from nature, which is more important than looking at the work of all the other painters.'

I notice that, while Monsieur Manet speaks, Alfred Stevens does not take his eyes off me.

'Where did you train, mademoiselle? Which studio? Who was your teacher?'

'I am self-taught, monsieur.'

Alfred Stevens looks surprised.

'Not many studios take women and, it costs a great deal of money to become a student.'

Alfred Stevens stares at me and then as he lifts his arm, he smiles: 'Mademoiselle, but that must be remedied. And it shall be. Mademoiselle Victorine. I have just made a decision and let me announce it here in front of the two of you, my dear friends. I have been thinking about it for some time, and now I am convinced: I am planning to open a studio for women painters. Mademoiselle, if there is anything you may like to study there, or use a model, I shall personally welcome you. And, let me add, anyone with a talent and determination will be able to join without a fee. Or, perhaps, in return, they could offer to model. What do you think, mademoiselle?' Is the passion in his voice genuine?

'That is very kind of you, monsieur,' I say.

'I am told that there are many young Americans studying painting in Paris, some from very rich families. They can pay.' Alfred Stevens watches me, seeking my approval. I nod and smile.

We move around the studio and stop in front of *Le Bain*.

'I admire this picture, Edouard.' Alfred Stevens says. 'You were misunderstood. That is all. Those silver heads on the jury and the ignorant public, what can you expect?' Then he turns towards me: 'Mademoiselle, you are like a muse to me. I need only to look at you and ideas develop in my head. Here is another one: please, please, do say that you will do it?'

Monsieur Manet interrupts: 'Alfred, you have to say what it is; you cannot expect mademoiselle to consent to something when she does not even know what it is.'

'Well, I would like to paint a picture on a large canvas with mademoiselle as an artist. I would like her to sit in front of an easel and paint while I paint her.'

He turns towards me: 'Please mademoiselle, do say yes. We can start next week. Edouard has never painted you like that, has he?'

I smile. Perhaps other artists can read my mind. But before I can say anything, Monsieur Manet interrupts: 'Alfred, it is a great idea, but it will have to wait. Mademoiselle Victorine is about to depart for Boston.'

Alfred Stevens' face becomes even more animated:

'For Boston? How exciting! Mademoiselle, when will you be back? I shall wait. We can start next month.'

'I am sorry to disappoint you, monsieur,' I say 'but I am not sure how long I shall be away. I may decide to stay for a very long time, possibly forever. I am told that French painters are in demand in Boston.'

'Then I shall have to visit you in Boston.'

I smile at him and nod.

Before I leave, Monsieur Manet wishes me well and gives me an envelope with several photographs of his painting in case I can interest dealers in his work. At the door, he says that if he makes any money, at any time later in his career, he will set up an annuity for me. He wants to acknowledge the contribution I have made to his work. I thank him and say that, for now, I do not need an annuity, but if I ever find myself in difficulties and unable to work, I shall be free to remind him of his offer.

We shake hands and he kisses me on both cheeks. So does Alfred Stevens.

'Do come back, mademoiselle, or if you don't, I shall make that trip to Boston,' he shouts as I walk downstairs.

On the way back to Maître Albert, it occurs to me that neither Monsieur Manet nor I mentioned Lola.

51

I walk all the way from the lawyers' offices to the studio. At least I can console myself that this is the last time I have to go there for this purpose. It is all in place now. The marriage contract is finally drawn.

It is a beautiful autumn day and I need to clear my head. Walking will help me relax. Mother has made all the decisions; I was hardly consulted on anything. I am glad Suzanne is not here. I would have not been able to hide my distress from her.

It has been a year since father died and mother has been looking after the family finances. She has always been generous to me and she is giving us a wedding present of 10,000 francs, so I do not have to worry unduly about selling pictures. If only she would treat my future wife with trust and respect.

The stark fact is that, if I die before mother, and without having children, all my inheritance will revert to her. Suzanne would be left penniless.

I know that mother has to keep an eye on expenses, but Suzanne is the last person I know who would be either extravagant or dishonest. She does not care for luxuries.

As I enter the studio, *Olympia* greets me. I have placed it near the entrance. In two days' time, Martinet's men will collect it. It will be on show at his gallery from next week. I smile at Victorine. It amuses me to think how shamelessly Alfred Stevens flirted with her. But then, she did look quite fetching in her new clothes, a beautiful bodice that showed off her bust. The clothes gave her a new air of confidence that made her more attractive than ever.

I sit down to write a letter to Suzanne. After this morning's business, I have a deep desire to be affectionate:

My dear Suzanne,

Last night, I spent a long time looking for your photograph that we had taken just before you left. I wanted to place it on the pillow next to me, so I can look at your comforting face whenever I am in bed. I eventually found the album in the table in the drawing room. Your image was the last thing I saw before I closed my eyes. Soon, it will be you that I see. Every day I shall wake up next to you. Your lovely face will be my first sight upon waking and the last sight before sleeping. That is a delightful prospect.

Thinking about our future, I fell asleep with you on my mind and then, in the middle of the night, I woke up dreaming I heard you calling my name.

There is knock at the door. Charles enters. He is carrying a bundle of newspapers. He asks who I am writing to.

'I am writing to my future wife,' I say proudly. Charles' forehead furrows. I know I owe him an explanation.

'I am engaged to be married,' I say.

'Oh, Edouard, I had no idea. When did this happen?'

'Well, we had to keep it secret. Mother wanted to wait for a year after father's death. And besides, Suzanne has been in Holland for a while. She is visiting her family.'

'Well done, Edouard.' Charles asks about Suzanne.

'She is a pianist, a very good one, and she is very beautiful.'

'Well, I really need to congratulate you on finding such a woman. When is the wedding?'

'I am off to Holland tomorrow and we shall be married soon after.'

'Tomorrow? And you kept it all secret from us. Well, well. Edouard, you old rascal.'

'I am sorry, Charles. Mother asked me not to tell anyone. She insisted on a proper period of mourning. There were to be no family celebrations until the year was up.'

'Of course,' Charles says. 'We have to preserve bourgeois respectability.' A contorted smile crosses his face. Why the sarcasm? He must be hurt that I have kept Suzanne secret from him. I am surprised that he is so affected by my news.

Suddenly, as if he has reached a decision, or as if he has to make an announcement, he turns on his heels and says: 'Edouard, listen to me. I have always loved you. I am glad about your news and wish you every happiness.'

'Thank you.'

'But, there is something else you need to know.' I glance at him. 'I am sorry to spoil your joy. Look at today's *Moniteur.*'

His face is grim as he passes the newspaper to me. Someone must have written something unpleasant about my art. That is no matter. I shall show Charles that his advice has worked. He must be testing me. It's my lot to be abused and I shall take it philosophically.

I smile: 'I am strong enough to face the scribblers criticizing my art. Thanks to you, my dear friend.' Charles' face remains serious.

The newspaper is already open on the page he wants me to read. I scan the text for my name. I cannot find what Charles wants me to read. I look at him. He lowers his eyes. I look at the page again and then I see it:

> *The body of a black woman has been discovered on the banks of the Seine. She has been identified by her former employers, Madame and Monsieur Demains, as Lola Sancho, a twenty-five year old black servant woman from Martinique. Mademoiselle Sancho is believed to have committed suicide. Heavy stones were found stitched into her clothing.*
>
> *In a statement issued by the gendarmerie, Monsieur Demains confirmed that Mademoiselle Sancho, who was brought over from Martinique five years ago, worked for his family for three years and left their employment*

of her own accord. After that, they had no contact with her.

Mademoiselle Sancho is believed to have had no family or friends in Paris.

I sit down. Numbness overwhelms me. Charles walks across the room to look out of the window. She is dead. But it is the last sentence that hurts most. For a few weeks while she lived here, I tried to be her friend. Now there is nothing left of her. If only my painting had survived... The portrait of Agnès was a portrait of Lola, a black woman, not a servant.

After a while, Charles comes to sit next to me. He says that I should not blame myself for what has happened. I could not have given her refuge for ever. He reminds me that she did destroy one of my paintings and threatened to do the same with the others. He says I had no choice but to throw her out.

'You are an artist. You have a responsibility to your work.'

I know that people would say that I exploited her and then cast her aside. That would hurt me even more than when they criticise my pictures. Contrary to what everyone thinks, I am not greatly interested in what is said about art, mine or anyone else's. But if I have to give an opinion on what is good, I would put it this way: everything that has a sense of humanity, a sense of modernity, is interesting. Everything that lacks these qualities is worthless. Humanity and modernity. Both were present in that portrait of Agnès.

From where we are sitting, I can see the canvas of *Olympia*. Does Victorine look at me with melancholy or contempt? I wonder how she feels about the news. There is only one course of action to take ... I ask Charles to accompany me to Martinet's gallery on the Boulevard des Italiens. I shall explain to Louis that I can no longer allow the painting to be exhibited. Not for a while, at least. Charles nods in agreement and we leave straight-away. Louis may not be so understanding but I shall not be open to discussion.

With Charles at my side, I walk through the streets, a man about to be married, numb with shock.

329

52

I stand on the deck and look down at the crowds waving to us. The ship has started to move. We are bound for Dover in England. The salt smell cuts through my nostrils.

I arrived in Le Havre yesterday morning. I took a room at the D'Angleterre, a small hotel not far from the port. Although it was comfortable, and I put out the light very early, I lay awake the whole night. My mind was on the voyage. It didn't help that the owner's wife told me, as soon as she heard that I was going to America: 'Oh mademoiselle, you look so young. Should you really be travelling alone? Such a difficult passage. So many dangers for a young woman on her own.'

I smiled. My burgundy brocade dress with its narrow waist and fitted jacket is too fashionable for people to think of me as a woman who can look after herself.

The sea is calm today and I don't have to worry about crossing La Manche. I am much more concerned about the travel across England. Everything has been organised by Monsieur Nouvel – he has done the same journey himself – but I'll still need to find my way from Dover harbour to the railway station. Mary has written down the English phrases I should use. I have to find a train bound for Liverpool. I'll stay two nights there, before sailing for Boston on an ocean paddle steamer. Fortunately, I have the address of a Liverpool guesthouse that Monsieur Nouvel has recommended. We should expect to be at sea for up to three weeks. The length of our voyage will depend on the weather.

Next to me stands a young man with his elderly mother. We nod at each other. I met them at D' Angleterre last night. They will be on the same steamer from Liverpool. 'I fear boredom more than anything else,' the man says.

'Don't worry, Jules, we can play cards.'

I have my drawing and painting materials with me and hope to do some work during the long voyage. I have packed the collapsible easel into my luggage and I plan to set it up on deck. They told me that my cabin will be cramped and dark, although the first class accommodation would be only slightly more spacious. There should be oil lamps on the ship but passengers won't be allowed to have them on for long, as they fear fire. Monsieur Manet did warn me that, at this time of the year, the sea can be very rough and that I might find it impossible to sit still, let alone hold a pencil or brush. It is likely that I'll suffer from sea-sickness.

'Most people do,' he said. 'It can be so bad that you will not care to do anything, not even paint. Or,' he joked, 'Mademoiselle Victorine, you may develop a strange walk, as I did.'

Monsieur Manet's rolling gait is part of his charm. I don't expect to start walking like him; he spent six months at sea.

'I am never ill, monsieur. I can cope with any affliction. A bit of rough sea should not bother me.'

'Trust me, mademoiselle,' he said, 'I am an old sailor.'

But, if there are periods of calm, Monsieur Manet said, I should be able to earn some money by painting portraits of my fellow passengers. Knowing his attitude to this kind of art, I wondered whether he was teasing me.

At the door, just before I left, he said: 'And don't forget mademoiselle, every trip, every voyage we make is a learning experience. For a painter, there is much to absorb. I learnt a great deal on my trip to Brazil. I spent endless nights looking at the play of light and shade in the ship's wake. And in the daytime, from the upper deck, I would keep my eyes on the horizon. That is how I learnt to capture a sky.'

In a few weeks' time, *Olympia* will be on display at the Martinet gallery. I don't expect the reaction of the public or the critics to be less hostile than to *Le Bain*. How will Monsieur Manet cope? One of the attendants at the Salon des Refusés claimed that he had seen him come in disguise. 'I recognised him,' the attendant, a short, elderly man, boasted. 'He would stand to the side, the only person who wasn't laughing. His collar was pulled up and he had a scarf tied around his neck, but I could see his red beard and knew it was him.'

I wonder whether Lola will visit Martinet's. Would the sight of *Olympia* remind her of me? Perhaps she will be encouraged to return to Maître Albert: Madame Conchis would tell her of the change in my fortunes.

'Do take me inside. This freezing wind doesn't agree with me.' The elderly woman standing next to me speaks to her son and, her arm resting on his, the two of them leave the deck.

The ocean paddle steamer has accommodation for around one hundred and thirty people travelling first or second class. There could also be up to four hundred steerage passengers – I was told that they would be poor Irish emigrants – but they would have no money for portraits.

As we sail further away from Le Havre, the people waving from the shore shrink, until they are tiny dots; eventually, they all merge. No one has come to see me off. A family, standing to my left and a couple on my right, wave frantically. A woman next to me is crying. Some hold large handkerchiefs in their hands. While waiting to embark, I saw them kissing and hugging the relatives who had accompanied them. Like me, those passengers must be going further than Dover.

Now that the people on land are anonymous and indistinguishable from one another, I join in and wave. My eyes are fixed on a tiny dot in the crowd. I imagine that Lola is there. I can hear her shouting over the sound of the sea and wind, wishing me a good journey. She cups her hands in front of her mouth as she screams: 'I'll miss you, Victorine. Come back soon.'

Next to her stands my mother. I see her lift a hand to wipe a tear from her cheek. She is crying from sadness and joy. She is proud that her only daughter is a painter and that she is being paid to go to America on a large ship. For the past week, she helped her daughter pack. She loved running her old hands over the shiny material of the new, fashionable dresses.

But these are illusions, shadows of my former life. I may never see them again, nor anyone else I have known.

Madame Conchis comes to mind and I remember the tears in her eyes as she hugged me. 'You've been a good lodger. I would always have you back.'

Soon, the French shore is distant and its outline blurred. When it completely disappears into the mist, I scour the horizon for signs of England, but I can't see anything. There is nothing but the sea all around us. Foamy waves splash sea water over the deck and toss the ship around. The skirt of my dress is damp. If only I could paint what I see now: the constant movement, the spray of water, the mist of little droplets. The excitement of a voyage. What colours, what brushstrokes should I use?

All my fellow passengers have gone inside. I stay outside, watching the sea rage. I don't think I'll be able to sleep tonight. So much is happening. I don't wish to miss it. For a painter, there is so much to absorb.

My journey to the new world has begun.

Post scriptum

Victorine Meurent returned from America and became a painter. In 1875, she attended evening classes at the Académie Julian. Her self-portrait was shown at the 1876 Salon; in the same year, Manet's submission was rejected. Her work was exhibited again at the Salon in 1879, 1885 and 1904. She was elected member of the Société des Artistes Français in 1903; she received financial support from them in 1909, and during the First World War.

For the last twenty years of her life, she lived with a music teacher, Marie Dufour, in the Parisian suburb of Colombes.

Victorine Meurent died in March 1927, at the age of eighty-three.

In 1930, her self-portrait was sold by auction at the Hôtel Drouot. Her only known surviving picture is *Les rameaux* (1885), which was bought by an unknown private collector at an auction in 2004. The whereabouts of her self-portrait and other works are unknown.

Edouard Manet died in April 1883, following complications caused by a new and unorthodox treatment for syphilis. He was fifty-one. While he sold very few paintings during his lifetime and for small sums, from the turn of the century his pictures became extremely valuable. He is regarded as the father of modernism in painting.

Olympia was exhibited at the 1865 Salon. The painting shocked the public and the critics alike.

Women were not formally admitted to the Ecole des Beaux-Arts until 1897.

Alfred Stevens opened a teaching atelier for women in the 1870s.

Acknowledgements

While most of the main protagonists are historical figures, my story is an artefact, not a historical reconstruction. Some of the events did take place, others are a product of my imagination.

In writing the novel, I have consulted a number of historical sources and academic books. These include: Beth Archer Brombert's *Edouard Manet*; Carol Armstrong's *Manet Manette*; T.J. Clark's *The Painting of Modern Life*; Pierre Courthion's and Pierre Cailler's, *Portrait of Manet by Himself and his Contemporaries*; Michael Fried's *Manet's Modernism*; Otto Friedrich's *Olympia*; Paul Hayes Tucker's *Manet's Le déjeuner sur l'herbe*; George Heard Hamilton's *Manet and His Critics*; Jacques Lethève's *Daily Life of French Artists in the Nineteenth Century*; Eunice Lipton's *Alias Olympia*; John Milner's *The Studios of Paris*; Henri Perruchot's *La Vie de Manet*; John Rewald's *The History of Impressionism*; Jane Mayo Roos' *Early Impressionism and the French State*; Lesley Stevenson's *Manet*, Adolphe Tabarant's *Manet et ses ouvres*; Juliet Wilson-Bareau's *The Hidden Face of Manet* and *Manet by Himself*. The novel is peppered with quotations from Manet's letters and from recorded memories of his friends.

I would like to thank Gérard Gabriel Kahn for his daily efforts to improve my French, to Gabriel Partos for his encouragement with my writing over the years, to Lesley Stevenson for her expert advice on the period, and to the members of Richmond Writers' Circle, who provided a critical audience for my work in progress.

Finally, my thanks are due to my first, and most critical, reader Peter Main.